Eggs in a Casket

Berkley Prime Crime titles by Laura Childs

Tea Shop Mysteries

DEATH BY DARJEELING
GUNPOWDER GREEN
SHADES OF EARL GREY
THE ENGLISH BREAKFAST MURDER
THE JASMINE MOON MURDER
CHAMOMILE MOURNING
BLOOD ORANGE BREWING

DRAGONWELL DEAD
THE SILVER NEEDLE MURDER
OOLONG DEAD
THE TEABERRY STRANGLER
SCONES & BONES
AGONY OF THE LEAVES
SWEET TEA REVENGE

Scrapbooking Mysteries

KEEPSAKE CRIMES
PHOTO FINISHED
BOUND FOR MURDER
MOTIF FOR MURDER
FRILL KILL
DEATH SWATCH

TRAGIC MAGIC
FIBER & BRIMSTONE
SKELETON LETTERS
POSTCARDS FROM THE DEAD
GILT TRIP

Cackleberry Club Mysteries

EGGS IN PURGATORY
EGGS BENEDICT ARNOLD
BEDEVILED EGGS
STAKE & EGGS
EGGS IN A CASKET

Anthologies

DEATH BY DESIGN
TEA FOR THREE

·LAURA CHILDS·

Eggs in a Casket

BERKLEY PRIME CRIME, NEW YORK

THE BERKLEY PUBLISHING GROUP
Published by the Penguin Group
Penguin Group (USA) LLC
375 Hudson Street, New York, New York 10014

USA • Canada • UK • Ireland • Australia • New Zealand • India • South Africa • China

penguin.com

A Penguin Random House Company

This book is an original publication of The Berkley Publishing Group.

Berkley Prime Crime Books are published by The Berkley Publishing Group.
BERKLEY® PRIME CRIME and the PRIME CRIME logo are trademarks of
Penguin Group (USA) LLC.

Library of Congress Cataloging-in-Publication Data

Childs, Laura.
Eggs in a casket / Laura Childs.—First edition.
pages cm
ISBN 978-0-425-25558-2 (hardcover)
1. Restaurateurs—Fiction. 2. Women detectives—Fiction. 3. Prison wardens—Crimes
against—Fiction. 4. Murder—Investigation—Fiction. I. Title
PS3603.H56E345 2014
813'.6—dc23
2013035912

FIRST EDITION: January 2014

PRINTED IN THE UNITED STATES OF AMERICA

10 9 8 7 6 5 4 3 2 1

Cover illustration by Lee White.
Cover design by Annette Fiore DeFex.
Interior text design by Kristin del Rosario.

*For the fine people of Scott County
who brought the Bookmobile to my hometown
when I was ten years old.
Finally, a real library at my disposal!
I'm pretty sure I read every book.*

Acknowledgments

A huge thank-you to Sam, Maureen, Tom, Bob, Jennie, Dan, and all the designers, illustrators, writers, publicists, and sales folk at The Berkley Publishing Group. You all do so much! And a special thank-you to all the booksellers, reviewers, librarians, bloggers, Facebook friends, and wonderful readers. I'm so glad you're still enjoying my crazy Cackleberry Club ladies—because I'm still thrilled to write these books!

Eggs in a Casket

CHAPTER 1

THE black wrought-iron gates of Memorial Cemetery loomed up through swirling fog like disapproving sentinels as Suzanne's Ford Taurus labored up the narrow, muddy road.

"There it is," said Toni, pointing. She was scrunched next to Suzanne in the passenger seat, her pert nose pressed flat against the steamed-up windshield. "Dead ahead."

"Lovely choice of words," said Suzanne, stealing a quick glance at Toni.

Suzanne Dietz, proprietor of the Cackleberry Club, and her business partner, Toni Garrett, were stuffed into her car along with four enormous baskets of fragrant flowers. The cemetery's Sesquicentennial Celebration, commemorating its founding one hundred and fifty years ago, was supposed to kick off tomorrow morning. And the plans called for a jubilant array of floral decorations, twenty-one gun salutes, and candlelight tours of some of the historic graves. But a nasty spate of rain and chilly weather had swooped in from the Dakotas three days earlier and taken up what seemed like permanent residence in the small Midwestern town of Kindred. Now, on this gloomy, rain-soaked Thursday morning, Suzanne wondered if the skies would clear and if the celebration would even happen.

"Careful, careful," Toni warned as Suzanne navigated the car along the slippery lane that wound past a stone statue of a kneeling angel. The angel was missing the top part of one wing and its sorrowful face was pitted with age.

"Poor thing," said Toni. "Got her wings clipped."

They were churning and chugging their way through the oldest part of the cemetery, the part where settlers and Civil War veterans lay in quiet repose. Here stood enormous first-growth oaks and cottonwoods, trees that had been shooting toward the sky ever since covered wagons had pushed across the prairies into what had been called the Big Woods. Now, spread out under these trees were ancient grave tablets, battered and bruised by the elements and canted so crazily they looked like rows of rotted teeth. Strangely, this part of the cemetery looked like it hadn't been maintained on a regular basis.

"Where are we supposed to drop these flowers again?" Suzanne asked as she peered out the front windshield. Weeping willows hung damply down and swept against the sides of her car, making strange whispering sounds. The overly fragrant aroma of the flowers in her backseat was starting to be a little too reminiscent of a funeral home. For Suzanne, the sooner they dumped these baskets and beat a hasty retreat, the better it would be. After all, Petra, the third member of their troika, was back at the Cackleberry Club, the little café they'd founded together a year or so ago on a wing and a prayer. Petra was prepping food and getting ready for breakfast service, which was—yikes!—supposed to kick off a half hour from now.

"We're supposed to set up the flowers near the Civil War memorial," said Toni. "At least that's what the folks at the Historical Society told me." The Historical Society was sponsoring the event and they'd been a little disorganized of late, what with a brand-new director coming on board and an influx of well-meaning but vaguely ineffectual volunteers.

"So where would that be?" asked Suzanne. She brushed back strands of her graceful, shoulder-length bob as threads of fog swirled outside the car like ethereal cotton candy. Being unfamiliar with this part of the cemetery, she had the feeling that she'd temporarily lost her way. For some reason, every time a marble obelisk or mausoleum floated into view, it gave her the jitters and sent a jolt of adrenaline shooting through her veins.

Easy, girl, Suzanne told herself. *Just focus on your driving.*

Suzanne was on the high side of forty, with silver blond hair and eyes a deep cornflower blue. She projected a low-maintenance ease and elegance, and her figure was strong and lean. Her shoulders, which peeked out from a sleeveless white handkerchief cotton blouse she'd teamed with straight-leg jeans, were just beginning to turn a burnished gold from spring days spent working in her beloved herb garden.

"I know the Historical Society folks were going to erect some kind of open-sided tent," said Toni. "So we should probably just stick the flowers in there. That way the poor little buds and blooms won't get pummeled by all this rain." Toni was short, stacked, and wore her frizzled reddish blond hair piled atop her head. Today she'd swept it into a red gingham scrunchie that matched her pearl-buttoned cowboy shirt. She was mid-forties, a self-proclaimed hottie patottie, and a crackerjack waitress to boot. Toni had grown up in a hardscrabble home life and was used to working her fingers to the bone.

"This weather is just plain awful," said Suzanne. Her windshield wipers slapped loudly as the back end of her car slewed slightly in the mud. Right now she was wishing Toni hadn't volunteered the two of them for this little task. Still, she was a business owner here in town and wanted to contribute something to the event.

As she rounded a hairpin turn, Suzanne's view was pretty much blocked by a copse of shaggy blue spruce. Which was why, when she spotted a small yellow car speeding directly at her down the single-lane road, she gasped in horror. With a mere two seconds to react, Suzanne cranked her steering wheel hard to the right and swerved awkwardly, barely avoiding a head-on collision!

"Whoa!" cried Toni, as she spun in her seat. Even though the yellow car had practically sideswiped them, it tore off without bothering to slow down. "Did you see that crazy driver? He almost creamed us!"

Suzanne's fingers turned white as she gripped her steering wheel and slowed the car. She felt more than a little unnerved. Because she was pretty sure she'd recognized the driver. "Wasn't that Missy's car?" she said. Missy Langston was a friend and one of their neighbors in Kindred.

"Huh?" said Toni, looking surprised. "Was it?"

"Yeah," said Suzanne, easing her car back into the muddy ruts. "I'm pretty sure it was her."

"What the heck would Missy be doing up here?" wondered Toni. "Shouldn't she be at Alchemy Boutique, hanging up clothes and getting ready to open the shop? Working like crazy under the unflinching eyes of her evil boss lady, Carmen?"

"I'm just wondering why Missy didn't wave hello," said Suzanne. "Or why she was driving so fast." *Or why she looked scared out of her wits.*

"She probably didn't see us."

"Maybe," said Suzanne. Her teeth gave a little chatter, partly because she felt chilled and partly as a result of their near-collision. Car accidents, real or just close calls, had a way of unnerving her. She flipped the heater on low and cranked up the defroster.

"Typical Missy," said Toni. "Always in a hurry."

But to Suzanne's eye, it looked more like Missy had been in a blind panic. Like she'd been speeding away from something scary. Something frightening.

"Pull in over there," Toni said now, cocking a finger. "Next to the Civil War graves and the old memorial marker. That's our drop point."

"And there's the tent you mentioned," said Suzanne. "Thank goodness." She exhaled slowly, trying to shrug off her unease as they rolled to a stop on damp grass. "Let's dump these flowers and hustle back to the Cackleberry Club. Petra's gonna pitch a fit if we're not back in time."

"Let's get 'er done," said Toni.

They scrambled out of the car, ducking heads and hunching shoulders as rain pelted down.

"This is miserable," said Suzanne, as she slipped on her jacket and pulled it tight. Then she flipped the seat forward and tried to muscle one of the baskets of peace lilies from her backseat. Unfortunately, the darned plant was wedged in tight and didn't want to cooperate.

"Good thing I brought my handy-dandy automatic umbrella," said Toni, grabbing a little black umbrella that looked like a bat with folded wings. Holding it out, she pushed the button, watched as the umbrella unfurled, then yelped in dismay as a gust of wind promptly grabbed it and sent it tumbling among the gravestones. "My umbrella!" yelled Toni. "I got it free with my subscription to *Hollywood Tattle-Tale!*"

"Better grab it," said Suzanne, as her basket of flowers suddenly popped free, almost sending her sprawling to the damp earth.

Don't want to do that, she told herself. *Not here. Not in this place. And certainly not after nearly getting smashed up in a car accident!*

"Aggh!" shrilled Toni from nearby. She was one step away

from grabbing her umbrella when it spun crazily and suddenly whooshed away from her again. "Suzanne, help!"

"Oh for gosh sakes!" exclaimed Suzanne. "If it means that much to you . . ." She set down her floral basket and chased after Toni, feeling a little silly as she capered across the wet grass. In record time, the downpour flattened her hair and soaked her to the bone. *I not only feel like a drowned rat, now I look like one, too*, she thought to herself.

"This is turning into a hare and hounds chase," said Toni, breathless and red-faced, as Suzanne caught up with her. "Every time I get remotely close, the doggone wind spins my umbrella away—kerflooey—just like a kid's toy top!"

"What we have to do," said Suzanne, trying to be practical, "is circle around. Try to get ahead of the darn thing."

"Outguess it," said Toni. "If that makes any sense at all."

They dashed across soggy ground and dodged around old graves, hot on the trail of Toni's dancing umbrella.

"There!" called Suzanne. "Over there. Your umbrella's hung up on that wrought-iron cross!"

Toni pushed herself into an all-out sprint. She stretched an arm out, got a good grasp on the handle, then swung the raggedy umbrella above her head. "Got it!"

"Excellent," said Suzanne, as she edged her way around a large granite tomb. "Glad to see you're . . ."

Suzanne suddenly skidded to a halt. There, directly in front of her eyes—six inches from where she was about to take her next step—was an open grave. Pitch-black earth yawned up at her, beckoning her, almost daring her, to come a little closer. The smell of fresh dirt, peat moss, and mildew assaulted her nose even as rain continued to patter down.

"Suzanne?" said Toni, walking toward her, twirling her umbrella lightly as if she were in a Gene Kelly movie. "You look like you just saw . . ."

"A body!" Suzanne gasped. She'd taken a hasty peek over

the edge of the gaping pit and was stunned at what she saw. A man was lying down there in a couple inches of water, crumpled on his side, not moving, seemingly not breathing. His clothes were soaked through, and his face and hands, what she could see of them at first glance, were practically bone white, leached of all color.

"What!" said Toni, seeing the look of horror and disbelief on Suzanne's face.

"There's . . . It's . . . You're not gonna believe this," Suzanne said, backpedaling away from the grave. Her voice was suddenly high-pitched and strangled. "Someone's down there!"

Toni moved cautiously toward her. "You mean like a *dead* body?" She reached out and grasped Suzanne's arm, then stood frozen in place, almost afraid to look down. "In a coffin?"

"No, not in a coffin!" said Suzanne. "That's the crazy weird thing. A man is just kind of . . . sprawled there."

"And you're sure he's dead?" Toni gibbered.

"Yes. No. I mean I *think* he might be . . . He didn't seem to be moving or breathing or anything." *And he's as white as a ghost . . . dead white.*

"Holy guacamole!" cried Toni. She gritted her teeth so hard she practically popped a filling. Then slowly, nervously, she shuffled forward and poked her head over the edge of the grave. "It *is* a body," she gasped after a few seconds. Her breathing was suddenly thready and ragged, like an over-wrought teakettle. "But . . . *whose* body?"

Suzanne's first thought was to dash back to her car and hightail it out of there. Go someplace safe, someplace warm and familiar where they could call for help. But a dreadful kind of curiosity had sunk its talons into her and she took a few hesitant steps forward to once again gape at the body. And, like a recurring bad dream that crept into the psyche every few months to haunt and terrorize, she knew, deep down in the limbic part of her brain, that this person was *familiar* to her. She recognized the knotted muscles, the tribal tattoo encircling one wrist, and the smooth, shaved head of this man who lay on his side, in uneasy and awful repose.

"I think I know who that is," Suzanne choked out hoarsely. "*We* know who that is."

"Who? Who?" said Toni, sounding like a startled owl from the nearby woods.

"It's Lester Drummond," whispered Suzanne.

"The prison warden?" asked Toni, stunned.

Suzanne gave a tight, wooden nod as she grabbed her cell phone. "The *former* prison warden."

SUZANNE'S breathless 911 call produced a flurry of activity. Molly Grabowski, the dispatcher at the Law Enforcement Center, listened to her frantic, slightly garbled plea and promised to send Sheriff Roy Doogie right away. Then Molly told her she was also going to alert the director of the Cemetery Society, as well as George Draper, proprietor of Driesden and Draper Funeral Home.

"Send them all," Suzanne begged into the phone. "And please hurry."

George Draper got there first, pulling up some five minutes later in a large black Cadillac Federal.

"Limo here," said Toni. She'd gotten over her initial shock at seeing the dead body and now, as they stood by the grave, felt brave enough to steal little peeks at the dead-as-a-doornail Lester Drummond.

"Draper," Suzanne said, under her breath. "I wish it had been Doogie who got here first." Sheriff Doogie was a friend, the duly sworn sheriff of Logan County, and generally the voice of reason. She knew he'd secure the scene, kick-start the investigation, and begin asking all the proper questions. Because—and Suzanne had pretty much accepted this in her head without yet voicing the terrible words—there was no question about it: this certainly had to be a wrongful death.

What else would account for such a bizarre scenario? How else would a dead man end up in a freshly dug grave? Even if Lester Drummond had passed away unbeknownst to them, no self-respecting funeral home would simply dump him in the ground and forgo a coffin, would they? No, of course not. It would never happen. So this had to be . . . an accident? Murder?

Suzanne and Toni stood like frozen statues in the continuing drizzle as George Draper hurried across the wet sod. He was tall and gaunt and dressed in one of his trademark black funeral suits as he walked stiff and stork-legged toward them. Reaching the edge of the freshly dug grave, Draper gave a brusque nod and peered down. He studied the body that lay on its side, pulled his face into a frown, and said, "That was dug just yesterday. That's Mr. Schneider's grave."

"Not anymore," said Suzanne. "Now it's Lester Drummond's grave."

CHAPTER 2

Sheriff Roy Doogie was the next one to arrive. His maroon and tan cruiser shuddered to a stop on the narrow road. Blue and red lights twirled idly atop his roof, but his siren was blessedly silent.

Doogie climbed slowly from his vehicle, hitched up his pants and utility belt, and headed across the soaked ground. He was a large man, broad in the shoulders, jiggly in the hips, with a meaty face and a cap of gray hair. But the glint in his steel gray rattlesnake eyes and the sidearm on his belt indicated he didn't take his duties lightly. Sheriff Doogie, with his hangdog face and outsized khaki uniform, only looked slow-moving. Truth was, not much got past him.

Toni spoke up first. "He's down there." She cocked a thumb. "We found him that way."

Doogie strode to the edge of the grave and gazed down. He frowned, walked around to the narrow end of the hole, and bent down. As he did, Suzanne could hear the cartilage pop in his knees.

"What do you think, Sheriff?" asked Draper. Of the four of them he was the least affected. After all, death was Draper's business. He handled pretty much all the body pickups, embalmings, and visitations in the small town of Kindred. He also provided sympathy cards, guest books, and memorial videos, and he honchoed funerals at the Lutheran, Methodist, Catholic, Baptist, and Episcopal churches. Draper was an equal-opportunity, nondenominational funeral director.

As Doogie straightened up, his eyes betrayed nothing. "Who discovered him?"

"I spotted him first," said Suzanne. "We were chasing Toni's umbrella and we . . ." She saw his brows beetle, so she quickly cut to a more abridged version. "We were delivering flowers for the Sesquicentennial Celebration and just happened to find him that way."

"It's Lester Drummond," said Doogie. "Right?"

"It certainly looks like him," responded Draper. He inadvertently kicked a clod of earth with his toe and Suzanne flinched as it tumbled into the hole.

"You're positive Drummond's dead?" asked Doogie. "He's not drunk or doped or anything?"

The notion startled Suzanne. "I think he's dead. But I never . . ." She hesitated as a wave of guilt swept over her. Should she have done more? *Could* she have done more? Should she have clambered down into that grave and checked his respiration or pulse? Done CPR or chest compressions or something? It hadn't occurred to her until this very second. Still, the notion of dropping down into that dank hole chilled her to the bone.

"He's deceased," said Draper. He spoke with authority as he stepped closer to the grave and pointed. "You see how one side of his face is dark, almost a purplish red? That's lividity."

"Lividity," Doogie repeated. "That means his blood has settled. That it's no longer circulating."

Draper bobbed his head, pleased that Doogie understood. "Correct. It's a general indication that a person has been deceased for a number of hours."

"How many hours would you think in this case?" asked Doogie.

Draper shrugged. "I'd be making a guesstimate, since I don't have liver temp or anything. But I'd say at least two or three."

"I wonder if that's what scared Missy away," said Toni.

Sheriff Doogie's head jerked sideways, as if he'd been touched with a hot wire. "What'd you say?"

Oh boy, thought Suzanne. *Here we go.* She drew a deep breath for what she knew was coming.

Toni looked sheepish now, as if she wished she could take back her words.

But Doogie wasn't about to let it go. "Explain, please," he said, waggling his fingers.

Toni tried to piece together their story. "When Suzanne and I were driving into the cemetery . . . um, to deliver the flowers, we saw Missy Langston driving out. She was in an awful rush. Fact is, she almost smacked into us. So now I'm thinking she might have, you know, seen this?"

"Is that true?" Doogie stared directly at Suzanne.

"Yes," said Suzanne. She knew she had to fess up, too. "We saw Missy back at that turn." She made a quick gesture over her shoulder. "Where the stone sundial is nestled in those cedar trees. Missy practically sideswiped my car." Suzanne fervently wished she had a reasonable explanation for why Missy had been fleeing the cemetery. Because, suddenly, their story seemed to be pointing toward Missy having some sort of involvement in Drummond's death!

"So she was in a rush," said Doogie. "I wonder why?" He rocked back on his heels and stared off into the nearby woods, allowing his thoughts to percolate. Then he said, "Didn't Missy and Lester Drummond go on a few dates together? Weren't they kind of sweet on each other?"

"No," Suzanne said in a firm voice. "No way. Drummond kept making passes at Missy, asking her out. But she was definitely not interested."

"You're sure about that?" asked Doogie.

"Absolutely positive," said Suzanne. And she was. She knew Missy had pretty much loathed Drummond. It wasn't a particularly Christian attitude, to be sure. But Missy had confessed to her that Drummond made her skin crawl. Actually, he'd made Suzanne's own skin crawl. There was just something about the man . . .

Doogie gazed thoughtfully into the grave. "Well, something pretty nasty went down out here. Something or someone killed Drummond. And, from the way you describe your near-collision, whatever it was must have scared the pants off Missy, too." He continued to mull over the strange circumstances. "I don't think it takes a genius to assume an incident took place between the two of them."

"You don't know that at all," said Suzanne. "There could have been two totally separate incidents. Drummond had some sort of freak accident or health crisis. Missy might not have even seen him. Maybe she was alone and felt scared or threatened and just took off fast."

"That seems awfully far-fetched," put in Draper. Much to Suzanne's consternation, he seemed almost amused at her attempt to conjure up a sort of alibi for Missy.

"It could have been . . ." Suzanne began. But her words were quickly drowned out by the blatting whine of the ambulance. They all stood in the mist and watched as a white ambulance roared up behind Doogie's cruiser. Then it turned and began to slowly nose its way down the slight hill and across the damp grass. It threaded its way among the markers and gravestones, headed for the open grave where they stood.

"An ambulance," scoffed Toni. "Lot of good that's gonna do. I'd say Drummond's way beyond resuscitation."

"We need to transport him," said Doogie, with sudden efficiency. "Bag his hands and feet, see what sort of evidence we can come up with. I'll need to get Deputy Driscoll out here to photograph the scene and . . ." He suddenly looked unhappy. "And then we're going to need an autopsy."

Suzanne glanced at George Draper. "Is that something you can do?"

Draper shook his head. "No, that's absolutely not within my realm of expertise. We'll have to bring in a medical examiner."

"You mean Sam?" Suzanne had been keeping company with Dr. Sam Hazelet lately. They were in like, definitely careening toward being in love. It was Sam's turn, this year, to serve as county coroner. So she figured he'd be the one they'd call.

"No, Dr. Hazelet can *pronounce* death," explained Draper. "And decide which cases should be autopsied. But he's not a trained medical examiner. We'll need a specialized forensic pathologist to determine exact cause of death."

"Who's best for this particular case?" asked Doogie.

"There's a fellow I know in Rochester by the name of Merle Gordon, Dr. Merle Gordon," said Draper. "He's awfully good. He's an expert in gunshots and toxicology."

"Is that what you think happened to Drummond?" asked Suzanne. "He was shot or poisoned?"

Draper looked vexed. "It's impossible to tell *anything* at this point, until we get him out of there."

"How are you going to do that?" asked Suzanne.

Draper spun on his heels and gazed at Doogie. "How are you going to do that?"

Doogie's hound dog face suddenly took on a sickly cast. "You want *me* to do it?"

"You're the one in charge," Draper snapped. "You're the duly elected sheriff." He edged away from the grave. "Once you get him up, you can deliver him to my back door."

Toni looked at Doogie. "I hope you haven't had breakfast yet."

Doogie didn't look happy. "Hash browns, bacon, and scrambled eggs," he mumbled.

"Scrambled eggs!" exclaimed Toni. "That's exactly what we're planning to serve at the Cackleberry Club this morning."

PETRA, their baker and short-order chef, stared at them, a look of disbelief on her broad Scandinavian face. "You found *what?*"

Suzanne and Toni had just returned to the Cackleberry Club and were hunkered in the kitchen. They spilled out their story, even as they got ready to dash into the café and take orders. The kitchen was already redolent with the aroma of sizzling sausage, peppery hash browns, and oatmeal muffins. Petra rattled pans and kept a watchful eye on her grill even as she gazed at them, a blue plaid apron wrapped around her ample waist.

Toni rapped her knuckles on the butcher-block table. "Were you not paying attention the first time we ran through this? I said we found Lester Drummond lying in an open grave!"

"I heard you just fine," said Petra. She was big boned and big hearted, favoring jeans and loose-fitting blouses, her size-ten feet shucked into comfy bright green Crocs. Her kindly face and bright brown eyes usually projected a hearty reassurance. But this sudden news had upset her. "Dear Lord, how do you suppose Drummond got there?" she asked. "Who put him there?"

"We have no idea," said Suzanne. She draped a long black Parisian waiter's apron around her neck and tied it in back. "Doogie's securing the scene right now. I'm guessing he'll drop by later and we can squeeze a few choice details out of him."

"Maybe he'll drop by for lunch," Toni cackled. "That's if he can keep breakfast down."

"What's this going to do to the Sesquicentennial Celebration?" worried Petra. "The festivities are set to kick off first thing tomorrow with the rededication ceremony. I mean, our church choir has been practicing for weeks." Petra was deeply religious and a pillar of the Methodist Church. She was also a volunteer with the sponsoring Historical Society.

"I have no idea how the event will be affected," said Suzanne. "I don't know if it will be cancelled or just proceed as planned."

"Drummond," said Petra. "Dumped in an open grave." She shook her head mournfully. "That's just plain awful."

Toni shrugged, then cracked open the door to the café and peered out. "We got customers," she announced. "And they look hungry."

Petra turned back to her industrial stove and sighed. "They always are."

SUZANNE and Toni got busy then, doing their morning meet and greet. They settled customers at tables, rattled off specials, jotted down orders, and poured steaming cups of French roast coffee and English breakfast tea. True to its moniker, the Cackleberry Club did indeed specialize in eggs. The café's creative repertoire included the heavenly Eggs in Purgatory, eggs Benedict, and Eggs Vesuvius, as well as more traditional breakfasts such as scrambled eggs, fried eggs, eggs over easy, and eggs on hash. On certain days, when the mood struck Petra and the stars aligned, she even whipped up specialties such as huevos rancheros, seafood omelets, and white bean breakfast hash.

And their customers, as well as folks who ambled down Highway 65 and stumbled upon the Cackleberry Club, pretty much adored the place. The whitewashed walls were decorated with antique plates, grapevine wreaths, old tin signs, and turn-of-the-century photos. Wooden shelves were jammed with clutches of ceramic chickens and forties'-era salt and pepper shakers. Besides the battered tables, there was a large marble counter and soda fountain backdrop that had been salvaged from an old drugstore in nearby Jessup.

The rest of the place, the Cackleberry Club in toto, was a homey, crazy-quilt warren of rooms that almost defied description. Across the hall from the café was the Book Nook, a small space that carried bestsellers and boasted a fairly decent array of children's books. Next door was the Knitting Nest, a cozy room packed with overstuffed chairs and stocked with a rainbow of yarns and fibers. Petra gave knitting and quilting lessons there and taught her occasional Hooked on Wool classes. Most of her customers were dedicated homemakers, a slightly crunchy-granola crowd that tended to favor nubby sweaters and Swedish clogs.

As Suzanne ferried orders from the kitchen to the café, she couldn't help but wonder about Missy Langston. Why had Missy looked so frightened this morning? What had she laid eyes on? And what part, if any, had she played in this morning's bizarre scenario?

There were a ton of questions to be asked and only Missy could answer them. Suzanne glanced around at the tables, deciding that once everyone was served, she'd slip into her office behind the Book Nook and give Missy a call. She hoped she'd reach her before Sheriff Doogie did.

"Suzanne," Petra called, hunching down to look through the pass-through. "Got your pancake order here."

Suzanne delivered a stack of buttermilk pancakes dripping with maple syrup, refilled coffee cups, and hastily put together an order of turkey bacon and English muffins for a take-out customer. She was especially happy that a few customers were ordering one of their newest side dishes, quinoa breakfast cookies. They were sweet and robust and healthy.

Then, when all her customers were finally enjoying their breakfasts, she dashed into the office to make her private call, away from prying eyes and ears that could launch an avalanche of town gossip. Punching numbers in by heart, she dialed Missy's cell phone. It rang six times, then went to voice mail.

"Missy," said Suzanne, keeping her voice low. "Call me. It's real important. I need to talk to you about this morning. Toni and I saw you, Missy. We were at the cemetery, too!"

Hustling back out to the café, Suzanne grabbed a fresh pot of coffee and made the rounds again, joking with her customers as she poured generous refills. But all the while she continued to think about Missy. And worried about the fact that Lester Drummond had hound-dogged after her for the last few months. He'd flirted with her constantly, asking her out, never wanting to take no for an answer. She wondered briefly if Missy and Lester might have had some terrible confrontation this morning. If so, Suzanne fervently hoped Missy hadn't been caught in some strange, compromising situation where she'd been forced to physically defend herself.

Suzanne grabbed a plate of fresh-baked strawberry muffins from Petra and began stacking them in the glass pie saver on the counter. And then was struck by the sudden notion that Missy might have been lured to the cemetery. Had Drummond tricked her somehow? And then threatened her? Had Missy been forced to act in self-defense?

Suzanne was also burning with curiosity about how Drummond had died. Could it have been a heart attack? Or an epileptic seizure? Maybe his death wasn't related to Missy at all. Maybe he'd been out jogging, minding his own business, and suffered some sort of desperate health crisis. Maybe, in his pain and delirium, Drummond had stumbled into the open grave and died. Or maybe he'd simply fallen into the grave and broken his neck. Could have happened.

Of course, Suzanne also knew it could have been a lot more sinister than that. Drummond could have been shot. Or strangled. Or something even worse. She also wondered if he'd died right there in the cemetery. Or had his body been transported and dumped there by some unknown monster?

These were the burning questions that whirled in her brain. The questions she wanted to discuss with Sheriff Doogie! These were the issues an autopsy would eventually reveal.

"Earth to Suzanne," said Toni. "You okay, girlfriend?"

Suzanne gazed at Toni, who'd dashed behind the counter to brew a fresh pot of coffee. "I've been better."

"You're pretty worried about Missy, huh?"

"Afraid so," said Suzanne. "Word is going to spread mighty fast about what happened to Drummond."

"It already has," said Toni. "Bob Krauser just asked me if I'd heard about it."

"And what'd you tell him?"

"I played dumb," said Toni, giving a wink. "I'm good at that."

"Don't say things like that," said Suzanne. Sometimes Toni could be a little too self-deprecating for her own good. "You're one of the smartest people I know. So please don't put yourself down."

"Thank you," said Toni. "I know I'm not book smart, but I consider myself to be people smart. Being a waitress teaches you a lot about people's moods, personalities, and quirks. It helps you come in on their vibe."

"Digging into your stash of anecdotal evidence," said Suzanne, "what does your inner vibe say about Lester Drummond?"

"Not too much," said Toni. "But as for Missy, I'd say she's got a boatload of trouble headed her way."

CHAPTER 3

WHEN Sheriff Doogie showed up just before lunch, as Suzanne pretty much knew he would, she pounced on him.

"Drummond," she said, before Doogie had even plunked his khaki-clad butt on a stool at the counter. "Are you any closer to figuring out how he died?"

"And good morning to you, too, Suzanne," said Doogie. He looked haggard, and the outer corners of his eyes were crisscrossed with tension lines.

"Sorry," Suzanne said. She realized she'd jumped on him like a rabid schnauzer. Grabbing a beige ceramic mug, she splashed in a generous serving of Kona coffee. She slid it in front of him, then set down a blue-checkered napkin and laid a knife, fork, and spoon on top of it. She pushed cream and sugar toward him and offered him her sweetest smile. "So?" She still wanted any nugget of information she could glean concerning Drummond.

Doogie glanced around the café. "Without giving away any state secrets," he said, "it looks like Drummond might have had some sort of cardiac incident. Maybe a heart attack or stroke."

"And you say that for what reason?" Suzanne asked, leaning her elbows on the counter as she looked at him.

"For one thing, he wasn't shot, stabbed, or hanged," said Doogie.

"You mean there weren't any obvious injuries to his body."

"I guess that's what I meant. Although I didn't examine him all that closely."

Suzanne grabbed a sweet roll dappled with slivered almonds and cream cheese frosting and plunked it on a plate. She did it because that's what she always did when Doogie came calling. Breakfast, lunch, or teatime, Doogie loved his sweet rolls.

"A cardiac incident, huh?" said Suzanne. She'd have to ask Sam about that. Being a doctor, he'd be able to explain the particulars. Such as, had it been ventricular fibrillation, coronary artery disease, or even a brain aneurism?

"We can't start the autopsy until Saturday," Doogie was saying. "Until Dr. Gordon shows up. Then we'll know a lot more."

"Let me ask you this," said Suzanne. "Does Drummond's death seem unusual to you? I mean, in your line of work you do see your fair share of strange and sudden deaths."

"Ayuh," said Doogie. "Far too many. Every time some poor soul gives up the ghost, the hue and cry is, 'Call the sheriff, he'll know what to do.' Problem is, all I can ever really do, besides perform rudimentary CPR or apply a tourniquet, is call an ambulance or life support helicopter."

"But Drummond always seemed to be in excellent physical shape," Suzanne went on. "He prided himself on his strict physical fitness regimen. He worked out constantly at the Hard Body Gym. He made a point of it, even bragged about it. Plus, you'd see him jogging all around town."

Doogie slurped some coffee and munched his sweet roll. "I hear you. He was an exercise fiend as well as a serious muscle builder."

"And he was fairly food conscious," Suzanne went on. "Whenever he ate here, he'd order vegetable soup with whole wheat crackers. Sometimes fish or chicken. But only if it was grilled, never fried."

"Then *boom*," said Doogie, widening his eyes and mouthing a kind of sound effect. "His ticker gives out and the guy keels over." He stared at Suzanne. "Into a convenient open grave." He hesitated. "Seems awfully suspicious to me."

"It does to me, too," said Suzanne.

"Which is why we need a trained forensic pathologist to give us his two cents' worth," said Doogie.

"I think that's smart," said Suzanne. "Heart attacks aren't always the primary cause of death. Sometimes there's an underlying cause."

"You think?"

"Sure," said Suzanne. "Like blocked arteries or even an allergic reaction."

Doogie tapped his own expansive chest. "You ask me, longevity is all wrapped up in the genes that are passed down to you by your folks and the folks before them. If they lived to a ripe old age, chances are you will, too."

"Maybe," said Suzanne. "Although it helps to eat right and keep your stress level in check." She kept talking because she was tap-dancing around the one question she really wanted to ask. And finally did. "So . . . what about Missy?"

"I'm gonna have a sit down talk with that lady," said Doogie. "I called her and she's going to meet me at the Law Enforcement Center this afternoon. We'll see if she can help fill in the blanks."

"Please tell me you'll treat her with kindness," Suzanne urged.

"I'll do my job," said Doogie, but there was an edge to

his voice. "I intend to ask her some very hard questions and in return I expect honest answers."

"I'm sure you'll get those answers."

Toni grabbed a ketchup bottle, slid down the counter, and grinned at Doogie. "How'd it go this morning?" she asked. "After we left."

"Don't ask," said Doogie, draining the last of his coffee.

"Ooh," said Toni, "your face is turning green again. Must have been awful trying to pull Drummond out of that wet grave."

"You don't want to know," said Doogie. Now he poked listlessly at what was left of his sweet roll. "We had to slide a backboard under him and then use the cemetery's coffin lift."

"You're right, I don't want to know," said Suzanne, as Toni wandered off. She hesitated. "Any idea on how long Drummond had been down there?"

"Draper made that guesstimate of two to three hours."

"That would mean Drummond died just before first light," said Suzanne, thinking it over. "What on earth would he be doing in the cemetery at five in the morning? Plus, the time frame doesn't jibe with Missy. We saw her leaving around seven-thirty."

"But what time did she *get* there?" asked Doogie. "And how long did she stay?"

Suzanne was momentarily confused. "But I thought you said Drummond had a heart attack."

"As you so helpfully pointed out, there are lots of ways to give someone a heart attack."

"Oh my gosh!" said Suzanne, gazing into Doogie's hard gray eyes. "You think Missy had a hand in Drummond's death." It was a statement, not a question.

"You have to admit, her presence at the cemetery paints a very suspicious picture."

"Which I'm sure she can easily explain," said Suzanne.

"You think so?" said Doogie.

No, but I hope so, thought Suzanne. *I really, really hope so.*

"OKAY, I've got some lunch specials for you," Petra called out.

Suzanne grabbed a piece of yellow chalk from a shelf behind the counter. "Shoot," she said. Each day, once Petra had the menu worked out, it was dutifully printed on the chalkboard for all to see.

"Chicken meatloaf," said Petra. "Although I suppose it's not really meatloaf at all."

"Chicken chickenloaf?" said Suzanne.

"Whatever," said Petra. "Along with stuffed green pepper soup, egg salad sandwich, and salade Niçoise."

"Is there gonna be pie?" Toni called from across the café, where she was setting out silverware.

"Rhubarb pie with vanilla ice cream," said Petra.

Toni smiled as she rubbed a spoon against her apron. "I have just one word for that. Yum."

Suzanne printed out the menu in block letters. And then, to better monetize the nearby cooler that held offerings brought in from some of their local vendors, she wrote down, Lemon Bread—$4.99 a loaf.

"We've got lemon bread?" asked Toni. She stared at the chalkboard as she stuck her hands into the back pockets of her skintight jeans.

"Our cooler is absolutely stuffed with food," said Suzanne. "Shar Sandstrom brought in ten loaves of bread, Ellen Hardy some jars of pickles, and Dan Mullin brought in a couple dozen wheels of his fabulous Swiss cheese."

The café's wall phone shrilled just then and Toni reached to grab it. She listened for a couple of seconds then passed the phone to Suzanne. "It's for you." She fluttered her eyelids. "Lover boy."

"Sam?" said Suzanne. She was surprised. Most mornings

his schedule was jammed with patients at the Westvale Medical Clinic. She took the phone. Said, "Sam?" again, this time into the phone.

His voice came to her, smooth and mellow with a hint of huskiness. "I heard you were in on the big excitement this morning," he said.

She was taken aback. "You're talking about Lester Drummond? How do you know about that? How on earth did you find out?" She worked hard to keep her voice low and turned her back to the room.

"I'd say the entire town probably knows by now," said Sam. "Plus, George Draper just called. He's decided he wants Lester Drummond's body transferred from his funeral home to the morgue at the hospital. So I'm on my way over there right now."

"No kidding."

"Yup. Draper pretty much gave me the whole story, blow by blow. Or at least as much as he knows."

"Did he tell you we saw Missy at the cemetery?"

"He seemed to take particular delight in relating that part."

"Obviously this is a very weird situation," said Suzanne, blowing out a long breath and running a hand through her hair.

"I'd have to agree," said Sam. "Although I can't say Drummond's death comes totally out of left field. From what I could see, he'd been aggressive and angry ever since he got fired from the prison."

"And then he was turned down for that big job at the bank," said Suzanne.

"Perhaps he was suffering from depression," said Sam. "I suppose he could have overdosed on some sort of medication."

"Was he taking something?" Suzanne asked suddenly. "Something strong?"

"No idea," said Sam. "But if he was, he sure didn't get his scrip from me."

Suzanne hesitated. "What worries me most is that Doogie is going to be questioning Missy. He finds it exceedingly strange that she was at the cemetery this morning."

"Well, so do I," said Sam.

"When Toni and I ran into Missy . . ." Suzanne began. "Or rather, she almost ran into us . . . with her car. She looked absolutely terrified." Suzanne knew her voice had risen an octave. Nowhere near hysterical, but edging into worry.

"Got any idea what she was fleeing from?"

"No. But I can take a wild guess."

"I can hear the concern in your voice," said Sam.

"Here's the thing," said Suzanne. "I think Doogie might be looking for a fall guy."

"Or girl," said Sam.

"But he's dead wrong about Missy."

Sam kept his voice neutral. "I'm sure he is."

"Do you have to work tonight?" she asked. She suddenly needed him. Wanted desperately to talk to him, longed to feel his arms wrapped protectively around her body.

"I'm on call tonight," he told her. "But tomorrow night, that's reserved strictly for us. No ifs, ands, or buts."

IF Suzanne had a dollar for every time one of her lunch customers asked her about Lester Drummond, she would have been well on her way to a very comfortable retirement.

"Drummond's death is all people seem to be talking about," Toni hissed when they met behind the counter. "The news has spread like wildfire all over town."

Suzanne nodded. "It sure has. Sam said they're talking about it at the clinic, too."

Toni cocked an eye toward a table of four older men. Two were dressed in overalls, while two wore T-shirts, jeans, and John Deere caps. "You see those guys over there?" she said.

"Yes?"

"Their theory is that Drummond got offed by some woman."

"Why would they say that?" asked Suzanne. *Why indeed?*

"They were kind of guffawing about the fact that he was such a notorious skirt chaser."

"Well, he was," said Suzanne. "And clearly lots of people knew that."

"Only problem is," said Toni, in an ominous tone, "the most recent skirt he chased belonged to Missy."

"I'm sure she has a perfectly good explanation for why she was in the cemetery this morning," said Suzanne.

"Let's *hope* she does," said Toni.

AT one-thirty that afternoon, Suzanne was standing in line at the bank. She'd been so busy she hadn't had time to deposit all their receipts from the previous week. So here she was, with a bulging blue plastic envelope stuffed with dog-eared ones, tens, and twenties as well as assorted checks.

"Hey, Suzanne," said the teller. She was a plump woman by the name of Jana Riesgraff. Jana had worked at the local bank for twenty years and probably should have been named as the new bank president, instead of the ineffectual young man who was in that position now. "I heard you were the one who found Lester Drummond this morning."

"Does everybody know about that?" Suzanne asked.

Jana nodded as she quickly counted bills, punched in numbers on her machine, and handed Suzanne a receipt. "Pretty much." Jana grinned. "That's the beauty of a small town."

"Or the *problem* with it," Suzanne murmured to herself as she turned to leave. But just as she got to the door, Havis Newton, the brand-new director at the Historical Society, flagged her down. As Suzanne could have predicted, Havis was also aflutter over Drummond's death in the cemetery.

"Fancy seeing *you*," said Havis, putting more meaning into her words than she ordinarily would. She was a young woman, just a few years out of graduate school. With her solemn eyes, straight hair, and no-nonsense horn-rimmed glasses, she was taking her job as seriously as if she'd just been appointed executive director of the Metropolitan Museum in New York.

Suzanne sighed inwardly. It was probably going to be like this for a few days. Until the shock of Drummond's death wore off, or his killer was apprehended. Or both.

"How are you doing, Havis?" Suzanne asked.

Havis just shook her head, looking exasperated. "What can I say? My plate is full."

Suzanne wasn't sure what that meant, so she said, "Is the rededication ceremony going on as planned tomorrow morning? In light of what happened at the cemetery?" She didn't want to talk about the fact that she'd been there. That would all come out soon enough.

"Yes, it's still happening," said Havis. "But I fear this strange death or accident or whatever it was may have frightened people. That it might keep them away."

"I don't think that's going to happen," said Suzanne. "For one thing, folks in Kindred are a curious lot. If anything, a mysterious death might actually bring even more people out."

"Really?" said Havis. "You think they'd come just to see the actual scene of the crime?"

"What's left of it anyway."

"What an awful thought!" said Havis, looking increasingly worried. "I better speak with the cemetery people. Make sure that grave is filled in immediately and the area secured!"

"Do that," said Suzanne. "Otherwise it will surely be a huge curiosity." She smiled warmly and reached a hand out to steady Havis, who looked awfully upset. "Really, it's going to be fine. Don't worry about it."

"But I do," said Havis. "I have to. The Logan County Historical Society is my first curatorial job. Actually, *director's* job. I don't want to blow it."

"That's not going to happen," said Suzanne, "because you didn't do anything wrong. You're just a victim of circumstances." *Kind of like Missy probably is.*

"Drummond's death in the cemetery just came whizzing out of nowhere," said Havis, shaking her head.

"Nothing you can do about it now," said Suzanne. "Except ride it out. Besides, I know tomorrow's rededication ceremony will be a lovely event. A lot of people in Kindred have relatives buried there, so your ceremony will be particularly meaningful to them."

Havis seemed to brighten at her words. "And we really have an entire *calendar* of events." She smiled. "Our candle-light tours on Saturday night, and then Sunday's Historical Society tea at the Cackleberry Club."

"Which we're looking forward to enormously," said Suzanne. "So please . . ." She stepped off the curb. "Don't worry about a thing!"

"You're too kind," said Havis, giving a little wave.

Not really, thought Suzanne, as she crossed the street to her car. *It's just that I'm worried enough for both of us.*

CHAPTER 4

HALFWAY across the street, Suzanne recognized Doogie's cruiser rolling toward her. She stopped and stood in the middle of Main Street, dodged a pickup truck with a sad-looking brown dog riding in back, avoided a hotdogging kid on a banana bike, and waved at Doogie.

She was rewarded with an acknowledging blink of his headlights as he pulled up alongside her, his driver's side window down.

"What's up?" Suzanne asked, leaning in slightly. Doogie was wearing mirrored aviator sunglasses, the kind state troopers favored, and his modified Smokey Bear hat was flopped on the passenger seat next to an open bag of Fritos. She had a sudden, wild flight of fancy. Maybe the sheriff had already figured things out. Maybe he'd already dismissed Missy as a possible suspect and resolved Drummond's death.

Yeah, right, and maybe pigs can fly.

Instead, Doogie removed his sunglasses and stared morosely at her.

"You look awfully down," said Suzanne. He hadn't looked this upset a few hours ago. Her nerves suddenly fizzed into overdrive as she took in the full measure of his face. "What's wrong? Did something else happen?"

"We've got a murder on our hands," said Doogie slowly. "A definite homicide."

Suzanne had been waiting for the other shoe to drop and now here it was. A size-fourteen clodhopper. "You found evidence to substantiate this? I thought you said you were going to wait for the forensic pathologist to make an exact determination."

Doogie put a meaty hand to his chest. "There are a couple of marks." His hand moved slowly in small, concentric circles. "On Drummond's chest."

"What kind of marks?"

"I got three people who believe the pattern is consistent with that of a Taser or stun gun."

"You can't die from a stun gun," said Suzanne. She took a big gulp and added, "Can you?"

"It's been known to happen in a few cases," said Doogie. "Especially if there have been rapid, repeated bursts."

"Wow," she said. Then, "Who are the three people who advanced this stun gun theory?"

"George Draper, Dick Sparrow, who is one of the paramedics, and your friend, Dr. Hazelet."

"And they all concur?" She suddenly wondered why her words sounded like a scripted line from *General Hospital*.

"Yes, they do," said Doogie. "And a Taser in particular can be especially dangerous if drugs or alcohol were involved, or the victim was in some way restrained."

"Do you think that's the sort of combo that killed Drummond?"

"I don't know."

"But now you're on your way to interview Missy," put in

Suzanne. She leaned back from his window. *Really, to interrogate her.*

"Absolutely," said Doogie. "Since she's our primary suspect."

This was unacceptable to Suzanne. "That's just plain crazy. There has to be a logical explanation for all this! For one thing Missy doesn't own a stun gun."

"You sure about that?" said Doogie.

"I don't know *anyone* who owns a stun gun," said Suzanne. "Besides, there have to be other suspects."

"Missy's what we got so far. You and Toni swear you saw her leaving the cemetery, so that places her directly at the scene of the crime."

"Not directly," said Suzanne. "There's that time difference."

"Doesn't matter," said Doogie.

"Sure it does. If Drummond died earlier and Missy was there later there's probably no correlation."

"That's not how I see it," said Doogie. His right hand wandered over and dug into his bag of Fritos.

"Missy's no killer," said Suzanne with exasperation. "I bet if we put our heads together we could figure out some *real* suspects. People who sincerely hated Drummond and wished him ill."

"That might be half the town," Doogie mused as he stuffed a handful of chips into his mouth and chomped noisily. "Since Drummond wasn't exactly Mr. Popularity." His gaze softened then as he looked at Suzanne. "I know Missy's a friend of yours . . ."

"What about Larry Chamberlain?" Suzanne proposed. "The deputy mayor? He sits on the board of directors for the prison. Didn't he pretty much spearhead the charge to get Drummond fired? Maybe he had it in for Drummond."

Doogie shook his head, totally unconvinced. "Chamberlain and some of the others got their way and Drummond *was* fired. So he had no beef with him anymore. There'd be no good reason for Chamberlain to kill him."

Suzanne racked her brain. "Maybe one of the prisoners? Drummond was the warden there for quite a while."

"Last time I looked," said Doogie, "all the prisoners were locked up in their cells or working in the foundry hammering out license plates. I doubt they were gallivanting through Memorial Cemetery early this morning."

"I meant an ex-prisoner," said Suzanne. "One who's out on parole or has been recently released."

"I'm already on that," said Doogie. "Warden Fiedler is drawing up a list for me."

"Well, that's good," said Suzanne. "Because it certainly could have been one of them. Someone who hated or despised Lester Drummond for whatever reason and wanted to get revenge. Maybe Drummond punished him harshly or . . . I don't know . . . sent him to the hole."

"I don't think they send prisoners to the hole," said Doogie, chuckling a little. "That's only in Clint Eastwood movies. This prison's not that hard-core."

"Then what do they do for punishment?" said Suzanne.

"I don't know," said Doogie. "Probably . . . take away their computer privileges?"

"What we need are a couple of good clues," said Suzanne.

Doogie leaned back and scratched his ample belly. "Oh, we got a clue or two."

"But you're still waiting for the autopsy," said Suzanne, mystified. "So what on earth did you turn up? Was there something else on Drummond's body besides the markings? Some strange hair or fibers?" *What have you got that you're not sharing with me, Doogie?*

"You've been watching too many episodes of *CSI*," said Doogie. "No, what we got is Drummond's cell phone."

Suzanne stared at him. "What? Where did you find it?"

"In Drummond's back pocket." Doogie's eyes flicked toward his rearview mirror then back at Suzanne. "We scrolled through his recent call list and emails. It seems that someone *invited* him to that cemetery."

"Just like that? There was an email invitation?"

"Well," said Doogie, "it was one of those short texty-type messages written as an email."

"What'd it say exactly?"

"It said, CU Memorial 0500." Doogie looked pleased with himself, as if he'd taken a giant stride into texting and technology. "See you at Memorial at five o'clock this morning," he said, deciphering it for her.

"I get it," said Suzanne. "But who invited him? That's the critical question."

"We don't know that yet. The sender's name was blocked."

"But you can get around that, right?" said Suzanne. "You can get some tech guy to figure it out for you?"

"Possibly," said Doogie, "I called a fellow who does technical forensics for the state police. He says it can be a complicated process. Sometimes an email even goes through a re-sender that's offshore."

"Offshore? What are we talking about—Europe?"

"More like the Caribbean," said Doogie. "Apparently it's a hotbed for resending and Internet scans."

"Kind of like Nigeria," said Suzanne. There wasn't a day went by that she didn't get some stupid scam letter in her email.

"But the Caribbean's closer," said Doogie. He snorted and grabbed another handful of chips. "And they got good rum and conch chowder."

TEN minutes later, Suzanne pulled in behind the Cackleberry Club and came flying through the kitchen door. Petra was busy chopping vegetables and Toni was munching a chicken salad sandwich and occasionally gazing through the

pass-through, keeping a watchful eye on a handful of lin-
gerers.

Suzanne dropped her suede hobo bag on the floor and
said, "Which do you want first? The good news or the bad
news?"

Petra looked up from her chopping. "Good."

"Bad," said Toni, ever the contrarian.

Suzanne drew a deep breath. "Okay, here's the scoop in
a nutshell. The rededication ceremony at the cemetery
is definitely still on for tomorrow, somebody attacked Lester Drummond with a stun gun, and Missy Langston has become Doogie's prime suspect in Drummond's
murder."

"That's totally whack," said Toni. "The part about Missy,
I mean."

"There's no way Missy would attack or even kill Drummond," said Petra. "She doesn't have a violent bone in her
body. She's a caring, gentle soul."

"You think everybody's a gentle soul," put in Toni.

"That's because most people are," said Petra. "Given half
a chance."

"Doogie's pretty adamant about this," said Suzanne. She
put a hand to the back of her neck and ruffled her hair.

Petra frowned. "You're still going to stand by Missy,
aren't you? I mean, we all have to."

"Darn tootin'," said Toni.

"Of course I am," said Suzanne. "It's just that Doogie . . ."
She frowned and shook her head. "I don't know."

Petra crossed the kitchen in two gigantic strides and
planted her hands on her ample hips. "Listen to me, Suzanne
Dietz, I don't want to hear 'I don't know' from you. You're
the one who reads all the mysteries we got stashed in the
Book Nook and figures them out by the time you hit chap-
ter three. So put on your Sherlock Holmes cap and start
figuring this thing out! You hear me?"

"You mean help Doogie?" said Suzanne, a little stunned at Petra's outburst.

"No, help Missy!" said Petra. "She hasn't had an easy life since her divorce from that no-good insurance huckster." She gave a satisfied nod. "There, I got that off my chest. I said my piece."

"You sure did," said Toni. "Jeez Louise." She stared at Petra. "I had no idea you were so tense."

Petra looked suddenly sheepish. "I'm not tense. I'm just terribly alert. And I didn't mean to attack you, Suzanne. It's just that you're so gol darn smart at figuring things out. So to see you kind of befuddled like this scares me a little. Rocks my world."

"Ditto that," said Toni.

"I had no idea you guys had that much faith in me," said Suzanne.

"You're our fearless leader," said Toni. "When Junior dumped me for the sixty-fourth time and poor Donny got Alzheimer's and stopped recognizing Petra's sweet face, you were the one who pulled this all together." She spread her arms to indicate that she meant the Cackleberry Club. "You made it possible for us to pick up the pieces and regain our confidence and self-worth."

"And live again," said Petra.

"And laugh again," added Toni.

"Plus, you did it all just weeks after burying your own husband," said Petra, remaining serious. "So, honey, that tells me that you've got beaucoup fortitude."

"And guts," said Toni. "Although I guess fortitude is a fancier word." She shrugged. "I better get me one of those 'learn a new word a day' calendars."

"You're doing just fine," said Petra.

"Oh my gosh," said Suzanne, totally blown away by all their words. "A girl couldn't ask for two better BFFs."

"Group hug?" said Toni, jumping up.

They clustered together, arms slung around one another's shoulders, squeezing hard.

"Always remember," said Petra, "a friend is someone who understands your past, believes in your future, and accepts you just the way you are."

"Amen to that," said Toni.

And a friend stands by you, Suzanne thought to herself, knowing she had to stand by Missy. No matter what it cost her.

STILL feeling at odds and ends, Suzanne threaded her way through the café and slipped into the Book Nook. With one glance around at the reassuring collection of books she felt instantly at peace. She loved the floor-to-ceiling wooden shelves with their orderly array of books. And she was especially proud of the little typewriter-typed signs that called out each of their various categories: Mystery, Romance, Fiction, Cooking, Crafts, and Children's. A few nights a week, Toni led a romance readers club in here while Petra gave knitting lessons next door. On those nights, Suzanne would stay late, too, fixing finger sandwiches for their guests or serving up wheels of cheese, sliced apples, and crusty baguettes. It was a win-win situation for everyone. The events were great fun for their customers and brought in a little extra money for the Cackleberry Club. Because, Lord knows, in this topsy-turvy economy, every nickel counted.

Suzanne grabbed a copy of *Winnie-the-Pooh* that had been left in one of the old maroon-colored velvet chairs and shelved it in its rightful spot. Then she glanced at her watch. Mid-afternoon already. Would Doogie have finished his interview with Missy by now? Was Missy suddenly free as a bird, cleared of any and all nasty suspicion, and already back at work as manager of Alchemy Boutique? Good question.

Stepping into her office, Suzanne dialed Missy's cell phone.

She got the same six rings and voice mail. Okay, that still wasn't working. So why not call Alchemy direct? She scanned the phone book and dialed their number.

"Alchemy," came a cultured voice. "How may I help you?"

Suzanne immediately recognized the voice of Carmen Copeland. Carmen was a local author blessed with a gift for writing semi-hot romance novels. Hence, her bodice busters were forever making the *New York Times* bestseller list and boosting Carmen's ego even more. Carmen lived in neighboring Jessup in a palatial Victorian home that looked like it had been airlifted in from Nob Hill in San Francisco. And a year ago, she had opened her edgy boutique here in Kindred, determined to jog everyone's Midwestern sensibilities with cutting-edge European fashion that included Miu Miu bags, huge statement rings, Prada blouses, and expensive designer jeans. Carmen's other calling card, the one that most folks knew her for, was that she was fabulously wealthy, arrogant, and insensitive. Not necessarily in that order.

"Is Missy there?" Suzanne asked, choosing not to identify herself.

"No, she's not," said Carmen in a clipped voice. "Who's calling, please?"

Rats, thought Suzanne. "This is Suzanne Dietz."

"Ah, Suzanne," said Carmen, her voice going a little smoother, a little silkier. "No, your little friend is not here right now. In fact, she left work mid-morning, claiming to be ill."

"That's too bad," said Suzanne. Obviously Missy hadn't clued Carmen in to any of the events this morning. Then again, why would she? If Carmen ever thought Missy was a suspect in a local murder she'd probably hand her a pink slip and boot her out the door.

"Yes, I was quite disturbed," said Carmen. "Since we're frantic here at the boutique. My new shipment of Cavalli just arrived, as well as two cartons of J Brand Jeans. Someone's got to steam out all the wrinkles and make everything presentable before it's put on display!"

Suzanne decided to go for it. "Carmen, did you hear about what happened this morning?"

Carmen sighed deeply. "Good gracious, of course I did. Who *doesn't* know? When I went out at lunch, the entire town was buzzing about Lester Drummond. That poor, dear man. Such a tragic, senseless accident."

"It might not have been an accident," said Suzanne. But she regretted her words almost instantly.

"Not an accident?" said Carmen, her voice rising a couple of octaves. "Suzanne, what do you know that I don't? What aren't you telling me?"

"I don't really have any specific details," said Suzanne, wishing she'd never even mentioned Drummond.

But Carmen was suddenly suspicious. "This doesn't have anything to do with Missy, does it?"

Darn Carmen and her sixth sense. "Oops, I need to go now," said Suzanne. "My other line is blinking."

Suzanne hastily hung up the phone, feeling lousy and wishing she hadn't uttered a single word. She hoped she hadn't gotten Missy into even more trouble.

Me and my big mouth. And why is it that Carmen always brings out the worst in me?

Suzanne wandered back into the Book Nook. Harvey, her favorite UPS driver, had dropped off two cartons of books this morning, so right now was as good a time as any to unpack them. The Cackleberry Club was relatively peaceful, with teatime starting to wind down in the café. Through the doorway, she could see Toni putting together a cream tea special: a bottomless pot of Assam tea along with a scone, jam, and Devonshire cream.

Grabbing a box cutter, Suzanne sawed open the cartons. She hoped they contained the children's books she'd ordered. They did. There were six copies of *Nighttime Ninja*, six copies of *Fancy Nancy* illustrated books, plus two oversized coffee table books titled *Craft Magic.*

Perfect.

In fact, in honor of their upcoming Hearts and Crafts Show, Suzanne decided she'd make a little assemblage on the display table that teetered between two rump-sprung chairs she'd salvaged from a friend's attic.

She covered the table with one of Petra's elegant pink afghans, added a vase of daisies, then began stacking up art books. She added two books on basic figure drawing, a craft manual that was supposedly for beginners, and then some books on decoupage, knitting, and oil painting. For a final touch she zipped into her office and grabbed a framed piece of needlepoint off the wall. Petra had embroidered a red heart with the words "2 hearts, 2 lives, 4ever entwined." It had been her anniversary gift to Suzanne.

SUZANNE rattled around for a good hour, fussing with the books, then wandered into the adjacent Knitting Nest. Colorful skeins of yarn and dozens of knitting needles were arranged here, along with towering stacks of quilt squares. Many of Petra's hand-knit pieces were displayed on the walls, including an azure blue sweater made from cuddly Sugarbunny Yarn, several knitted scarves, and a lovely pink afghan of baby alpaca yarn. Armchairs were draped with knitted shawls and afghans and pulled into a cozy semicircle so customers always felt welcome to sit and stay awhile.

In the relatively short time they'd been open, the Cackleberry Club had emerged as the apex for food, books, knitting, quilting, and good old-fashioned female bonding that drew fans not just from Kindred but from all over the tri-county area.

"Suzanne." Toni stood in the doorway. "We're about ready to lock up."

Suzanne glanced up, surprised. She'd been toying with a set of birchwood knitting needles. "You are? Already?" It seemed as if the afternoon had pretty much whizzed by.

"Yup. Petra's heading out to visit Donny at the nursing home and Junior's taking me to the stock car races at the Golden Springs Speedway over near Cornucopia."

"Yee gads, Junior's not racing one of his beaters, is he?"

"Not that I know of," said Toni. "Although it's always been his dream." Junior Garrett was Toni's on-again, off-again husband with a penchant for juvenile delinquency. They'd been married for three years but had lived apart for more than two and a half of those years. Even with their quickie Vegas wedding and immediate separation, Suzanne didn't doubt they loved each other. But Junior had serious commitment issues. In other words, he was seriously committed to sticking dollar bills in the skimpy costumes of the girls who danced at Hoobly's Roadhouse, despite his till-death-do-us-part vows to Toni.

"Okay," said Suzanne. "Have fun, then. Try not to get hit in the head by a flying tire or something."

"Want me to lock you in?" asked Toni.

"Naw, I'll be outta here in five minutes," said Suzanne.

Back in the Book Nook, she fussed with her arrangement for another two minutes, shelved another handful of books, then flipped off the light and walked out into the café.

As Suzanne glanced at their antique soda fountain and rows of colorful ceramic chickens, she couldn't help but grin. When her husband, Walter, had died a little more than a year ago, she'd taken a giant risk and, like a female Don Quixote, rushed full tilt into this crazy venture. She'd been determined to carve out a future, make a difference, and have more than a few giggles along the way.

And, with the help of Toni and Petra, the Cackleberry Club had become an instant hit. Part café, part social club, part successful event venue, it was a modest little operation, but it made money. Even in their first year of business, they'd not just earned a living but turned a small profit, which was practically unheard of these days, especially when so many small businesses struggled just to keep the lights on.

Yes, other than finding a dead body this morning, things were pretty much right with the world for Suzanne. The Cackleberry Club was steaming along, her love life was simmering, and somehow, she'd managed to lose three pounds so her skinny jeans fit like a glove. So hallelujah and pass the chocolate chip cookies.

"Cackleberry Club," she murmured as she looked around the cozy café. "You are my lifeline."

Footsteps sounded outside. Suzanne turned and cocked her head, wondering what traveler might be rattling her doorknob, hoping for a cup of coffee and a slice of pie. Well, it was too late now. She'd have to tell them they were closed. But as she stepped toward the door, it suddenly flew open and smacked hard against the wall. And Missy Langston walked in.

Bright circles of pink blazed high on each cheek and her eyes shone with outrage. In her mid-thirties, Missy possessed fair, almost porcelain skin, hair the color of fine corn silk, and a full, ripe figure. She'd caught the eye of more than a few men in Kindred but hadn't been seeing anyone lately. At least Suzanne didn't think so.

"Guess where I just came from!" Missy sputtered to Suzanne. And then, in a more plaintive voice, "Guess where I've been all afternoon!"

CHAPTER 5

SUZANNE stared at Missy, trying to gauge her friend's mood as well as her words. Of course, she had a fairly good idea exactly where Missy had been. "Um . . . the Law Enforcement Center?" Suzanne said. "Talking to Sheriff Doogie about Lester Drummond?"

"Yes!" Missy shrieked. "How on earth did you know that?"

Suzanne shrugged. Missy obviously hadn't had time to check her voice mail. Or listen to the buzz of town gossip.

"And you know what?" Missy continued, practically sputtering to get her words out.

Suzanne wanted to say, *You're a suspect.* Instead she said, "What?"

"I'm a suspect!" Missy wailed.

"Missy," said Suzanne, knowing in her heart she had to be up front about everything. "I know a little about what's going on. Toni and I saw you this morning. When you were racing out of the cemetery. In fact, you almost plowed into us."

Missy peered quizzically at her. "That was you?" Her jaw

suddenly clenched tight. "So *you* told Doogie I was at the cemetery?"

"Uh . . . Toni mentioned it to him, yes." When Missy's eyes turned cold as frosted pennies, Suzanne added, "She . . . we . . . pretty much had to. Especially after we found Lester Drummond lying in a grave."

Missy's mouth closed with a snap.

Suzanne continued, "Besides, honey, Doogie would have figured it out for himself eventually. There's a good chance someone else saw you, too. I figured telling the truth was the aboveboard thing to do."

"You didn't do me any favors, Suzanne," said Missy. Her voice was chilly, veering below zero degrees Celsius.

A tiny line insinuated itself between Suzanne's brows. Something felt off Missy wasn't usually this hostile. In fact, she was one of the sweetest people she knew. "We told Sheriff Doogie because we knew it wouldn't be a problem for you." She hesitated, let a couple of beats go by, and said, "It isn't really, is it?"

Missy blew out a glut of air and plunked herself down in a wooden chair. "It's just that . . ." She lifted a hand, then let it flop in her lap.

"What, Missy? What's going on?"

Missy pressed her lips together and shook her head. She looked annoyed. But beneath the tightness in her face she seemed frightened, too.

Suzanne marched over to the counter and poured a glass of water. She carried it back to Missy and sat down at the table across from her.

"Why do people always bring you water when you're upset?" Missy asked, taking a tentative gulp.

"I don't know," said Suzanne. "It's just what you do." What she didn't say was, *It's what you do to buy time in mixed-up situations that you don't understand. In situations where you're afraid for your friend.*

"Well, thanks," said Missy, taking another sip.

Suzanne decided to take a softer approach. "So you had a conversation with Sheriff Doogie . . . ?" Her voice trailed off.

Missy narrowed her eyes and said, with bite in her voice, "Seems to me you've grown awfully close to that old toad."

Suzanne was suddenly defensive. "Don't call him that. Sheriff Doogie is a good man. He looks after our town."

"He's completely misguided," Missy snapped. "He thinks I murdered Lester Drummond, which is absolutely preposterous! You know I wouldn't hurt a fly! Even though I despised Drummond!"

"I know that," said Suzanne. "But try to see it from Doogie's point of view. You were at the cemetery, Drummond was at the cemetery." She lifted her hands, spread her fingers apart in a gesture of appeal. She was hoping Missy might fill in some of the blanks and explain herself. And certainly, there were significant blanks to be filled in.

Instead, Missy grew wary. "Why were *you* there, Suzanne?"

"Because Toni roped me into delivering a bunch of flowers for the Sesquicentennial," Suzanne replied. "But my guess is, you already know that. Sheriff Doogie probably mentioned all that to you."

Missy gave a tight nod.

"Okay," said Suzanne. "Now I want you to listen very carefully to me. I need you to know that I seriously went to bat for you this morning. Yes, we told Sheriff Doogie that we saw you leaving the cemetery. But I also told him, in no uncertain terms, that there was no way you could be involved in Lester Drummond's death."

Missy stared at her. "You really told him that?"

"Yes. Of course I did," Suzanne said with great intensity.

"He didn't believe you," Missy said in a soft voice, a voice filled with pain. Her eyes sparkled with tears and she let loose an anguished sound in the back of her throat.

"Then tell me what happened," said Suzanne. "Tell me what went on up there this morning. And then let me help you!"

Missy put a hand up and pushed away a hunk of blond hair, revealing a furrowed forehead. "Suzanne, do you remember when Ozzie was killed?" Ozzie had been Missy's sweetheart after she'd divorced her husband, Earl Stensrud.

Suzanne nodded. She remembered.

"Sheriff Doogie questioned me about that murder, too!"

"For about two seconds as I understand it. And it was only pro forma, since you were one of any number of people who were close to Ozzie."

"But I'm pretty sure Doogie still doesn't trust me. In fact, I'm pretty sure he hates me!"

"Doogie doesn't hate you, Missy. He barely even knows you."

But Missy just shook her head mutely and stood up. Seconds later, before Suzanne could ask any more questions or elicit any responses, she was out the door.

SUZANNE was three blocks from home when she flipped a U-turn in the middle of Hayworth Avenue and gunned her engine. She'd just decided that Baxter and Scruff, her trusty watchdogs, could cool their paws for a few more minutes. Because, for some strange reason, the thought had come crashing into her brain that she should return to Memorial Cemetery. To take another look.

She didn't want to. No, she really did not. In fact, Suzanne repeated that negative litany to herself as she threaded her way down Main Street, navigated a residential district known as The Oaks, then finally made her way out of town and up the narrow road to the cemetery.

And when she drove through the gates, that same jittery feeling she'd experienced this morning came flooding back to her. She drove down the narrow lane between marble tombs and whitewashed headstones. The sun, which had peeped out for all of three minutes this afternoon, was now secluded behind layers of thick clouds, and the chill wind was back. Trees thrashed overhead, low branches *tick-ticked* their skeletal fingers against the sides of her car, and the windshield began to fog. It was like some strange entity was trying to warn her or keep her away.

Silly girl. Stop imagining things, she told herself.

Turning down a muddy lane, Suzanne noticed a few people wandering among the stone markers. Clad in sweaters and jackets, they were hurriedly placing flowers on some of the graves.

Good. At least I'm not alone here.

But when Suzanne got to the old part of the cemetery, the part where they'd dropped the flowers and discovered Drummond lying in the grave, she discovered she was quite alone.

Just my luck. Doesn't anybody have relatives buried over here?

She sat for a full minute, engine still idling, defroster sputtering, her hands gripping the steering wheel. Then she drew breath, shut off her engine, and got out.

Squishing across the grass, her shoulders hunched to the wind, Suzanne headed for the flutter of yellow crime scene tape some fifty yards away. When she reached the grave, she decided it didn't look all that different than it had this morning. Except now it was just an empty dark hole. There was no waxen-looking Lester Drummond crumpled on his side, only the persistent bad memory of seeing him that way. The town's tough guy laid low.

But by whose hand?

Certainly not Missy Langston's. Missy may have been harassed by Drummond, but she'd never retaliate with violence. It just wasn't in her nature. Then who else? Who in this small town, where calm and collegiality were so preciously valued, would do such a terrible thing?

As Suzanne stood there, shivering, thinking dark thoughts, she was suddenly aware of a low, throaty rumble. Startled, she whirled around, feeling a jolt of panic. But all she saw was a small, dirty yellow Bobcat tractor bumping its way toward her.

It's coming to fill in the grave, she told herself. *A sort of burial without the body.*

And with that bizarre thought buzzing inside her brain, Suzanne couldn't get out of the cemetery fast enough.

WHEN she finally arrived home, Suzanne wasn't very hungry. Somewhere along the line (she wondered where!) she'd lost most of her appetite. So after fixing bowls of kibble for Baxter and Scruff, she made herself a small bowl of tomato soup and grabbed a couple of crackers. She put her meager meal on a tray and carried the whole shebang into Walter's former office, the spot that was fast becoming her cozy library/den/computer room.

Setting everything on a small spinet desk, Suzanne opened her laptop computer and, after a moment's thought, pecked in the words "stun gun."

A whole world of companies offering self-defense and personal safety devices was suddenly revealed to her.

Is protection that big a business?

She decided it certainly must be, judging by all the stun guns, Tasers, stun batons, canisters of Mace, and pepper sprays that were readily available to wary, security-minded individuals. There were even voice changers, listening devices, tap detectors, and (who would seriously use this?) invisible ink! The ad copy on all the websites seemed to have the same fear-mongering message: Times are getting tough! You'd better be prepared!

As Suzanne started clicking around, trying to find a local dealer, she came upon Billy's Gun Shop in neighboring Jessup. Turns out they carried Tasers and stun guns. And wasn't this interesting. You didn't even need a carry permit. Really, just cash-and-carry, Suzanne thought.

Suzanne ate her soup thoughtfully as she perused a few more websites filled with so-called protection devices as well as amateur spy paraphernalia that even included wrap-around camcorder sunglasses.

Trying to shake off a growing sense of unease, Suzanne finished her soup and decided to take her dogs out for a long walk. A little physical exercise was always helpful in relaxing the brain and dissipating negative energy.

After much wagging of tails and spinning in circles, leashes were clipped onto Baxter and Scruff and they all headed out into the misty evening. Suzanne, wearing leggings, a Windbreaker, and Reeboks, kept up a steady, fast walk-jog pace. The three of them splashed across nearly deserted streets, spun past homes that all seemed to be battened down for the night, and brushed down alleyways where rain dripped off giant lilac bushes. After a spin through Founder's Park, which was also deserted, the swing sets and slides looking a little forlorn, Suzanne slowed her pace and turned for home.

Now that Baxter and Scruff had sufficiently blown out the carbon, they padded along slowly, sniffing and snuffling at every little patch and parcel of wet grass. And, as Suzanne approached her home, she saw that someone was waiting on her front steps. Sitting there, hunched over, as rain continued to patter down.

Was it Toni? Had she had a fight with Junior and was in need of a little gentle commiseration? Along with a glass or two of pinot grigio?

But when Suzanne got closer, she saw that it was Missy.

"Hi there," Suzanne said, as she turned up her walk.

"Hi," said Missy. She was dressed in jeans, short boots, and an olive drab anorak that was cinched at the waist with a wide black leather belt. She looked, Suzanne thought, like a stylish commando.

"You're sitting in the drizzle," said Suzanne, diplomatically. "So whatever you want to talk about, it must be pretty important." She stepped past Missy, stuck her key in the lock, and pushed open her front door. Then she dropped the leashes and let the dogs wander in themselves. "Come on in," she called to Missy.

"You're being very nice about this," said Missy. She ducked her head, looking a little embarrassed.

"You're my friend," said Suzanne. She gave a lopsided smile. "I have to be nice. It's the law."

"At least you haven't lost your sense of humor," said Missy.

"Believe me," said Suzanne, as she hung up her jacket and stepped out of her damp shoes, "I try not to."

Once they'd grabbed drinks, orange juice for Suzanne and white wine for Missy, they settled on the sofa in Suzanne's living room. Suzanne, who was burning with curiosity now, didn't waste any time. She asked Missy point-blank if she owned a stun gun.

"No!" Missy cried in a strangled voice. "And I wouldn't even know where to buy one." She grabbed a pink and white pillow that had the words Keep Calm and Carry On stenciled on it and hugged it to her chest. "Why do people keep asking me about that?"

"Who else asked you about it?"

"Sheriff Doogie did," said Missy. "This afternoon."

"During your interview."

"More like an interrogation!" Missy flipped the pillow aside and grabbed her glass of wine off the coffee table. She drew a deep sip and held on to her glass.

"I'm sorry this is so painful for you," said Suzanne. "But you did show up on my doorstep tonight, so there must be something on your mind." She sat back and waited for Missy to explain herself as Baxter and Scruff watched with solemn, worried dog expressions.

Missy seemed to weigh Suzanne's words for a while. She

put her wineglass down and said, "You're right. I came here for a reason. The simple fact is . . . I need your help."

"Okay," said Suzanne, trying to put a note of encouragement into her voice, hoping to draw Missy out more.

"I went to the cemetery this morning because someone called and asked me to meet them there."

"Explain please," said Suzanne.

Missy drew a deep breath. "Lately, I've been doing volunteer work at the women's shelter over in Jessup."

"Harmony House? The one what's-her-name . . . Sookie runs?" said Suzanne.

"They've got a new executive director now," said Missy. "A woman by the name of Marcia Schutte. Anyway, I've been helping with a program called Best Foot Forward. It's a self-esteem program that deals with how to interview for a job and how best to present yourself in a business situation."

"Wait a minute. Are you saying that one of the women in the program called and said she needed your help?"

"I *thought* she did," said Missy. "I was pretty sure I recognized her panicked voice."

"But you don't know exactly who made the call?"

"Not really."

Suzanne stared at her, completely at a loss for words. "You went to the cemetery on the basis of what was pretty much an anonymous call? I find that hard to believe. Didn't you think someone was trying to set you up?"

"They *did* set me up!" shrilled Missy.

"But what did this person—the woman on the phone—say to you?"

"She said she was in trouble and needed my help."

"So you jumped in your car and took off not knowing who it was or what sort of trouble she was in? Jeez, Missy!"

"What can I say? I'm the trusting sort." Missy looked deeply embarrassed. "I don't even lock my door at night."

Suzanne was dumbfounded. "Not even when Drummond was harassing you? Asking you to go on dates and such?"

Missy shook her head. "No."

This didn't make sense to Suzanne. So she decided to get right to the heart of the matter. "Do you know what happened to Lester Drummond this morning?"

"No! Of course not!"

"You didn't have anything to do with his death?"

Missy was practically wild-eyed. "Absolutely not!"

"Did you see him lying in the grave?"

Missy's eyes slid sideways and she hesitated for a moment. That's when Suzanne knew she'd seen him. Missy hadn't had a direct hand in Drummond's death—but she'd certainly seen the man lying in the open grave.

"You *did* see him," said Suzanne.

Missy took a gulp of wine and nodded. "I did. I was scared out of my wits, but in a strange way I felt relieved, too."

"How so?" Suzanne asked. She was worried and curious about Missy's conflicting emotions.

Missy hugged herself. "Drummond had become like a dangerous animal who'd slipped his collar. He was acting crazy, like he was on his own personal rampage."

"Did Drummond ever threaten you?"

"Sort of," said Missy. "But he was always cagey about it. Some nights when I worked late, he'd wait for me outside Alchemy. And it was always the same. Come have a drink with me. Let's go out to dinner. Come over to my house for a relaxing evening, wink wink." Missy shivered. "One night, when I told him to take a flying leap, he grabbed my arm so hard it left a big purple and green bruise." She snuffled hard now and a tiny tear trickled down her cheek.

"Did you do anything about all this?" Suzanne asked. "Whip out your cell phone and call 911? Talk to Sheriff Doogie on the QT? I mean, you could have gotten a restraining order or something."

Missy ducked her head and wiped her tears. "I didn't. I know I should have acted right then and there, but I didn't." She sighed. "The truth of the matter is, I was embarrassed by the whole thing. I just wanted it to go away."

Suzanne reflected on what Missy had just told her. Probably, there were any number of women who were embarrassed by unwelcome advances that escalated too fast, too violently. Unfortunately, many of the women who *didn't* act sometimes suffered at the hands of angry husbands, boyfriends, or stalkers like Drummond. They died, quite literally, of embarrassment.

Leaning in urgently, Suzanne said, "You have to tell Sheriff Doogie about this. You have to lay this out logically, give him all the facts, and help him understand your mindset. Explain what really happened."

"I *did* tell him!" said Missy. "I went through the whole story with him but he didn't believe me."

"Then *I'll* tell him."

"Suzanne, please! You've got to do more than that!" Missy grasped Suzanne's hand and squeezed it tight. "You've got to make him *believe* me!"

"I'll try my best."

"Really, you have to help me!" Missy continued tearfully. "You're the only person I know who can help me!"

CHAPTER 6

WITH Petra attending the rededication ceremony at Memorial Cemetery this Friday morning, it was up to Suzanne and Toni to whip up some breakfast magic. Luckily, Suzanne had thought to bring in Kit Kaslik, a young woman who'd helped them out before, to wait tables in the café. So as Suzanne reigned supreme at the stove, frying strips of turkey bacon and flipping mounds of hash browns, Toni and Kit scribbled orders, poured coffee, and ferried out plates of pancakes, French toast, and Suzanne's special breakfast BLT.

Wondering how Petra kept all the orders straight, Suzanne popped two orders of eggs and hash browns onto plates, then leaned down and called through the passthrough, "Pick it up!"

"Got it," said Kit swinging by. She was a stunning young woman. Her almond eyes were tipped with full lashes, her hair had recently been colored a rich chestnut, and she possessed a lush body. Until six months ago, she'd made her living as an exotic dancer at Hoobly's Roadhouse, a disreputable joint out on County Road 18. Now Kit was working odd jobs and attending medical reporting classes at a trade school over in Jessup. She'd also found herself a steady boyfriend. She was rehabilitated, as Petra liked to say.

"Hey, you're pretty good at this cooking stuff," Toni said as she bumped her way into the kitchen amidst a mélange of aromas that included fried onions, bacon cornbread, scones, and crazy-quilt bread.

"You think?" said Suzanne. She was secretly pleased that she was able to keep up with the morning mayhem as well as turn out a few pans of baked goods, too.

"Oh yeah," said Toni. "You're doing great. Plus you don't yell at us like Petra does."

"Petra doesn't yell," said Suzanne with a smile.

"Okay then," said Toni. "Let's just say you're not quite as *enthusiastic* as Petra. You're more—contained."

"And that's a good thing?" said Suzanne. She poured a mixture of eggs, cream, mushrooms, and red peppers into an omelet pan, swirled it all around gently, and said, "So how were the car races last night?" She figured a little light conversation might take her mind off worrying about Missy, which she'd been doing practically since she woke up.

"Noisy but actually kind of cool," said Toni. "The whole evening was basically a series of stock car events."

"And what's that, exactly?" asked Suzanne.

"A bunch of junkers flying around an oval racetrack," said Toni. "And then, of course, there was the requisite guzzling of beer and eating of hot dogs."

"Fun," said Suzanne as she tossed a handful of grated pepper jack cheese on top of her omelet.

"Junior was pretty much hysterical the entire time. He kept jumping up and down like a wild mongoose, spitting little hunks of peanuts as he screamed at the drivers."

"Now there's enthusiasm," said Suzanne, shuddering inwardly.

Toni shook her head. "Junior surely does love cars. You know, he's even bragging about entering his old Chevy Impala in a demolition derby?"

"Don't let him," said Suzanne. "He'll just go and get himself killed. Or, worse yet, permanently paralyzed."

"I know, I know! That's exactly what I told him! Junior may be a fairly decent mechanic, but he's not that skillful a driver. He never wears his glasses and his reaction time is shot to crap. And, to tell you the truth, I don't think he even has a legal driver's license." Toni suddenly lifted her nose and sniffed. "What smells so dang good? Your bacon cornbread?"

"No, it's Petra's pork roast. She left me two full pages of explicit instructions on how to slow-cook it in a Dutch oven so we can serve pulled pork sandwiches for lunch."

"Love it," said Toni.

"Hey," said Kit, popping into the kitchen suddenly. "Do we serve something called a Nest Egg?"

"Why?" said Toni. "Is somebody asking for one?"

Kit nodded. "Yeah."

"That's a poached egg served in a popover," said Suzanne. "But we're not doing popovers today."

Toni glanced at the top of the stove where Suzanne was working. "Looks like we're not even doing poached eggs."

"We leave the fancier stuff to Petra," Suzanne explained to Kit.

"So just what's on the chalkboard?" said Kit.

"That's right," said Suzanne. "Until Petra shows up and takes over for lunch, anyway."

"Hey, Kit," said Toni. "You heard about Lester Drummond getting killed and all, didn't you?"

Suzanne glanced sharply at Toni, wondering where she was going with this loose talk.

Kit nodded eagerly. "I sure did. I also heard you guys were the ones who found him."

"You heard right," said Toni. She stuck her hands in her

apron pockets, trying to look casual. "Say, didn't you have some trouble with him? When you were dancing at Hoobly's?" Kit's career as an exotic dancer had concluded when Suzanne and Petra had a heart-to-heart talk with her and convinced her to pursue a more appropriate line of work. Which, in Kit's case, was anything else.

Kit looked suddenly unhappy. She lowered her voice conspiratorially. "I could tell you stories about Lester Drummond that would curl your hair."

Toni looked intrigued. "Really? Like what?"

"Oh," said Kit, "for one thing, he was forever pestering the dancers."

"I think Drummond pestered quite a few women," Suzanne murmured.

"Like, what did he do?" asked Toni.

"He'd sit on the runway flashing a wad of cash and—"

"Kit," said Suzanne, interrupting, "do you think you could help out again on Sunday? We're hosting a formal tea for the Historical Society."

"Sure, I think I could do that," said Kit.

"Appreciate it," said Suzanne.

"But what about . . . ?" said Toni.

Suzanne slid her omelet onto a plate, added two slices of turkey bacon, and handed it to Kit. "This is for the gentleman at table six, if you don't mind."

BY late morning, the café had pretty much cleared out. This was the quiet time when a few of the Cackleberry Club regulars stopped by to grab an early take-out lunch or have a quick cup of coffee. Which meant Suzanne was pretty much freed from her kitchen chores and able to wander out to fix a nice cup of tea.

Just as she was brewing a pot of oolong, Dale Huffington sauntered into the Cackleberry Club.

"Hey, Dale," said Suzanne. Dale Huffington was a behemoth of a man, one of the locals who worked at the Jasper Creek Prison, the private prison run by Claiborne Corrections Corporation that Kindred's town council had hailed as a wellspring for new jobs when it opened a few years ago. "You just get off your shift at the prison?"

"That's right," Dale said as he slipped onto a stool at the counter.

"Fix you a cuppa?"

"Why not?" said Dale.

Dale was one of Suzanne's recent converts. He'd once been a confirmed coffee-and-donuts type of guy. But, over a period of repeat visits to the Cackleberry Club, Suzanne had converted him to tea and scones. Dale was Suzanne's bright spot among the men of Kindred, who tended to favor coffee, black, with six lumps of sugar along with bear claws, glazed donuts, and sticky buns.

Working quickly, Suzanne placed a small pot of Darjeeling tea in front of Dale along with a cup and saucer.

"Thanks, Suzanne." Dale peeked under the teapot's lid and decided to let his tea steep a minute longer.

"I suppose everyone out at the prison is all atwitter over Lester Drummond's death," said Suzanne.

"It's all anybody's been jawing about," agreed Dale. "Guards, administration, inmates. Even the guys who are confined to their cells are passing kites."

"What are kites?" Suzanne asked.

"Little folded-up notes," said Dale. He poured out his tea in a golden stream, added two lumps of sugar, stirred gently, and took an appraising sip. "Good," he said.

"You want a scone, too?" Suzanne asked. "We've got fresh-baked maraschino cherry scones."

Dale's right hand strayed unconsciously to the ample tummy that hung over the belt of his blue prison-issued slacks. "I shouldn't. But . . . okay, you talked me into it."

Suzanne plated a scone and added a small dish of Devonshire cream.

"You're fairly close to Sheriff Doogie," said Dale. "Does he have any idea what happened to Drummond? Or even a wild card notion?"

Suzanne wasn't about to breathe a word about Missy. Instead she said, "I don't think so. All I know is he is bringing in a forensic pathologist to examine Drummond's body and run some tests."

Dale looked surprised. "That so? That's kind of big-time, isn't it?"

Suzanne shrugged. "I guess." She knew it was.

"They expect to find something unusual?"

"I suppose they expect to find cause of death," said Suzanne carefully.

"It was murder, wasn't it?"

"Probably," said Suzanne. "But no one knows *exactly* how Drummond died." She thought about the strange marks on his chest that Doogie had discussed with her. "Or if there are any clues that might lead to his killer."

Dale ducked his head right, then left, then hunched forward slightly toward Suzanne. "I got a kind of theory on that."

"Is that so?" Suzanne was suddenly dying to hear it.

"If I were going to go looking for suspects, I'd take a good, hard look at Karl Studer."

Suzanne shook her head. The name meant nothing to her. "I don't think I know who that is."

"Sure you do," said Dale. "Ornery-looking guy with long gray hair. Drives a red rattletrap pickup and makes his living selling firewood and poaching deer out of season."

Thinking about it, Suzanne did recall a skanky-looking guy who favored camo shirts and vests and stumped around town looking generally unhappy.

"You probably saw him at Schmitt's Bar or Hawley's Place," said Dale.

"Okay," said Suzanne. "I guess I've seen him around."

"Anyway," said Dale, "his son, Dwayne, is incarcerated at the prison and old Karl pretty much hated Drummond with a passion."

"Why?" Suzanne asked. "Drummond was just the warden, not the judge and jury that sent his son there."

"Those facts don't matter to Studer," said Dale. "He isn't your logical, linear thinker. The thing is, Studer lives right near that cemetery where Drummond was found."

"He does?"

"As the crow flies anyway," said Dale. "If Sheriff Doogie is still fishing around for a suspect, I'd recommend he go talk to Karl Studer."

"He *is* looking at a number of suspects," said Suzanne.

She wondered, could Studer be an actual suspect? Could he be Drummond's killer? Was this mystery not such a big mystery after all? Could it all be wrapped up and tied with a bow in a matter of, well, minutes?

"If Doogie wanders in here," said Dale, "you might want to put a bug in his ear."

"I think I might do that," said Suzanne.

WHEN Petra finally blew into the kitchen just after eleven o'clock, they were all thrilled—and a little relieved—to see her.

"Whew," said Toni, dumping a stack of dirty plates into the sink. "I'm sure glad you're back."

"Hey, it's the Kitchen Queen!" said Suzanne. She was happy to relinquish her post at the stove. Better to work the front of the house where she could chat up the customers and keep things humming.

Petra smiled her crooked, knowing smile. "You guys couldn't do it without me, could you?" She reached into her pocket for a tortoiseshell barrette and poked it into her short hair.

"Oh, we can do it, we just don't *like* to do it," said Toni.

"So tell us," said Suzanne. "How was the ceremony?"

"Yeah, did anybody show up?" asked Toni. "Did you guys warble your little hearts out?"

"The cemetery rededication turned out to be quite lovely," said Petra. "And surprisingly well attended."

"I figured it would be," said Suzanne. She decided there was nothing like the scene of a crime to ensure a full house.

Petra opened the oven door, peered at her pork roast, and smiled. "Lookin' good. Smellin' good, too."

"I did everything exactly as you instructed," said Suzanne.

"I bet you had to sit through all sorts of boring speeches," said Toni, wrinkling her nose.

"There were a couple of speeches, yes," said Petra, ever the diplomat. "But they were really quite moving, talking about the early settlers and how the people of Kindred have been tasked to carry on their hopes and dreams."

"And what else?" said Toni. "Besides singing and speeches?"

Petra draped a red calico apron around her neck. "Oh, let's see. One of the Boy Scout troops carried off a rather snappy flag ceremony, and the vets from the VFW gave a twenty-one gun salute."

"Hah!" said Toni. "Considering what happened out there, maybe you shoulda had a twenty-one *stun* salute!"

"Toni!" admonished Petra. "That's an awful thing to say."

"I thought it was kind of funny," said Toni.

"No, it just makes me sad," said Petra.

"But even *you* didn't like Drummond," said Toni, back-pedaling. "And you hardly dislike anyone!"

Suzanne stepped in. "At least the weather cleared a little and your choir was able to sing."

"Thanks goodness," said Petra. "After all the practicing we did."

"What songs did you sing?" asked Suzanne.

" 'Shout from the Highest Mountain' and 'I Will Remember You.' "

"Nice," said Toni. "The feel-good churchy songs."

"I'm just glad the whole thing wasn't cancelled," said Suzanne. She knew a lot of people had been planning hard for this celebration and the nasty business with Drummond could have easily derailed it.

"I hope it's going to be sunny and warmer tomorrow," said Petra. "It would be nice to have the weather cooperate for the candlelight walk."

"What's that?" said Toni. "This is the first I've heard of any candlelight walk."

"Don't you read the *Bugle?*" asked Petra.

"Sometimes," said Toni. "When they print, you know, horoscopes and winning lottery numbers and stuff." She wiped her hands on her apron. "So what's this candlelight walk all about, anyway?"

"It's going to be very solemn and lovely," said Petra. "There'll be candles flickering throughout the old part of the cemetery and guides dressed in Civil War–era costumes to give tours and point out historic markers."

Toni looked suddenly intrigued. "Sounds sort of spooky."

"Everything sounds spooky to you," said Petra. She slipped out of her loafers and into a pair of size-ten green Crocs, what she called her cookin' shoes. "I'm afraid you have a profound sense of the macabre, Toni."

"What's macabre?" said Toni. She thought for a minute, then snapped her fingers. "Wait a minute, it's that island right by Hong Kong, right?"

"That's Macao," said Suzanne politely. "Macabre means gruesome or ghastly."

Toni considered this. "I guess that might describe me. Since I kind of groove on scary movies like *Halloween* and *Final Destination.*"

"Dreadful fare," shuddered Petra.

"What about the *Twilight* movies?" said Toni. "At least there's a little romance tossed in among the vampires and werewolves."

"Doubtful," said Petra.

"Suzanne," said Toni, a little jacked up now, "let's go to the candlelight walk tomorrow night. Okay?"

But Suzanne wasn't all that anxious to make yet another trip to the cemetery. And weren't her nerves frazzled enough?

"Come on," said Toni, sensing her mood and trying to cajole an answer out of her. "It'll be fun."

"Maybe," said Suzanne, caving a bit, wondering how much fun it would be to visit graves in flickering candlelight. "I suppose we could."

"Suzanne," said Petra, "better do the chalkboard."

"What's on tap for lunch?" asked Toni.

"Let's see," said Petra. "Pulled pork sandwiches, personal pan pizza with pancetta and caramelized onions, and egg salad sandwiches. And maybe, if I hustle my buns, I can manage a couple pans of cranberry muffins."

AT exactly twelve noon, amid the clanking of dishes and clacking of silverware, Sheriff Doogie shuffled through the front door. He gazed around with his cool law enforcement gaze, gave his sidearm a perfunctory pat, then ambled over to the counter and slid onto the end seat. It was Doogie's regular seat, the one with the permanent tilt to it.

"How's it going?" Suzanne asked, looking him straight in the eye. "The investigation, I mean."

"Cooking along," said Doogie. "I got that list of recent parolees that we're trying to run down. Those who still reside in the area, that is."

"And how many would that be?" Suzanne poured Doogie a piping-hot cup of coffee and slid it across the counter.

Doogie winked one eye shut, thinking. "Looking at the surrounding counties, probably . . . a half dozen?"

"So not too difficult to follow up on."

"Of course, the list could always turn out to be a dead end," said Doogie, pulling his cup closer.

"Is there anything else on your radar?" Suzanne asked.

Doogie sucked air in through his front teeth. "There's a halfway house over in Cornucopia."

"No kidding." That was news to her. "With ex-cons?"

"That would be the general idea."

"You think one of them could have killed Drummond?" she said, working hard to keep her voice low. I mean, are they dangerous guys?"

"There hasn't been any trouble up until now," said Doogie. "But . . ."

"But you never know," said Suzanne, interrupting him. "So you have to check it out."

"Correct."

Suzanne decided this was as good a time as any to bring up her conversation with Dale. "Hey, one of the prison guards was in here this morning, after his shift ended. Dale Huffington?"

Doogie took a sip of coffee and nodded. "Sure, I know Huff."

"Anyway," said Suzanne, "Dale happened to mention a guy by the name of Karl Studer. Are you familiar with him?"

Doogie stared blankly at her. "Can't quite place him."

"Apparently Studer sells firewood and has been known to poach a few deer."

A look of distaste suddenly dawned on Doogie's doughy face. "Oh jeez, *that* son of a gun!"

"Apparently Studer's son is currently incarcerated at the prison," said Suzanne. "And, according to Dale, there was no love lost between Karl Studer and Lester Drummond."

"Huh," said Doogie.

"And Studer lives close to the cemetery," said Suzanne, pretty much repeating word for word what Dale had told her. She was leaning on the counter now, her elbows squarely placed.

"And this is all Huff's theory?" said Doogie.

"It is, but I think it could hold water."

"Sounds like a stretch," said Doogie. "But . . . it *might* be worth a look-see."

"I thought it would tweak your interest," said Suzanne. She glanced over at her chalkboard. "If you're hungry, and I'm guessing you are, we've got pulled pork sandwiches, little pizzas, and egg salad today. But the pulled pork's really the best."

"Then that's what I'll have."

"Got it," she said. And then added, "I talked to Missy last night."

"Yeah?" Doogie shot her a wary look.

"She told me she thought she was responding to a call from one of the women from Harmony House."

"Already spoke to their director," said Doogie. "Nobody there called."

"How would their director know that?" asked Suzanne.

"Because the phone is closely monitored," said Doogie.

"But someone could have . . ."

"Someone didn't," said Doogie. "But just to make sure, we've subpoenaed all their phone records." He smiled coldly at Suzanne. "No stone unturned."

CHAPTER 7

SUZANNE was standing behind the counter, fixing a ham and Swiss cheese sandwich for a take-out order when Gene Gandle walked in. Gene was the *Bugle*'s intrepid reporter, really their only reporter, who was always on the hunt for a scoop. Tall and gangly, with a square head that seemed to bob on his thin stalk of a neck, Gene slumped at the counter, staring at her as she spread mustard onto the ham sandwich. When Suzanne didn't acknowledge him, Gandle said in a mournful voice, "I feel like a total doofus."

"What's wrong now, Gene?" asked Suzanne. Gene was always at the Cackleberry Club complaining about something or other. He fancied himself Kindred's answer to Woodward and Bernstein.

Gandle threw up his hands. "Are you kidding me? I just missed the story of the century!"

"What are you talking about?" said Suzanne.

Did something major happen that she wasn't aware of? Like the start of World War III? Suzanne sliced the sandwich and slid it into a plastic bag. Then she popped that into a brown paper bag along with a small bag of barbecue-flavored chips.

"I'm talking about Lester Drummond!" Gandle said with great exasperation.

From her few but intense dealings with Gene Gandle, Suzanne keenly suspected him to be a wonked-out drama queen. "You really think Drummond compares to Pearl Harbor or the Kennedy assassination?" she asked. "No, of course it doesn't. Drummond's death, sad as it may be, strange as the circumstances are, is just a small-town incident."

But Gandle was clearly reveling in his own pity party. "Why does the major news in this town always happen on a Thursday, just hours *after* our paper comes out?"

"I think people do it to spite you, Gene," Suzanne said, tongue planted firmly in cheek. "Just so you won't get your scoop. Everyone holds off on car crashes, arrests, drug busts, and all the really grisly news until Thursday afternoon."

"Now you're mocking me," said Gandle.

"I wouldn't do that," said Suzanne. *Hee hee.*

"And you were the one who *found* Lester Drummond! You could have at least *called* me. Given me a heads-up. Throw me a bone of some kind."

"It wasn't the first thing that came to mind," said Suzanne. "Besides, I didn't know you had your own personal tip line."

"Face it," Gandle sighed. "I'm just unlucky. Maybe it's because I'm a Gemini. There's too much duality in my life."

"Maybe it's because you wear too many hats at the paper," suggested Suzanne. "What with reporting hog prices, softball scores, and holes in one at the country club, handling ad sales, and everything else."

Gandle's face suddenly brightened at her mention of ad sales. "Why don't you place an ad in the *Bugle*, Suzanne? I'd cut you a real sweetheart of a deal." He pulled a calculator from his shirt pocket and began punching numbers like crazy. Suzanne decided Gene must be figuring his commission.

"I could let you have a quarter page for the price of an eighth of a page. For around the price of . . ." His fingers worked overtime as he punched more numbers. "Two hundred bucks."

"Look around, Gene," said Suzanne. "The Cackleberry Club has plenty of customers. Running an ad isn't going to bring in any more. Besides, I'm already writing a tea column for Laura." Laura Benchley was the editor and publisher of the *Bugle*. Gene's boss. "So I already get a byline and a little blurb about afternoon tea service."

"I happen to know you're late with your column," said Gandle, in a self-induced snit now. "Weren't you supposed to turn it in last week?"

"I had two bridal showers and a catering gig at the library last week," said Suzanne. "But I'll get to it. In fact, I did get to it. My column's pretty much written."

"It's a matter of honoring deadlines, Suzanne," said Gandle, tapping an index finger against the counter. "Journalistic integrity. That's what counts!"

"Gene," said Suzanne, "it's not like you work for the *Washington Post*. And covering high school baseball scores and hog reports isn't going to win you a Pulitzer."

Gandle leaned back on his stool and puffed out his chest. "Oh yeah? Well, I'll have you know, Miss Smarty Pants, that I have a rather juicy interview scheduled for later today."

Suzanne's antennae perked up. "What are you talking about, Gene? With who?"

"Wouldn't you like to know," Gandle chortled.

"I bet you're talking to Doogie. Getting all the facts about Drummond's murder." She regretted being so flippant with him earlier. It was fun, but not exactly a charitable thing to do.

Gandle flapped a hand disdainfully. "No, no. Not Doogie." A glint suddenly appeared in his wary eyes. "Guess again."

"I have no idea."

Gandle leaned forward over the counter and said, in a stage whisper, "I'm going to interview Lester Drummond's ex-wife."

Suzanne's eyebrows rose in twin arcs at this bombshell. "Seriously? I had no idea Lester Drummond even had an ex-wife."

This was news. Really big news.

Gandle saw her surprised reaction and smiled a cat-who-ate-the-canary smile. "Oh yeah. I'm gonna get the scoop."

Suzanne waited a couple of beats, then said, "So who is this woman? Tell me more."

"Her name is Deanna Drummond," said Gandle, pronouncing each syllable very deliberately.

"And she's here right now, in town? Are you telling me the poor woman's come to plan her ex-husband's funeral? And you're going to harass her?"

Gandle looked thoughtful. "Not exactly. From what I understand, Deanna Drummond's been living here for the past couple of weeks. Staying in Drummond's house." The corners of Gandle's mouth pulled up in a smarmy smile. "Cohabiting."

"Does Sheriff Doogie know about this ex-wife?" asked Suzanne.

"I have no idea. But I imagine you're going to blab it to him," said Gandle, suddenly sounding cross.

"Well, somebody should tell him," said Suzanne.

"And why would that be?" asked Gandle.

"Because . . ." said Suzanne. She thought for a few moments. "She could be a suspect."

SMACK dab in the middle of lunch, just when Suzanne was balancing a tray with three orders and a fresh pot of coffee, the phone rang.

"Get that, will you?" Suzanne called to Toni.

Toni grabbed the wall phone off the hook, listened for a few seconds, and aimed a finger at Suzanne. "It's for you, cookie."

"Give me a minute," said Suzanne. She delivered the luncheons to table five, poured a refill for the adjacent table, and handed the pot to Kit. Then she pirouetted across the café and snatched up the phone. "'Lo," she said. "Suzanne here."

"Sweetheart," came Sam's low purr.

A broad smile lit up Suzanne's face. "Hey! What's up?"

"I've got car trouble," said Sam. "Beamer's in the garage for the rest of the day, so I was wondering if you could pick me up after work and give me a lift?"

"Of course I can. What's wrong with your car?"

"Oh, I don't know. I think the carburetor has to be retooled in Stuttgart or something like that."

"But it'll be ready tonight," said Suzanne.

"Fingers crossed," said Sam. He chuckled. "Or maybe not."

PETRA was sitting on a bench in the kitchen, wiggling her toes and eating a slice of pizza, when she said, "You know, we have to get organized for our Hearts and Crafts Show next week."

The Hearts and Crafts Show was one of Suzanne's brainstorms. They were asking local artists and crafters to donate handmade goods to be displayed, gallery style, at the Cackleberry Club for a week and sold through a silent auction. All the proceeds would go to the local food bank.

"I thought we were all set," said Toni. She glanced sharply at Suzanne. "Aren't we all set?"

"Our posters have been hanging in every storefront window in Kindred for a month now," said Suzanne. "So I'm expecting a fair number of donations. Oh, and the show's been mentioned in the *Bugle*, too."

"Did you ask Paula Patterson to mention it on her morning radio show?" asked Petra.

"Yes, I did," said Suzanne. "She promised to really talk it up."

"That's good, huh?" said Toni.

"That's great," said Suzanne. "Anyway, I've got the donation forms all printed and ready and we've got drop-off times for the artwork scheduled for tomorrow, Monday, and Tuesday."

Petra slapped her hands against her knees and stood up. "Okay, good. So we're further along than I thought. Now if we can pull off the Historical Society tea on Sunday and this art show next week I can die happy."

"Don't talk old," said Toni.

"Then I won't die, I'll just go into hibernation like a bear. Man, they have it made. Bears get to eat themselves stupid and then take a nice long sleep for six months."

"Guys," said Suzanne, aiming to redirect the conversation, "have either of you heard anything about Deanna Drummond?" She'd been turning her conversation with Gene Gandle over and over in her mind and decided she had to mention it.

Toni grabbed the last slice of pizza. "What's a Deanna Drummond?"

"Apparently she's Lester Drummond's ex-wife," said Suzanne. "And she's here in town."

"Get *outta* town!" said Toni. "There's an ex-wife in the picture?"

"I suppose she's here for the funeral?" said Petra.

"Noooo," said Suzanne tantalizingly. "According to Gene Gandle, the ex-wife has been living at Drummond's place for the past couple of weeks."

"You mean they were going to get back together?" said Toni, going pop-eyed now. "Wow, it sounds like the plot of a soap opera. Star-crossed exes about to reunite—then POW! Tragedy strikes!"

"With an imagination that vivid, I think you could *write*

soap operas," said Petra. She pulled on an oven mitt and peeked inside her oven. "Mmmmn."

But Toni was still demanding the 411 on Deanna Drummond. "So what else do you know about this Deanna person?" she asked Suzanne. "Come on, girlfriend! Start dishing some dirt!"

"I just told you everything I know," said Suzanne, suddenly aware of a loud rumbling coming from their back parking lot.

"Which wasn't very much," said Toni.

"What *is* that awful noise?" asked Petra. "It sounds like some kind of heavy machinery."

Toni pressed her nose to the window. "Yee gads, it's Junior."

"Did he steal a tractor or something?" asked Petra as the noise got louder. "Or a forklift?"

"Naw, he's just driving some rotten old blue car," said Toni. "Probably something he found in *Auto Trader*." Then she did a kind of double take and said, "Oh shoot!"

"What's wrong?" said Suzanne.

"I hope that isn't what I think it is!" said Toni, grabbing Suzanne's hand and pulling her out the back door.

Junior Garrett grinned when he saw them. He was nothing less than a vision in saggy blue jeans, white T-shirt, and scuffed black motorcycle boots. He swept his grease-stained trucker cap off his head and said, "Afternoon, ladies."

"What. On. Earth," said Suzanne. She turned an inquiring gaze at what almost passed for an automobile.

"Isn't she something?" said Junior. He was practically bursting with pride. "My blue beater. I've been working on this for quite some time." His hand coasted along the front fender in a loving caress. "I plan to enter it in the demolition derby Sunday night!"

Suzanne and Toni stared in horror at Junior's car. It was an old Chevy Impala, but that's where the similarity to a street-legal car ended. The blue paint was mostly chipped or worn off, leaving the car with a fine patina of rust. The front bumper was reinforced with what looked like heavy-duty bedsprings, the windshield as well as side and rear windows had been chipped out, and the roof was punched in.

"You can't race that car in a demolition derby," said Suzanne. "You'll be disqualified on the basis that it's *already* demolished."

"It's a total wreck," agreed Toni.

"Naw," said Junior. "What you see here is a car that's been stripped down to its bare essentials and customized with special reinforcements." He grabbed a metal strut that had been welded from the driver's side door to the roof. "See? Genuine steel rebar."

Suzanne thought the strut looked suspiciously like a metal crowbar.

"And the doors have been welded shut, too," Junior continued. "For added strength and safety."

"Safety?" squeaked Toni.

"How on earth do you get in and out if you can't open the doors?" Suzanne asked. She knew she shouldn't indulge Junior with such questions, but, like a mongoose drawn to the cobra, she was fascinated by his demented dreams of speedway glory.

"Simple as pie," said Junior, giving his hips a little shake. "I just shimmy through the open windows. See, that's the beauty of my unibody modifications. There are no pesky doors to come unhinged or fly off at critical moments during the race."

"You're the one who's unhinged," cried Toni, who couldn't stand it anymore. "Junior, you're gonna *kill* yourself!"

"If you flame out," said Suzanne, "there's absolutely no way for you to escape!"

Junior reached inside the car and pointed to a small red fire extinguisher that had been crudely wired to the dashboard. "Then I just pull that thing out and extinguish the flames."

Toni shook her head. "In between the rolling of the car, the crunching of metal, and flames singeing your hair and flesh, do you really believe you'll have the wherewithal to operate a fire extinguisher?"

"Sure," said Junior. "What's the big deal?"

"Junior," said Toni, practically hyperventilating now, "you barely have the wherewithal to operate a pencil sharpener!"

Stung by her words, Junior's face darkened. "You see why we can't make a go of our marriage?" he cried. "You're constantly picking at me and finding fault! It's 'Junior, this won't work' or 'Junior, you can't do that.'" He shrugged his forelock off his face. "Sometimes it feels like I can't do anything right!"

"That's because you *can't*!" Toni shot back.

BACK inside the comfy café, in the zone of safety and sanity, Suzanne said, "You're not really going to let Junior race that thing, are you?" They were setting up for afternoon tea, covering the battered wooden tables with linen tablecloths, adding crystal sugar bowls and small tea light candles. Petra had baked two more batches of cranberry scones.

"What can I do?" said Toni. "Junior may act like a dim bulb juvenile delinquent, but he's a grown man. I can't tie him to a chair or lock him in his room. I can't idiot-proof his life!"

"But Junior would seriously be risking his fool neck," said Suzanne. She wasn't all that crazy about Junior, but she didn't want to see him end up in a full body cast, either. Plus, he was her friend's husband, even though the two of them were estranged. She cared because she cared about Toni.

"Maybe on the night he races I could hire an ambulance to stand by," muttered Toni.

"Expensive," said Suzanne.

"Life insurance?" said Toni. She frowned, thinking. "Although shouldn't they really call it death insurance?"

"That might make it a harder sell for the agents," said Suzanne.

"Ah man, Junior's so poor he can barely afford the free clinic."

"Hold that thought," Suzanne said, as the phone started to ring. She scampered a few steps and snatched up the receiver. "Cackleberry Club."

"Suzanne?" said a small voice.

"Yes?"

There was a choking sound and then Missy Langston said, "Suzanne, I'm so sorry to interrupt your day. But I didn't know who else to call."

"What's wrong, Missy?"

"I just got some really bad news."

"What happened?" asked Suzanne, fearing the worst.

"I've been fired."

The wire that was strung tight around Suzanne's heart loosened just a bit. At least Missy hadn't been arrested. "Oh no, Missy. Just now?"

Missy sighed. "Carmen waited until I'd unpacked about fifteen boxes of clothes, steamed everything, and carefully hung it all on racks. *Then* she canned me."

"That's awful. In fact, it's practically sadistic."

"We always knew she was a little crazy," said Missy.

"Did Carmen give you any severance pay?"

"Not a dime."

"Well, can you apply for unemployment?"

"Carmen warned me that I better not try. She said it was a disciplinary firing, so I wouldn't be eligible for unemployment. Now I don't know *what* I'm going to do!"

"It wasn't disciplinary." Suzanne snorted. "You were a model employee who received rave reviews from all your customers. This firing was based on Carmen paying too much attention to town gossip, then having a snit fit and completely overreacting."

"You know that and I know that," said Missy. "But what am I going to tell the people at the unemployment office?"

"You don't need to tell them anything," said Suzanne. "Just go and apply first thing Monday morning. If Carmen tries to deny your unemployment claim, you can appeal it. You just write out exactly what happened and let the unemployment people sort it out."

"Really?" said Missy.

"Of course," said Suzanne. "And if Carmen still tries to deny it, then she will have to sit down with you and a mediator. That's the way it works. Respectful and fair."

Missy gave a huge sigh of relief. "Thank you, Suzanne. Thank you so much for telling me all of that. At least now I feel a little more hopeful."

"What happened?" Toni asked when Suzanne hung up the phone.

"Carmen fired Missy," said Suzanne, shaking her head.

"I can't say I'm surprised," said Toni. "Carmen's a real witch."

"Ah . . . she's just been listening to stupid rumors. And letting her emotions get away from her. Maybe, hopefully, when Drummond's killer is finally caught, she'll see her way clear to hiring Missy back."

"You think Drummond's killer will be caught?"

"Of course he will," said Suzanne. "And I hope sooner than later."

"What if—" Toni stopped abruptly.

"What if what?"

Toni waved a hand in the air, as if to erase her thoughts.

"No, go ahead," said Suzanne. "Say it." *Because I think I know what you're going to say. And I think I want to hear it.*

"What if Missy really *was* involved?" said Toni. "Then what?"

"Then . . ." Now it was Suzanne's turn to hesitate. "Then she's really cooked."

CHAPTER 8

SUZANNE swung into the parking lot at the Westvale Medical Clinic and tooted her horn. About two seconds later, Sam came striding out the front door, zipping a light green Polo jacket over his blue scrubs. Tall and in his early forties, with tousled brown hair and blue eyes, he was good-looking in an earnest boy-next-door kind of way.

"You're like a bad date," Sam said, a smile curling his lips, as he jumped into Suzanne's car. "You just pull up and honk. Don't come in to meet the folks or anything."

"Because that's what you told me to do!" Suzanne protested.

"Kidding," said Sam. "Kidding." He leaned across the console and gave her a nice, long, lingering kiss. No quick, perfunctory peck, so, okaaaay.

"Your, um, car is ready?" Suzanne was suddenly feeling all warm and tingly and slightly discombobulated.

"Naw, not until tomorrow."

She gave him an expectant look. "So you want me to drive you . . . where?"

"Home," said Sam. "Preferably *your* home if you don't mind."

"Dr. Hazelet," said Suzanne, smiling now, "I don't mind a bit."

As they bumped across the parking lot, which was jointly shared by the Hard Body Gym, Sam lifted a hand and waved at Boots Wagner, the owner. Wagner, a fit-looking man of sixty with ropey, sinewy arms and buzz-cut gray hair, was stomping out to his car, a little red two-seater Miata.

"That's the guy Doogie should be talking to," said Sam, as they watched Wagner fold himself into his car. "If he wanted to get a line on Lester Drummond's comings and goings, that is. I swear Drummond spent half his waking days at that gym. Mornings, when I'd come in to work, Drummond's black SUV would be parked outside. When I'd leave at night, it would sometimes be back again."

"Drummond was working out twice a day?" said Suzanne. "Isn't that bad for you? Isn't that awfully hard on your spine and joints? I thought the smart thing to do was let your body rest a bit between workouts."

Sam cocked his head and winked at her. "Depends on what kind of workout you do, baby."

Suzanne smiled. It might have been springtime, with the weather still cool, but suddenly it felt like the heater was going full blast.

BAXTER and Scruff were over the moon to see Sam. They whirled and twirled and licked and kissed him in greeting.

"Whoa," said Suzanne. "I never get that much attention when I come home."

"That's because they're used to you," said Sam. "To them, I'm still the new flavor of the month."

Yes, you are, thought Suzanne happily.

"So maybe a glass of wine?" said Sam. "To celebrate TGIF?"

He'd brought over a case of assorted wines a couple of weeks ago and they were slowly working their way through it.

"Sounds perfect," said Suzanne. "You go ahead and do the honors while I season and grill a nice piece of swordfish for us."

"White wine then," said Sam, reaching for a bottle of chardonnay.

As Suzanne worked on her fish, chopped vegetables, and tossed together a simple salad, Sam popped the cork and they shared a glass of wine.

"Good," said Suzanne taking a sip. Then she reconsidered. "No, better than good. This is really quite exceptional." The wine felt silky but robust on her tongue with hints of berry and citrus that lingered pleasantly.

"You can always count on Cakebread Cellars to be lush as well as bright." Sam took a sip and paused. "You know, you really should get a wine and beer license for the Cackleberry Club."

"Heaven forbid," said Suzanne. "Then we'd have to be open evenings, too."

While the swordfish sizzled on the Jenn-Air grill and Suzanne stirred a pan of beurre blanc sauce on the stove, Sam gave her the update on Lester Drummond.

"He was definitely Tasered," said Sam. "A number of times. Which I think might have sent his heart into cardiac arrest."

"Wow," said Suzanne. "That sounds like a terrible way to go."

"But that's not all," cautioned Sam. "He had drugs on board, too."

"You already ran a toxicology test? I'm surprised. I thought that was something the medical examiner would handle."

"It is and he will when he gets here tomorrow. I just ordered a couple of basic tests to make Doogie happy and satisfy my own niggling curiosity."

"So what were the drugs? Can you say?"

"Looks like a psychostimulant. An amphetamine."

"Drugs," said Suzanne, cocking her head. "I find that awfully strange. I always pegged Drummond as being fairly health conscious. What with the jogging and the incessant working out he did."

"There's more. He'd also suffered a nosebleed."

"What would that indicate?" asked Suzanne.

Now Sam looked a little concerned. "Generally it's a sign of intracranial pressure."

"Which means what exactly? Talk to me in layperson's language, please," Suzanne reminded gently. "Explain it in terms I can understand."

"Well, I'm no ME so I can't make a final determination about cause of death. But I'd say that Drummond's breathing had been seriously compromised."

"No kidding." Suzanne gave a low whistle. This news pretty much turned her on her ear. "How would that happen? Him pitching into the grave and lying on his side with his mouth stuck in the mud?"

"Possibly."

"And this is on top of the Tasering?" said Suzanne.

Sam took a sip of wine. "Yup."

Suzanne stirred her sauce thoughtfully. "Who would have a Taser in their possession, besides Sheriff Doogie and a few of his deputies? I mean, I know you can order one through the Internet and all, but who'd want to? They just seem so . . . dangerous."

"But easy to get," said Sam. "Much like buying an assault weapon. I hope someday we'll put laws into place to prevent the purchase of nasty items like that."

They were quiet for a minute, thinking things over but also just enjoying each other's company. "So," said Suzanne, "did anything else jump out at you?"

"To be honest, I only took a cursory look at Drummond.

Partly out of curiosity and partly because I knew you'd pester me about it."

"You're right," said Suzanne. "I would have." She turned this over in her brain while she picked up a small baguette and buttered it. "I am pestering you."

Sam nodded. "Yes, you are. But it's okay, since you're also making me this lovely dinner. It's a fair enough trade."

"So it's looking more and more as if Drummond was murdered."

"The evidence is piling up," Sam affirmed.

"And you were the one who discovered the Taser marks in the first place?"

"No, no," said Sam. "George Draper did. That's why he wanted Drummond's body moved to the hospital morgue. He wanted me to take a look at the marks, too, so we could give Doogie a heads-up. Plus, I don't think Draper really wanted the autopsy to take place in his embalming room. He probably thought Drummond would take up valuable table space. Just in case he suddenly got a couple of customers."

Suzanne wrinkled her nose. "The autopsy is tomorrow?"

"Right. The ME's doing it on a freelance basis, so Saturday worked out perfectly for him."

"Does anyone else know that Doogie is bringing in a forensic pathologist?"

"Just you and maybe Deputy Driscoll. Oh, and George Draper."

"Maybe we should keep this whole thing under wraps."

"I pretty much thought we were," said Sam, looking at her, his eyebrows raised.

She nodded. "So . . . a day or two for the autopsy results. And then I suppose a funeral. I wonder if anybody's even planning that far ahead?"

"Funny you should mention that," said Sam. "Apparently there's an ex-wife."

"Yes!" Suzanne cried. "I know. I just found out about her. Gene Gandle dropped by the Cackleberry Club this afternoon and bragged that he'd wangled an interview with her."

"And she's been seen around town," Sam continued. "I know Doogie was trying to get ahold of her earlier today."

"An ex-wife," Suzanne murmured. "The plot definitely thickens."

Sam gazed over her shoulder where a pan bubbled on the stove. "But not as delightfully as your white wine sauce."

"There's another casualty in all this, too," said Suzanne, as she set out place mats.

"What do you mean?"

"Missy Langston. Carmen fired her today."

"Oh no."

"Carmen listened to a bunch of rumors that have apparently spread like wildfire and then she completely overreacted."

Sam fixed her with a steady gaze. "But Missy *was* seen at the cemetery."

"How did you know that?"

"Sweetheart, everybody knows."

THEY let all talk about Lester Drummond go then. And sat down at the table to enjoy dinner and each other. Everything turned out to be a hit, especially Suzanne's tasty beurre blanc sauce.

"Sorry the dogs keep nudging your elbow," said Suzanne. "They're hoping for scraps."

"Which they'll undoubtedly get," said Sam. "But tell me, why does Baxter keep looking up at the skylight? What's *that* about?"

"Oh, he sees people and dogs reflected up there and thinks it's some kind of parallel universe."

"That's a pretty metaphysical thought for a dog," said Sam.

"Well, that's Bax for you. Mmn, would you like more sauce? I see it mysteriously disappeared from your plate."

"I'd love some more."

When Suzanne returned with the sauce, Sam gazed into her eyes and said, "Thank you."

"No problem."

"No," said Sam. "I mean thank you for this. For you. It's all wonderful. And you're really quite a genius with food."

"No problem," said Suzanne, blushing a little. Direct compliments always embarrassed her.

"And now a personal question."

"Shoot."

"When did you first realize you were a foodie?" Sam asked his question with utter seriousness, as if he were asking about the first time she'd ever had sex.

"Oh, I don't know," said Suzanne, waving her hand.

"Sure you do. Go ahead, you can tell me."

"Promise you won't laugh?"

Sam nodded as he made a quick cross-my-heart motion.

"Okay," said Suzanne. "It was probably the first time I tasted really good prosciutto with figs and balsamic vinegar. That's when my mind sort of traveled to another place and I realized there was more to eating than hot dogs and beans."

"Don't kid me, lady. Your diet didn't really consist of hot dogs and beans."

"No, of course not. But when you grow up in a small Midwestern town it isn't easy to break away from traditional dinners like hotdish, pot roast, and baked ham decorated with canned pineapple rings."

"But you still serve comfort food at the Cackleberry Club," said Sam.

"Sure we do, but it's comfort food that's been kicked up a notch. Not just baked eggs, but Eggs in Purgatory with chorizo and hot sauce. Grilled chicken breast topped with sun-dried tomato and pesto sauce instead of mayo. And rather than a fried fish sandwich we bake our salmon in puff pastry."

Sam nodded his approval as Suzanne grew more and more intense.

"And we try to source all our ingredients locally. Cheese, eggs, veggies, fruits, even meat. It has to be fresh and organic. No preservatives, hormones, antibiotics, or factory processing."

"Tell me, my dear, do the good folks of Kindred know you're such a sneaky gourmet?"

Suzanne put a finger to her mouth and smiled, the corners of her eyes crinkling. "Shhh."

CHAPTER 9

"THANK goodness Saturdays are half days," said Petra, as she stood at the stove, one-handedly cracking fresh white eggs and plopping them into a large blue-speckled ceramic bowl. "Especially since we've got the tea tomorrow."

"Yesterday was a half day for you, too," Toni pointed out.

"That was different," said Petra. "I had a mandatory event."

"Well, what if I have an event?" Toni asked, a mischievous gleam in her eye.

"Then Suzanne and I would have to step it up," said Petra. "Just like you did."

"Aw, that breakfast service yesterday wasn't so tough," said Toni. "Especially since we had Kit to help out."

"How's she doing anyway?" asked Petra. Since she'd had a hand in convincing Kit to quit dancing at Hoobly's, she felt she had somewhat of a stake in the girl's future.

"She's doing okay, I guess," said Toni. "She has a new boyfriend."

"I hope it's not a former Hoobly's customer," said Petra.

"Who's a former Hoobly's customer?" asked Suzanne as she bumped her way into the kitchen.

"Hopefully not Kit's new boyfriend," said Petra.

"No, I think he's a good guy," said Suzanne. "He works over at the post office."

"A postal worker?" said Toni. "Yeah, it's hard to resist a man in uniform."

Now Petra leaned forward and peered through the pass-through. "Suzanne, I think two of your craft ladies just wandered in. At least they look like they might have brought things for the Hearts and Crafts Show."

"Wonderful," said Suzanne. She wiped her hands, then rushed out to greet them. After a moment of small talk, she steered them into the Book Nook.

"We didn't know if you were interested in jewelry or not," said a dark-haired woman by the name of Marilyn Ferris. "But Sherry and I took this neat jewelry-making class and bought a bunch of beads and metal findings and, well . . . the whole thing just kind of got away from us."

"And then we saw your posters," said Sherry. "See?" She carefully pried open one of the boxes she was carrying. "We did about a dozen beaded stretch bracelets, using beads of all colors, and some nice pendants to match."

"They're beautiful!" Suzanne exclaimed. And they truly were. Marilyn and Sherry had combined Czech glass beads with antique beads to create some stunning pieces of jewelry. One necklace featured a cameo, while a couple of bracelets had dainty little charms dangling from them. "You ladies have a real talent for putting together color and different types of stones."

"Does that mean you'll accept them in your show?" asked Marilyn.

"Absolutely," said Suzanne. She slipped behind the counter and grabbed a stack of entry forms. "In fact, let's get you signed in right now."

"How many entries do you have so far?" asked Sherry.

Suzanne tapped her pencil and thought for a minute. "Maybe . . . two dozen pieces?"

"But you're expecting more?" said Marilyn.

"Oh sure," said Suzanne. "Lots more. I expect next Monday and Tuesday the entries will pretty much pour in."

"This is such a fun idea," said Marilyn. "Especially since half the proceeds go to the food bank and the other half to the artists. You know, we don't have many art or crafts shows around here."

"Well, we're going to do something about that," said Suzanne. "Seeing as how we have such a talented pool of artists and artisans to draw from."

The two women beamed at her words.

"HEY," said Toni, when Suzanne returned to the kitchen. "We're still on for the candlelight walk tonight, aren't we?"

Suzanne remained reluctant about the whole thing. "You're sure you want to go?"

"You better believe it," said Toni. "In fact, I'm counting on it. So . . . you can pick me up?"

"Ah, sure," said Suzanne. "If you want me to." She was giving in to Toni because, well, because friends did that sometimes.

"The thing is," said Toni, "Junior's got my car." She rolled her eyes. "I think he's stealing parts from it."

"Better your car than mine," Petra muttered as she unwrapped a piece of goat cheese.

"Oh no," said Suzanne. "Junior's not still under the delusion that he's going to race that old beater, is he?"

"I think he's planning to race it tomorrow night," said

Toni. "He's all jacked up because the grand prize for the demolition derby is something like five hundred dollars."

"That much?" said Petra. She dumped her cheese into an aluminum bowl and began to mash it.

Toni nodded. "It'd be a huge bump in Junior's bank account."

"It'd *be* his bank account," said Petra.

"Junior's dream is to win enough prize money so he can buy a Softail or a Fat Bob."

"I think I used to date a guy named Fat Bob," said Petra. "Back in high school. Seems like yesterday . . ."

"What *is* a Fat Bob anyway?" asked Suzanne.

"A Harley," said Toni. "A Harley-Davidson. Where've you been, girl? A Softail's a Harley, too. Except it has all these springs and things, so you take the road softer."

"How much does one of those Fat Bob bikes cost?" asked Suzanne, totally confused.

Toni thought for a minute. "A lot. Something like fifteen grand? Depends on how loaded it is."

"Awfully pricey either way," said Suzanne. "Junior would have to win a whole lot of races."

"That's if he doesn't get killed first," said Petra.

Suzanne's eyes fell on Petra and stayed there for a moment. "Petra? Are you okay? You seem a little edgy this morning."

"Edgier than usual," agreed Toni.

"Don't mind me," said Petra. "I'm just fretting about tomorrow's tea, that's all."

"But we've got it all planned out," said Toni.

"Up to a point," said Petra. "The thing is, I'm working on a new tea sandwich filling." She tilted her bowl. "See? I'm whipping up a test batch."

"What's the problem?" said Toni. "It doesn't taste so good?"

"I think it's going to be absolutely delicious," said Petra. She opened a small jar of something red, dumped it in, and continued to stir. "But I'm worried other folks might not see it that way. I'm afraid they might think it's too much of a radical departure from cucumbers and cream cheese."

"How radical is it?" asked Suzanne.

"Goat cheese and pimento," said Petra.

"That *is* a little kinky," said Toni.

"Tell you what," said Petra, dipping a knife into her bowl and spreading a dollop of her new mixture onto a slice of bread. "I'll make a sandwich and you can taste for yourself." She popped a second piece of bread on top, deftly sliced off the crusts, then cut the sandwich into four triangles. "Here, tell me what you think."

"Uh-oh," said Toni as Suzanne accepted a triangle. "Drumroll, please."

Suzanne took a bite. Then her eyes widened and she grinned at Petra as she swallowed. "This is delicious!"

"You think?" said Petra, delighted.

"I know it is," said Suzanne.

"Let me try, let me try," piped up Toni.

"Here." Petra handed her a triangle, too.

Toni popped the whole thing into her mouth and chewed. "Mmn," she said, rolling her eyes. "Mmn, mmn."

"I don't know if that's good or bad," said Petra. "She looks like she's throwing a fit."

Toni chewed vigorously, gave a fist pump, and swallowed hard. "It's good!" she said. "I really like it."

Still, Petra was nervous. "But will everybody else like it?"

"Tell you what," said Suzanne. "Try it out on Doogie. Let Sheriff Doogie be your focus group of one."

"What will that accomplish?" asked Petra.

"If Doogie likes your concoction, you're home free," said Suzanne. "Once he gives it his blessing, you can serve your sandwich spread to anyone."

"Are you trying to tell us that Doogie is picky?" said Toni.

"On the contrary," said Suzanne. "Doogie doesn't have a

picky bone in his body. He's one of those men who'll eat pretty much anything that's slapped in front of him. But"— and here she held up a finger—"Doogie has finely tuned Midwestern sensibilities. If he's not put off by your tea sandwich, then you'll know it's safe to serve."

"That's smart thinking," said Petra. "I'll make Doogie my personal guinea pig."

"Just don't call it a tea sandwich," warned Toni.

"And don't cut it into dainty little triangles," said Suzanne. "Just . . . slice it in half."

A loud voice suddenly blurted out, "Anybody here?"

"Speak of the devil," said Petra.

Suzanne went out to greet Doogie. "Good morning, Sheriff. I bet you're looking for a spot of breakfast."

"Ayup," said Doogie as he grabbed his usual seat at the counter. "Got any French toast?"

"French toast," said Suzanne, jotting it down on her order pad.

"And bacon."

"A side of bacon," said Suzanne.

"Better throw on a couple fried eggs."

Suzanne watched him, her pencil poised. "Anything else your little heart desires?"

"Maybe one of those sticky buns while I'm waiting," he said.

"You know what? I've got something even better." Suzanne smiled sweetly then called, "Petra! Why don't you let Sheriff Doogie try your new sandwich!"

As if on cue, Petra hustled out into the café bearing half a sandwich of her goat cheese and pimento spread.

"What is it?" asked Doogie as she placed the food in front of him like some kind of sacrificial offering.

"A sandwich with cheese spread," said Petra. "Go ahead and give it a try. I'd love your opinion."

Wary, sensing some kind of trap, Doogie poked a stubby finger at it. "Is it an appetizer?"

"Something like that," said Petra, watching Doogie closely.

"And it's not weird? You're not trying to slip me beef tongue or Rocky Mountain oysters, are you now?"

"We wouldn't do that," said Suzanne. "Really, it's just cheese spread."

Doogie picked up his sandwich and took a bite. Chewing resolutely, discovering it wasn't strychnine laced, he managed another bite. "Good," he finally mumbled. With his mouth full it sounded more like, "Guuh."

"See?" Suzanne said to Petra. "I told you."

Doogie stopped chewing, suddenly suspicious. "Did I just miss something here?"

"Not at all," said Petra smoothly. "You look extra hungry today, Sheriff. How about I fix you a whopper of a breakfast?"

"Now you're talkin'!" said Doogie.

Suzanne poured him a cup of fresh, hot coffee. "I heard the most interesting rumor from Gene Gandle when he was in yesterday. It seems Drummond's ex-wife is in town."

"Funny you should mention her," said Doogie, "since I had the pleasure of interviewing Deanna Drummond last night."

"You did, really?"

"Yup." He finished his last bite of sandwich.

"Apparently she's been living at Drummond's house?"

"Looks like."

"And?" said Suzanne, trying hard to restrain herself. "How did your interview go?"

"The woman claimed to be utterly heartbroken."

Suzanne peered intently at Doogie. "Wow. So she must have still loved him. Do you think she and Drummond were trying to work things out and get back together?"

Doogie's expression shifted and he suddenly looked uncomfortable. "Maybe," he said slowly. "It was kind of hard to tell what their relationship was. Deanna Drummond was fairly open and friendly to me at first. And then when we got to the business of Drummond getting killed she became extremely emotional . . . There were quite a few tears."

"That's understandable," said Suzanne. She thought about how awful it would be to reconcile with an ex, to finally work out your differences, only to have it all end in a brutal murder!

"Still . . ." said Doogie, trailing off. "She was difficult to read."

"Really?" said Suzanne. Doogie might look placid and plodding, but his years in law enforcement had made him an excellent judge of character. "You don't, um, see her as a suspect, do you?"

"At this point . . ." Doogie seemed to pick his words carefully. "I'm not ruling anything out."

"Wow." Suzanne decided that Gene Gandle might get his scoop after all.

"Let me ask you something," said Doogie. He hesitated, then said, "Can a woman be completely brokenhearted and still parade around in a leopard-print blouse, tight pants, and sky-high stiletto heels?"

"I'm not sure there's a strict correlation between heartbreak and wardrobe," said Suzanne.

"Except," said Doogie, "that she knew I was paying an official visit and she still dressed up like some kind of hoochie momma." He ducked his head, a little embarrassed now. "I heard that phrase on TV."

Something pinged in Suzanne's head. "Wait a minute. Are you saying she *flirted* with you?"

"Let's just say that after we got the serious discussion and the tearful part out of the way, Deanna Drummond was somewhat, um, playful," said Doogie.

"With you?" Suzanne instantly regretted the shock she'd let creep into her voice.

"I ain't *that* bad lookin'," said Doogie with a small smile.

"I didn't mean it like that," said Suzanne, backpedaling mightily.

"Go ahead, put your foot in your mouth, Suzanne. You're doing a fine job of it already."

"Okay, okay, let's get back to Deanna Drummond," she said. "If you're not ruling her out as a suspect, does that mean you picked up some kind of vibe?"

"A vibe," said Doogie, looking perplexed. "Why do women always talk in terms of vibes and hunches?"

"I guess what I'm really asking," said Suzanne, "is do you think she might have *wanted* her ex-husband dead?"

"That's . . . difficult to say. I mean, the two of them were legally divorced, so she was already receiving alimony."

"But you are suspicious of her," said Suzanne. "A little bit anyway." Something about Deanna Drummond had apparently set off Doogie's internal cop-o-meter.

"Somewhat, yes."

"Maybe if Drummond were dead, she'd inherit his entire estate?" said Suzanne. "Not just half but the whole enchilada?" She thought for a moment. "Or would she? Do you know if Lester Drummond has any other heirs?"

"We don't know at this point," said Doogie. "I need to have my investigators do some forensic work on Drummond's finances and gather a lot more background information. Even though he lived and worked in our midst, there's a lot we don't know about him."

"I wonder," said Suzanne, reflecting. "Could Deanna Drummond have made those two phone calls?"

Doogie just stared at her with his flat, gray eyes.

"Could Deanna have sent those textlike messages and asked Lester Drummond to come to the cemetery last Thursday morning? And then also called Missy?"

"Probably not if she was in the same house with him," said Doogie.

"Cell phone?" said Suzanne.

"Ah jeez," said Doogie, shaking his head. "I suppose. It's kinda convoluted, but it could have happened."

"And then Deanna Drummond set up Missy?"

"You'd come up with any excuse to get Missy off the hook, wouldn't you?" said Doogie.

"No, I wouldn't," said Suzanne. "But I know this Drummond case is a tough nut to crack. It's probably going to call for some out-of-the-box theories."

"I guess so," agreed Doogie. "Because there ain't much in the box to go on."

"While we're on this, did you pay a visit to that halfway house in Cornucopia?"

"Aw, those guys are mostly small potatoes. Nary a bank robber or murderer among them."

"How about Karl Studer? Have you talked to him yet?"

"I'm still getting around to that," said Doogie.

"The sheriff's breakfast is up!" Petra suddenly shrilled through the pass-through.

Suzanne grabbed a steaming platter and set it in front of Doogie. Then, as theories spun like windmills in her head, she hustled off to take orders from their breakfast customers, who had been filing in faster than she realized. As Suzanne brewed tea, poured coffee, delivered breakfasts, and joked with their customers, Doogie seemed to pick and poke at his enormous breakfast.

"Not to your liking?" Suzanne asked, as she swung by him a few minutes later.

"It's good, all right," said Doogie, putting down his fork for a minute. "It's just that I got to thinking about all the weird little permutations in this case. If I could just get a fingernail under one single thing, I'd be off and running. Anyway . . ." Doogie leaned back and adjusted his utility belt. "I guess I'm not as hungry as I thought I was."

To Suzanne this was code for, "I'm worried sick."

"Then how about something sweet?" Suzanne asked. She knew that sweet things always had a soothing effect on Doogie.

That seemed to perk him up a little. "You got any pie?"

THIRTY minutes later, Doogie was still sitting at the counter, sipping coffee. He'd long since polished off his piece of blueberry pie, and now was staring into space. It was as if he was hesitant to go out and honcho a full-scale investigation. Or maybe he was just chewing everything over.

"Is Doogie okay?" Toni whispered to Suzanne in the kitchen.

"I think he's just mulling things over," said Suzanne.

"Mulling what things?" put in Petra. "Shouldn't he be out chasing down clues, sniffing out sources—trying to solve a murder?"

Suzanne decided she might as well tell them what she knew. "Doogie's kind of befuddled because he interviewed Deanna Drummond last night."

"What's going on with her?" asked Petra.

"Apparently," said Suzanne, "after she forced out a bucket of crocodile tears she kind of came on to him."

Toni looked stunned. "Came on to him? You mean, like, flirted?"

Suzanne nodded. "Something like that."

Petra frowned and said, "Wow. Talk about messing with the law."

"So is this Deanna Drummond person an actual suspect?" asked Toni. "Or a potential hot date?"

"I think she's firmly in the suspect category for now," said Suzanne.

"Let's hope so," said Petra. She leaned to one side and

peered out the pass-through. "Suzanne, I think another artist just showed up. And it looks like he brought in a couple of paintings."

JAKE Gantz was a sometime customer of the Cackleberry Club. He was a big man whose wardrobe stylist must have been the slacker kid who worked at the local Army-Navy Surplus Store. Because that's how Jake dressed. Army jacket, baggy olive drab slacks, web belt, steel-toe boots. In winter he switched it out for a padded anorak and white Arctic pac boots.

"Jake," said Suzanne, greeting him. "I see you brought us a couple of your paintings." Jake was what an art critic at a big city newspaper might term an "outsider artist." His work consisted of slashes of bright color laid over almost primitive motifs. Paintings that were compelling, prosaic, and just plain fun.

Jake gave a shy nod. "I've been seeing your posters all around town and thought I might bring in these paintings for your show. That's if you'll have them."

Suzanne waggled a finger. "Come on in to the Book Nook and let's see what you've got." She gave Jake an encouraging smile as she noticed Doogie peering at him with hooded eyes.

Jake followed Suzanne into the Book Nook and carefully placed his paintings on the counter. "They're acrylics," he said. "I like to work with acrylic paint 'cause it dries nice and fast."

"These are wonderful," said Suzanne, holding one up. The first painting was a landscape of an old hip-roof barn done in purples, reds, and bright oranges and featuring a herd of purple and green dairy cows. The second painting was a lot more abstract with some graffiti thrown in for good measure.

"So you'll take 'em for your Hearts and Crafts Show?" Jake asked.

"Absolutely," said Suzanne. "In fact, it's very kind of you to bring these in."

"And half the proceeds go to charity?" said Jake.

"To the food bank," said Suzanne. "And the other half goes to the artist."

"That's good," said Jake. "I can always use a little money."

"If you'll just write down your information," said Suzanne, sliding two entry forms across the counter, "then we'll be set." She punched out two crack-and-peel tags, wrote P-11 and P-12 on them, and adhered them to the backs of the paintings. Then she jotted those same codes on Jake's entry forms.

"Thank you, ma'am," said Jake. He lifted his head and smiled. "I have to say, it sure smells good in your café. You must be cooking up some wonderful things."

"We may be on the far side of breakfast," said Suzanne, "but we have plenty of food left if you're interested."

Jake dug a hand into the pocket of his saggy pants and pulled out a single crumpled dollar bill. He looked at it carefully, almost hopefully, then said, "Nope, not today, ma'am. Looks like I'm a little tapped out. No offense."

"None taken," said Suzanne, trying not to be embarrassed for him.

"But I'll drop by some other time."

"Do that," said Suzanne. She gave a wave. "Maybe next Thursday when everything's on display."

She carried Jake's paintings into her office and leaned them carefully against the wall. She was hoping that, over the next few days, they'd be inundated with lots more artwork and handicrafts. Hopefully, the Cackleberry Club would, with all good luck, be filled to the rafters and the fund-raiser would be a roaring success.

When Suzanne stepped back into the Book Nook, Doogie was standing there. His khaki bulk was pressed up against the counter and he was frowning at the entry forms that were spread out.

"You seem a little more upbeat," Suzanne told him. She knew it was a lie, but figured if she dished out positivity, some goodness and light, some of it might stick.

"Yup," said Doogie, practically ignoring her. Then he pressed his big paw down on the papers and spun them around so he could read them.

CHAPTER 10

"EXCUSE me," said Suzanne. "Just what do you think you're doing?"

"Taking a look." Doogie said it with such forced nonchalance that she was instantly suspicious.

"Because you're so curious about the artwork that's been donated?"

"Because I'm investigating," said Doogie.

"Well, I doubt you'll find anything of great importance there," said Suzanne. "Those are just entry forms and copies of receipts for the folks who brought in artwork for our Hearts and Crafts Show."

Doogie gave her a placid look. "I know that. And I just recognized a name that's on my list."

"Your list? Which list?"

"The list of local parolees that Warden Fiedler gave me," said Doogie. "Your artist friend who just left? Guess what?"

"What?" said Suzanne. A low tickle of apprehension started to build inside of her.

"He's an ex-con."

"Jake?" said Suzanne, startled. "He's not . . . Are you sure? Well, for heaven's sake, what'd he do?"

"I don't know offhand," said Doogie. "Though it couldn't have been too serious. He was only in the joint for a few months."

"But you *know* Jake!" said Suzanne, trying to quell her rapidly blipping heart. "He's an okay guy." Why was Doogie suddenly so focused on Jake? The man was harmless, wasn't he? At the very least, he'd always struck her as a man who could use a break.

Doogie shook his big head. "I really don't know Jake, but he does seem familiar to me. I'm pretty good at remembering faces. In my line of work you have to be."

"Maybe Jake's just a type," said Suzanne. "That's why you remember him. In his case, a down-at-the-heels starving artist type."

"The fact remains," said Doogie, "his name is on my list."

"So you're telling me you have to check him out."

"That's right," said Doogie.

"Well, do me a favor, will you?"

Doogie stared at her.

"Don't be too hard on him. I think Jake's kind of wounded. I don't mean physically, but . . . psychologically. I don't want you to beat him up too badly."

"And if he turns out to be the killer?"

"He won't," said Suzanne.

"Heck," Doogie snorted. "You don't think *anybody's* a killer!" And with that he spun smartly on his heels and clomped out to his car.

WHEN Suzanne told Toni and Petra about Jake being on Doogie's parolee list, they both pooh-poohed it.

"I can hardly believe it," said Petra. "Jake's a pussycat! He's always so sweet and polite. If you meet him at the drugstore or something he greets you politely and holds the door open for you. You know how many people still do that these days?"

"Like, zero," said Toni. "Chivalry is kaput."

"Well, Jake's on Doogie's radar now," said Suzanne. "Big-time."

"You really don't think Jake had anything to do with Lester Drummond's death, do you?" said Toni.

"No, not really," said Suzanne.

"What do you think he was in jail for?" pressed Toni. "I mean what crime did he commit that landed him in the slammer?"

"I don't know," said Suzanne. "But Doogie said it couldn't have been too major. He was only in for a few months."

"I feel sorry for Jake," said Toni. "He always seems so down-and-out."

"That's probably because he really is," said Suzanne. "I think he wanted to stay and have breakfast but couldn't afford it. All he seemed to have on him was a dollar—literally."

"Good gracious," said Petra. "Then you should have given him a coffee and a sweet roll to go."

"Even though he's an ex-con," said Toni, nodding. "Yup, they have to eat, too."

"And he's a veteran," said Suzanne. "I know for a fact that Jake was in the Gulf War." She figured that Jake's military service might account for his slightly drifty nature.

That cinched it for Petra. "In that case you should have definitely offered him a sandwich!" Petra had a soft spot in her heart for veterans. She routinely delivered homemade chicken dinners and baskets of cookies to two old World War II veterans who lived out on Stonybrook Road and a Korean War veteran who'd been missing a leg ever since the landing at Inchon. She had her own little private meals-on-wheels.

"I suppose you're right," said Suzanne, feeling regretful now. "I should have been a little more hospitable."

"You realize," said Petra, "a veteran is someone who wrote a blank check to this country for an amount up to and including his life."

"Now I really feel bad," said Suzanne, vowing to make it up to him somehow.

As soon as they locked the doors of the Cackleberry Club, Suzanne drove over to the Hard Body Gym. She had it in her head to talk to Boots Wagner, the owner. Maybe he could offer a different perspective on Lester Drummond. Or maybe he'd witnessed some sort of conflict that had gone on at the gym. A grudge or a misunderstanding that might have festered and somehow led to murder.

The Hard Body Gym smelled of dirty socks, manly sweat, and Lysol. Lots of Lysol. A young man in a faded Maroon Five T-shirt sat at the front desk, munching a PowerBar and talking on a cell phone. When Suzanne mouthed "Boots Wagner" to him, he nodded, hooked a thumb, and pointed to the doorway.

Suzanne drifted past displays of knee braces, yoga mats, and weight belts as she stepped into a large, well-equipped, but mostly empty gym. Two men were huffing like mad on rowing machines, looking like prisoners on a Roman slave galley, going nowhere fast. Wagner was kneeling next to a machine, tinkering with some kind of cog. When Wagner finally looked up and spotted her, he raised a hand and stood up.

As he strode toward her in his tight T-shirt and gray gym shorts, Suzanne decided he looked like a Marine Corps drill sergeant straight out of central casting. All muscle and sinew and silver brush-cut hair.

"Have you come to join up?" Wagner asked her.

"Thinking about it," said Suzanne. The words popped out of her mouth before she could give them careful consideration. She hadn't been thinking about joining until she stepped inside his gym. Now the idea of working out, of pumping a little iron, suddenly appealed to her. It would be one way to hopefully lift her derriere and keep her arms from developing little underarm pudding sacks, which was the term Petra used for hers.

"Well, good," said Wagner, giving her a broad smile.

"But what I'm after right now," said Suzanne, "is a little information about Lester Drummond."

Wagner's smile slipped a few notches. "Why is that? If you don't mind my asking."

Suzanne had figured he'd question her motives, so she gave him what she thought was a logical, straightforward answer. "Because I'm the one who found Drummond in that grave. Early Thursday morning when Toni and I were delivering flowers to the cemetery."

Wagner looked surprised. "I didn't know that. That must have come as a real shock to you, huh?" He looked both curious and profoundly sad.

"It wasn't the best way to start the day," said Suzanne. She looked past him at shiny Nautilus and Cybex machines, several StairMasters, a huge free-weight setup, and a number of bright blue punching bags that dangled from chains in the ceiling. "So," she said, "Drummond worked out a lot, huh?"

"I'd have to say he was one of my best customers," said Wagner.

"What kind of workouts did he do?" Suzanne hoped her questions seemed more like basic curiosity.

"Mostly with the free weights, although Drummond liked doing crunches on the Nautilus and leg work on the Cybex machines."

"I heard he was a jogger, too."

"Now that was unusual," said Wagner. He picked up a bright blue ten-pound barbell and idly did a few curls. "Usually hard-core body builders don't bike or run. Truth is, they get so muscle-bound they lose a lot of their flexibility. But once or twice a week Drummond did a little jogging, just to stay loose."

"I understand he might have had a bad heart," said Suzanne.

"Is that what your doctor friend thinks?"

Suzanne smiled. He'd obviously seen her picking up Sam at the clinic next door. And more than a few times. "It's one theory."

Wagner's gaze suddenly wavered and he fell silent for a few moments.

"What?" said Suzanne.

Wagner just shook his head. "I shouldn't tell tales out of school."

"But if it's something that might lead to solving a crime and, um, explain how Drummond died . . ." said Suzanne.

"This is on the down low?" said Wagner. He stopped doing curls and moved a step closer to her.

Suzanne nodded. "Of course." *Unless it's something Sheriff Doogie needs to know.*

"Here's the thing of it. You don't gain that much muscle mass simply by working out. It doesn't just happen that way, if you catch my drift."

Suzanne stared at him until the pieces suddenly clicked into place. "You think Drummond was taking drugs." Her words came out in a slow, measured statement that surprised even her.

Wagner shrugged. "Not that I ever saw any evidence of

it. If I had, he'd have been out on his tail. Banned forever. We don't tolerate that kind of thing here."

"But you saw his progress in developing his body," said Suzanne.

"Rapid progress," said Wagner.

"Weight training, exercise physiology, that's what you do. That's your expertise. So you had a fairly good idea that Drummond might have been taking performance-enhancing drugs."

Wagner spread his hands apart. "I'm just saying . . ."

Suzanne thought for a minute. "This adds a new dimension to things. Would you be willing to share your theory, your suspicions, with Sheriff Doogie?"

"Why?" asked Wagner. "Are you working with him or something?"

"Are you kidding? Doogie probably thinks I'm working *against* him," said Suzanne, trying to lighten the mood a bit. "No, but I have an ulterior motive. What I'm really trying to do is clear a friend of mine, Missy Langston." When Wagner looked a little confused, she continued. "Missy was spotted at the cemetery right around the time we found Drummond. So, in Doogie's mind, she's become a kind of suspect."

Wagner's brows pinched together. "That little girl? She'd be no match for a big guy like Lester Drummond. She couldn't have done anything to him." He paused. "She *wouldn't* have . . ."

"My point exactly," said Suzanne. "So I've been asking around, trying to develop a different perspective on the investigation. Really, an amateur's point of view."

"I see," said Wagner. He reached up and scratched an ear. "I suppose I could talk to the sheriff. Tell him what I observed in Drummond's case, though I don't know it to be gospel truth."

"Still, it might be a great help," said Suzanne.

"Okay then," said Wagner, as they walked slowly toward the door. "Tell the sheriff to drop by. I'll be here."

"Thank you," said Suzanne. "I appreciate your help."

"And I'd still love it if you'd think about joining," said Wagner. "We're not just a bodybuilding studio, you know. We've got plenty of classes for the ladies, too. Cardio Bounce, Tai Chi, Zumba . . ."

They were standing in the outer office when the door burst open and a small, dark-haired woman came steaming toward them.

"Oh, hey," said Wagner. "Speaking of which . . . Here's someone you should definitely meet. Suzanne Dietz, meet Carla Reiker."

"Hi," said Suzanne.

"Nice to meet you," said Reiker, extending a hand. She was short and compact, with spiky black hair and warm brown eyes. She seemed bubbly, bordering on high-strung, and filled with boundless energy.

"Carla teaches a number of our classes," said Wagner.

"Right. When I'm not teaching phys ed at the middle school over in Jessup," said Reiker.

"Carla is also going to be teaching a new self-defense course starting next week," said Wagner.

"Self-defense for *women*," said Reiker, giving Suzanne a quick smile. "You ought to sign up. Our first class is this Monday. You look like you might enjoy it."

"The only workout I get these days is tossing hay bales and riding my horse," said Suzanne.

"There you go," said Reiker. "Instead of tossing hay bales wouldn't you like to learn how to toss an attacker to the ground?"

"Actually, that sounds like fun," said Suzanne.

"It's a blast," said Reiker. "It's physical as all get-out and you really feel pumped once you learn a few basic moves."

"And your class starts next week?"

"Monday afternoon at five," said Reiker, sensing more than just casual interest. "Tell you what . . ." She dug into her gym bag and pulled out a brochure. "Take one of my flyers. And if you decide to come, I promise you'll learn some killer moves and have the time of your life."

CHAPTER 11

THE sun hadn't bothered to peep out once all day long. And with an unsettled sky full of dark, low-hanging clouds, the night seemed to press down with ominous intensity.

"This is gonna be fun, huh?" said Toni. She was riding shotgun, primed and ready for adventure, as Suzanne's car crawled back up the road to Memorial Cemetery.

"It's a cemetery," said Suzanne, shrugging. "A candlelight walk where a lot of dead people are buried. How much fun can it be?" They were both bundled in boots, jeans, and sweaters, in anticipation of the chilly evening.

Toni glanced over at her. "You, my dear, are in a grouchy funk."

Suzanne decided she *was* being a grouch. Probably because Doogie was pressuring Missy so hard and it offended her sense of fair play.

"Apologies," she said. "It's just that . . ."

"Yeah, I know," said Toni, reading Suzanne's mood and

mind. "It's that we're back in the cemetery. I know you think it's all creepy and weird, and that the memory of finding Lester Drummond is still really fresh in our minds."

In a fresh grave, Suzanne thought to herself. "Yes, I suppose that's it." She left it at that.

"But the good thing is we're not alone tonight," Toni pointed out, as they drove past dozens of parked cars. "It looks like lots of people have showed up for this candlelight walk."

"Peachy," said Suzanne.

"Petra's been talking it up like it's really going to be a big deal. Lots of history, a little bit of mystery."

Suzanne shook her head. "Sorry. I guess I'm *still* being a grouch."

"You sure are."

"So I hereby promise to kick my dumb mood and try to get into the spirit of things."

"Interesting choice of words," said Toni.

They bumped past graves, statuary, and little groves of trees, heading for the oldest part of the cemetery, pretty much exactly where they'd dropped the flowers two days ago. Close to where they'd found Drummond. Had it really only been two days, Suzanne wondered? It seemed like . . . forever.

"Over there," said Toni, pointing and swiveling in the passenger seat. "You can slide in right there. There's an opening."

Suzanne angled her car between two cedar trees and shut off the motor. She sat with her hands clutching the steering wheel for a moment, took a deep breath, and said, "Okay. I've got this."

Toni flung open the passenger door. "Whoa!" she cried. "Look at all the candles. And there are some of the guides, dressed in period costumes. Come on, Suzanne, shake a leg and let's hit the trail!"

Together, the two women crossed the damp grass and headed for the white tent that seemed to be command central tonight.

But when they arrived at the check-in table, illuminated brightly by a bunch of portable lights borrowed from the City Works Department, they were in for a surprise.

Cheryl Tanner, one of the volunteers who was dressed in a calico bonnet and long prairie skirt, said, "I'm really sorry, ladies, but we're backed up like crazy right now. Every one of our guides has just left with a group in tow, so now there's almost a forty-minute wait."

"Oh man," said Suzanne. It was dark, getting chillier by the moment, and the hundreds of little candles strobing off nearby tombstones were making her feel jittery.

"We have to wait?" said Toni, supremely disappointed.

"We had no idea the candlelight walk would be so popular," Cheryl apologized.

"Now what?" said Toni.

"You could wait and hope one of one guides finishes early," Cheryl told them. "Or you could take our self-guided tour." She handed Toni a printed sheet. "Which is basically a map with all of the salient points marked off."

Toni held the paper at arm's length and squinted, the better to read it. "It follows the same trail?"

Cheryl and her bonnet nodded. "Oh, absolutely. And there are signs and markers everywhere to guide you and tell all the unique stories of the settlers who are buried here."

"What do you think?" Toni said, glancing at Suzanne. "Should we do the self-guided trail?"

"Sure," said Suzanne, shivering. "I'm game."

"Excellent," said Cheryl, handing a sheet to Suzanne, too. "The first marker is right over there"—she pointed—"at the Settlers' Monument."

Suzanne and Toni padded over to a six-foot-high obelisk that was surrounded by a low black wrought-iron fence. Just inside the fence, two dozen red pillar candles flickered and danced against the dark.

"The Settlers' Monument," said Toni, reading from her sheet. "Huh. I guess nobody's buried here per se. But they're buried all around here in unmarked graves." She scanned the rest of the notes in front of her. "Apparently, most of the people died from smallpox."

"There's a happy thought," said Suzanne.

"Next marker," said Toni. Some of the wind had gone out of her sails, too.

They eased their way down a hillside slick with wet leaves, passing a guide and a large contingent of people who were following like ducklings, all of them huffing back up the hill.

"The second marker," said Toni. "General Josiah Seville, who was the commander at nearby Fort Sandstone."

"Is he buried here?" asked Suzanne.

"Let me consult the old cheat sheet," said Toni. "Yes, he is." She glanced up at Suzanne. "This isn't quite as fun as I thought it would be."

"You want to bail?" asked Suzanne. *Please?*

"No, we said we were gonna do it, so we should do it," answered Toni. "Besides, I don't want to disappoint Petra. She was so gung ho when we told her we were going to do the candlelight walk."

"You were gung ho, too," said Suzanne. Toni had burned with the unbridled enthusiasm of a cheerleader hyped on a double espresso.

"Maybe things will pick up," said Toni.

"Maybe," said Suzanne, as they turned and trudged their way to the next marker.

But in the dark, with low-hanging tree branches and shrubbery all around, the next marker wasn't so easy to find.

"I thought it was over there," said Toni, pointing. She stopped, scratched her head, and tried to peer through the thick darkness. "On the other hand, we might have taken a wrong turn."

"I think we came too far," said Suzanne. "We should retrace our steps and . . ."

"Looking for something, ladies?" came a loud male voice.

Both Suzanne and Toni jumped as if an air horn had exploded behind them.

"Jeez!" Toni yelped as she spun around. "You scared the bejeebers out of me!"

Allan Sharp, Kindred's local lawyer and right-hand man to Mayor Mobley, stepped out of the bushes. Tall and angular, Sharp had his greasy black hair slicked back from his receding hairline. Wearing a dark suit that seemed two sizes too big for him, Sharp's stomach pouched out strangely, as if he'd just swallowed an entire rump roast. Suzanne always thought of him as a first-class weasel who favored gold neck chains and multiple rings on his spidery fingers.

"Allan Sharp!" said Suzanne, feeling as cross as she sounded. "What are *you* doing here?"

"Probably the same thing you're doing," said Sharp. He was tough, tenacious, and took no guff from anyone. There wasn't much that unnerved him or caused him to back down.

"We're looking for the Pembley grave," said Toni.

"Back that-a-way," said Sharp, jerking his chin to the left. "Right close to where you ladies found Lester Drummond the other day."

Suzanne's head swiveled in shock. "How do you know about that?" she asked.

Sharp gave her a look of superior amusement. "Everybody knows about that. Besides, not much goes on in this town that *I* don't know about. You should know that by now."

"Who gave you a crown and scepter?" said Toni. But when Sharp angled his head and glared darkly at her, she took a step back, suddenly intimidated.

Sharp now heaped all his attention back on Suzanne. "I

even know that your little friend is Sheriff Doogie's prime suspect." He seemed to smile then, his teeth gleaming white and nasty in the darkness. "On the plus side, Drummond's murder couldn't have happened at a more opportune time. Wouldn't you say?"

"What on earth are you talking about?" said Suzanne, genuinely puzzled.

Sharp's answer was a harsh bark. "Because Lester Drummond was on a collision course with this town. One he wasn't going to win."

"I don't think anybody wins in a situation like this," said Suzanne evenly. She recalled that Sharp had been one of the board members who'd helped oust Drummond from the prison. *No wonder he sounds so gleeful. So why am I even talking to this guy? What am I, the jackass whisperer?*

Sharp looked like he was about to say something else, then thought better of it. Instead, he touched a finger to his forehead in a mock salute and said, "Good night, ladies. Happy cemetery walk."

"What a dirtbag," muttered Toni under her breath once Sharp had moved on.

"There's no sense in even talking to the man," said Suzanne. "Any conversation on his part is always cryptic and nasty. I think he honestly tries to intimidate. The best thing to do is just . . . ignore him."

Toni had her nose buried in the map again and said, "You were right, Suzanne. We have to do a little backtracking."

They did so and quickly located the next marker. Oddly enough, it was close to the site where they'd discovered Drummond's body.

"I'd call this a creepy coincidence," said Toni. "It's like we're somehow back where we started."

"Please don't say that," said Suzanne.

Toni took a few tentative steps and pointed. "See? The grave's right over there." There was an oval mound of fresh dirt that wasn't quite level with the earth around it. She sucked in her breath and added, "At least they filled it in."

"Thank goodness for that."

Toni moved closer. "You think anybody's down there?"

Suzanne thought about the muddy Bobcat tractor she'd seen humping across the grass late Thursday afternoon. "No, I'm pretty sure it's empty. Nobody home."

"Look at that," said Toni. "Somebody even set a candle on top of the grave. But I guess the wind must have snuffed it out." She glanced around. "Who would have done that? Do you think the mysterious ex–Mrs. Drummond was prowling around here?"

"Maybe," said Suzanne, though it didn't feel right to her.

"Still . . . it's awfully strange," said Toni.

The more they talked about it, the jumpier Suzanne felt. "We should really keep moving."

But Toni seemed compulsively drawn to the gravesite. "Suzanne, come look at this," she said in a low voice.

"What?" Suzanne stepped closer to see what Toni was so jazzed about. That's when she saw a creamy parchment envelope, a corner of it stuck into the dirt.

"What *is* that?" Toni hissed.

Suzanne blinked. "It looks like . . ."

"Some kind of note?" said Toni.

"Maybe it has something to do with the Sesquicentennial Celebration?"

"No," said Toni, "I don't think so." She looked around quickly. "I think we should take a peek at it. Do you see anybody? Anybody on the tour? Is anyone watching?"

"Do you really think this is a good idea? It could be personal," said Suzanne.

But Toni's hand had already snaked out and grabbed the envelope. Hastily stuffing it inside her jacket, she reached out and yanked Suzanne's hand. "Come on, let's get out of here!"

When they arrived at the next marker, a large square

mausoleum bathed in the light of a hundred tiny vigil lights, they opened the note.

"I don't think we should be doing this," Suzanne whispered. "It feels awfully . . . intrusive."

Toni gazed at her. "Why are we whispering?"

Suzanne let out a deep sigh. "Because that's what people do when they're in a cemetery at night poking their noses into somebody else's business."

"Is that what we're doing?"

"Oh . . . just open it," said Suzanne. Truth be told, even though she had a terrible case of the guilts, she was as eager as Toni to read the darned note.

Toni tore open the envelope and scanned its contents. "Holy muckluck!" she exclaimed.

"What?"

"Here, take a look."

Suzanne grabbed the note. There was but a single sentence: *And he slipped sadly away.* It was signed with a single letter, a *G*. "Wow," she breathed. "That's weird."

"Isn't it?" said Toni.

"I mean, I wonder who . . . ?"

"Who on earth is *G*?" said Toni. She thought for a minute. "Do you think it could be Greta Jones who works at the stationery store?"

"No, I don't think so," said Suzanne. Greta Jones was seventy-five if she was a day. She doubted the septuagenarian would be cavorting with the likes of Lester Drummond, seeing as how she could barely heft a ream of paper.

"Well, what about Grace Hammond?" said Toni.

"She's married," said Suzanne.

"Still," said Toni, "she could have been having an affair."

"Doubtful," said Suzanne. Grace and her husband, Stanley, raised standard poodles and seemed dedicated to each other as well as to their adorable dogs.

"Then who?" said Toni.

Suzanne shook her head. "No idea."

"And what's this about slipping sadly away?" asked Toni.

"It sounds as if whoever wrote the note is feeling sad and mournful," said Suzanne.

"Or maybe whoever wrote this is sad because they killed him!" said Toni. "I mean, this is seriously freaky stuff."

"I think it's just a bad coincidence," said Suzanne. "Did you ever consider that the note might have been intended for some other grave and the note writer got turned around in the dark?"

"I suppose that could have happened," said Toni. "Or . . . or what if somebody was *supposed* to find this?"

"What do you mean?"

"What if the note is really written in code?"

"Why would someone do that?" said Suzanne. That didn't seem at all logical.

"I don't know," said Toni. "What if there was some kind of illegal deal going on? Something like that?"

"Interesting theory."

"Think maybe we should pass this note along to Sheriff Doogie?"

"Maybe so," said Suzanne. But first she wanted to think about it. And more than anything else, she wanted to get the heck out of here.

THEY called off the rest of their candlelight walk and ambled back to the tent. While they'd been out tiptoeing through the tombstones, volunteers had set up a long trestle table where hot cocoa and hot cider were now being served. So Suzanne and Toni grabbed paper cups of cocoa and stood on the sidelines, sipping and watching people come and go, wondering if the note might have been left by one of them.

When Suzanne had an inch of sludgy cocoa left, she said, "Time to pack it in?"

"There's just one more thing," said Toni. "I'd like to visit the meditation garden."

"What meditation garden?" This was the first Suzanne had heard of any such thing.

Toni smoothed her crumpled map, held it up to one of the portable lights, and read the short blurb aloud. "On the southwestern boundary of Memorial Cemetery, down a path through a quiet woods, a small meditation garden has been established. This garden, enhanced by stones, a small pool, and unusual plants, is intended to promote inner peace and serenity." She paused. "Doesn't that sound nice?"

"It sounds like it's off in the woods," said Suzanne.

"But doesn't it sound tranquil?"

"It sounds remote," said Suzanne. "The only reason I came here tonight was because you promised me we'd be surrounded by people. You know, strength in numbers and all that jazz?"

"I get it, I get it," said Toni. "Still, wouldn't it be nice to visit an area that wasn't filled with *dead* people? Doesn't that sound like a good way to cap off the evening?"

In the end, Suzanne relented. They climbed into her car, drove half a mile through the cemetery, and parked next to a small brick building, what was probably a maintenance shed.

"Jeez," said Toni, "I hope that's not where they store the dead bodies."

"I'm sure it's a maintenance shed," said Suzanne.

"Hope so."

"I was afraid of this," said Suzanne, as they climbed out of the car. "There's nobody here."

"That's a good thing," said Toni. "Seeing as how it's a meditation garden, the emphasis should be on peace and quiet."

"I had no idea you were so interested in meditation," said Suzanne, as they walked down the path.

"I watched an old kung fu movie the other night," said Toni. "And I decided it wouldn't be a bad idea to tap my inner Zen. I think being around Junior has an adverse effect on my brain waves."

"Oh, grasshopper," Suzanne laughed. "You just said a mouthful."

"This sure is pretty," said Toni as the woods closed in around them. "Look at all the ferns and hostas. And I love those glowing little garden lights."

"Solar lamps," said Suzanne, squinting in the dark. She decided the solar lamps, which led down the path, were indeed a lovely touch. Unfortunately, because this area was so densely wooded, the little lamps hadn't been able to absorb their full quota of sunlight. So for now they just glowed eerily.

"And there are wood chips on the path, too," said Toni. "This is really well done."

Suzanne had to agree. It was a nice winding path, and, as they meandered along, there were plantings of Japanese maple trees and winter-hardy bamboo, as well as several wooden benches.

"But where's the little pond?" Toni wondered.

Where are all the people? Suzanne wondered. It bothered her that they were so alone out here in the woods.

Toni was studying her map again. "It should be here somewhere."

"We're probably getting close," said Suzanne. They rounded a turn and her toe snagged on something. "Agh," she cried, flailing out, almost stumbling.

"What?" said Toni. She halted alongside Suzanne, putting an arm out to steady her.

"Something on my shoe."

"Aw, you're caught on a hunk of plastic," said Toni. She bent down and snatched at a plastic bag, then crumpled it up and stuck it in her jacket pocket. "Probably from when they brought in all the plants."

Suzanne lifted her head and, as she did, caught a reflective glint of something. The little pond? Yes, there it was. Just ahead, a small oval body of water was surrounded by rocks and tucked into a small grove of birch trees. "There's your pond," she told Toni.

"Ooh, this is so neat," said Toni, rushing over to kneel on a large, moss-covered rock. "Do you think there are goldfish?"

"If there are, they'd be a sushi dinner for all the raccoons, foxes, and woodchucks that live out this way," said Suzanne.

"Maybe it's a wishing pond, then," said Toni. She dug into the pocket of her slacks and came up with a few pennies. She stood up, spun around, and tossed the coins over her shoulder. Tiny splashes echoed as they plunked into the water.

"What did you wish for?" asked Suzanne.

Toni wrinkled her nose and gazed at her. "World peace."

"Well, that's . . ."

"Are you kidding?" said Toni, laughing. "I wished for a new refrigerator! Mine is totally on the fritz. My milk curdles so fast it looks like pancake batter."

"You tossed in more than one penny," said Suzanne. "So I'm guessing you've got more than one wish coming."

"In that case," said Toni, "world peace, a new refrigerator, and maybe a Wonderbra thrown in for good measure."

"Now you're talking," said Suzanne. She decided the meditation garden was having a slightly soporific effect on her. She did feel more relaxed and relieved. *Go figure.* Or maybe she was just getting tired.

"I think if we keep meandering this way," said Toni, flapping a hand, "the path will lead us right back around."

"Okay," said Suzanne as they continued walking on a slightly narrowed path. "I have to admit, this garden is very cleverly done. I think, during the day, with sunlight filtering down through these stately oaks and pines, it will feel almost cathedral-like."

"And this is just the first season," said Toni. "When there's some real growth to the garden, then we'll start to . . ."

"Whoa!" said Suzanne.

Toni halted in her tracks. "Huh?"

Suzanne clutched Toni's arm. "Did you hear something? In the woods?"

Toni frowned. "Don't be so jumpy. It was only a matter of time before some other folks showed up to check this out."

"I guess you're right," said Suzanne as they continued on. "Sorry."

"No problem," said Toni. "It's not like we're gonna . . . What the heck!"

A man suddenly stepped out onto the path in front of them. A big man, dressed in a camo jacket and carrying a 12-gauge shotgun.

"Oh, jeez Louise!" cried Suzanne. She tried to say more, but nothing came out. It was as if the back of her throat had gone as dry as the Gobi Desert.

CHAPTER 12

"WHAT do you think you're doing on my property!" the man bellowed at them.

Still taken aback, Suzanne fought to find her voice. "*Your* property?" she finally squeaked out. "I thought we were on cemetery property."

"You thought wrong," snarled the man. His eyes smoldered from within the deep creases of his face. His hair was long and unkempt and he wore a scruffy four- or five-day beard.

"Isn't this the meditation garden?" Toni stammered.

"Property line's back there," said the man, gesturing with the butt of his shotgun. "Which means you're on my land!" He cocked his head and shook it hard as if he were having a philosophical argument with himself. "This is private property," he muttered. "And I won't put up with people wandering around or driving cars in here all hours of the day and night!"

Suzanne held up both hands in a placating gesture.

"Okay, okay. We'll go back the way we came. No harm done." Suzanne wasn't one to easily back down, but in this situation she decided it was the smartest thing to do.

"Harm?" said the man. He turned his head, made a nasty, wet noise, and spat at their feet. "There's been harm done all right."

Horrified and upset, Suzanne and Toni continued to back up. Then, in one coordinated move practically worthy of the Radio City Rockettes, they spun like tops and broke into a fast trot. Shaken and unnerved, all they wanted to do was get out of there!

"Is he following us?" Toni asked. Her teeth chattered as they jogged over uneven ground.

Suzanne ventured a quick look over her shoulder. "I don't see him."

"Who the Sam Hill *was* that jerk?" Toni reached out and grabbed Suzanne's hand as they ran along. "He lurched out at us like some kind of crazed zombie."

"I think," said Suzanne, slightly breathless by now, "that we just made the acquaintance of Karl Studer."

"Who's that?" Toni cried. They ran another hundred feet, then slowed down. Toni suddenly stopped and bent forward. In a shaky wheeze, she said, "Man, I gotta quit smoking."

Suzanne fought to catch her breath, too. "What are you talking about? You don't smoke."

"Then it must be secondhand smoke that's got to me," Toni gasped out. "Because my lungs feel like somebody's old duffel bag. So, *who'd* you say that guy was?"

"I'm pretty sure that's the man Dale Huffington warned me about. Don't you remember? I told you about Karl Studer, the guy whose son is incarcerated at the prison."

"Oh yeah, yeah," said Toni, practically hyperventilating. "You think that was him?"

"Probably. Studer's property supposedly borders the cemetery."

"Hence his obvious fixation on boundaries," said Toni.

"To say nothing of his lack of hospitality. But you know what the really strange thing is? What's really frightening?"

"There's more?" said Toni, finally straightening up.

"Dale told me that Karl Studer *hated* Lester Drummond!"

"Excuse me," said Toni, "but I think everybody in town hated Lester Drummond."

"But everybody in town doesn't own land close to where Drummond's dead body was found!"

"Jeez," said Toni, suddenly catching on. "You don't think Drummond was trespassing just like we were and . . . and Studer blew his top, do you? Like . . . *kaboom!*" She glanced back over her shoulder. "I mean, you saw that gun."

"I don't know if he's a killer," said Suzanne. "But Studer struck me as one angry man."

TWENTY minutes later they were back in the safety of the yellow brick buildings and sparkling lights of downtown Kindred. Toni, feeling much braver now, said, "Well, that was kapow crazy. Like being on a new ride at the State Fair—a cross between the Wild Mouse and House of Horrors."

"To say the least," said Suzanne, as they coasted down Main Street past Kuyper's Hardware and Albright's Dry Cleaning.

"You want to stop at Schmitt's Bar and have a bump? I sure could use a little liquid refreshment."

"After our adventure in never-never land," said Suzanne, "I think I'd rather just go home and wind down. Try to get a good night's sleep. Don't forget, tomorrow's a big day. We're hosting the Historical Society's tea party."

"Aw, that'll be a slam dunk," said Toni.

"Don't let the Historical Society people hear you say that," said Suzanne. "They're expecting lavender, lace, and super luxe treatment. They really want us to knock ourselves out."

"And that's exactly what we'll do," said Toni. "What we always do!"

Suzanne drove down Maple Street, dropped Toni off at her apartment, and headed for home. Halfway there, her curiosity kicked in big-time, even though she was craving some zzzz's by now, and she took a short detour past Lester Drummond's house. It was a nice-looking, white Cape Cod–style home set on a corner lot and surrounded by a dozen towering blue black pines.

As she slowed down, Suzanne could see that lights burned brightly in the downstairs windows. *Was Deanna Drummond in there?* If so, what was she doing? Sitting there mourning her dead husband? Or something else?

Suzanne was tempted to park her car in the shadows, tiptoe up to a side window, and venture a quick peek. But something inside her said *no.* There'd been enough strangeness and drama for one night, enough skulking through the dark.

As Suzanne rounded a corner and headed down her own street, lights suddenly blazed behind her. Temporarily blinded, she saw that a car had nosed right up to her rear bumper. As she turned into her driveway and pulled up to her garage door, she held her breath, wondering who in the world it could be. Then she glanced in her rearview mirror and recognized a familiar blue BMW.

Sam! Whew.

She jumped out of her car and ran to greet him. "Hey, you got your car fixed. What are you doing here, anyway?"

"I'm here on official business," said Sam. He opened his arms and Suzanne stepped happily into them.

"What's kind of business is that?"

"Neighborhood watch." His cheeks dimpled. "I've been watching for you."

"In that case, you better come in."

They walked, arm in arm, into her home, and Suzanne finally found herself relaxing after all she'd been through. Baxter and Scruff, roused from their slumber, were sleepy but interested. The dogs circled them, lazy and stiff-legged, as Suzanne and Sam pushed their way through the entryway and into the kitchen.

"I've got news," Suzanne told him as she plunked her bag on the counter and kicked off her shoes. Being back in her kitchen, the heart of her house, made her feel safe and secure. She was so glad to be away from that cemetery! And it didn't hurt that Sam was with her, too.

"I've got news, too," said Sam, as he helped Suzanne out of her jacket. "You want me to open a bottle of wine?"

"I'm not sure I'm up to wine tonight," said Suzanne. "But I could definitely brew a pot of tea."

"Tea," said Sam. "That sounds rather enchanting. What kind of tea?"

Suzanne glanced at her kitchen clock, a Felix the Cat clock with ticktocking tail and eyes. Felix said it was quarter after ten and getting near bedtime. "I'm thinking a nice chamomile."

"What magic will that golden elixir work?" asked Sam. "Besides being tasty?"

"It should make you feel relaxed and a little sleepy."

Sam tilted his head and made a mock snoring sound. "Okay, count me in."

Suzanne washed her hands at the sink, trying once and for all to shake off tonight's strangeness. Then she filled her teakettle with water and set it on the stove to heat. She grabbed a tin of chamomile tea, a small yellow teapot, and two matching teacups.

"So fancy," said Sam appreciatively.

Suzanne raised an eyebrow as she measured out her tea. "Would you rather have a paper cup with a snap-on lid?"

"No, I meant that this is all very nice . . . homey. You have to remember, I'm a single guy. Living alone. A tray of Lean Cuisine on a place mat is my idea of formality."

She smiled to herself. *Maybe one of these days we're going to have to do something about that.*

Once the tea was brewed, Suzanne placed everything on a silver tray and pointed the way to the living room.

"I have a feeling there's something you want to tell me," she said, glancing at him sideways. They sat down on the couch and she poured him a cup of tea.

"You first," said Sam. He took a sip of tea, swallowed hard, and managed to choke out the word, "Good." What he really meant was, "Hot!"

"You know that Toni and I went to the candlelight walk tonight," Suzanne began. It was a statement, not a question.

"Up at the cemetery," said Sam.

"Well, it was not without incident," Suzanne said as she poured a cup for herself.

Sam leaned forward, interested. "What happened? Tell me."

"Let's see," said Suzanne. "Where should I start? First we were accosted by that sleazeball Allan Sharp, who was practically chortling over Drummond's demise."

"Lovely fellow. Always the town charmer."

"Then," said Suzanne, "we stumbled across the very same grave where we found Lester Drummond the other day . . ."

"I'm assuming the grave had been filled in?"

"Yes, but there was a note stuck on top."

"A note? What did it say?"

Suzanne was just about to take a sip of tea herself when she stopped and looked at him. "What makes you so sure we read the note?"

"Come on," said Sam. "This is me you're talking to."

"Okay," she said, unable to resist a grin. "So we grabbed the note and read it."

"And?"

"The contents were short but sweet. All it said was 'And he slipped sadly away.'"

"Poetic. But what's it supposed to mean?"

"No idea," said Suzanne. "But it was signed with the initial *G*."

"Gee," said Sam.

"Then, just as I was poised for a clean getaway, Toni wanted to visit the new meditation garden."

"Toni being so totally chill and Zen."

"Right. Anyway, we walked a little too far and a crazy redneck straight out of *Deliverance*, complete with camo gear and shotgun, threatened bodily harm to us if we didn't get off his land."

"What!"

"What part didn't you understand?" said Suzanne.

"*Deliverance?*"

"Yes."

"Shotgun?"

"I'm guessing it was a 12-gauge," said Suzanne.

"Woof," said Sam, furrowing his brow. "That doesn't sound good."

Suzanne aimed a finger at him. "Exactly my take. Thank you, Dr. Hazelet."

"Do you know who it was?"

"I'm guessing it was a guy by the name of Karl Studer. Apparently his property borders Memorial Cemetery." She debated telling Sam about Dale Huffington's take on Studer, that the man hated Drummond with a passion. Then she decided that might complicate the story. Or her own investigation.

"Are you going to tell Sheriff Doogie about all this?" said Sam.

"Which part of my sad tale do you think I should lay on him?"

"All of it!" said Sam. "Your entire evening sounds a little off-kilter."

"My world and welcome to it," she said.

"Suzanne," Sam said, assuming his clinical, no-nonsense, doctor's voice now. "I want you to sit down with Sheriff Doogie and tell him exactly what you just told me. And give him the note—you still have it?"

"Yes."

"Okay, then. Let Doogie sort it all out. That's his job. Yours is to go on living."

"You think?"

"I know," said Sam.

Suzanne pulled her feet up and snuggled closer to him, feeling his warmth and inhaling his scent. She felt a tad bit guilty that she hadn't told Sam about the information Dale had passed on to her. That Studer hated Drummond. She shook her head. But telling Sam might complicate things. To the point where he wouldn't want her involved at all. "Now. What was your news?" she asked him after a few more moments of snuggling.

"It concerns the autopsy that was done today."

Suzanne un-snuggled in a jiffy and carefully swung her feet back on the floor. "Oh." She decided she needed to have her feet planted on solid ground for this.

"You have to swear not to breathe a word of what I'm about to tell you. I mean, you can't tell another soul."

"How about if I swear an oath on one of my Alice Waters cookbooks?"

"This is serious." Sam cleared his throat. "As you know, the visiting medical examiner, Dr. Merle Gordon, began Drummond's autopsy today at the hospital."

"Were you there? Was it awful?"

"Yes and no," said Sam. "Realize, please, that I had no real interest in being a part of it. But once Dr. Gordon came up with a few preliminary findings, Sheriff Doogie called me in and requested that I be a witness. In case he needs a second opinion when this case goes to court."

"Dear Lord," said Suzanne. This sounded serious. "What on earth did your Dr. Gordon discover?"

"Bear with me," said Sam. "Because some of this is fairly technical."

"Okay."

"Do you know what a petechial hemorrhage is?" asked Sam.

"Not exactly. Should I?"

"No reason you should know. But here's the thing. They're small blood leaks that Dr. Gordon found behind the victim's eyes."

"Meaning Drummond got smacked in the eye, too?"

"Not exactly," said Sam. "Petechial hemorrhages are often present when someone has been a victim of hanging or suffocation."

Suzanne gave him a sharp look. "You just told me last night that Drummond might have gone into cardiac arrest from some kind of intracranial pressure. Now you're saying he was . . . what? Tasered and then strangled? Were there bruises around his neck? Was he beaten?"

"No, absolutely not," said Sam. "There's no indication of strangulation at all. No skull fracture, no vestiges of bruising, no sign of ligature marks. In fact, Drummond's hyoid bone, the bone directly at his neck, was quite intact."

"I don't understand," said Suzanne. "So Drummond *wasn't* strangled? Then how did he get those . . ." She fluttered a hand in front of her eyes. "Those eye hemorrhage things?"

"Best guess? He could have been smothered."

"You mean like a pillow jammed over his face or something?"

"Or something," said Sam. "If Drummond was seriously incapacitated by a high number of Taser bursts, he would have been at his attacker's mercy."

"So first Drummond was Tasered like crazy," said Suzanne, not quite believing they were talking about this so matter-of-factly. "And then when he collapsed, someone smothered him?"

"It's pointing in that direction," said Sam.

"Wow," said Suzanne as she digested this new information. "Didn't this just turn into a murder and a half!"

He reached over and grabbed her hand. "Sorry. I know it's late at night and this is all quite unsettling. Not exactly the stuff dreams are made of."

Suzanne had to agree. For the last two nights her dreams had been haunted by visions of cemeteries and open graves, of earthen holes and bleached white bones.

"Then let's change the subject," she said.

"To trout fishing," said Sam suddenly. Which made Suzanne giggle. "No, seriously," he said. "I read that book you gave me, cover to cover. And I've been practicing my casting techniques."

"You're telling me, right here and now, that you want to go trout fishing," said Suzanne.

Trout fishing was a sport she'd shared with Walter. But when she'd mentioned trout fishing to Sam in passing one day, he'd jumped at it. And now he seemed intent on venturing out and hooking himself a brook trout or two.

"There's supposed to be a mayfly hatch in a few days," said Sam. "That's according to Burt Finch at the Sports Shack."

"Do you even know what a mayfly looks like?" asked Suzanne.

"No, but I'm very perceptive," said Sam. "If I can find one in a book, I'm sure I can spot one in the outdoors."

"Well . . . okay. We'll go next week. I'll dig out my waders."

Sam pulled her closer and gently kissed her neck. "Do I know how to set the hook or what?"

"Oh yes, you do, Dr. Hazelet. You most certainly do."

CHAPTER 13

PETRA stuck her hands on her broad hips and pulled her normally placid face into a frown as she stood squarely in the middle of the kitchen and surveyed the grocery-strewn countertops. "Do you think we ordered enough bread?" she asked. But before Suzanne or Toni could muster an answer, she said, "That's it. We didn't order enough bread. We're going to be short."

"We'll be fine," said Suzanne. "Bill Probst delivered twelve fresh loaves yesterday. That should be enough to feed six teams of hungry Little League baseball players, never mind a women's tea group."

It was ten o'clock on Sunday morning at the Cackleberry Club as the three friends fussed about the kitchen, getting ready for the tea party. It should have been a snap with their preplanned menu of scones, tea sandwiches, quiche, and cake. But these days, everything seemed fraught with worry and second-guessing. Things that should be straightforward and simple seemed . . . not simple at all.

"I see egg twist, sourdough, rye, and honey wheat bread," said Petra, scanning a pile of loaves. "But no cinnamon bread. I need that for my chicken spread. The spice always adds an extra punch."

"That bread's probably still in the cooler," said Toni as she juggled a stack of dessert plates. "Want me to go look?"

"I'll do it," offered Kit. Per their request, Kit Kaslik had shown up to help set tables, prep food, serve, and do whatever was needed to help the day run smoothly.

"Thank you, Kit," said Petra. "I'm glad someone's on their toes."

"You're nervous as a dog at a flea market," Toni said to Petra. "What's the problem, lady? Usually you're all cool and collected and I'm the one who's stressing."

"I don't know," said Petra. "I'm just upset about . . . things."

"What things?" Suzanne asked, her eyes squinting at her dear friend. She and Toni hadn't told Petra about their shadowy cemetery encounter last night, so that certainly couldn't be what was eating her.

"For one thing," said Petra, hesitating, "I got a phone call about ten minutes ago . . ."

"Go on," said Suzanne, her antennae suddenly perking up.

"It was Missy."

"Okay," said Suzanne. Now the story was going to spill out.

"And she said she wasn't coming to the tea," said Petra.

Suzanne gave Petra a quizzical look. "What? Wait a minute . . . Why isn't Missy coming? Last time I talked to her, she was looking forward to the tea."

Petra's face turned downward in a glum look. "Not anymore, I'm afraid. Missy said that wherever she goes, people give her funny looks. Suspicious looks. She said things have been really tough for her."

"You're telling me the entire town knows that Sheriff

Doogie is talking to Missy?" Suzanne couldn't quite believe that.

Petra hefted her serrated bread knife and began shearing off crusts from an unsliced loaf of bread, the teeth of the knife making clear, straight cuts. "I guess that's about the size of it."

"But how did people find out about it?" Suzanne wondered. "I know it wasn't Doogie. He's trying to keep things under wraps."

"How much you want to bet it was George Draper?" said Toni. "Doogie probably mentioned it to him—and you know how George *loves* to talk. He's the Chatty Cathy of the funeral industry! Pull the string in the back of his sedate black undertaker's suit and he drones on about death being so peaceful then immediately segues into all the hot town gossip. It's almost like he's got a split personality."

"That snarky little crepe hanger!" said Suzanne bluntly. She thought about how, only a few months ago, Draper had been romantically linked to Claudia Busacker, the wife of the former bank president. And how the snooty, snotty Claudia had quietly skipped town to avoid getting caught in a scandal. Talk about serious gossip!

"Anyway," said Petra, slicing away mechanically, "Missy told me she feels like persona non grata."

"Not around here, she shouldn't," said Suzanne. "She knows I'm sticking up for her."

"Ditto that," said Toni.

"I found your cinnamon bread," said Kit.

"One mystery solved," said Toni, snapping her fingers.

Kit dropped two loaves onto the butcher-block counter and suddenly slumped forward.

"Honey, what's wrong?" Suzanne asked, alarmed. She stretched out an arm to support Kit and decided the poor girl was looking a little green around the gills. A thin sheen of sweat dampened her forehead.

Kit folded an arm across her stomach, looking nervous

and slightly chagrined. "You're not going to believe this," she said. "I can't quite believe it myself . . ."

"What?" said Petra, looking concerned. "If you think you might be coming down with something . . ."

"I'm not sick, if that's what you mean," said Kit. "I'm not contagious."

"Then what?" asked Suzanne. She reached over to the sink and turned on the cold water so she could fix Kit a cold compress.

"I might be pregnant!" Kit blurted out.

Suzanne turned off the water and gazed at Kit. "You *think* you might be pregnant or you really are?"

"Well," said Kit, swallowing hard and wiping the back of her hand across her forehead. "I used one of those home pregnancy tests yesterday and the result was positive. I saw a little blue arrow."

"Then you probably are," said Suzanne. "Those things are pretty accurate." *Oops.*

But Toni had a completely different take on Kit's rather dramatic announcement. "Wow!" she said, letting out a raucous whoop. "That's super! So who's the lucky baby daddy? Is it . . . ?" She suddenly snapped her mouth shut, cowed by withering looks from Suzanne and Petra.

"Sorry," Toni murmured quickly. "I shouldn't have . . . um, presumed."

"It's okay," said Kit.

"Is it really?" said Petra, who was coming from a slightly different position. She was deeply religious and believed in the sanctity of marriage before starting a family.

Kit managed a weak smile. "Everything's going to be fine because I'm actually engaged to be engaged." At that, she held out her left hand and waggled her fingers. An oversized silver ring with a black stone and wad of tape wrapped around its shank bobbled on her ring finger. "See? Ricky gave me his class ring to wear as a promise ring."

"Ricky Wilcox?" said Toni. "He's a good kid."

"Does a class ring really count?" asked Petra. She sounded less than thrilled.

"Sure it does!" said Toni. "It means Kit is engaged to be engaged. That she won't be an unwed mother."

"I'm not sure anyone uses that term anymore," said Suzanne.

"How about baby momma?" said Toni. "You hear that a lot on *Jerry Springer.*"

"Well, there's a chance I might not be married before the baby comes anyway," said Kit. "Since Ricky's National Guard unit was just called up."

"Oh no," Suzanne said with dismay. "Oh, Kit!"

Now Kit looked a little less sure of the situation herself. "I think Ricky might get sent to Afghanistan."

"Can't you guys get married right away?" asked Toni. "Book a church and have a . . . What's the expression I'm looking for?"

"Shotgun wedding," said Petra.

"A *quickie* wedding," said Toni. "A speedy one. You know . . ."

"I suppose we could," said Kit.

"Or better yet," suggested Toni, "you could dash off to Las Vegas and get hitched at the Elvis Wedding Chapel, like Junior and I did. You could get married by the King of Rock and Roll himself—or, rather, one of his handsome look-alikes."

"And we all know how well *your* marriage turned out," said Petra.

"Yeah—but I'm still all shook up about it!" finished Toni.

KIT pulled it together then, as they all did. And, at precisely quarter to twelve, Havis Newton, the director of the

Historical Society, waltzed through the front door. She wore a black-and-white houndstooth jacket over a black skirt, her hair was perfectly wound on top of her head, and she tottered on high heels. Instead of her usual denim skirt and nubby sweater, she'd dressed to the nines in honor of the tea party.

"Havis," said Suzanne warmly, going over to greet her. "Everything's just about ready." She took a step back so Havis could feast her eyes on the new, improved Cackleberry Club.

"Oh my gosh," said Havis as her eyes roved about the café. "What'd you do? The place is absolutely gorgeous. It looks just like a proper tea shop!"

Suzanne smiled. *Yes it does*, she thought to herself. With white linen tablecloths draped over the tables, crisp silk bows tied onto the chair backs, and huge bouquets of colorful spring flowers on every table, it looked as if a wonderful English tearoom had been magically transported from the Cotswolds of England to right here in comfortable Kindred.

Havis took a step closer. "The glassware, the china . . . everything is sparkling!" She sounded thrilled.

Suzanne had selected their best china, polished the silver to a high luster, and put out their nicest cups and saucers. Then she'd added cream pitchers, sugar bowls, and glass tea warmers with small flickering votive candles. So, yes, the tables looked highly inviting and even—dare she say it?—a touch glamorous.

Toni came flying through the swinging door, saw the wonderment on Havis's face, and said, "Oh, you like what we've done?"

"I like it very much," said Havis. "You ladies have created a beautiful setting for our tea."

"Wait until you get a load of the food," said Toni. "Petra's really knocked herself out."

"If you don't mind . . ." Havis dug a hand into her tote

bag. "I brought along some place cards. Is it okay . . . May I go ahead and arrange them?"

"You can do anything you want," said Suzanne. She liked the notion of having place cards at each setting. And Havis obviously wanted to ensure that friends sat with friends, and that potentially shy and uncertain newcomers were tucked happily next to chatty, welcoming volunteers who could share everything they knew about the society and today's tea.

As Havis consulted her seating chart, she slowly picked her way around the tables, precisely arranging place cards. When she was done, she glanced across the room and gave a self-satisfied nod. Along with the cemetery's Sesquicentennial Celebration, this was one of the first major events she'd organized as the society's new leader, and she was pleased at how well Suzanne and her Cackleberry Club partners had brought her wishes to fruition.

The clock struck twelve noon and, as if on cue, the front door flew open and half a dozen women spilled into the café. From then on, it was nonstop commotion as Historical Society volunteers and guests continued to arrive, greeting one another warmly, exclaiming over the beautiful tables, and eventually finding their places. Purses and coats were plopped down as the women settled in.

"Do you think we should start pouring tea?" Toni asked Suzanne, as they stood shoulder to shoulder near the kitchen, taking it all in.

"Sure, let's start," said Suzanne. There were still four vacant chairs, but she figured the missing guests would wander in shortly. She hoped they would, anyway.

While Toni began serving tea on one side of the room, Suzanne started on the other side. As she was pouring tea for Lolly Herron, the front door flew open and two more guests breezed in from outside.

Turning around, a smile on her face, ready to greet the

newest visitors, Suzanne said, "Welcome, you're just in time for . . ."

She stopped suddenly as she recognized the somewhat smug countenance of Carmen Copeland. Tall, slender, her dark hair twisted up in a topknot, Carmen, always the fashion plate, wore a butter-soft suede tunic, slim black slacks, and impossibly high heels, and she carried a shiny red designer handbag that was roughly the size of a picnic cooler.

Then, before Suzanne could say another word, Carmen announced, in her cool, breezy manner, "Suzanne, dear, I'd like you to meet Deanna Drummond."

You could have heard a pin drop in the room. Every woman's face suddenly turned toward the newcomers. And every emotion seemed to be expressed on those faces—curiosity, concern, bewilderment, shock. Then, just as quickly, the moment passed. The guests seemed to lose interest in scrutinizing Carmen and Deanna, and hastily resumed their animated conversations.

Suzanne, however, was still riveted.

"I had no idea you two knew each other," Suzanne blurted out. Then she thought to herself, *What an inane thing to say. Why on earth did I say that? Why didn't I simply offer my condolences to Deanna Drummond?*

"Deanna's one of my best customers," said Carmen. "We only met a few weeks ago, but we've already become best friends. BFFs, you might say."

Suzanne nodded at Carmen's words but turned her attention to Deanna, who was practically a petite carbon copy of Carmen. Dark hair, bright eyes, elegant black sheath dress, shiny patent leather high heels, and glittering jewels to match.

"Please accept my condolences," Suzanne told her. "And

I . . . I apologize for my earlier comment. Your recent tragedy should have been the first thing that came to mind."

Deanna stared at Suzanne for an impossibly long moment, looking her up and down. Then she said, "You're Suzanne, aren't you?"

"Yes, I'm Suzanne Dietz," said Suzanne, with all the warmth she could muster. "How nice to finally meet you."

"You were the one who found Lester," said Deanna with a sudden and strange formality. Her eyes blazed with a kind of inner light and her body language was suddenly stiff and formal.

"I'm afraid so," said Suzanne. "You see, Toni and I were . . ."

Deanna held up a manicured hand. "Please. I've heard the story," she said in a crisp, no-nonsense tone. "No need to go into it again."

"I didn't mean to dredge up . . ." Suzanne stopped and looked at her. Deanna was gazing about the café, no longer paying attention to her. It was as if she'd been summarily dismissed and Deanna had more important things on her mind.

Deanna jabbed impatiently in the air with an index finger. "Are those our places over there?"

"Yes," Carmen chimed in, picking up on Deanna's change of focus. "Suzanne, we'd prefer to join our group, if you don't mind."

"Of course," said Suzanne, feeling about six inches tall and not liking it one bit. "Come right this way," she managed to say with slightly clenched teeth.

Once Carmen and Deanna had been seated, Suzanne hurried to the counter to grab a pot of tea.

"Hey," said Toni, "what the heck just happened over there?"

"What do you mean?" said Suzanne, working hard to shake off the encounter, fighting to regain her normal calm and poise.

"You and Deanna Drummond looked like you were

about to face off against each other like a pair of hissing wombats."

"Was it really that obvious? I mean . . . that she didn't like me?"

Toni's mouth twisted into a crooked grin. "Well . . . yeah."

As soon as all the guests were settled in their places, Havis stood up and smiled, spreading her arms in a friendly wave as she tried to get the attention of everyone in the room. Gradually the guests settled down and Havis began a short welcoming speech. She talked about how delighted she was to serve as director of the Historical Society, thanked all the volunteers for their tireless work on the Sesquicentennial, and welcomed them all to the tea. As she spoke, Suzanne moved around the tables, quietly refilling teacups.

"And now," said Havis, wrapping up her remarks, "I'm going to ask Suzanne Dietz, our gracious hostess, to say a few words."

Suzanne blinked and straightened up suddenly. "Me?" she mouthed to Havis, while Havis gave a hearty bob of her head. Suzanne had no idea she was going to be called upon to perform. *Nothing like short notice*, she thought as she steadied herself.

"Go get 'em, tiger," Toni mumbled under her breath as she grabbed Suzanne's teapot.

Suzanne scooted up to the front of the café, paused to catch her breath and calm her nerves, and smiled warmly at all the women who gazed at her expectantly. "Welcome to the Cackleberry Club," she began. "We're delighted to host this tea luncheon sponsored by the Logan County Historical Society. I know you're all looking forward to enjoying some delicious food today, so why don't I run through our menu very quickly. The tea Toni and I have just poured for you is a Nilgiri black tea from the Blue Mountains of southwestern India. It's a smooth, mellow, non-astringent tea that's absolutely delicious. If you'd like, you can add a little milk or even lemon to it. We'll also be serving a jasmine tea and an orange blossom tea this afternoon as you make your way through each succeeding course."

She paused slightly and smiled again at those who watched her. "If you've taken tea with us before, you know that we always begin with a scone. Well, today you have your choice of cream scones or blueberry scones, both served with Petra's homemade Devonshire cream." She took another breath. "Our second course will be a lovely array of savories served on three-tiered trays. Tea sandwiches will include cucumber and cream cheese, chicken salad spread, and goat cheese with pimento. We'll also be serving miniature cheese quiches. And finally, for dessert, we have a delicious carrot cake with cream cheese icing." At that, some of the women oohed and aahed. Suzanne glanced toward the kitchen door as—right on cue—Toni and Kit stepped out, each carrying large silver trays piled high with scones. "So please enjoy!" added Suzanne. People clapped politely as she ducked hastily into the kitchen.

"Nice speech!" said Petra. "How's it going out there so far? Are we off to a rousing start?"

"It's okay," said Suzanne, breathing deeply. "Good."

Petra turned to look at her. "Just good? Or . . ."

"Deanna Drummond showed up with Carmen," Suzanne blurted out. "And meeting her like that kind of took me by surprise."

"It was only a matter of time," said Petra as she spread chicken salad onto slices of cinnamon bread.

"What do you mean? Just a matter of time before I met her?"

"Face it," said Petra. "It's a small town—and you're a big personality."

"No, I'm not," countered Suzanne. *Am I?*

Petra glanced up and lifted an eyebrow.

"Okay, okay," said Suzanne, backing down a little, catching Petra's drift. "So maybe I am a tad involved in this investigation. But that's only because I was involved in finding Lester Drummond's dead body!"

"Which is going to make his ex-wife feel extremely uncomfortable around you."

"She didn't seem one bit uncomfortable," said Suzanne. "In fact, she acted cool and aloof, as if she had the upper hand."

"Oh, that's what you're upset about," said Petra. Now she deftly quartered the sandwich and placed the pieces on a tray. "But come on, Suzanne, did she really have the upper hand?"

"I suppose not, but it *felt* that way."

"Now we know why Sheriff Doogie found her behavior a little strange. Because she *is* strange."

"You make a good point," said Suzanne.

"Which is why," added Petra, "Deanna Drummond has probably earned a spot on Doogie's short list."

"You mean . . . ?" Suzanne hesitated. "As a murder suspect."

Petra nodded. "Don't the police always look at the spouse first? Isn't that the most logical thing in an investigation?"

"Or ex-spouse in this case," said Suzanne.

"Either way," said Petra, brushing crumbs off her apron, "you should probably steer clear of her."

"Right." But Suzanne knew that steering clear of someone was no way—no way at all—to crack a murder case.

CHAPTER 14

WITH Petra's advice ringing in her ears like a noontime chime, Suzanne steamed back into the crowded café to check on the progress of the luncheon. And was promptly rewarded with warm greetings and lots of compliments.

Dede Meyer, who was a world-class baker herself, couldn't say enough about the cream scones. In fact, she wanted to buy a dozen to take home. And Laura Benchley, the *Bugle*'s editor, was raving about Petra's Devonshire cream and asking if she could please, please, please get the recipe so she could put it in the newspaper as soon as possible.

As Suzanne wove her way among the tables, pausing here and there to say hello, Paula Patterson reached out a hand to greet her.

"Just who I wanted to buttonhole," said Paula in her husky radio announcer's voice. She was a languid, long-haired blond with big eyes, and she sounded as interesting as she looked. "I was wondering if you'd like to be a guest on my *Friends and Neighbors* show this Tuesday morning."

"I . . . I'm not sure," stammered Suzanne.

Paula grinned at her. "You're not nervous about going on the air again, are you?"

"Not really." *Sure I am. Of course I am. It's not every day I have to talk live on radio waves that seep into hundreds of homes.*

"Because it seems to me," Paula went on smoothly, "that you did a fine job when you filled in for me a few months ago."

"Actually, no," said Suzanne. "That was a disaster of epic proportion. All those buttons to push and headsets to wear." *And airtime to fill, because, face it, I'm just not that glib. I'm not a motormouth DJ type of girl.*

"Well, this wouldn't be at all complicated," said Paula. "You'd just be my studio guest, no strings attached, no buttons to push."

"And we'd talk about . . . what exactly?"

"How about we hustle up some interest in your Hearts and Crafts Show," said Paula. "It's for a great cause and I'm guessing you could use more publicity. Right?"

"We really could," acknowledged Suzanne. She very much understood the value of PR and marketing, especially for a small enterprise like the Cackleberry Club or an event such as the Hearts and Crafts Show.

"You could mention some of the art pieces that'll be for sale and explain how a silent auction works," said Paula. "So . . . it's settled! Nine o'clock Tuesday morning in Studio B. I'll be counting on you."

"Gulp," said Suzanne.

IT wasn't until Suzanne and Toni delivered the three-tiered trays laden with tea sandwiches and miniature quiches that Suzanne realized Carla Reiker was also among the guests at the tea.

"Hey there!" said Reiker, her spiky black hair barely

moving as she turned in her chair to greet Suzanne. "We meet again."

"Carla!" said Suzanne. "Fancy seeing you here."

"You didn't recognize me without my cross-trainers and Lycra workout clothes?" She laughed. "The truth is, I got roped in by some of these crazy teachers I work with." She waved a hand at the group of smiling women that surrounded her.

"We're glad you made it," said Suzanne. "All of you."

"I hope you're still coming to my class on Monday," said Reiker.

"What class is that?" asked Toni, who was working her way around the table, pouring out piping-hot cups of jasmine tea.

"Carla teaches a self-defense class for women," Suzanne explained. "Over at the Hard Body Gym."

Toni's eyes lit up like a pinball machine. "For real?" she squealed. "That sounds absolutely rockin'!"

"I take it you're interested, too?" said Reiker, looking pleased.

"I'm into anything that involves kicking, punching, or releasing my inner aggression," said Toni.

"What ever happened to cultivating a more Zen attitude?" asked Suzanne in a teasing voice.

"I think self-defense is better suited to my personality," said Toni.

"Fantastic," said Reiker. "Then I'll be expecting you both!"

EXCEPT for the little blip of excitement when Carmen and Deanna Drummond first walked in, Suzanne decided the tea party was pretty much a runaway success. Havis seemed over-the-moon pleased as she hopped from table to table, chatting amiably with all the well-fed guests and volunteers. Toni and Kit were smoothly efficient in clearing away dishes and ferrying out fresh cups and saucers. And any troubleshooting Suzanne thought she might have to deal with never really materialized.

So when the carrot cake was finally sliced and served, and everyone was sipping orange blossom tea, kicking back in their chairs a bit, Suzanne ducked into the Book Nook. Because, you never know, a few guests might want to wander in and purchase a book or two. Or three or four.

After clearing the counter, Suzanne grabbed a half dozen of Carmen's romance novels and stacked them carefully, their spines clearly showing. Carmen would be pleasantly surprised to see the display, and some of the guests might even want her to inscribe a book for them, Suzanne thought. She also added a few books on tea and some cookbooks to her arrangement.

Then, just as she was about to pop back into the kitchen to check on Petra, Carmen drifted in.

"Hello, Suzanne," said Carmen. "I see you have some of my books front and center." She sounded pleased.

"I thought some of the guests might want to purchase signed copies," said Suzanne. "You don't mind signing a few, do you?"

"Mind?" said Carmen. "Darling, it's what I *live* for. In fact, I may as well sign your entire stock."

"Perfect," said Suzanne. She plucked the rest of Carmen's books off the shelf and placed them on the counter. Carmen, meanwhile, had uncapped a black Montblanc pen and was busily signing books with a dramatic flourish.

"You have lovely handwriting," said Suzanne, watching over Carmen's shoulder. "A lot of authors start out signing their names and then lose interest and flatline like a bad EKG."

"Not me," said Carmen. "I work way too hard to just dash off my name any old way." She peered through the open doorway into Suzanne's office and said, "By the way, Suzanne, those two paintings you have stashed in there? Were they by any chance done by Jake Gantz?"

"Yes, they were," said Suzanne. "Jake brought them in yesterday. I take it you're familiar with his work?"

"Absolutely I am," said Carmen. "I have two of Jake's pieces hanging in my office. Did you know there was even a small sidebar about him last month in *Midwest Art Scene* magazine? They called him an up-and-coming outsider artist. One to be *noted.*"

"And that's what you collect?" Suzanne asked. "Outsider art?" She found the term to be both interesting and quaint.

Carmen gave an almost imperceptible shrug. "Among other types of art and photography, yes."

"Jake's work doesn't appeal to everyone, of course," said Suzanne. "But I think his freewheeling style is pretty amazing. His use of bright colors and wild slashes conveys tremendous emotion."

"Yes, it does," said Carmen, suddenly adopting a slippery-smooth, nicey-nice voice. "You know," she added quickly, "I could save you some time and effort by writing a check right now for those two paintings."

"I'd like to say yes," Suzanne said carefully, "but the paintings have already been entered into our silent auction. Which means they'll be hung on our walls so everyone has a fair chance to bid on them."

Carmen's eyelids drooped. "You're telling me I have to come *back* here to bid on them?"

"That would be the general idea, yes. Since the auction doesn't start for a few days."

"And I'm off to New York tomorrow for a week," said Carmen with a sniff. "Really, couldn't we work out a more favorable arrangement? I have my checkbook with me now. We could wrap this whole thing up in mere minutes."

"Tell you what," said Suzanne. "If you give me your topmost number, I'd be happy to bid in the silent auction for you."

"Why do I feel like this is highway robbery?" protested Carmen.

"Really, Carmen," said Suzanne. "We're just trying to earn a little money for the food bank. I'm sure you can understand."

"It just seems unfair to me," said Carmen, unwilling to let the subject drop.

"You know what's unfair?" said Suzanne. She swore she wasn't going to bring this up, but now seemed like an opportune moment. "The fact that you fired Missy."

"That's a private business issue," Carmen snapped. "One that's not up for discussion. So kindly keep your nose out of it!"

"Missy's my friend," Suzanne continued, undaunted. "And I take umbrage that she's been treated so badly."

"Oh for goodness' sake!" hissed Carmen. "I can't have a woman who's a murder suspect managing my boutique. That would be utterly ridiculous! It would drive customers away and damage my reputation!"

At that Suzanne practically lost it. "But you can sashay in here with Deanna Drummond on your arm!"

"She's not a murder suspect!" cried Carmen.

"I wouldn't bet on that," said Suzanne.

Carmen stood stock-still now, practically quivering with anger. "Why is it you constantly pick at me, Suzanne? Why does every conversation we have always end in an argument?"

That stopped Suzanne in her tracks. Carmen was right. They did argue constantly. And she wasn't proud of that fact. She wasn't really a hectoring, lecturing person—not really. It was only when she was around Carmen that she seemed to fly off the handle. Carmen just . . . pushed her buttons.

"Truce," said Suzanne. "Détente, okay?"

Carmen continued to glare at her. "On the artwork, yes. But when it comes to Missy, absolutely not."

Still feeling the need to make her point, Suzanne dialed back her anger and forced herself to speak in a pleasant, almost conciliatory tone. "You know as well as I do, Carmen, that Missy's not a killer. She's a sweet and decent human being who's somehow caught up in trouble she had nothing to do with." Maybe she had to deal with Carmen the same way one would handle an aggressive dog. Show no fear, don't back down, remain perfectly calm.

Carmen bristled. "I really *don't* know that."

"Sure, you do," said Suzanne, trying to get Carmen to see her point. "If you look deep into your heart you'll realize what a good person Missy is. How loyal she's been to you and your boutique. How hard she's worked for you. And you'll see that you acted impetuously. Probably out of fear and worry—and I certainly understand that. But, Carmen, you did the wrong thing. Missy didn't deserve to be fired from your shop."

Instead of getting angry, Carmen fixed Suzanne with a nasty smile. "Typical Suzanne," she almost spit out. "Always pleading the case of the underdog."

"Well, somebody has to!" Suzanne snapped back.

CARMEN slipped out of the Book Nook in a huff, just as a few women came spilling in. One of them was Carla Reiker.

"Whoa," Reiker said bluntly to Suzanne as her eyes darted around the room. "Are you okay? I don't know what just happened here, but it looked like you and that author lady were close to a knock-down, drag-out fight."

Suzanne waved it off. "I shouldn't let her get under my skin like that."

Reiker grinned. "See, you really do need a self-defense class."

"Carmen's just . . ." Suzanne drew a shaky breath. "A basket full of crazy."

"Tell me about it," Reiker was saying. "Whenever Queen

Carmen comes to the gym, she expects someone to go ahead of her and wipe down all the handles and seats on the machines before she climbs on. I think she's deathly afraid of someone else's sweat!"

"Aren't we all?" said Suzanne, which somehow made them both giggle.

"So," said Reiker, "I understand you've been asking about Lester Drummond."

Suzanne looked at her. "Did Boots Wagner tell you that?"

"Not in so many words, but I heard via the local gossipmongers that you're following the case pretty closely."

"Just trying to clear my friend," said Suzanne.

"Nothing wrong with that," said Reiker. "I know Missy and I think she's a great girl."

"You spend a lot of time at the gym," said Suzanne. "Did you ever have any nasty run-ins with Lester Drummond? I'm curious."

"Not me, personally," said Reiker. "But I know that a lot of our members did. In fact, truth be known and all cards on the table—I wouldn't have blamed Wagner for wanting Drummond gone permanently. The man caused *so* many problems."

"When I talked to him, Wagner was fairly closemouthed about Drummond," said Suzanne.

"Aw, that's just because Boots is a good guy," put in Reiker. "He's got kind of a Marine code of ethics. Loyalty and *Semper Fi* and all that. But, really, he pretty much despised Drummond." She turned and smiled as Toni walked in, dangling a white bakery bag in one hand. "Please tell me that's for me."

"I snuck away with the last four blueberry scones for you," said Toni. "But do not tell a soul!"

"Bless you," said Reiker. "I rarely eat carbs, but for these little puffs of goodness I'll make a huge exception. Even though I'll have to do a gazillion crunches to make up for it."

Toni nudged Suzanne's arm. "Did you ask her about Lester Drummond?"

Reiker answered for Suzanne. "She did. And my personal take on Lester Drummond is that he was a major pain in the butt for everyone at the gym."

"I think everyone in town felt the same way," said Toni. "He wasn't exactly Mr. Popularity." She glanced at Suzanne. "Have you heard any word on the autopsy yet?"

"Not really," said Suzanne, wishing Toni hadn't brought it up out of the blue like that.

"We're lucky," said Toni, giving a slow wink. "Suzanne has a direct pipeline to all the hot news."

As Suzanne's stomach did a little somersault, Reiker said, "Oh, you mean from Dr. Hazelet? I suppose he would be involved in this."

"In the autopsy," Toni said in hushed tones, drawing out the word again, making it sound alien and threatening, "They're running all sorts of special tests to help determine who killed Drummond!"

"Well . . . that's good," said Reiker, looking a little taken aback at Toni's dramatics and hyperbole.

But Suzanne wasn't about to set the record straight concerning Sam deferring to a visiting ME. It was bad enough that Drummond's autopsy was even being discussed at what had been a perfectly lovely tea party.

Toni still wasn't finished. "You know they actually take teeny little slices of a person's liver, kidney, and brain and look at them under a microscope?"

"You must be a huge fan of *CSI*," said Reiker, looking a little askance.

"Nah," said Toni. "I think I saw that on an old episode of *Quincy*."

"How awful is it out there?" asked Petra. The tea was officially over and all the guests had departed in a sugar-induced, carbo-zonked haze. Suzanne, Toni, and Kit had gathered in the kitchen, picking at what was left of the sandwiches and cake. "Is the café pretty messy?" Petra asked again. She was a neat freak with a touch of OCD. She liked things to be clean, organized, and in good repair.

Playing to Petra's insecurities now, Toni gave a huge grimace. "Do you remember those old films of Woodstock? When the concert was over and everyone had cleared out and there was so much trash and garbage left it looked like a neutron bomb had exploded?"

"Oh no," said Petra. "It can't be *that* bad."

"I think it's worse," said Toni.

"It's not that bad," said Kit.

"In that case," said Toni, "*you* can give me a hand with the cleanup."

"But only if she feels okay," said Petra. "Kit, *do* you feel okay—are you better now?"

"I'm fine," said Kit. "That piece of quiche you gave me kind of settled things down."

"Eggs have a way of doing that," agreed Petra. "They're kind of a magic elixir."

"So what's our plan of attack?" asked Toni.

"Petra stays in the kitchen to tidy up her domain," said Suzanne. "And the three of us tackle the café. We'll bus dirty dishes, gather up tablecloths, put away candles and stuff, and handle whatever else needs doing."

"Got it," said Toni, pushing open the door. "Come on, Kit Kat."

"What *are* we going to do about that poor girl?" asked Petra once she and Suzanne were alone in the kitchen.

"You mean Kit?"

"Yes. Who else?"

"I don't know," said Suzanne. She stood up just as the wall phone shrilled. "Maybe . . . throw her a baby shower?" She grabbed the receiver off the hook and said, "Hello?"

"Suzanne."

"Sam!" she said, recognizing his voice and suddenly feeling badly that she hadn't thought about him all day. Well, since they kissed each other good-bye this morning, anyway.

"Hey," he said, "I'm going to be hung up at the hospital for a while."

"Okay," she said. They had planned to go out for a burger tonight, but she understood. The life of a doctor could be—interesting.

"I'll probably be stuck here until around nine. Can I call you later?"

"Of course," she said. "No problem." She hesitated. "Is everything all right?"

"Um," said Sam. "I promise I'll call you later."

"SUZANNE," said Toni. She jabbed a broom under one of the tables in the café, trying to snag a few errant crumbs. "I have a favor to ask."

"What's that?" asked Suzanne. She was at the counter, stacking teapots into a gray plastic tub.

"Come along with me to the race tonight," said Toni.

Suzanne turned, a blank look on her face. "What race?" She wondered if there was something she'd missed. Maybe a 10K for the Sesquicentennial?

Toni wrinkled her nose. "You know . . . with Junior? The demolition derby over at Golden Springs Speedway?"

"He's really racing tonight? Oh dear."

"Tell me about it," Toni said in a small voice.

"Why exactly do you want me to come along?" Suzanne decided that Toni either wanted her to mumble prayers for Junior's safety—or try to talk him out of racing.

Toni shrugged. "Let's just call it moral support."

"Won't Junior think it's weird if I tag along?" *And mumble prayers? Or try to talk him out of racing?*

"Aw, he'll be thrilled. We'll give you a trucker cap and tell him you're part of the pit crew."

"Does Junior have a pit crew?" asked Suzanne.

"You're lookin' at her."

Kit, who'd been listening to their exchange, said, "You really should go, Suzanne. Those races are a lot of fun."

"You think?" said Suzanne. But deep down she knew it would be a horrible experience. Cars buzzing around a track like angry hornets, rollovers, crashes, sirens and red lights . . . injuries.

"Come on, Suzanne," said Toni. "Do you *really* have something better to do?"

Sensing Toni was in desperate need of company, Suzanne gave in and said, "Okay, if you absolutely insist." But deep down she was really thinking, *Yes, I have something better to do. A lot of things would be better. Like reading a book, watching TV, maybe even scrubbing the kitchen floor!*

FORTY minutes later, the café was sufficiently restored to its normal state of readiness and Kit was sent on her way home. As Petra and Toni poked around in the Knitting Nest, marveling over a new shipment of alpaca yarn, Suzanne worked in the kitchen, wrapping up leftover tea sandwiches and carrot cake to take home with her.

Maybe, she decided, she could bring some of the food with her to the demolition derby tonight. Then she wondered if a pit—is that what you really called it?—was really the idyllic spot for a picnic.

A *tap, tap, tap* on the back door brought Suzanne out of her reverie.

Who's there? she wondered. Then she scrambled to the back door and peered through the screen at a shadowy, looming figure.

Which turned out to be none other than Sheriff Doogie.

"What's up?" Suzanne asked him, as she opened the door and let him in. Had something happened? Had he been at the autopsy and learned something new and important?

"I've got a heads-up for you," said Doogie, mincing no words. His gray eyes bounced around the kitchen, studiously avoiding hers. His mouth was pulled into a tight line.

"What's going on?" Suzanne asked suddenly.

Was there big news? While tea kettles hissed and burbled at the Cackleberry Club, had Doogie finally nabbed the killer? Was this nightmare finally over? But no, if that's what had happened, wouldn't there be a look of supreme relief on his face? Wouldn't he'd be acting a lot more cocky than he was right now?

"I'm only doing this because we're friends," said Doogie. "And because the two of you are friends."

A warning bell sounded loud and clear in Suzanne's head. "What are you talking about?"

Doogie rubbed a meaty hand over his mouth, then focused sad eyes upon her. "We found a Taser stashed in Missy's apartment."

His words hit Suzanne like the proverbial ton of bricks. Her mind reeled with disbelief, as if the world had seriously tilted on its axis. Then, in a voice filled with gravel, she choked out, "What?"

CHAPTER 15

"Don't make me say it again, Suzanne. It was hard enough getting it out the first time."

"Doogie, no!" Suzanne cried. "I don't believe it!" She stared at Doogie's mottled face and suddenly realized that he looked as lousy as he probably felt.

"Believe it," he said. "It was there. Top drawer of her dresser. Saw it with my own two eyes."

"What were you doing prowling around Missy's apartment?" Suzanne demanded. "In her *dresser*, for goodness' sake! Isn't that a little—I don't know—beyond protocol? A little too personal?"

"Not prowling, searching," Doogie corrected. "And it was all carried out exactly by the book. We had a search warrant signed by Judge Carlson. Had everything all sewed up just like we were supposed to."

"Why on earth did you go to a judge for a search warrant?"

"Because we had probable cause," said Doogie, like it was the most reasonable thing in the world.

Suzanne wasn't buying it. "You had nothing of the sort!"

"Yes, we did," said Doogie, trying to keep his voice level. "We have two other witnesses, besides you and Toni, who swear on a stack of Bibles that they saw Missy driving out of that cemetery Thursday morning. You all placed her there without question. So that was good enough for me and a few other people."

"Who are the other witnesses?"

Doogie shifted from one foot to the other. "I'm really not at liberty to get into specifics . . ."

"Come on, Doogie," said Suzanne. "That's a bunch of hooey and you know it. If you drove all the way over here to tell me about finding the Taser, then you can sure as heck reveal who your witnesses are."

"I suppose," said Doogie slowly. It was clear he wasn't happy with the way this conversation was going. "One of them is Mrs. Haberle. And the other is Allan Sharp."

"Mrs. Haberle!" Suzanne blurted out. "The woman is eighty-four years old, wears glasses with Coke-bottle lenses, and is hardly the poster child for most reliable witness." She could feel the outrage bubbling inside her now. And it was about to pop and ooze all over the place.

"Still," said Doogie, "Mrs. Haberle was working in her tomato patch and she recognized Missy's car."

"Excuse me, but Mrs. Haberle wouldn't recognize a VW Bug from a Rolls-Royce Phantom," said Suzanne, really steamed. "And how did Mrs. Haberle come to be a witness in the first place, pray tell? This I'd really like to hear."

"Because of smart and solid investigative techniques."

"Meaning?"

Doogie studied his boots. "I sent all my deputies out to question the folks who live along Monarch Road."

"And just how was Allan Sharp's keen observation called into question?" Suzanne asked.

"Turns out the man was right there when it all went down."

"Isn't that convenient," Suzanne snapped.

Doogie held up his hands. "It was all aboveboard. Allan Sharp and Mayor Mobley were out scouting a plot of land near the Sunnyside Daycare Center. Apparently, Sharp has big plans to develop that area. He's gonna put up some more of his ticky-tacky town houses, I guess."

"And Sharp just happened to see Missy drive by," said Suzanne.

"Yup. He swears he saw Missy drive by that morning, and Mobley backs him up."

"That's not backing someone up, that's collusion!" exclaimed Suzanne. "You know what a dirty dealer Mayor Mobley is—and Sharp isn't any better. Shame on you for taking their word for it! For swallowing their story hook, line, and sinker!"

Doogie tried to muster a dollop of patience, but he seemed less and less sure of himself with each passing moment. "I don't know why Allan Sharp would lie about something like this."

"Sure you do," said Suzanne. "Allan Sharp despised Lester Drummond. Sharp was one of the board members who voted to fire Drummond from the prison, remember?" She stopped and tried to pull her scattered thoughts together. "Doogie, listen to me, Toni and I ran into Allan Sharp last night at the cemetery walk. He was chortling like mad about Drummond. About what a dreadful person he was. On and on. For all you know, Sharp could be the killer!"

"That's doubtful," said Doogie. But he looked like he was ready to wobble.

"Come on, Doogie, you know for a fact that Allan Sharp and Mayor Mobley stuffed the ballot box last November to get Mobley reelected. If they're not above that kind of shameless tactic, obviously they wouldn't think twice about coercing you into getting a warrant!"

Doogie's face turned red as a chili pepper.

Of course, they did, thought Suzanne. *I can see it large as life on Doogie's face.*

"It's out of my hands now," said Doogie with some resignation. "We went in, did our search, and found a Taser." Looking dejected, he turned and stepped back outside.

"So what are you going to do now?" Suzanne shouted out after him. "Arrest her?"

"We already did," answered Doogie. "Missy's being arraigned first thing tomorrow morning."

"Then I'll be there to post bail," Suzanne snapped back.

"Be careful, Suzanne," warned Doogie. "Be careful who you take sides with in this thing."

But Suzanne had already taken sides. And slammed the door in his face.

THREE minutes into Suzanne's recounting of events to Toni and Petra, the phone rang. Petra picked it up, listened closely for a couple of moments, then silently held out the receiver to Suzanne.

"Suzanne!" came Missy's hollow, strangled voice. "I . . . I . . ."

That was all she managed to get out. The rest of her words were lost behind pitiful sobs.

"I know, I know," Suzanne cooed into the phone. Even though she was angry and frustrated to the point where she wanted to let out a good long scream, she tried to hold it together for Missy. "Sheriff Doogie just stopped by and told me you'd been taken in." She couldn't bring herself to say the word "arrested."

"I need your help!" wailed Missy. She sounded frantic and desperate. "I need to make bail tomorrow. I just have to. I know this is a lot to ask and all, but I've got to, Suzanne. Can you . . . Will you . . . ?"

"Of course," Suzanne answered without hesitation. "You know I will. But, um, what do I do exactly? Who do I speak with?" She wasn't sure how this whole process worked. She'd never posted bail for anyone before. In fact, she'd never even known anyone who'd been arrested. Except maybe Junior.

"They tell me there's an arraignment tomorrow morning," Missy stammered out. "So that's when you have to post bail."

"What about a lawyer?" said Suzanne. "Do you have one?"

"Yes," said Missy. "I called Harry Jankovich over in Jessup. So he'll be there, too. In fact, I can give you Harry's phone number if you need it. He said it'd be okay if you called him at home. He'll tell you how everything works." She sniffled loudly.

"Good. Okay. I'll give Harry a call. And I'll *be* there tomorrow."

"You promise?" Missy's voice was a hoarse whisper.

"You better believe it," said Suzanne. She was dying to ask Missy why she had a Taser in her possession—she still couldn't get over that fact. But she figured she'd let it go for now. *One thing at a time. I'll put one foot in front of the other and forge ahead step-by-step.*

"Now what do we do?" Petra asked, once Suzanne had hung up the phone. Petra and Toni had remained at Suzanne's side during the entire conversation with Missy.

"There's nothing to do," said Suzanne, "until I go to the Law Enforcement Center tomorrow morning."

"It's a good thing Missy didn't come to the tea," said Toni. "Imagine if Sheriff Doogie had come busting in on all those ladies like some kind of crazy storm trooper!"

"Don't even think about that," said Suzanne. "All we can do is try to stay positive."

"And pray," said Petra. "Ask the Good Lord for help."

"Do you think He'll hear us?" asked Toni.

Petra's face softened. "Honey, the Lord hears us whenever

we pray. That's one thing in this world you never have to worry about."

SUZANNE'S arms and legs felt leaden and her brain felt as soggy as a bowl of day-old oatmeal as she stumped to her car. Climbing in, she tossed her bag on the seat next to her, gripped the wheel, and gritted her teeth, trying to cut through the fog and kick her brain into overdrive. There had to be a reasonable explanation as to why Missy owned a Taser. There had to be! Most women didn't have a nasty thing like that tucked in a dresser drawer next to their slip.

Even if Missy had bought the Taser for self-protection, wouldn't she have dumped it right after Drummond's death? Just in case something like this happened? Sure she would have. Of course, that supposition was based solely on the premise that Missy was innocent.

So, what if she wasn't? What if she was guilty?

Suzanne didn't want to contemplate that possibility. Her brain just didn't want to go there. No, there had to be something else going on. A clever killer who had schemed to set Missy up? But who—and why?

Suzanne racked her brain for answers. Was there some critical clue that she or Doogie had missed? There had to be. She tried to concentrate, tried to think outside the box, but no brilliant thoughts appeared in a cartoon bubble above her head. No blinding flash lent any new insight into the murder. Not right now, anyway.

Feeling dazed and a little helpless, Suzanne put her car into gear. But instead of creeping around the Cackleberry Club and onto the main road, in a spur-of-the-moment decision she eased her way past the back shed and through the woodlot at the rear of her property. Then she bumped across the dirt road that led to the farmyard across the way.

It was really her farm, bought and paid for by her dear

Walter as an investment of sorts. Now she was leasing it to a farmer named Reed Ducovny. He put the rich acreage to work by growing bumper crops of soybeans and Jubilee corn.

Suzanne topped a small hill and was rewarded with a panoramic view of a lovely faded red, hip-roof barn, three small outbuildings, and a white American Gothic farmhouse where Reed and his wife lived. No cattle, pigs, chickens, or dairy cows inhabited the old farmstead at the moment. Just her beloved horse, Mocha Gent, and a mule by the name of Grommet.

I might be busy with the Cackleberry Club—and now I'm smack dab in the middle of a murder mystery—but I'll never, ever forget about these critters. They mean the world to me.

Thinking about Mocha and Grommet soothed her, helped her respiration slow down and her racing mind find some comfort.

Parking her car next to the barn, Suzanne stepped out of the car and glanced at the sky. A sultry haze hung over the fields as far as she could see, and the temperature had climbed into the low eighties. But the air carried an electrical feel, almost as if a big storm might be brewing to the south. Storm clouds hunkered over Kansas, trying to suck up moisture from the Gulf and spin it into something fierce. Or maybe, she decided, the rain would just move in harmlessly and give the fields a much-needed soaking.

Sliding open the barn door, Suzanne breathed in the rich mingled scents of fresh hay, oiled leather, and horses. She drifted past the long row of empty stanchions, heading for the back of the barn and the two large box stalls.

Mocha was the first one to hear her coming. He'd probably picked up her scent. Or perhaps he was a psychic horse. Either way, there was a low, welcoming nicker, then the echoing stomp of a hoof.

"Hey, guy," Suzanne called to him, a smile spreading across her face. "Hey, Mocha boy."

Mocha pushed his chest up against the gate and thrust his head out for Suzanne to pet. He was a stocky, blocky quarter horse, a reddish brown chestnut with large brown eyes and a crooked white blaze that splattered down the center of his Roman nose. He'd been with her for five years now and she loved him dearly.

Suzanne scratched behind Mocha's ears, then ran her hand down his cheek, tracing down the side of his nose and ending up under his chin in a field of prickly stubble. In appreciation, Mocha gave a vigorous snort.

Grommet, the mule, pushed his head across his gate, too. He was shiny black and enormous, almost seventeen hands high. Bobbing his head, he thrust his huge ears forward, eager for her touch and attention. She'd bought him in a sheriff's auction a year ago and never regretted it.

"I was getting to you, boy," said Suzanne, rubbing his nose just the way he liked. Suzanne didn't ride Grommet: his gait was a little too slow and shambling, but he made a dandy roommate for Mocha. The two guys seemed to get along just fine as stable buddies, and Suzanne was grateful that Ducovny took such good care of his equine guests.

Popping the lid off a metal container, she grabbed a scoop of oats and fed it to Grommet. Mocha, worried he wouldn't get his fair share, let loose a nervous whinny.

"Not to worry," she told him. When Grommet was finished munching, she dipped the scoop back into the oats and fed some to Mocha. He chowed down noisily, chewing, drooling a little, all the while keeping a watchful eye on her. When he was finished, he nudged the scoop, trying to cadge a second serving.

"No, you don't. In fact, in another week, you're going to be spending a lot more time out in the pasture. Be good for you. You could stand to lose a couple of pounds."

Mocha just stared at her, as if to say, *Please. I'm perfect just the way I am.*

"You do want to do some barrel racing this summer, don't you?" Suzanne asked gently.

Mocha backed away.

"Ooh, you know exactly what I'm talking about! Well, buddy, you and I are going to start doing some serious workouts. I can promise you that." Suzanne unbolted the gate and slipped inside Mocha's stall. She threw her arms around his shoulders and buried her face in his rough, tangled mane. Big horse, comforting horse, she thought to herself as she inhaled his pungent horsey scent. In a world gone a little bit crazy, it was pure joy to have a creature like this to love.

And know that he loved you back. No matter what.

BACK home some twenty minutes later, Suzanne felt calmer and more centered than before. Her little detour had worked wonders. And as she hummed about the bathroom, freshening up, she wondered what on earth one should wear to a demolition derby. Was there even "proper" attire?

Then she decided that whatever threads she threw on would work just fine. In this case a navy T-shirt, blue jeans, and short black leather boots.

Back downstairs, Suzanne fed Baxter and Scruff, let them romp around outside in the backyard for ten minutes, and bribed them with jerky treats to get them back inside. Their paws were mud-caked because of the previous day's rain, so she got bowls of warm water then knelt down on the floor and sat back on her heels.

"I know this looks like I'm ready to do a Japanese tea ceremony," she told Baxter, "but I really need to dip and scrub each of your paws. You, too, Scruffer."

At eight o'clock, Suzanne turned off all the lights in the house and stood in the entryway, checking her wallet for money. Two twenties—that ought to do it. She glanced idly out the narrow window next to the front door and watched a car slide slowly up to the curb.

Is that Toni?

Peering out her front window into the dusk, Suzanne squinted to see who it might be. But it was so dark she couldn't really tell. The car sat there, the engine rumbling, the lights turned off. Hesitating, her heart suddenly thumping in her chest, Suzanne watched the car idle at the curb. It sat there for another thirty seconds or so—then abruptly pulled away.

Well, Suzanne thought, *it's obviously not Toni. But who then? Was it a case of mistaken address? Or was the lone person sitting in that car somehow connected to all the craziness that's been going on?*

Or—gulp—could someone be stalking me? I know I shouldn't be jumping to crazy-quick conclusions, but I can't help it!

Feeling more than a little jittery now, Suzanne craned her neck to make sure the car had vanished down the street. Then she stepped gingerly outside to wait on her front steps, hoping Toni would hurry along soon.

She heard Toni's car before she saw it—a rattling, shaking cacophony that sounded like a medieval instrument of torture. Then a horrible-looking cat-urine-yellow car pulled to the curb and shuddered to a stop. Suzanne turned around to her front door, locked it securely with her key, and skittered down to Toni's car.

"This isn't what you usually drive," were Suzanne's first words as she opened the creaky passenger door and clambered in.

"Ah, you know Junior," said Toni, with a wave of her hand and a big smile, almost as big as the reddish blond clip-on hairpiece on top of her head. "He's always stealing pieces and parts to make do."

"And he jacked *your* car?"

"Just for a couple of days."

"And this is what you get in trade?" said Suzanne, thinking Toni had gotten the raw end of the deal.

"Hey," said Toni, "I'm just lucky this junker runs."

"What is this thing, anyway?" Suzanne had a vague memory of this particular make of car being popular when she was in high school.

"An eighty-one Plymouth Fury."

"Didn't Detroit stop making these babies?" Suzanne asked.

"Yup. Hence its enormous appeal to Junior."

"How many cars does Junior actually own?" asked Suzanne, fishing for the seat belt. This car was so ancient the seat belts were the old-fashioned kind that strapped across your lap.

"At least a dozen," said Toni as they screeched away from the curb. "But I'm not sure Junior has a pink slip on every one." She was struggling to find second gear and couldn't seem to come up with it. The car grunted and groaned until Toni finally revved the engine and popped it into third gear.

"So this is like Frankencar," said Suzanne. "Rebuilt with random pieces."

"Good one," Toni chuckled.

"What time does the race start?" Suzanne asked. "Or, rather, Junior's demolition event?"

Toni grimaced. "I think Eve of Destruction starts around eight-thirty. But I got a call from Junior a little while ago telling me he might be a little late. He had a flat tire."

"On his race car?" said Suzanne. She decided this might be a piece of good luck. A reprieve of sorts.

"Not on his car," said Toni. "On his house."

Suzanne's head spun sideways so fast she almost gave herself whiplash. "Excuse me?"

"Oh, you don't know about that, do you?" Toni chuckled as she checked her rearview mirror. "Junior bought himself a used double-wide trailer a couple weeks back."

"No kidding," said Suzanne. "So that's where he's living?" She knew he wasn't with Toni. Toni had kicked him out more than a year ago.

"You got it," said Toni as they careened around a corner, a cloud of blue exhaust belching from the tailpipe, laying a smoke screen worthy of James Bond.

"So I guess that means that Junior's the newest resident of the Essex Motor Park," Suzanne mused. She tried to picture Junior fitting in there with the retired bridge and bowling folks. "Isn't that place kind of ritzy for Junior? I hear they even have a swimming pool."

Toni snorted. "Hah! Junior should be so lucky. No, his trailer's parked illegally out on Revere Road. Just down from the town dump."

"Well, that's, um"—Suzanne searched for an appropriate word—"convenient."

CHAPTER 16

TWENTY minutes later they pulled into the parking lot at the Golden Springs Speedway. The place was teeming with tricked-out pickup trucks, souped-up cars, and classic muscle cars. From the scream of engines and the roar of the crowd, it was obvious the races were well under way.

These people are all gearheads, Suzanne thought to herself as she looked around at the crowd. So what was she doing here? A dyed-in-the-wool . . . um . . . bookhead? Egghead? She decided there really wasn't a toned-down, normal equivalent to gearhead.

"Here we are," Toni crowed as she pulled into a parking space. "Take a gander at all the denim tuxedos!"

"Denim . . . what?"

"You know, denim jackets and jeans," said Toni.

"Okay," said Suzanne as she climbed out. Suddenly she was feeling *over*dressed. "And we're going . . . where?"

"Over this way," said Toni, tugging at her arm. "No grandstand for us tonight. We gotta hook up with Junior in the racers' lot!"

When the two women reached a large, flat, weedy lot out back, Junior was just pulling in. Driving a beat-up pickup truck, he was towing his demolition derby car on a rickety wooden trailer.

Junior grinned when he saw them. "Glad you guys made it. I can really use your help!"

"What can we do?" asked Suzanne. On the walk back here, she'd made up her mind to remain positive. She'd come here to lend a hand for Toni's sake, and that's exactly what she was going to do. No judgment, no snide remarks. Just a good time with one of her BFFs, even if the venue was a bit on the wild side.

"Suzanne, grab those cans of motor oil and brake fluid," said Junior. He was dressed in saggy jeans and a ripped Pennzoil T-shirt. "And Toni, if you can get that spool of electrical wire. Oh, and the wrenches and socket set, too."

While they gathered equipment, Junior backed his car down off the trailer. "Wiggle in if you want," he invited them. "You girls are skinny enough to squeeze in through the back windows."

"That's okay," said Suzanne. "We'll just follow you over."

"Don't get lost!" warned Junior.

How could they? As they huffed their way along behind Junior's car, the noise from the track got even more deafening. It started out as a throbbing rumble then built to the ear-piercing, bone-shaking roar of a freight train.

"Is it always this loud?" Suzanne mouthed to Toni, thinking this was eardrum-splitting territory.

Toni nodded. "That's because the Thundercars are racing now," she said. "Their souped-up engines are crazy loud. Some of the fans even wear earplugs, like they do at rock concerts."

Once they were in the pits, lined up alongside a dozen or

so other demolition derby cars, Suzanne found herself growing strangely fascinated by this race-night spectacle. Brightly
painted and decaled cars, so vivid they looked like neon-
colored parakeets, thundered past them on the high-banked
asphalt track. People cheered, the jacked-up crowd seemed
lost in an endless human wave, and loudspeakers blared with
a fuzzy announcer's voice that went virtually ignored. It was
an amalgam of carnival, pageantry, and theater all rolled
into one.

"What do you think?" Toni asked, a gleam in her eye.

"It's crazy," said Suzanne. "This is practically . . . epic!"

"Hey!" called Junior. "I could use a little help over here."

They got busy then, arranging gear, sorting out Junior's
flame-retardant jacket and jumpsuit, and watching breath-
lessly as two Thundercars dueled their way to the finish line
while a great roar went up from the crowd.

"That's it," said Toni. "There's the checkered flag. That
means our race is next." She was quivering like a Chihuahua
caught in a snowstorm.

"We got time," said Junior. "They gotta award prizes
first." He pointed a greasy finger toward a small stage in
front of the grandstand. "See? They've even got tire models
here tonight!"

Suzanne peered across the hazy track and saw two women
dressed in tight white tank tops, impossibly short leather
skirts, and white go-go boots, and decided those must be
the tire models.

"That's big-time," Junior assured her as he undid a latch
and flipped up his hood. "Whenever companies send tire
models to these races, you know there's decent prize money
involved."

Toni handed Junior a can of motor oil and watched him
pour it, the engine gulping hungrily. "Might have a leak,"
said Junior. "And Toni, grab me a ratchet, will you? I wanna
tighten up the screws on this gasket."

She grabbed a tool and handed it to him.

"That's a wrench," said Junior. "I need a ratchet."

"Um . . ." said Toni, rattling around in the tool kit. "I don't think we brought those."

"You *forgot* my ratchet set?" barked Junior. He ran his fingers through his dark, unruly hair and breathed out a stream of air. "Ah, man, that means they're sitting in the back of my truck, in the parking lot."

"I'll run back and get your tools," Suzanne volunteered. "No problem."

"Just the ratchet set," said Junior.

"Thanks, girlfriend," said Toni, as Junior made a whirring motion with his finger, indicating he wanted her to peel off a strip of electrical tape.

Suzanne dodged through the waiting fleet of demolition derby cars and headed back out to the racers' lot. It was full-on dark now, with gray, bubbly-looking clouds hanging low in the sky, making the atmosphere feel more than a little oppressive. Suzanne wondered if the soft purple evenings of early summer were ever going to arrive. Then she decided she'd better worry about that later and kick it into high gear if she wanted to get Junior's tools back to him.

When she reached the truck, she found the ratchet set right where Junior said it would be. Lying in the truck bed. Suzanne stuck a toe into the wheel rim and found a toehold on a bolt. Then she hoisted herself up so she could lean over and grab it.

Just as her fingers made contract with the plastic box that held the tools, she heard the sharp clunk of metal. Grabbing the toolbox, she scrambled down and whirled around. Her eyes searched the dark. And saw . . . absolutely nothing.

But I heard something, didn't I?

Suzanne stood in the dry grass, trying to relegate the dull

sounds of cheering and rumbling engines to background noise. She tuned in to her immediate environment of dry grass and parked trucks, listening for the smallest sound.

The sudden ring of her cell phone shattered the silence and almost scared the daylights out of her!

She fumbled in her pocket for it, pressed the On button, and managed a squeaky, "Hello?"

It was Sam.

"Hey," he said. "You sound funny."

"I'm at the car races with Toni and Junior."

"Car races?"

"I'll explain later. What's up?"

"Suzanne . . . there's something weird going on that I have to tell you about."

Suzanne was instantly on alert. "Sam, what is it? What's wrong?"

"Not over the phone. When I get to your place, okay?"

"Sure." She glanced at her watch. "I'll be home in a couple of hours, okay? Come over then."

"Got it," said Sam.

Suzanne stood there, nerves amped, suddenly wondering what was on Sam's mind. Had he discovered something during this second and final day of Lester Drummond's autopsy? Or was something else going on? If so—what?

She gulped, blew out a glut of air, and heard . . . another clunk.

There was that sound again! Almost as if a metal crowbar had ticked against the side of a truck.

Someone else come back to grab some gear?

Shoulders stiff, head cocked, Suzanne stood stock-still. Then, almost out of nowhere, a puff of wind arose and tiny bits of dust blew up into her face. She wrinkled her nose to keep from sneezing and wiped at her eyes. All the while she continued to listen.

Someone had crept back to grab some gear, she decided. Or . . . hold on a minute . . . what if someone had followed her back to this seemingly deserted parking lot?

But why?

Her thoughts drifted back to the car that had pulled up outside her house tonight. Dark car, no lights. Who had it been? And could they have followed her here?

Gripping the socket set tightly against her chest, Suzanne took off running and didn't look back.

WEARING his flame-retardant jacket and gripping a toothpick between his teeth, Junior grabbed the ratchet set from Suzanne's hands and set to work.

"Did I miss anything?" Suzanne asked.

Toni looked worried. "They just called the demolition cars onto the track."

"So when does this crazy derby officially start?" asked Suzanne.

Toni looked at her watch. "Like, in two minutes." She glanced up at Suzanne and noticed her friend's shakiness. "Hey, are you okay?"

Suzanne nodded. "Fine." This wasn't the time or place to explain her sudden paranoia.

"Done!" said Junior. He snatched up his helmet and plopped it onto his head.

Toni squinted at him. "Is that regulation?"

Junior spat out his toothpick and tapped a finger against his helmet. "High school football."

"Dear Lord," said Toni as Junior slithered into his car and settled into the driver's seat. "Buckle up tight!"

"Don't worry," said Junior as he turned the starter. There was a clicking sound, a loud sputter, and a series of nasty backfires. Then Junior was put-putting his way into the center of the track.

"Be safe!" Suzanne called. But who was she kidding, really? Was anybody safe in this wonked-out demolition derby that actually went by the name Eve of Destruction?

Thirty seconds later a starter gun exploded and the demolition derby began in earnest. Suzanne decided it was like watching the Keystone Cops, only with hideous cars. A yellow and black car that looked like an angry beetle took aim and promptly smashed into a white car. The beetle car shivered, shook, backed up twenty feet, then crashed into a blue car. It was chaos, pandemonium, and flying auto parts. She also noticed there were a few cars whizzing around the outer perimeter, wisely staying out of the fray.

"There's Junior!" cried Toni. "Oh jeez, he's sandbagging it."

"What's that mean?" asked Suzanne.

"He's trying to avoid getting hit, hoping he can keep going until the end of the race."

"That's good, huh?"

"No, that's bad," said Toni. "The judges might disqualify him for not participating."

"We can only hope," said Suzanne.

But Junior wasn't out of the action for long. A red Chevy with yellow flames painted on both sides was suddenly dogging him. Junior zigged and zagged and spun and turned, but he couldn't shake the aggressive Chevy. Finally, as Junior was charging down the straightaway in front of the grandstand, the red Chevy powered straight at him and struck him broadside. Junior's driver's side door crumpled like a piece of tinfoil and a tire flew off the rim!

"Come on, Junior, move it!" Toni screamed. "Get your butt outta there!"

But try as he might, Junior couldn't get his car started again. The Chevy had struck a death blow. Junior's engine was shot and he was out of the race.

"Now what?" asked Suzanne. "Junior just sits there like a squished bug until every last car is out of commission?"

Toni looked morose. "Those are the rules. In this derby anyway."

"But isn't he a sitting duck?"

"Aw," said Toni, "the other drivers don't care about him anymore."

"Isn't that what you wanted?"

Toni frowned. "I didn't want Junior to enter, but now that he's out of the money I feel kind of sad for him." She shook her head and said, "I guess that's why they call it the pits."

SAM was waiting in his car, parked neatly at the curb, when Suzanne arrived back home an hour later.

"Lucky you," said Toni, pumping the brakes on her hunk of junk. "You'll have sweet dreams tonight!" She giggled as Suzanne jumped out of her car.

"Thanks! See you tomorrow."

Suzanne sped toward Sam as he stepped out of his car. "What's up?" she asked.

He put his arms around her and gave her a quick kiss. "Better we should go inside."

Suzanne shook her head to clear it. *Right.* She was so wound up over Missy's arrest, her argument with Doogie, Junior's stupid contest, and the scare she'd had in the parking lot that she wasn't processing things very well.

"Did you hear about Missy?" Suzanne asked once they were in the kitchen and the dogs had been let out into the backyard. She stood at the sink, washing her hands and drying them with a crisp dish towel.

Sam shook his head. "No. What?"

Over glasses of Cabernet, sitting at the counter, she filled him in on the sad events of the day, especially her news about Missy.

"Arrested her," said Sam, whistling. "Wow. I didn't see that one coming."

"I think I kind of did," said Suzanne. "Even though I tried to push it to the back of my brain." She took a sip of wine for courage. "I'm going to post bail for her tomorrow. And please don't tell me I shouldn't, because my mind's already made up."

Sam lifted both hands in a show of no protest. "Hey, you'll get no argument from me."

"If the tables were turned, she'd do the same for me in a heartbeat."

"If the tables were turned," said Sam, "I'd beat her to it."

Suzanne smiled and touched his cheek. "Thank you." The flutter in her stomach seemed to subside a little. "Now, what were you all fired up about?"

"Dr. Gordon finished the Drummond autopsy this afternoon."

Uh-oh, here it comes, Suzanne thought to herself. "And let me guess—he was finally able to determine the cause of death?"

"First things first," said Sam. "What he discovered were additional hemorrhages on Drummond's heart and lungs."

"Which means what?" said Suzanne. "Remember, please, I never went to medical school."

"Internal hemorrhages like that are usually caused by stress-induced arrhythmia."

Suzanne peered at him. "Drummond had a heart attack?"

Sam continued. "There was no indication of that, but his breathing was definitely compromised and the rhythm of his heartbeat was either slowed considerably or sped up. Which meant his heart couldn't pump enough blood to his body."

"So what killed him, then?" asked Suzanne, puzzled.

"We don't have conclusive evidence, since we don't have

all the test results. But I have a rather intriguing theory for the actual cause of death. Really, a fairly straightforward theory."

"Tell me," said Suzanne. Now she was hanging on his every word.

"After Drummond was Tasered and fairly incapacitated, I think someone held a plastic bag over his nose and mouth."

Suzanne's hand inadvertently went to her own mouth. "That's awful!" She could almost feel a burning sensation in her lungs. "And then his heart went into arrhythmia?"

"Probably."

"Does Doogie know all this? I mean, you shared your theory?"

"I did," said Sam. "We had a confab with him earlier this afternoon."

"And then Doogie got a search warrant and went to Missy's apartment," Suzanne said bitterly.

"My guess is he probably had one already, he just hadn't executed it yet. Was holding off, I guess."

"But your information really didn't point toward Missy," said Suzanne.

Sam shook his head. "Not really."

"So Doogie bulldozed his way into her apartment and discovered a Taser. Hmm." Suzanne took a sip of wine and rolled it around inside her mouth, thinking.

"There's more," said Sam. "More about the autopsy, I mean."

Suzanne's mind suddenly leapt to the last time she'd seen Drummond. Alive, that is. He'd acted frazzled, angry, and hopped up. "Drugs," she said suddenly. "He was taking drugs."

Sam cocked a finger at her. "Bingo."

"What kind?"

"It's way too early to tell. But something unusual, since it didn't show up on the first tox screen."

"When will you know?" Suzanne asked.

Sam shrugged. "Another few days. A week at the most, depending on how backed up the state lab is."

Suzanne looked at him with a penetrating gaze. "Keep me in the loop, will you?"

"Sweetheart," said Sam, leaning in close to her, "I'd rather keep you safe."

CHAPTER 17

NERVES fizzing, shoulders hunched forward, eyes darting from side to side as if she were casing the joint, Suzanne pushed her way through the double doors of the Law Enforcement Center. She'd been to this building many times before, but never for official business that meant posting bail for a friend and springing her out of jail!

Suzanne's pumps clicked efficiently against the marble floor as she hurried along. She'd dressed with care today in a navy blue suit with a sedate white blouse underneath and a string of small white pearls draped professionally about her neck. She hoped her formal business attire made her look competent and maybe even a little intimidating. Like she'd just walked out of a Wall Street firm and sealed the biggest deal since the financial crisis!

Luckily, before she was forced to intimidate anyone, Missy's attorney, Harry Jankovich, appeared in the hallway and hailed her.

"Suzanne?" Jankovich, in a pin-striped suit and clutching

an overstuffed briefcase, looked expectant but friendly as he stuck out a hand.

Suzanne shook his hand firmly. "Mr. Jankovich, has Missy been arraigned yet?" she asked directly. She saw no need for idle pleasantries, since this wasn't a pleasant situation—but she was careful to stay on the right side of rudeness, too.

Jankovich gave an affirmative nod. "That's right, it's over and done with already." He was short and portly with a ruddy, red face. But it was also a kind face.

"That was awfully speedy, wasn't it?" Suzanne said. She'd never known the wheels of justice—good, bad, or indifferent—to turn quite that fast.

"I think Sheriff Doogie . . . ah . . . facilitated a few things," Jankovich told her.

Suzanne shook her head in bewilderment. "First he arrests Missy—and then he greases the slides and arranges special treatment." It didn't make sense. Then again, this whole situation was most peculiar. "So . . . what do we do now?"

"Now we pay her bail," said Jankovich.

"What's her bail set at?"

Jankovich shepherded her into a nearby office. "Fifty thousand dollars," he said crisply. "But the court only requires you to post ten percent." He stepped to the counter and had a mumbled conversation with a stern-looking woman who sat behind a sturdy set of bars. When she passed him a set of papers, he looked them over hastily and said, "Suzanne?" He stepped aside so she could slide in next to him. He pointed to two red Xs. "You need to sign here and here."

"Oh dear," said Suzanne.

Jankovich dug in his jacket pocket. "Need a pen?"

TWENTY-FIVE minutes later, the transaction completed, Suzanne and Missy walked out of the Law Enforcement Center.

Head down, shoulders slumped, her long blond hair looking clumped and straggly, Missy said, in a barely audible voice, "I've never been so humiliated in my entire life."

Suzanne saw the circles under her eyes and the way her clothes were wrinkled and rumpled. "I'm so sorry you had to go through that," she said. "It was . . . unconscionable on Doogie's part."

"I'm never going to speak a civil word to that man again," said Missy, a few tears leaking down her face.

When they reached her car, Suzanne pulled open the passenger door for Missy. "Get in and let's talk." She hurried around to the driver's side and climbed in.

Missy sat with her face buried in her hands. "It was awful, Suzanne," she said in a muffled voice. "You have no idea!"

"No, I don't," said Suzanne. "And I know you're feeling terribly scared and fragile and wounded right now. But we do have to talk."

Missy dug in her pocket, found a single Kleenex, and blew her nose. Then she said, "About what?"

Suzanne turned in her seat so she could face Missy. "I need to ask you something, and I'd like you to answer me as honestly as you can. Was that your Taser that Sheriff Doogie found?"

"No!" Missy cried, yanking her hands away from her face and throwing Suzanne an anguished look. "Of course not! What do you think I am? Some kind of crazy weirdo?"

"Then where did it come from?" Suzanne pressed. "I mean, something like that doesn't just magically appear." That one indisputable fact had been gnawing at her all night long. "There has to be a logical explanation. The object came from *somewhere*."

"Isn't it obvious?" said Missy. "Someone put it there."

"How do you know that?"

"Because I sure didn't!"

"You're positive about that? There's no doubt in your mind?"

"Yes! Of course!"

Suzanne leaned in closer. "Hey, Missy, this is me—Suzanne. I'm your friend. I'm here for you. You can level with me."

Missy's distress was palpable. "I *am* leveling with you!" A fresh sob escaped her throat and hot tears coursed down her cheeks.

Suzanne dug in her purse and pulled out a small pack of tissues. She passed it to Missy and said, "I want you to be scrupulously honest. If you did something a little crazy, if you made some sort of mistake—I need to know about it."

"Jeez, Suzanne." Missy blew her nose with a forceful honk. "I know it sounds crazy and I wouldn't blame you for doubting me. But somebody really did call and ask me to come to that cemetery last Thursday. And then . . . and nobody *believes* me on this . . . but I think that same person snuck into my house and planted a Taser!"

"If that's what really happened then I believe you," said Suzanne. She knew Doogie was still working on getting that call traced. Once they had that information, this whole bizarre incident would probably be over.

"I'm pretty sure that's what really happened," said Missy, intensity etched into her face. "I want you to believe that. I *need* you to believe that!"

"Then I do," said Suzanne. She still had questions—but she also saw how much Missy needed her buy-in on this. She hesitated. "You told me you rarely lock your front door."

"Stupid of me," admitted Missy. "And I guess I'll be lots more careful from now on." She let out a deep sigh and bowed her head. "Please, Suzanne, will you just take me home?"

They were both silent on the drive to Missy's house. Suzanne coasted along, turning all the events of the past four days over in her mind. She wondered who could have set Missy up. Who had rather effectively incriminated Missy while deflecting blame for their own dastardly actions? What was this about?

When they were a half block from Missy's house, Suzanne said, "Now don't do anything crazy, okay?"

"What do you mean by crazy?" asked Missy. Her eyes were red and swollen and continued to leak a steady stream of tears.

"Don't leave town or anything like that. Just stay put." Suzanne rolled to a stop in front of Missy's small bungalow.

"Where would I go?"

"I don't know. It's just . . . It just seemed like good advice." She bounced her fingers lightly against the steering wheel. "Sorry I couldn't come up with something better."

Missy smiled wanly and leaned over to give Suzanne a heartfelt hug. "You did come up with something better," she said. "You came up with the bail money."

BREAKFAST was in full swing when Suzanne came flying in the back door of the Cackleberry Club some ten minutes later. Petra was rattling her cast-iron pans, sizzling eggs, red peppers, and thick slabs of Canadian bacon. Toni worked diligently at the countertop, setting out plates and adding garnishes of sliced strawberries and orange wedges. The aroma of breakfast fixings and baked goods permeated the small kitchen.

"Hey," said Toni, turning when she saw Suzanne. "Is Missy a free woman again?"

"For now anyway," said Suzanne.

"I think it was very sweet and loyal of you to post bail for her," said Petra, turning and wiping her hands on her apron. "You're a good friend. Better than most."

"I bet you'd do the same for us, huh?" said Toni. "If Petra or I were ever arrested and tossed in the clink?"

Suzanne furrowed her brow. "Depends on what the charges were."

"Haw!" said Toni.

"Really," said Petra. "Is Missy okay?"

"Her pride is severely damaged," said Suzanne. "But other than that I think she'll be just fine."

"Unless she's convicted in court," said Petra.

"We're not going to let that happen," said Suzanne.

"Did she, um, say anything about what happened?" asked the ever-curious Toni. "How she thinks that Taser got into her house?"

"Only that she thought she'd been set up," said Suzanne. "Correction, she said she *knew* she'd been set up."

"That's exactly what she said before," said Toni. "I mean about being called to the cemetery that morning."

"Well, now she thinks somebody slipped into her house and planted the Taser," said Suzanne. "As a kind of coup de grâce."

Petra flipped a couple of pancakes onto a plate. "Do you think that's what happened?"

"I think I believe Missy," said Suzanne.

"She sure doesn't strike me as a killer," said Toni.

Petra pursed her lips. "Who in town does?"

"I have no idea," said Suzanne. "But I'm not going to stop investigating until I get to the bottom of this. No matter what Doogie says. There are just too many unanswered questions." She hesitated. "Besides, it's personal now."

"Atta girl!" said Toni.

"Changing the subject to the here and now," said Petra. "We're going to be offering a new menu item this morning and I wanted to clue you ladies in."

"What is it?" asked Suzanne. With all the egg and breakfast permutations Petra had dreamed up, it was hard to believe she'd invented something new.

"Drumroll please," said Toni.

"A Cackleberry Sunset," said Petra. "A fried egg on a fluffy baked potato, drenched with melted cheddar cheese."

"Holy calorie count!" blurted out Toni. "That's more like a Cackleberry Carb Explosion!"

"Oh foo," said Petra. "Who counts calories or carbs or fat grams when it comes to breakfast?"

"But you said your pants were getting all tight and uncomfortable," Toni pointed out.

Petra put a hand on her hip. "That's because my stupid clothes dryer shrank every last pair."

Toni eyed her warily. "Did you ever think of just cutting back on chocolate?"

Petra set her jaw. "Not really."

"You do eat a lot of chocolate," ventured Toni.

"Seriously," said Petra, "I don't think chocolate chip pancakes, truffle cake, and peanut butter fudge are that far out of line, do you?"

"Noooo," Suzanne and Toni echoed together. They knew when to drop a touchy subject. Or at least let it lie there.

"Anyway," said Petra, "melted cheese is always a big seller."

"You got that right," said Toni. "You could probably put melted cheese on an old shoe . . . or a tire . . ."

"Dead carp?" said Petra.

Toni nodded. "There you go."

"Carburetor?" laughed Petra.

Toni giggled. "That'd for sure be a hit at the Golden Springs Speedway!"

Which dredged up a whole raft of bad memories for Suzanne. She hadn't told Toni about how she'd felt menaced during her little foray to the parking lot to grab the ratchet set. Maybe it had been nothing at all, just her imagination working overtime. Or maybe it *had* been something. Maybe it was . . . what? Somebody who didn't want her to get too close to discovering the truth . . . about Drummond or Missy?

SUZANNE tucked that thought in the back recesses of her brain as she joined Toni in the café. They did their whirling, twirling breakfast ballet, greeting customers, taking orders, hyping the new Cackleberry Sunsets, and ferrying plates to and fro.

Later that morning, after breakfast was wrapped up and the room was made spick-and-span again, Pat Shepley stopped by with a few bags of potato rolls for their little market area. And then two of Petra's dyed-in-the-wool (no pun intended) knitters carted in a half dozen scarves and shawls for entry in the Hearts and Crafts Show.

"These are amazing," Suzanne told Sasha, one of the knitters, as she held a soft and gorgeous cream-colored shawl in her hands. "I can't believe you're willing to part with these creations." The women were in the Knitting Nest now, going over all of the items.

"Oh, we'll just knit new ones," said Andrea, Sasha's sister-in-law. "You'd be amazed how fast these items fly off my fingers. All I need is a squishy movie on Lifetime and I'm good to go."

"Your pieces are the perfect addition to our Hearts and Crafts Show," Suzanne told them. "Thank you."

"You're sure?" said Sasha. "They're not too crafty?"

"Not at all," said Suzanne. "We seem to be getting a nice mix of things. A few paintings and sculptures, some crafts and lovely needlecraft items."

"Maybe," said Sasha, glancing around eagerly, "we should do a little fiber and yarn therapy while we're here?"

"For sure," said Andrea. "In fact my doctor told me I should definitely get more fiber!"

AROUND eleven o'clock, Suzanne had her morning confab with Petra over their luncheon menu.

"I think we'll keep the Cackleberry Sunsets on the menu and just add a nice piece of summer sausage to make it a slightly heartier entrée," said Petra.

"Works for me," said Suzanne. "We'll just raise the price two or three bucks."

"Make it three," said Petra.

"So what else?"

"Chicken and waffles," said Petra. "Plus egg salad sandwiches on rye, a fruit salad plate, and curried carrot soup. Plus Toni's hard at work in the kitchen, whipping together her infamous dump cake for dessert."

"The one with the pineapple chunks?"

"And the angel food cake mix," said Petra. "Though you know I'm not a big fan of packaged mixes."

"Hey!" Toni called through the pass-through. "Don't dump on my dump cake! Not everybody's a gourmet baker. Some of us have to cut a few corners here and there."

"What if we top your cake with vanilla ice cream and call it Angel Ice Cream Dream or something like that?" said Suzanne.

"What?" said Toni. "Dump cake doesn't sound classy enough?"

"No!" came Suzanne and Petra's blended voices.

THE first one in for lunch that day was Dale Huffington.

"You're getting to be a regular," Suzanne told him.

"Ah, it's this crazy shift I'm on."

"So you're ready for breakfast? Or something heavier?" Suzanne asked.

Dale shrugged. "Maybe just a tea and scone." He patted his stomach. "I'm cutting back."

"I can see that," she said, as the door opened and customers began to trickle in.

Suzanne hastily began taking orders, poured coffee, and hyped the specials. And, wouldn't you know it, right at the peak of the lunch hour, Jake Gantz came ambling in with another painting.

"Toni?" called Suzanne. She nodded toward Jake as she refilled Dale's teacup. "Can you check him in?"

"Will do," said Toni, scurrying off.

Chewing his last bite of scone, Dale gazed across the café at Jake. "I know that guy," Dale said to Suzanne. "He was at Jasper Creek for a while."

Suzanne decided to play it cool. Maybe she could pick up some information. "That's Jake Gantz. He's a pretty decent painter."

"That a fact?"

"Looks like he brought us another donation for our Hearts and Crafts Show. So . . . do you know what Jake was in for?"

Dale hunched forward and stuck his elbows on the counter. "Jake's not exactly the brightest bulb in the box. Basically, he's a Gulf War vet who never plugged back into society when he came home."

"Unfortunately, I think that happens a lot," said Suzanne. "But what exactly did Jake do to end up in prison?"

"It's a sad story," said Dale.

"I've got a full box of Kleenex," said Suzanne.

"As best as I recall," said Dale, clearing his throat, "he was hanging with a bunch of guys one night—guys he met in a bar somewhere who started pumping him for war stories. You know, military wannabes who'd never think of enlisting but could spend all night listening to tales about night patrols, ammo loads, and AK-47s. Anyway, it turns out these yahoos popped into the Quick Stop over in Jessup to grab a pack of Marlboros. And while they were getting their smokes they decided to grab a little unauthorized pocket money out of the cash register. Poor Jake is sitting in the backseat minding his own business when they came running out with a handful of cash and two twelve-packs of Budweiser. Long story short, they all got caught and soldier boy over there was sentenced to eight months at Jasper Creek."

"Didn't he have a lawyer?" asked Suzanne. "I mean, it sounds like there were extenuating circumstances."

Dale tilted his head. "Probably just a first-year public defender. And, last time I checked, being dumb as a sack of hammers doesn't count as an extenuating circumstance."

"Maybe Jake isn't dumb," said Suzanne. "Maybe he's just . . . numb." She knew Petra had volunteered with a couple of Vietnam veteran organizations and that a few of those poor men were *still* traumatized, fifty-some years later.

Toni came hurrying back to the counter. "Okeydoke," she told Suzanne. "All checked in and good to go."

"Great," said Suzanne, as two more newcomers settled at the counter. One of them was Allan Sharp, the lawyer they'd had the contentious run-in with on Saturday night. Then again, Sharp always acted contentious.

"Howdy-do," Toni greeted the two men. Sharp was seated next to Dale, the other man farther down the counter. She gave them both ice water and coffee, then set about taking orders. When Toni got to Allan Sharp he was his usual brusque self.

"Just a bowl of soup," Sharp told her.

"You don't want to hear the specials?" said Toni. "We've got egg salad sandwiches plus chicken and waffles."

"Chicken and waffles?" said Sharp. "That's an unusual combination."

"It's Southern," said Toni. "Kind of a comfort food thing. Besides, Allan, it's always good to get a fresh perspective on different cuisines."

"I prefer my own perspective," said Sharp. "Just the basics, nothing too wild or crazy."

"Whadya think?" asked Toni, sidling closer to him. "You think we're the kind of café that serves crap like deep-fried jalapeno poppers? Junk food that comes frozen from a restaurant supply company in fifty-pound sacks?"

"Uh, okay," said Sharp, drawing back a little.

"This is a *real* café," said Toni. "Didn't you ever hear of the locavore movement?"

"You're the one who's loco," snarled Sharp.

SUZANNE wondered if today's lunch crowd would ever end as customers continued to pour in. It was great for the bottom line, but she was beginning to feel a bit frazzled. She took another dozen orders, shoved them through the pass-through to Petra, and drew a deep breath. Then she poured herself a cup of coffee and practically inhaled it. *I need a hit of caffeine*, she decided. She stood there, gulping her coffee, trying to muster her energy. And as she did, became aware that Allan Sharp was saying something to Dale about Lester Drummond.

What?

Suzanne edged closer to the two men, hoping to catch Sharp's words. Instead, Sharp muttered a few more words, chuckled nastily, then did a mock wipe of his brow.

"I guess so," said Dale, sounding agreeable.

Then Sharp stood up, tossed a five-dollar bill on the counter, and quickly left.

Suzanne glanced at Dale, who was hitching up his belt, also ready to depart, and said, "Um, what was *that* all about?" She was beginning to realize that Dale was a bit of a gossip.

"More drama and intrigue," said Dale, smiling and shaking his head. "It never seems to stop."

"Do enlighten," said Suzanne.

"Here's the thing," said Dale, in a conspiratorial tone. "It seems that Allan Sharp and two other prison board members were named in a three-million-dollar lawsuit over Lester Drummond's firing. Now, with Drummond dead, Sharp is off the hook. No longer liable. End of story."

"Just like that," said Suzanne.

"Like water off a duck's back," said Dale. "A lucky duck."

"Maybe," said Suzanne. But she was instantly suspicious. Because if Allan Sharp was now free and clear of a multi-million-dollar lawsuit—and openly celebrating it—didn't that make him a suspect, too?

CHAPTER 18

ONCE lunch was finished and every last bit of Toni's dump cake had been polished off, the floodgates seemed to open for donations to the Hearts and Crafts Show. At least a dozen or so artists popped in to drop off contributions.

"This is fantastic," Suzanne told Agnes Bennett, who served as part-time organist at Hope Church. She was gazing with an appreciative eye at the canvases in front of her. "I had no idea you were such a skilled painter."

"I'm not really," said Agnes. "I think of myself more as a dabbler. I just like the way colored paint looks on canvas."

But Suzanne had to disagree about the dabbling. Because Agnes's landscape painting of nearby Bluff Creek Park, done in muted browns and greens with sharp, clean brushstrokes, perfectly captured the majesty of the rocks and towering cliffs so familiar to everyone in Kindred.

"I'm going to hang this one up right away," Suzanne told her. "And everything else, too. It'll give our teatime customers a real treat while they're munching their goodies."

"And get everyone thinking about placing their bids," said Agnes, smiling.

"Absolutely," said Suzanne.

She hopped into overdrive then, removing painted plates and metal signs from the café walls, working feverishly to hang up the paintings and quilts and knitted shawls and scarves. She even moved a few of her precious ceramic chickens off the lower shelves so she could carefully display memory boxes, velvet handbags, and beaded jewelry. Sometimes, Suzanne decided, even chickens had to yield the floor.

MID-AFTERNOON, pleased that the Cackleberry Club had taken on the patina of a real-life art gallery, Suzanne ducked into the cozy kitchen for a five-minute break.

"Perfect timing!" said Petra. "You want a raspberry scone? I just baked a batch. Teatime is busier than usual for a Monday."

"I'll take a scone," said Suzanne.

"With a heaping of Devonshire cream?" asked Petra.

Suzanne held up a hand. "Hold the cream. I'm good with just a plain scone."

"No wonder you stay so thin," said Petra. "You never *eat*!"

The swinging door suddenly banged open and Toni came in.

"Hey!" she enthused. "I love what's going on out there with all the artwork. It looks just like the Louver."

Suzanne and Petra exchanged glances.

"Excuse me?" said Suzanne. She wasn't sure she'd heard Toni correctly.

"You know," said Toni. "The Louver. That fancy French museum. In Paris. Where the *Mona Lisa* lives."

"You mean the Louvre," said Petra, struggling to keep a straight face.

Toni looked suddenly stung. "Louver, Louvre, what's the difference? Our café is suddenly filled with art!"

"It's filled with something else, too," Petra muttered.

Toni jabbed a finger at her. "I heard that, lady. And don't think I don't know you were poking fun at my French."

"Why, Toni," said Petra, suddenly apologetic, "I didn't know you studied French in school."

Toni cocked her head to one side and grinned. "Sure did. French kissing."

When Petra looked surprised, Toni giggled wickedly and said, "Ha-ha. Gotcha!"

"Oh you!" shrilled Petra, as Toni's slim form slipped through the swinging door.

SUZANNE was pouring cups of Keemun tea for two customers when Doogie came stomping in through the front door. His face was beet red and his sparse gray hair stuck up like somebody had rubbed a balloon against the top of his head.

"Where is she?" Doogie thundered. "Is she here?"

"Is who here?" asked Suzanne, glancing over at him. What on earth was going on? Why was Doogie so hot and bothered? And then it dawned on her, just as Doogie shouted . . .

"Missy!" The name came flying angrily out of Doogie's mouth. "She's disappeared! Gone. Her car's gone, too, and she's not answering her phone!"

Suzanne settled her teapot onto a tea warmer and flew across to room to intercept him.

Before he could say anything more, she grabbed Doogie's sleeve and yanked him into the Book Nook, which was no easy feat since he was almost double her size. But she was anxious to get him away from whatever prying eyes and interested ears might be waiting in the restaurant. Amazingly, he took the hint and followed her.

"Are you sure she's disappeared?" Suzanne asked.

"Yes, I'm sure," said Doogie. He was hopping mad and ready to blow a gasket.

Missy's disappearance, if that's what it really was, was unsettling news for Suzanne. *Because now it looks as if Missy really does have something to hide.* Her brain was turning somersaults as she tried to process everything Doogie's message implied.

"She's probably just scared," Suzanne said finally, scrambling to be logical and pacify Doogie at the same time. "That's why she's probably hiding out somewhere. Maybe at a friend's house or something?"

"She hasn't been seen around town since she left the Law Enforcement Center this morning with you," said Doogie, his voice shaking with anger. "And in my book that makes her a fugitive!"

"She's nothing of the . . ." Suzanne began.

"And I don't want to hear any excuses from you." Doogie waved a stubby index finger in warning.

"Okay," said Suzanne. Truth be told, she was more than a little shaken by all of this. Missy had been instructed to stay put, and now it looked as if she might have slipped out of town. What could it mean? Suzanne really didn't want to go there.

"Would it make you feel any better if I went looking for her?" she asked, having a sudden brainstorm. "Maybe I could try to find her, figure out where she went."

"Are you suggesting I don't know how to do my job?" said Doogie. Now he turned suspicious and defensive.

"Not at all," said Suzanne, trying to stay calm. "I know you have your hands full, so I'm simply trying to help out."

"You can pitch in," said Doogie, "just as long as you don't interfere with the law."

"I wouldn't do that," said Suzanne.

Doogie cocked a wary eye at her.

"Look, I want this mystery solved just as much as you do," said Suzanne. "Missy's a friend and I'd like to bring this to a close once and for all. Do you think I enjoy having my friend in the middle of a big mess like this? Well, the answer is no. So I don't see any harm if I poke around town and try to find her."

"I'm warning you, don't step on my toes."

"Absolutely not."

"Because this is my jurisdiction."

"Clearly it is."

Doogie let out a long, heavy sigh and hitched up his utility belt. With the gun, flashlight, nightstick, and radio he wore on it, the whole getup made him look like a human Swiss Army knife.

Satisfied that Doogie's famously red-hot temper had been dialed back a few notches, Suzanne said, "Look, why don't we go back out to the café and get you a nice cup of chamomile tea." *The better to calm you down.*

"Coffee's better," Doogie muttered as he followed her out, his footsteps heavy and loud.

"Coffee then," said Suzanne. She led Doogie to the counter where he settled his considerable bulk onto his favorite stool. "And maybe a scone?" she added.

He shook his head. "Make it a donut. They're better than those dainty little tea pastries you serve."

Suzanne turned slightly so he wouldn't see her eye roll. She reached into the glass pie saver and selected a large donut covered with chocolate frosting and colored sprinkles. After a moment's hesitation, she added a second donut to his plate. She placed the pastries in front of him, poured him a fresh cup of coffee, and said, "There you are. Donuts with your favorite sprinkles."

"Jimmies," Doogie said with relish as he took a big bite. A miniature avalanche of red, pink, and white sprinkles coursed down the front of his khaki shirt. He didn't care.

"Good?" said Suzanne.

"Guuh," Doogie replied, attempting to talk and chew at the same time.

He took a sip of coffee, and when he'd polished off the first donut and was tearing into his second, Suzanne decided it was safe to broach a couple of other subjects with him.

"Sheriff," she said, "Toni and I went to the cemetery walk on Saturday night."

"Uh-huh," said Doogie, still focusing on his donut.

"And we came across something kind of strange. Something we thought we should run past you."

Doogie stopped chewing. "What are you talking about?"

Suzanne reached back to the counter and grabbed the parchment note they had plucked from the filled-in grave. She placed it on the counter and slid it toward him.

"What've you got there?" he asked warily, swallowing hard.

"It's a note," said Suzanne. "A note that somebody left on top of the grave where Lester Drummond was found."

"Huh?" Doogie wiped his sticky fingers on a napkin, dabbed at his mouth, and picked up the note. His brows beetled together as he read the mournful words printed on it—*And he slipped sadly away.*

"What's it supposed to mean?" said Doogie.

"That's what we were wondering," said Suzanne. "That's why I thought we'd show it to you. We don't have a clue."

"You say this was left on a grave?"

"Not just any grave. The one where Drummond died. The one that got filled in."

"Huh," Doogie said again. "This is pretty dang strange." His flat eyes stared at Suzanne. "You didn't see who left it?"

"No."

"You didn't notice anybody messing around there?"

"Not really," said Suzanne.

"You mind if I keep this?" asked Doogie.

"I was hoping you would," said Suzanne. She thought for a moment. "It would be interesting if it could be scanned for the original fingerprints or maybe for the type of paper it is. Or if a handwriting expert looked at it, that would be good, too."

"Maybe," said Doogie. "Of course, this could mean absolutely nothing."

"I suppose that's true."

"It could have been written by anybody. The whole thing could be totally random."

Suzanne gazed at him. "You think so?"

Now it was Doogie's turn to mull things over. "Maybe . . . not. Drummond wasn't all that well liked around town. And this note is what you might call a . . . warm sentiment."

"There's something else I need to run by you," said Suzanne.

He looked at her. "You're just bursting with interesting bits of information, aren't you?"

"Now that you mention it, yes," said Suzanne. She looked around the café to make sure the customers were fine and no one needed her. Gazing back at Doogie, she said, "Allan Sharp came in for lunch today."

Doogie nodded. "Yeah?"

"And I kind of overheard him talking to Dale Huffington."

Doogie continued to stare at her.

"I hadn't realized it until Sharp mentioned it, but apparently he was named in a three-million-dollar lawsuit that Drummond brought against three of the prison board members."

"You mean Drummond was suing because he was fired?" said Doogie.

"That's right," said Suzanne. "But it was a civil lawsuit, against Sharp and two other board members. So it wasn't exactly public knowledge."

"First I've heard of this," said Doogie, scratching his big head.

"Anyway," Suzanne continued as Toni slid behind her with a tray of dirty dishes, "Sharp seemed greatly relieved."

"Because Drummond is dead, so the suit will be dropped," said Doogie.

"That's what I took away from it."

"So you're asking me what?" said Doogie. "To take a closer look at Allan Sharp?"

Suzanne met his gaze square on. "If you could do that," she said, "it would be great."

"It would be great," echoed Toni.

"I suppose I could do that," said Doogie. "But it doesn't mean I'm going to let Missy Langston off the hook."

"Is Missy . . ." Toni began. But Suzanne waved her off.

"I hear you, Sheriff," said Suzanne.

The coffee and donuts he'd eaten seemed to pacify Doogie for the moment, but he was definitely still in a grousing mood. When his cell phone rang, he answered promptly— "Sheriff here"—and responded to whoever was on the other end with monosyllabic grunts and harrumphs. He didn't look one bit happy. The call ended when he muttered, "To top it off, I gotta take the cruiser in 'cause the brakes feel mushy."

When he hung up, Toni sidled up next to him. "I couldn't help but overhear . . . Why don't you let Junior take a look at your car?"

Doogie held up a big paw in protest. "I don't need that overage juvenile delinquent tinkering with my official vehicle." He pronounced it "ve-hi-cle," as most folks in law enforcement did. "Besides, it's county property and we've got a contract with a *legitimate* garage."

"Aw, come on," Toni urged. "Give Junior a chance. He's a crackerjack mechanic."

"Huh," said Doogie as he slid off his stool. "It's more like he found his auto repair certificate in a Cracker Jack box!"

"Sticks and stones!" Toni called out in Doogie's considerable wake.

"Didn't Junior attend the vo-tech school over in Jessup?"

Suzanne asked as she and Toni watched Doogie leave. She'd always figured that Junior, with his keen love of cars, had done fairly well there.

"He was at the top of his class," said Toni. "Of course, his attendance was court remanded."

Suzanne frowned. "Meaning . . ."

"That the judge ordered Junior to learn a meaningful trade or go to the workhouse."

"Was Junior ever *in* the workhouse?" asked Suzanne.

Toni shrugged her shoulders. "Years ago. Only problem was, it never stuck." The corners of her mouth crooked up in a mischievous grin. "Because Junior's never done an honest day's work in his life!"

WHEN Suzanne told Toni and Petra about Missy's sudden disappearance they were appalled.

"I was wondering what Doogie was yelling about," said Petra.

"Where could she be?" Toni asked. "Do you think Missy might have fled the state?"

"No idea," said Suzanne, feeling a little heartsick. Fresh in her mind were her words admonishing Missy not to do anything foolish, like leave town. And now it looked like—not four hours later—Missy had gone and done exactly that.

"Do you think Missy really is guilty?" asked Toni, almost whispering her words.

"Of course she's not," said Petra quickly. "She's just scared, right, Suzanne?"

"Right," said Suzanne.

"What's she scared of?" asked Toni.

"I think she's . . ." Petra stopped, suddenly unsure of where she was going.

"Maybe she thinks the killer's going to come after her," put in Toni. "Chase her down on the street or something. Or show up at her house!" Her eyes went round as saucers. "Do you think?"

"Really," said Suzanne, "I don't want to think about it at all." She felt tired and jittery and confused all at once.

"But we have to think it through so we can help her," said Petra, always the practical one.

Suzanne gave a defeated shrug. "And I opened my big mouth and asked Doogie if it was okay for me to go look around town for Missy."

"Then what are we waiting for?" said Toni, suddenly excited. "Let's jump in the car and motorvate."

"You really want to?" asked Suzanne. She felt a little bit heartened by Toni's offer.

"Sure," said Toni. She glanced at her watch. "We've got almost an hour and a half before our self-defense class starts."

"I forgot about that," said Suzanne. At the moment it was the last thing on her mind.

"You two are really going to that class?" asked Petra.

"Absolutely we are," said Toni. "I have to find some way to release my inner aggressions."

"For the most part," said Petra, "I'd say you do just fine."

"But I don't get to actually *kick* things," said Toni. "Or punch." Toni executed a quick little bunny hop and shot her leg out, striking the oven door. "Ya ha!" she cried in victory.

Petra frowned. "Promise me you'll be careful. Because the last thing you want to do is break a hip!" Falling and breaking a hip were Petra's biggest fears. She was always worrying about fracturing a vital bone and being laid up for months.

"She won't break a hip or any other bone," Suzanne promised. "Besides this is just the first class. It's basically an orientation, an introductory lecture. We'll probably just sit around in a circle and listen to Carla Reiker explain everything. No kicking or punching or tossing of perceived predators."

"Like a Girl Scout meeting," said Toni. "We'll all hold hands and sing 'Kumbaya.' That's a lot better than flaking out in front of TV with a mound of Doritos on a paper towel!"

Petra still wasn't convinced. "Face it, ladies. We have to take it easy because we're all getting a little older. Just the other night I saw a TV commercial with Henry Winkler pitching reverse mortgages for seniors." She tapped her wooden spoon against a metal pot for emphasis. "Can you believe it? The Fonz? Instead of oozing cool and picking up chicks, he was talking about financial security in your old age? Honestly, what's this world coming to?"

CHAPTER 19

SUZANNE and Toni cruised up and down the streets of Kindred, craning their necks as they drove along. Once they hit Main Street, Suzanne slowed her car so they could peer at each person strolling past the yellow brick buildings. They cast their eyes into storefront windows filled with wares and topped by colorful curved awnings, but they saw no sign of Missy. They even detoured down narrow back alleys, navigating twists and turns, and poked into cul-de-sacs. Still, nothing.

After a good twenty minutes of searching, they were feeling slightly defeated.

"Maybe she's at Root 66?" said Toni. "Getting her hair done?"

So they parked quickly and went into Root 66, Kindred's premier hair salon owned by Gregg and Brett, two chatty owners who kept tabs on everybody in town. Brett, resplendent in a bright yellow T-shirt and stylish black jeans, rushed up from the back where he'd just finished putting a blue-

haired client under an old-fashioned monster-sized hair dryer.
He greeted them with his trademark hugs and air kisses.

But when they asked him about their missing friend, his
smile turned into a frown. "I haven't seen her in a few weeks,"
he said. "Not since her last trim and blowout, anyway."

"Not the answer I was hoping for," said Suzanne. "Well,
thanks anyway. Call me if you see her, okay?"

"Is she in trouble?" asked Brett.

"Hopefully not," said Suzanne, unwilling to say any more.

Once outside, Suzanne and Toni climbed back into her
car. "Could she be hanging out at Alchemy Boutique?" wondered Suzanne.

So they stopped out front and Toni ran in. But when she
came dashing back a minute later there'd been no sign of Missy.

"The salesgirl reiterated the news that Missy was fired,"
said Toni, a little breathless. "So I guess there's no chance
she's been hiding out there."

"Then where?" Suzanne wondered. "She can't just disap-
pear into thin air. She's got to be around somewhere."

"Maybe somebody—" Toni began. Then suddenly she
snapped her mouth shut.

"Maybe somebody *what*?" prompted Suzanne.

"Um . . . I'd rather not say."

"What?" Suzanne pressed.

Toni hesitated, then said in a small voice, "Don't jump
on me or anything, but maybe somebody kidnapped her?"

"Don't say that!" said Suzanne. "Don't even think that way."

"I'm sorry, I really am," said Toni. "It's just that . . ."

"Say a little prayer," Suzanne said feverishly. "To make it
all okay."

THEY drove along Catawba Parkway, searching along the banks
of Catawba Creek as well as the park with its picnic pavilion,
and made quick stops at Kuyper's Hardware, Rexall Drugs,

and Schmitt's Bar. Finally, with time running out, they abandoned their search and drove over to the Hard Body Gym.

"At least we tried," said Suzanne. They were in the wom-
en's locker room, getting changed. She felt deflated and
worn out and not sure she was up to this class.

"We gave it our best shot," said Toni. She sat down on a
hard bench and kicked off her scuffed cowboy boots. "Whew.
I'm glad we signed up for this class after all. I think it'll do
wonders for us."

"You think?" said Suzanne, taking a gulp of bottled
water. She'd been ready to throw in the towel before they
even started, so Toni's enthusiasm was heartening.

"Sure," said Toni. "We're both frustrated and upset, but
now we'll have a chance to blow off steam." She was changing out of her cowboy shirt and boots into something fuzzy
and pink. When she saw Suzanne glance at her, she said,
"You think this is okay?" Toni had pulled on a pink velour
tracksuit and ratty sneakers.

"I think it's just fine," said Suzanne. She was tugging on
black yoga pants and a gray T-shirt. "After all, this is the
Hard Body Gym in Kindred, not SoulCycle in New York."

Toni spun around and stuck out her butt. "Even with
this on back?" Glitzy, bouncy letters on Toni's backside
spelled out the word "Princess."

"It's cool with me."

"Yowza, you're a good friend," said Toni. "You never crit-
icize me, or bash me, or try to change me. You just accept me
for what I am."

"Because I love you just the way you are," said Suzanne.

"BFFs forever," said Toni. She held up her pinkie finger.
"Pinky swear we'll stay that way forever?"

"Forever," said Suzanne, locking pinkies with her dear
friend.

They walked out of the locker room and into a good-
sized workout room, joining a small group of women who

were perched expectantly on metal folding chairs that had been pulled into a circle. They recognized most of the women and spoke with them in excited, anxious voices.

"This is gonna be so much fun," Toni whispered to Suzanne. "I can't wait to vent my frustrations."

"Besides not being able to locate Missy," said Suzanne in a low voice, "just who is it you're frustrated with?"

"Junior," said Toni. "Who else? That dumb bunny was supposed to bring my car back and never did. Now I'm stuck driving a clunker that shimmies and shakes like a cement mixer."

"I hate to sound like a broken record," said Suzanne, "but that car is the least of your problems. It's only the latest symptom of your difficult relationship with Junior. And for the last few months you've been seriously talking about filing for divorce . . ."

"I know, I know," said Toni. "But dissolving a marriage just seems so doggone drastic."

More like realistic, thought Suzanne.

"There's a part of me that just wants to hang on to what I know," Toni confided. "And deep down, Junior's basically a sweet guy. A little loony, but well-meaning."

"What about the time he raided your savings account and tried to start a gerbil farm?" said Suzanne.

"That was ill conceived," admitted Toni.

"And the time he tried to sell Ginsu knives door-to-door?"

"Okay," said Toni, "it's all coming back to me now. You've got me all fired up and ready to smash a board with my bare feet."

"You know," said Suzanne, "self-defense isn't just physical. You have to protect your feelings, too."

Tears swam in Toni's eyes. "I hear you. Loud and clear."

THE class was fun. More fun than Suzanne had experienced in a long time, excluding her evenings with Sam. Carla

Reiker was a terrific teacher and she did, indeed, begin with a nice, tame orientation talk.

"This is a safe spot," Carla told them, her dark eyes twinkling, her lithe body encased in a black leotard, spiky hair gelled into place. "A place for women to learn some basic fight-back techniques."

"Woo hoo," said Toni, raising a fist.

"But first," said Carla, "we're going to talk about how to *avoid* being a target and how to de-escalate a potentially dangerous situation. Then we'll move on to handling confrontations—verbally, mentally, and, if need be, physically."

After Reiker's twenty-minute talk, the class segued into basic warm-up exercises. And as the women puffed and panted, Reiker drove home the critical points. "We're going to focus on your core and lower body strength," she told them, "because that's where you generate the most power."

When they were warmed up and ready to go, Reiker moved on to instructing them in basic moves. How to deflect choke holds, wrist grabs, and grabs from behind.

"Come over here, Suzanne," Reiker instructed. "Come up behind me and, in slow motion, put your arms around my neck. Try to grab me."

Suzanne did so and was surprised when a deft move on Reiker's part immediately disengaged her arms.

"Okay, once again," said Reiker. "Watch carefully." When everyone in the class had committed her arm-slapping and hip-thrusting moves to memory, she said, "Now grab a partner and let's practice this for real!"

Suzanne and Toni paired off together, Toni assuming the stance of aggressor.

"I'm gonna get you!" she called out to Suzanne as she lunged at her from behind. But Suzanne, always a quick study, pulled off a maneuver that sent Toni tumbling to the rubber mat.

"Whoa!" said Toni, looking a little wobbly as she picked herself up. "You got moves, girl!"

THE hour-and-a-half class pretty much flew by, and by six-forty-five, after showers and quick primping in the locker room, Suzanne and Toni walked out the door into a rain-slicked night.

"You think we should hunt for Missy some more?" asked Toni.

"I was kind of thinking I'd stop by the visitation for Lester Drummond," said Suzanne. "Over at the Driesden and Draper Funeral Home."

"Let's be serious about this, my friend. You don't care a lick about Drummond." Toni gave her a sideways glance. "You just want to go over there and sleuth around, try to get a bead on things."

Suzanne raised an eyebrow. Toni, of course, could read her fairly well. "If that's what you think, maybe you should tag along."

"Do you think I can go like this?" asked Toni. She was still wearing her pink velour tracksuit.

"I see no reason why not," said Suzanne. "It's always good to shake things up with the locals now and then. And this is the perfect opportunity."

THE Driesden and Draper Funeral Home was a big old rambling place. It was mostly American Gothic with a fanciful array of turrets, finials, and balustrades, and a few touches of Victorian tossed in for good measure. Set back from the street, the wooden clapboard building was a somber gray with decorous white trim. To Suzanne, it looked like the kind of place where the Addams Family could have settled in rather nicely. And with a backdrop of rain and lightning, and booming thunder that sounded like kettledrums, well, it was all just a little too *House on Haunted Hill*.

"This place always smells weird," said Toni, as they pushed their way through the front door. "Like overripe flowers and chemicals and . . ."

"Please don't say any more," said Suzanne.

"Whatever," said Toni.

Suzanne didn't mind the smell so much as the creepy interior. Plush gray and mauve carpets and draperies that muffled footsteps as well as, she supposed, the sad sounds of mourning. Brocade fainting couches, small tables with boxes of Kleenex, and large funereal-looking bouquets were everywhere. There was also a de rigueur guest book on a fake walnut stand complete with fake quill pen.

"I guess we ought to sign the guest book, huh?" said Toni.

Suzanne sidled over and glanced at the names. Then she turned back to the previous page and studied those, too.

"If you're here for Mr. Drummond's viewing," said a sad-eyed young man in a slightly oversized black three-piece suit, "you'll find him in slumber room two."

"Do you work here?" Toni asked. "Or are you one of the mourners?"

"I'm employed here, ma'am," said the man. His eyes flicked away from Toni, sending a message that he didn't appreciate any more questions.

"C'mon," said Suzanne. "Let's just get this over with." She didn't quite know why she was here, but something had compelled her to attend Drummond's wake. So she was going to play it by ear.

But when they walked into slumber room two, Toni's

knees buckled and she slumped hard against Suzanne's shoulder. "Oh no," she whispered. "It's an open casket!"

"Take it easy," said Suzanne. "You've already seen Drummond at his worst, lying in that awful grave. This should be a cinch for you."

"But I can't stand looking at this kind of dead guy!" Toni protested. "When they're all duded up with pancake makeup and stuff."

"Kind of like aging rock stars," said Suzanne, trying to make a joke of it.

Toni managed a weak smile. "I guess." But she was still rooted in her tracks, unwilling to take a single step forward.

"Come on," Suzanne urged again. "One quick walk by and then we'll be free to mingle." She paused. "You're tougher than you think. Take a deep breath and we'll do this."

Toni shook her head. "It still freaks me out to see guys propped up in caskets."

"Drummond's just lying there like a beanbag," Suzanne told her in a low murmur. "Looking relatively peaceful. Really, it's not *Weekend at Bernie's* or anything crazy like that."

"Still," said Toni.

They finally managed a quick and respectful walk by, Suzanne casting a glance at a waxy-looking Drummond while Toni kept her eyes planted firmly on her feet.

This is awful, Suzanne thought to herself. Not only did the sight of Drummond once again dredge up memories of his terrible death, but Toni was like some awkward child, totally dependent on her to shuffle them past the casket and into the receiving line.

Which turned out to be a receiving line of one.

Deanna Drummond, Lester Drummond's ex-wife, stood a few feet from the casket, watching Suzanne and Toni intently. She wore a black silk sheath dress that Suzanne thought was just this side of a cocktail dress, and strappy black stilettos. A large ruby ring glinted on her finger. The outfit was not exactly what one might think of as wake appropriate.

"My condolences again," said Suzanne, shaking Deanna's hand. She nudged Toni, but Toni was still focused on her shoes. "*Our* condolences," she added.

"Thank you," Deanna Drummond said in a near monotone.

"Snap out of it, will you?" Suzanne said to Toni when they were a safe distance away.

Toni shook her head and gazed at Suzanne. "Sorry about that. I think I put myself into a catatonic state or something, just to get through it."

"Well, you're home free now," said Suzanne. "And, not that you were paying particular attention, but Deanna Drummond seemed awfully matter-of-fact about this visitation, didn't you think?"

"I *was* paying attention," said Toni. "And I thought she acted bored. Politely bored."

"Not that polite," said Suzanne. She'd just spotted Mayor Mobley across the room. "C'mon," she said to Toni, "let's go speak to our illustrious mayor."

"That blowhard?" said Toni. "Why do you want to talk to him?"

"Because I have a few questions for him."

Dressed in his typical khaki slacks and golf shirt, Mayor Mobley was busily glad-handing everyone in the room. He was a barrel-chested man with muscle that was slowly turning to lard. His hair was thinning and his pink scalp was keenly visible beneath a self-conscious comb-over.

"Good evening, Mayor," said Suzanne, stepping directly in front of him.

Mobley gazed at her with piggy little eyes. "Suzanne!" he said effusively, though his eyes remained hard and his expression was one of distaste. "One of our outstanding business owners. Excuse me, *female* business owners. Kindred could certainly use a few more entrepreneurs like you."

Suzanne wanted to tell him to stuff it. Instead, she said, "I wanted to ask you about the lawsuit Lester Drummond filed against three members of the prison's board of directors."

"This is not the time nor place," Mobley wheezed, trying to maneuver away from her.

"Actually, it is," said Suzanne, moving to block his path.

"Well, it's all water under the bridge now," said Mobley. "Because the suit's been dropped."

"Really," said Suzanne. "You're sure about that?"

"Positive," said Mobley. "Even the ex–Mrs. Drummond doesn't want to dredge up that sad affair."

"I heard that Allan Sharp was really sweating it there for a while," said Suzanne.

Mobley glared at her. "I suppose he was. Then again, *any* lawsuit is stressful."

Suzanne gestured toward the very deceased Drummond lying in his gunmetal gray casket and said, "You don't think Allan Sharp could have had a hand in that, do you?"

Mobley sucked in a glut of air and took a step backward, looking shocked. Looking as though he could never imagine the slippery Sharp doing a dastardly deed in his life.

"Allan?" said Mobley. "Are you serious? Allan is above reproach. Why, I trust that man like a brother. He even served as my campaign manager last year!"

And Sharp helped you stuff the ballot box, Suzanne thought to herself as Mobley skittered away. *And if you had a tail it'd be tucked between your legs.*

INTERESTINGLY enough, more and more people poured into slumber room two. The place was getting crowded and the noise level was steadily rising.

"Lots of folks came to say their farewells," said Toni.

"Or maybe they showed up out of sheer curiosity," said Suzanne.

"Like us?"

"You got it."

"Hey," said Toni, "there's Boots Wagner and Carla Reiker over there. Looks like they've changed clothes since we last saw them. Maybe I should've changed into something more presentable, too."

"You're just fine," said Suzanne. "Besides, we're leaving soon anyway."

"And there's Sheriff Doogie," said Toni.

Doogie had spotted them and was elbowing his way through the crowd. "You spot her anywhere?" were his first words. He was obviously referring to Missy.

"Not yet," said Suzanne. "Sorry."

"But we're not giving up hope," said Toni.

"I wanted to ask you something, Sheriff," said Suzanne.

Doogie pulled his mouth into a grimace. "Huh?"

"Were Missy's fingerprints found on that Taser?" said Suzanne.

"No," said Doogie. "But that doesn't mean anything. She could have wiped it clean."

"And then didn't bother to ditch it?" said Suzanne. "That makes no sense at all."

Uncomfortable with the direction of the conversation, Doogie turned his gaze on Toni and frowned. "What are you wearing, anyway?" he barked. "Pajamas?"

"Workout clothes," said Toni, stiffly.

"Huh." Doogie hitched up his belt and eyeballed the crowd. "Anyway, they sure drew a crowd for this wingding."

"For a guy who wasn't exactly well liked, Drummond's suddenly very popular," said Suzanne.

"Most people who are curious," said Doogie, "are morbidly curious. They're looky-loos. In it just for the thrill."

"Have you expressed your condolences to Deanna Drummond yet?" Suzanne asked him.

Doogie gazed at her sharply. "No. Why?"

"I was just wondering if you had any further impression of her," said Suzanne.

"And had any idea if she intends to hang around town?" Toni said.

"I believe she does," said Doogie. "Although it's kind of strange since she doesn't really know anyone." He thought for a few moments. "Actually, her relationship with Drummond seemed a little strange, too."

"Maybe they had an open marriage," Suzanne mused.

"And now they've got an open casket," said Toni.

SUZANNE and Toni hung around for a few more minutes, talking to Molly Grabowski, the woman who supervised the 911 responders at the Law Enforcement Center. She was planning a bridal shower tea for her daughter and wanted to know if Suzanne and the ladies could cater it. Then they got caught up in talking cake decorating and menus and, before they knew it, slumber room two had pretty much emptied out.

"Oops, time to go," said Molly, glancing around.

"Us, too," said Suzanne. "We stayed a lot longer than we intended."

"Call me with that estimate," said Molly as she dashed out the door ahead of them.

Suzanne and Toni followed the last of the crowd out into the anteroom of the funeral home.

"I'm gonna take one of these memorial cards," said Toni, plucking a card from a metal rack. "Don't know why . . ."

"Souvenir?" said Suzanne, lifting a brow.

"That does sound kind of creepy," said Toni. "Maybe I'll just . . . put it back."

They pushed their way out the door and were instantly pelted with a cold drizzle.

"This weather is getting monotonous," said Toni.

"Tell me about it," said Suzanne.

"I was gonna plant some . . ." Toni suddenly stopped short and plucked at Suzanne's sleeve. "Whoa, take a gander at that!"

Suzanne peered through the rain and suddenly saw Deanna Drummond sliding into Boots Wagner's little red car. He waited until she was settled in the passenger seat, then closed the door carefully and scooted around to the other side.

"What's that about?" wondered Toni.

"I don't know," said Suzanne. "But why is it I get an uneasy feeling about that woman?"

"Maybe because she killed her husband?" said Toni. "Look at her, all flirty and cute in her little lounge lizard dress." She stuck an index finger up to her open mouth and made a poking motion. "Makes me want to gag."

"Where do you suppose the two of them are going?" Suzanne wondered.

"Out for a drink?" said Toni. "Or over to Drummond's house?"

"Said the spider to the fly?" said Suzanne.

Toni grinned wickedly. "Hey, you wanna follow them and see if that's where they end up?"

Suzanne thought for a few moments. Wondering about Deanna Drummond, finding it strange that she was suddenly chummy with Boots Wagner. Or was she? Maybe he was just being kind to her. Or maybe she was flirting with him, the same way she'd flirted with Sheriff Doogie. Maybe Deanna Drummond was just that kind of woman. A tease.

"Well?" said Toni. "I'm waiting for an answer."

"Okay," said Suzanne, her curiosity suddenly kicking in. "But let's just do a drive-by. Nothing tricky." Toni had roped her into secret missions before—and they'd never ended well.

CHAPTER 20

WITHIN minutes they were back in Suzanne's car, driving over to Lester Drummond's house in the northern part of town. The pavement hissed beneath her tires as they sped along well-kept streets on a reconnaissance mission that Suzanne knew—right down to the tips of her pink painted toenails—had all the makings of a disaster with a capital *D*.

What made me say yes to this knuckle-brained idea? she wondered. *Who do I think I am, Nancy Drew for the new millennium? Trixie Belden? Don't I have my hands full with everything else that's going on?*

She knew the answer was a resounding yes. Still, curiosity had sunk its talons into her. And she wondered—would Deanna Drummond be there? Would Boots Wagner be with her? What the heck were they *doing* together?

As Toni craned her neck from side to side, keeping her eyes peeled for Lord knows what, the two women cruised past block after block of homes. Some were stately Georgian-style homes replete with columns, some of the older ones were stark American Gothic, and a few were small, cute Queen Anne–style homes.

Finally they spotted the Drummond residence up ahead on the corner. Tonight, with rain sluicing down, his Cape Cod–style home seemed dark and foreboding while the blue black pines surrounding the house lent an ominous forested look.

"This is it," Toni said in a whisper. "Pull over."

Suzanne slid to a gentle stop at the curb, her lights splashing against the house. They sat there for a few moments, gazing at Drummond's house. The front door was a slab of oak with just a tiny peephole of a window at the top. A large *D* was draped to the side, above a copper mailbox.

D for Drummond, Suzanne thought. Or maybe, she thought ruefully, it could stand for deceased. Or dead as a doornail. She shivered involuntarily. Now that they were here, she wasn't sure what to do.

"Hmm . . ." said Toni. "The place looks dark as a tomb."

"No lights on," said Suzanne, "means nobody home." Truth be told, she felt a little relieved.

"Guess not," said Toni.

They sat there for another thirty seconds, eyeballing the dark house and the empty street. Literally, not a creature was stirring.

"They probably went for a drink somewhere," said Toni.

"Or maybe just a talk," said Suzanne.

She was about to put her car back in gear and take off when Toni said, "Hold up a minute."

"Why? What?"

Toni suddenly thrust open the passenger door and jumped out. "I want to check something."

"What are you *doing*?" Suzanne hissed, as a gush of rain rushed in.

With a smirk on her face, Toni leaned back in and said, "Aren't you coming?"

Suzanne's heart did a sudden flip-flop.

"I thought we'd have ourselves a little look-see," Toni continued. "Peek in the windows, see what's shakin'."

"Toni, we can't do that. Somebody might see us!"

"Hey, we're just two neighbors worried sick about poor Deanna Drummond. I mean, even though they were divorced, Lester's death must have come as a terrible shock to her."

Suzanne blinked at her friend. "You scare me, you know?" she said. "You really do. You're such a good liar."

"I think it's from watching so much TV," said Toni. "You kind of pick up sneaky techniques on how to act and what to say. It's amazing what you can absorb by osmosis, just sitting there like a blob on the couch."

Suzanne looked concerned. "Toni, you don't fib or playact when you're at the Cackleberry Club, do you?"

Toni looked shocked. "No! Never!" Then: "If you're coming, Suzanne, you better step on it!"

Suzanne felt slightly ridiculous as the two of them scampered across the damp grass. When they got within a few feet of the front porch, they jogged around the corner of the house and ducked into the shadows.

There, under cover of darkness, with damp bushes hiding any view from the street, they hesitated.

"What exactly are we doing?" Suzanne whispered.

In response, Toni grabbed her hand and pulled her toward a side window. "Let's just look inside," she whispered back.

The two of them crouched beneath the window, staring at each other. Then, like a pair of wide-eyed gophers peeking out of a hidey-hole, they popped their heads up and stared in the window. Inside, the house looked dark, empty, and completely devoid of people.

"Like I said before," said Suzanne, "nobody home."

"But that's good," purred Toni. Then, grabbing hold of the bottom of the window, she let out a small grunt and pushed with all her might. There was a small squeak and then the window rose a good three inches.

"This is so dangerous!" said Suzanne. But Toni was putting even more muscle into it now and had shoved the window up another ten inches.

Toni's face took on a cunning look as she turned toward Suzanne. "What are we waiting for?" she said. "Let's creepy crawl this joint."

Suzanne's heart was thudding in her ears. "You mean . . . go inside?"

"Sure, why not? Nobody's home and I think I'm skinny enough to fit through that window." She paused. "I think *you're* skinny enough."

"I can't!" said Suzanne.

"Sure you can. Just hoist one leg over the windowsill and . . ."

"What if Sheriff Doogie drives by and sees us?" said Suzanne, working hard to keep her voice low. "Or one of his deputies? Driscoll or one of the other guys? They could have this house under surveillance, you know."

"We'll just say we saw suspicious activity and had to check it out."

"But we're the suspicious activity!" said Suzanne.

"They won't know that," said Toni. "They'll just think we're doing a good deed. Tell you what, lace your fingers together and give me a little boost. I'll go in first."

"Apparently the word 'trespass' means nothing to you," said Suzanne before she did any lacing of fingers.

"Not in my vocabulary," said Toni. "Now c'mon, boost me up!"

Suzanne let loose a sigh as she gave Toni her boost. Skinny Minnie that she was, Toni was up and over the windowsill faster than you could say "breaking and entering."

"Now you," said Toni, reaching a hand down for Suzanne.

Suzanne looked around, saw a small red garden gnome, and

quickly put a foot on its pointy little head. Within moments, she was hoisted up, up, up, and suddenly, with only a couple of muffled thumps, found herself inside Drummond's house.

Wide-eyed, their breath coming quicker now, the two of them looked around.

"Whoa," said Toni. "This is some spiffed-up hacienda."

And she was right. They'd landed in Drummond's living room, a space dominated by tufted leather couches, a large chair covered in some kind of animal hide, and an enormous red lacquered coffee table. On the wall were oil paintings in Baroque frames and a Chinese coromandel screen.

"This guy lived like a plutocrat," said Toni, impressed. "Or . . . was that the right word? Maybe some kind of Russian oligarch."

"Whatever he was," said Suzanne, "Drummond clearly had money."

"You can afford this kind of stuff on a prison warden's salary?" asked Toni.

"Apparently, yes," said Suzanne. "Remember, Jasper Creek Prison is a for-profit prison. It's privately operated, not a state-run institution."

"Now we know where some of the profits landed," said Toni.

And why Deanna Drummond is sniffing around, thought Suzanne.

Toni stuck a hand out and touched one of the paintings on the wall. "This is the real deal," she said. "Not just some crap on a cracker paper poster." Then, moving stealthily across the Oriental carpet, she disappeared into the darkened dining room.

"Where are you going?" Suzanne asked, her adrenaline pumping, her nerves jangling like crazy. But as her eyes became more and more accustomed to the low light, she saw that Toni was bent over a massive dining room table.

"Come take a gander at this," called Toni.

"What?"

"There's like bank statements and stuff." Toni gave a low whistle. "I'd say Deanna Drummond's been rummaging through Drummond's personal papers."

Suzanne dug in her purse and pulled out a Maglite. She aimed it at the table and switched it on.

"Ah," said Toni. "Good girl. You're in cat burglar mode."

"What papers?" Suzanne asked, squinting.

Toni waved a hand over the dining room table. "Take a look at all this stuff."

Suzanne did take a look. And saw that someone, probably Deanna Drummond, had been pawing through stacks of what must be Lester Drummond's personal papers. Spread out on the table were his bank statements, 401(k) papers, life insurance policy, statements from Fidelity and Vanguard, and credit card bills of all kinds. Even property tax receipts had been tossed into the mix.

"What do you suppose she's looking for?" asked Toni.

Suzanne thought for a few moments. "Maybe to see if she's the beneficiary of some of his insurance policies? Or to see how much money he had stashed in his bank accounts and mutual funds?"

"Whoa!" said Toni. "You really think that's it? That's her motivation?"

"Well . . ." Suzanne was reluctant to look closely at the paperwork—it was, after all, Lester Drummond's personal business. But, finally, driven by curiosity and suspicion, she sifted through the papers.

"You're good at figuring this stuff out," said Toni. "Because you've got business smarts." She dug around on the table and grabbed one of the papers. "Maybe take a look at this life insurance policy?"

Just as Suzanne was about to shine her light on the paper, the front doorbell rang—a long, insistent buzz that made them practically jump out of their skin!

"Holy shitake!" Toni blurted in a harsh whisper. "Somebody's here! Hit the deck!"

They dropped to the floor instantly, Suzanne snapping off her flashlight as she went down. Crouched on the hardwood floor, amidst a small nest of dust bunnies, Suzanne said, "This is crazy. We shouldn't be here!"

So, of course, the doorbell rang again!

"Yee gads, that's annoying," Toni whispered.

"Never mind that," said Suzanne. "We need to know who's at the door! Or if they've got a key!"

"Well . . . heck," said Toni. "I can go take a peek."

"No!" Suzanne hissed. But she was too late.

Like a human inchworm, Toni slowly crawled her way through the dining room, across the living room rug, and over to one of the front windows. Then, hearing nothing further at the front door, she poked her head up for a split second. "Dang," she said.

"Who is it?" Suzanne whispered from where she lay on the floor. "Is it Doogie? Or somebody else? Did you recognize them?"

"I kind of did," said Toni. "I think it's Mrs. Klingberg who works over at the Pick Quick . . . Doesn't she live on this block?"

"Maybe," whispered Suzanne. "The question is, what's she *doing* here?"

"I'd say she's carrying either a dirty bomb or a Tater Tot hotdish," said Toni. She lifted her nose and sniffed the air. "Yup, probably Tater Tots."

"For crying out loud . . ." Suzanne whispered. She'd known this crazy escapade would be a huge mistake. And now here she was, cowering in the dark, sweating bullets over a neighbor lady and her hotdish.

After what seemed like an eternity, the very charitable Mrs. Klingberg retreated with whatever she was carrying.

Peeking out the front window together, Suzanne and Toni watched her go.

"Okay," said Suzanne. "We're outta here right now!"

"Wait!" pleaded Toni. "You gotta look at that insurance policy. It could be, you know, evidence!"

"Evidence of what?" said Suzanne. She was ready to strangle Toni.

"Of greed or murder or who knows what!" said Toni.

Every brain cell pinging in her head warned her not to do it, but Suzanne snapped on her flashlight and crept back to take a final look through the papers. After she'd perused a half dozen or so documents, she said, "Yes, I think Deanna Drummond is definitely the beneficiary."

"Told you so!" said Toni. "What else did you find?"

"There's lots of personal stuff here, too," said Suzanne. "Cards, notes, that kind of thing." She picked up an envelope with Deanna's name scrawled on it and pulled out a square card. It was a personal note that Drummond had written, but, for whatever reason, hadn't mailed. As Suzanne scanned it, she saw that it was a birthday note, wishing Deanna a happy day. He closed with the words, *Good night, Gracie*, the same as the famous George Burns and Gracie Allen end-of-show gag.

"What's it say?" asked Toni.

"Nothing much," said Suzanne. But the word "Gracie" pulled at her, did a tippy-tap at her memory bank. Could that be Drummond's pet name for his ex-wife? Okay, maybe. Then could that account for the *G* on the note that was left on Drummond's grave in the cemetery? If it was, then . . . holy cow!

"Suzanne, you're right," Toni said suddenly. "We gotta get out of here! We've been in here *forever* and pretty soon our luck's going to run out!

They tiptoed back to the window and Toni hopped out

first. "Now you," she said. "Just kind of slither down and I'll catch you."

But just as Suzanne landed on top of a juniper bush, her cell phone buzzed.

"Oh no!" said Toni, glancing around.

Suzanne fumbled for the phone to silence it. "What if it's Doogie calling to check up?" she whispered excitedly to Toni. "What if he's got some crazy sixth sense and knows we're messing around where we shouldn't be?"

"Doogie's not that intuitive," said Toni. "Just answer the phone."

"Hello?" Suzanne warbled into her phone.

It was Sam.

"Oh my gosh," said Suzanne, hugely relieved. "Hi there. We thought maybe . . ." She suddenly stopped and listened. He was talking low and urgently to her, saying words like "accident" and "injury."

"Wait a minute," said Suzanne. "Say that again. I didn't quite catch . . . sideswiped?"

"There's been an accident," Sam told her. "Doogie's hurt. In fact he's rather seriously injured."

"What happened?" Suzanne cried.

"Better you should just come to the hospital," said Sam. "Let me explain there."

"Oh my gosh!" said Suzanne. She yanked on Toni's arm, hurrying her toward the car. "There's been an accident! And Doogie's hurt bad!"

THEY threw themselves into Suzanne's car and, within seconds, were careening their way to the hospital.

"What happened? What's the story?" Toni asked anxiously.

"I don't know," said Suzanne, her teeth chattering. "Sam just said Doogie was in some sort of accident."

"Wow," said Toni. "That's weird."

Arriving at the hospital, Suzanne parked in the lot closest to the ER. "C'mon," she said to Toni as she jumped out. "Let's hurry up and find Sam."

But Suzanne and Toni were abruptly halted at the door leading into the ER. It would appear hospital security was on high alert.

"Hold on, ladies," said a gruff-looking guard in a maroon uniform. "Nobody's allowed in this way. We've got police business going on."

"I know that!" said Suzanne. "That's precisely why we're here. We got a call that Sheriff Doogie was hurt!"

The guard was unfazed. "Sorry, there's still no access. But if you want to go around to the front . . ."

Before Suzanne could launch a protest, Sam suddenly appeared. Wearing blue jeans, a T-shirt, and a white coat, he'd obviously just been called in from home.

"Sam!" said Suzanne. "We came as fast as we could!"

Sam elbowed his way past the guard and gave Suzanne a hug. "Hey you," he said.

"What's going on?" asked Toni, dancing around. "Is Doogie okay?"

Sam broke off his embrace and said, "Sheriff Doogie has two cracked ribs and a concussion." His voice was calm and authoritative, as if this were an everyday routine for him. "They're taking him up for a head CT scan shortly."

"But is he gonna be okay?" asked Toni.

"He'll be in some pain for a while," said Sam. "But he'll recover, for sure."

Still stunned by this news, Suzanne's mind was working overtime, thinking: Who? Why? How? "You said on the phone that he was sideswiped?"

"That's what he told the EMTs," replied Sam. "Apparently, he was getting out of his car to help somebody change a tire or something to that effect."

Suzanne instantly thought about the yellow car—Missy's car—that had almost sideswiped her. Had it been the same car? Was Missy really the killer, trying desperately to knock Doogie out of action? Were all these things connected in some terrible, twisted way?

"Was Doogie able to give a description of the car or the driver?" Suzanne asked.

Sam shook his head. "No, Deputy Driscoll tried to question Doogie, but he was too out of it. Tomorrow, though. I expect he'll be more coherent tomorrow."

"Is there anything we can do?" asked Suzanne. For some reason she felt guilty, sad, and anxious, all rolled into one.

Sam furrowed his brow. "What you can do is be careful," he told them. "Whatever's going on in Kindred is serious business. All of these things can't just be coincidences, so I want you two to really watch your backs."

Suzanne gulped. *Imagine if he knew where we'd just been and what we were up to!* She wasn't going to blab it to him right now, that's for sure.

"Maybe I should stay overnight at your place?" said Toni, glancing at Suzanne.

"That's a smart idea," said Sam. "And be sure to keep those guard dogs nice and close."

"Sure," said Suzanne. "Of course we will."

"Anything else we can do?" asked Toni.

"The hospital staff has things under control," said Sam. "But maybe you could say a little prayer? Doogie can use all the help he can get."

Couldn't we all? thought Suzanne.

CHAPTER 21

SUZANNE'S first thought when she sprang out of bed on Tuesday morning was to check on Sheriff Doogie. How was he? What kind of night did he have? And who in the name of creation had sideswiped the sheriff?

All night she'd tossed and turned, worrying, praying that he'd make a full and speedy recovery with no complications. So after feeding the dogs, downing a cup of industrial-strength coffee, and getting dressed, she bid good-bye to Toni and rushed off to the hospital. Rain was still pelting down from a gray sky and her windshield wipers squeaked loudly, barely able to hold their own against the downpour. And when she pulled into the hospital parking lot, she found it was not only half flooded but almost completely filled with cars!

Did everyone choose this day to get severely ill or visit a loved one?

After circling the packed lot three times, she finally inched into a spot that was barely legal. With her raincoat abruptly thrown on, she stepped out into what felt like hurricane-force winds and, with her umbrella flapping like a crazed bat, rushed for the front door.

Stopping at the reception desk, feeling like she'd just endured her washing machine's spin cycle, Suzanne was told that Doogie had been moved into room 432, a private room. But the volunteers who staffed the desk could offer no word on how he was doing. They didn't know if he was awake or still unconscious.

Feeling anxious, Suzanne took the elevator to the fourth floor. Then she raced down the hall past bustling nurses, nervous-looking visitors, and breakfast carts that smelled vaguely of scrambled eggs and toast. Arriving at Doogie's room, she hesitated at the closed door and drew a sharp, shaky breath. Then she knocked softly. There was no answer. Was he being seen by a doctor or nurse? Was he maybe undergoing some kind of procedure? Taking another deep breath and hoping for the best, Suzanne grasped the handle and pushed the door open.

The room was in semidarkness and Doogie was alone, lying in his hospital bed absolutely motionless. He was surrounded by beeping, blinking monitors and looked pale and unnaturally white beneath a mound of blankets. An IV was hooked up to his arm and led to a hanging bag filled with clear liquid, while another cord—a pulse oximeter—was clasped to his finger. Suzanne took a few baby steps into the room.

Is he sleeping? Suzanne wondered. *Or still unconscious?*

She glanced around for a nurse, but none of them were nearby.

There was only one way to find out.

Suzanne tiptoed slowly to Doogie's bedside, never taking her eyes off his face. After a few seconds, she grasped the metal rails of his bed and whispered, "Sheriff?" She leaned forward slightly, hoping to catch his answer, but there was nothing. No movement, no response. "Doogie," she said, a little louder. "How are you feeling?"

This time his eyelids fluttered ever so slightly.

Suzanne reached over and touched an index finger to the chubby hand that lay on top of the blanket. "It's Suzanne," she said gently. "I just stopped by to see how you're doing."

Doogie's hand twitched slightly. He gave a long moan and, with what seemed like tremendous effort on his part, partially opened his eyes. He held her gaze for a couple of seconds then his eyes closed again.

"Hey," Suzanne said, trying to sound upbeat but really wanting to burst into tears. "Looks like you're doing much better." The words felt dry and empty in the back of her throat.

Doogie tried to open his eyes again but seemed overcome with sleep. Then his lips moved soundlessly.

"What?" said Suzanne, leaning closer. Was he asking for something? Trying to tell her something?

"It's . . ." Doogie began. Then he stopped abruptly.

"It's what?" Suzanne prompted.

"Hard to . . . Drugs," he finally whispered.

"I know it's difficult," she said. "And the drugs they gave you aren't making it any better." She patted his hand. "Better that you just rest for now. I'll stop by later to see how you're doing." She waited for his response, any response at all, but Doogie seemed to have retreated into the netherworld of sleep.

Suzanne backed away from the bed and grabbed a tissue. Dabbing at her eyes, she turned and left the room.

Back out in the hallway, it was still a hub of activity. Laundry carts rumbled past, patients in wheelchairs were being taken to labs, nurses snapped out orders. And, in all of this chaos, there was one bright ray of sunshine for Suzanne. Because Sam was suddenly striding down the hallway toward her, looking fresh and crisp and efficient. In the middle of her sadness, he seemed a vision of hope.

"Did he say anything to you?" were Sam's first words. A shock of brown hair fell over his forehead and his eyes sparkled. Dressed in blue scrubs and a white coat, he clutched a stack of clipboards. Obviously making early morning rounds.

Suzanne shook her head. "Not a thing. He just mumbled something about drugs."

Sam nodded. "Yes, he still has some heavy drugs on board. We gave him several meds last night to reduce cranial pressure, and then Versed this morning for sedation. But I think he's kind of fighting them, as many patients do."

"When do you think Doogie's going to be fully conscious?" Suzanne asked. "When do you think he'll be able to talk?"

"It's hard to say," said Sam. "And, truth be told, we prefer to keep him a little groggy and as quiet as possible for now."

"So he still hasn't said anything about what happened last night?"

"No, and he won't be able to for a while."

Suzanne sighed. "I'm really worried about him."

"I know you are, sweetheart," said Sam, touching her arm. "But Sheriff Doogie has a very strong constitution. His respiration and blood pressure are good, his pulse ox is right up there. Really, he's probably going to make a full recovery."

"Then why is he just lying there?" said Suzanne, sniffling again.

"Because he was struck on the head and it's going to take a little time for his brain to recover. But it will recover. *He* will recover. Just at his own pace."

"Thank goodness," said Suzanne. She was nearly close to tears.

Sam grasped her by the hand and gently but firmly pulled her down the hallway. He stopped suddenly, opened a door, and pulled her into a small, dimly lit room. Suzanne peered around. The place was stocked with towels and cleaning supplies. She whirled around to face him and suddenly found herself being held protectively in his arms.

"You worry too much," Sam told her.

"Doogie's really going to be fine?" Suzanne was amazed by her own depth of emotion.

"Yes, of course he is. You trust me, don't you?"

"I trust you implicitly," she said. "I'd trust you with my life."

"Well, there you go," said Sam. He kissed her on the forehead. "Just like I trust you. I'll tell you what—if there's any change, any change at all, I'll call and give you a heads-up. Okay? Will that set your mind at ease?"

Suzanne looked up at him and nodded. "It's a start. And I'm definitely going to stop back here again this afternoon."

"That's good," said Sam. "I'm sure Sheriff Doogie will appreciate that."

"Maybe not if he can't hear me," said Suzanne.

"We don't know that for a fact," said Sam. "I've seen lots of patients who've been placed in drug-induced comas following a heart attack or major trauma. And the gentle words or just the presence of a loved one has aided greatly in their recovery."

Suzanne sniffled. "Even though the people in comas couldn't talk to their visitors or see them?"

"The thing is . . . people in comas or deep sedation seem to know *instinctively* that someone's there, loving them, praying for them, encouraging them. They can sense other people's presence. You'd be amazed."

"That makes me feel a lot better," said Suzanne.

Sam leaned down and gave her another kiss. "So cheer up, okay? Hey, did you forget I'm taking tomorrow afternoon off?"

"For trout fishing," said Suzanne, finally managing a smile.

"That's right," said Sam. "I get off at two and then we

head out to the wilds of Logan County, just you and me. I can't wait to fish that little creek you told me about."

"Rush Creek," said Suzanne. "Back in the really hilly section of the county."

"And it's no doubt teeming with rainbows and brookies." Sam cocked his wrist sharply and made a fly-casting gesture. "I've got my bamboo rod primed and ready to go."

"If it doesn't rain," said Suzanne.

"You've never fished in the rain?" said Sam, feigning surprise. "C'mon, be a sport. That's the best time to fish!"

ON her way out of the hospital, Suzanne ran into Deputy Driscoll. Young, lanky, and earnest-looking, wearing his uniform and hat, Driscoll was known for doing the administrative grunt work in the department.

"Oh, hey," Driscoll said when he spotted Suzanne in the lobby. "Have you been upstairs to see the sheriff?"

Suzanne nodded. "I was just in his room, yes. But he's barely awake. In fact, Dr. Hazelet said Doogie's been given some fairly heavy medication so he might not wake up for a while."

"Jeez," said Driscoll, digesting this information, shaking his head. "That's tough. It's not what I was hoping for, not what any of us were hoping for."

"How are *you* faring in all of this?" Suzanne asked. He seemed to be the next in line after Doogie. But even to her untrained eye, Deputy Driscoll looked scared and nervous. Not exactly the picture of authority.

"Well, I don't mind telling you I'm worried," Driscoll admitted. "I've always looked to Sheriff Doogie to lead the way on things. He's been on the job a long time, while most of the other deputies are fairly new. I've been here two years, but the other guys are basically green recruits."

"You're saying they lack confidence," said Suzanne. "And experience."

"I guess you could say that," said Driscoll.

Suzanne reach a hand out and touched his arm. "Don't worry. I know the investigation has landed squarely on your shoulders, but you've been well trained. You're smart and resourceful and I'm sure Sheriff Doogie has every confidence in you."

"Thank you, ma'am," said Driscoll, tipping his hat to her. "Coming from you, that means a lot."

"I want to ask you about a couple of things," said Suzanne.

"Shoot," said Driscoll.

"Will you keep an eye on Allan Sharp?"

Driscoll squinted at her. "You mean that slimy lawyer? The one who hangs out with the mayor?"

Suzanne stifled a giggle. "That's right. I have the strangest feeling he's somehow involved in all this."

"You mean in Lester Drummond's death?" said Driscoll.

"Yes. Did Sheriff Doogie mention anything about it?"

Driscoll shifted from one foot to the other. "Somewhat."

"So he sees him as a suspect, too?"

"More like a person of interest," said Driscoll.

"Okay," said Suzanne. She knew that was cop-speak for suspect. "So he is on your radar. And what about Missy Langston?"

Now Driscoll looked a little uncomfortable. "What about her?"

"I take it the search is still on?"

"It's our first priority," said Driscoll. Now his words seemed to carry a harder edge.

Suzanne studied his grim expression. Then a look of recognition dawned on her face. "Oh no," she said finally. "You think Missy might have engineered Doogie's accident last night!"

Driscoll's gaze never broke from hers. "It's certainly possible, ma'am," he said diplomatically.

"No," said Suzanne. "It really isn't."

The deputy edged away from her. "Count on us to be on the job, ma'am," he told her. "Count on us to find her."

I sincerely hope not, thought Suzanne. *Because we are not on the same page with this. Not at all.*

CONSUMED with worry over Missy as well as Doogie, Suzanne knew she wasn't even halfway through her busy morning. Braving the rain once again, she guided her car over to the east side of town where station WLGN was located in a bare-bones cinder-block building with a transmitter tower on top.

Breezing past the reception desk, brushing raindrops from her coat, Suzanne made a beeline for Studio B. And just as she was about to scoot inside, Paula Patterson emerged from the office across the hall.

"Oh my gosh," said Paula, giving her a big smile. "I was afraid you wouldn't make it. That you'd gotten cold feet or had a change of heart."

"I had to stop by the hospital first," Suzanne explained.

Paula's face fell. "Oh no. Who . . . ?"

"You mean you haven't heard?" said Suzanne.

Paula shook her head. "No. What happened? I've been stuck in a recording session and haven't had a chance to swing by the newsroom yet."

"Sheriff Doogie was involved in some kind of hit-and-run accident last night."

"For goodness' sake," said Paula, looking concerned. "Was he injured? Is he okay?"

"He's in the hospital," said Suzanne as calmly as she could. "Still mostly unconscious. But a lot of that's because of the drugs they gave him."

"The poor man," said Paula.

"So other than the fact that Doogie got hit and the unknown driver drove away, the answer is he's probably going to be fine," said Suzanne, trying to appear upbeat but feeling empty inside. "At least that's Dr. Hazelet's opinion."

"*Your* Dr. Hazelet," said Paula, smiling. "God bless him."

Amen, Suzanne thought to herself.

"So," said Paula, switching gears, "are you ready to handle a quick interview?"

"I guess I'm as ready as I'll ever be," said Suzanne. *Which is basically not ready at all.*

But that wasn't about to stop the efficient and ever-cheerful Paula. She bustled Suzanne into a small studio with low lighting, baffled walls, and a large, blinking console. Once the two women were seated in comfy chairs adjacent to one another, Paula plopped a set of headphones on Suzanne's head. Wiley VonBank, one of the sound engineers, quickly appeared and adjusted Suzanne's microphone, then did a voice level check. After that she sat there, nervously twining her feet, hoping she wouldn't come off like some kind of ditz.

"There's going to be three sixty-second commercials," Paula told her as she settled in her chair and pulled her microphone close. "Then, after the bumper, I'm going to do my intro and come directly to you."

"Bumper?" said Suzanne, puzzled.

"The theme music that opens and closes my show," said Paula.

"Right," said Suzanne. "Got it."

And just a few minutes later, Paula's *Friends and Neighbors* theme music came on— a little bit country western with a hint of salsa for good measure. Paula's fingers danced across the soundboard as she punched buttons and spun dials. Then, as the last notes sounded, she said in a booming, over-the-top voice, "Good mornnnnnning Logan County! And welcome this Tuesday morning to *Friends and Neighbors*. I'm Paula Patterson and I've got a terrific show in store for you today."

Alert now, nerves fizzing, knowing she was seconds away

from being live on the air, Suzanne sat up straight in her chair.

"For those of you who haven't ventured outside yet, it's raining cats and dogs," said Paula, smooth as silk. "And the temperature's hovering at a chilly fifty-two degrees." She paused and glanced over at Suzanne. "But nothing's going to dampen our community spirit when it comes to helping out some of our dear friends and neighbors. As many of my listeners know, I've talked about the Hearts and Crafts Show that's going to take place later this week at our own Cackleberry Club café. The proceeds from this arts and crafts show are earmarked to benefit our local food bank. And it's just our luck to have Suzanne Dietz, the majordomo of the Cackleberry Club, here in studio with us today! Suzanne, welcome!" Paula nodded at Suzanne.

"Thanks, Paula," said Suzanne, taking the cue. "It's great to be here."

"So tell us, Suzanne, about the Hearts and Crafts Show."

Doing her best to sound articulate despite jittery nerves, Suzanne explained about the paintings and the needlework and the crafts, with Paula cutting in now and then, lending an encouraging word, making the interview sound relatively flawless.

"And half the profits go back to the artists?" said Paula. "While the other half . . ."

"Will go to support the food bank," Suzanne answered. "I know a lot of your listeners might think that fall and winter are the key times when the food bank needs to be well stocked. Unfortunately, in our county—and so many other places, too—hunger is a year-round issue."

"It sure is," said Paula, nodding encouragement at Suzanne. "So I'm urging all of our listeners today to visit the Cackleberry Club this Thursday through Saturday. Look over all the wonderful arts and crafts and place your generous bets in the silent auction."

"That's exactly what we're hoping for," said Suzanne.

"Now let's take a few calls," said Paula. "I'd love to get some reactions from our listeners."

Within just a few seconds, three of the call lights on the phone immediately lit up.

Paula punched button number one and said, "Good morning, you're on the air."

"I just want to thank Suzanne," came a woman's voice. "It's so nice when someone in the community steps up to help."

Suzanne smiled at the woman's words. "You can really thank all our artists and crafters," she said. "They're the ones who are making this possible."

Paula punched another button. "And *you're* on the air, my friend!"

This time it was a man's voice. "I just want to know, Suzanne, if you're going to be serving those caramel rolls— the ones covered with pecans?"

"They're one of our breakfast favorites," Suzanne answered. "So we pretty much bake a couple pans of sticky buns every morning."

"Thank you for that," Paula said to the caller. "Let's see who else has a question or comment." She punched another button.

"I'd just like to thank Suzanne for all her good efforts," came a soft voice.

Startled, because the voice was so achingly familiar, Suzanne blurted out, "You're so welcome." *Is that Missy's voice?* she wondered with a start. *Could that be her? Because it sure sounds like Missy!*

"Thank you," Paula said abruptly, ready to cut to another call.

"I'd like to say one more thing," said the woman. "And that is . . . please don't worry."

Puzzled, Paula shook her head and said in a breezy voice,

"And now a word from the fine folks over at Chalmers' Feed Store." She hit a button and a prerecorded commercial blared in their headphones. "Weirdo," Paula muttered over the canned spot. "We get a lot of those."

"No problem," said Suzanne. But more than ever she was pretty sure this last cryptic caller had been the missing Missy!

CHAPTER 22

THIS was Chicken Pickin' Tuesday at the Cackleberry Club, one of their most popular days when they cooked up a number of signature dishes. And when Suzanne stepped through the back door into the kitchen, there was Petra, hovering at the stove, tending to sizzling chicken breasts and links of rice sausage in a black cast-iron pan while also stirring a pan of chicken gravy to grace her potato cakes.

"Smells good in here," said Suzanne, eyeing the food. "Looks good, too." She realized she hadn't eaten breakfast yet. Just no time.

"We had the radio on!" Toni told her proudly from nearby. "And listened to your whole interview!"

Petra turned and smiled at Suzanne. "You did good, girl."

"You think so?" said Suzanne. "It didn't seem a little strange?" She was referring, of course, to their final caller of the show.

Petra turned back to the stove. "Sounded fine to me." She

flipped a dozen or so sausages onto a platter, then said, "How's Doogie doing?"

"Looking a little battered," Suzanne admitted. "But he's still feisty as all get out," she fibbed.

"Doogie's feisty?" said Toni. "Really? Lying there in the hospital?"

"Did you actually *talk* to him?" asked Petra. She grabbed a dish towel and twisted it nervously. "Was he able to tell you what happened? About the accident, I mean."

"Well, not exactly," Suzanne hedged. "Doogie was still a little out of it."

"So he didn't ask you to take over the investigation?" said Toni. "Pick up where he left off?"

Suzanne was taken aback. "No, of course not!"

"But he gave you some clues?" said Petra.

"Not really," said Suzanne.

"Oh," said Toni. She sounded deflated.

"But I talked to Deputy Driscoll and he seems to be stepping in nicely," said Suzanne. It was a little white lie but she figured it would make them all feel better. Why admit the dreary truth about how Doogie really looked?

"Eddie Driscoll?" said Petra. "Is that who you're talking about? Seems to me I had him in school back when I taught sixth grade. He had trouble diagramming sentences."

"I could never do that, either," said Toni. "Nouns, verbs, adjectives, adverbs, it was all very confusing. To say nothing of dangling participles." She laid out six white plates on the butcher-block countertop, ready for Petra to fill.

"You're still serving breakfast?" said Suzanne. It was after ten o'clock.

"We had a few latecomers," said Petra. "Probably because of the bad weather. Hey, I heard you two had fun at your self-defense class last night."

"I was telling her all about it," said Toni to Suzanne. "Hey!" she grabbed at Petra's apron string. "Did you know that shouting actually adds thirty-three percent more power to your blows and throws?"

"I did not know that," said Petra. She shook her head. "How in the world I lived this long without that piece of information I'll never know."

Toni babbled on. "And we learned how to go after our opponent's natural soft spots, too. Really kick or gouge 'em in the eyes, throat, nose, shins, and—"

Petra held up a hand. "Stop right there. I think I can guess the rest."

"Well, yeah," said Toni. "Obviously."

BEFORE they knew it, rain or no rain, it was time to get the place spiffed up for lunch.

After their last breakfast customers departed, Suzanne and Toni whirled through the café like a pair of crazed dervishes, scooping up dirty plates and wiping tables, pushing in chairs and sweeping up errant crumbs. Then they set out fresh silverware, napkins, and glasses, and put fresh coffee on to brew.

"Got a jelly donut left over," said Toni.

"I think it's got your name on it," said Suzanne.

Toni reached into the glass pie saver and grabbed it. "You got that right."

"Suzanne," Petra called from the pass-through. "Time to do the menu."

"On it." Suzanne grabbed a piece of yellow chalk and stood poised.

"Beer-battered chicken with a zucchini and corn medley," said Petra. "Cheddar and broccoli quiche, and curried chicken salad on seven-grain bread."

"And the pie you've got bubbling away in the oven?" said Suzanne. She made a cartoon drawing of a piece of pie.

"Blueberry," said Petra. "We'll serve it with vanilla ice cream."

"And we're off to the races," said Toni, peering out the window. "Because here come our first customers now."

BUT even as Suzanne served her customers and tended to a hundred little details, she continued to worry about Missy. Where was she when she made that phone call to the radio station? Where was she hiding out? And, since Missy was listening to the radio, did that mean she was nearby? Had she snuck back to her home? Or had she found a little bolt-hole somewhere else?

"Earth to Suzanne," said Toni. They were standing behind the counter and Toni was holding up a plate with a chicken salad sandwich on it. "Maybe you should eat something while our customers work on their desserts?"

"Thanks," said Suzanne. "I am feeling a little hungry." She took a bite of sandwich and chewed. "Mmn, good."

"Uh-oh," said Toni.

Suzanne stopped chewing. "What?"

The front door banged open and Junior walked in.

"It's okay," said Suzanne. "We've only got a few customers left."

"Still," said Toni. She didn't look happy as Junior, in ripped jeans and a dingy T-shirt, strode across the café carrying what looked like a car battery.

"You can't bring that in here," said Toni.

"Oh no?" said Junior. He hoisted his package up for them to see, grinning proudly, like he was showing off a new puppy.

"So you've got a car battery," said Suzanne. "So what?"

Junior did a little tap dance, then doubled over and laughed soundlessly, still holding the case. "Gotcha! I did it! I got you girls!"

"What are you talking about?" said Toni, sorely irritated now.

"I want you to take a gander at this here battery," said Junior. He shuffled over to the counter and hefted it up.

"Big deal," said Toni. "What's so special about it?"

"Just watch this," said Junior. He pulled off what turned out to be a metal shell that replicated the look of a car battery. Underneath was a six-pack of Budweiser. "Now ain't that something?" he chortled.

"Uh, no," said Toni, staring at it. "Not really."

"Sure it is," said Junior.

"What's the point?" said Suzanne.

"The point is," said Junior, sounding frustrated now, "you buy this handy-dandy fake battery cover and then you can sneak your own six-pack into anyplace your heart desires and enjoy a refreshing libation. A restaurant, the movies, a concert, you name it."

"You don't think hefting a car battery into the local Cineplex is going to look a little strange?" said Suzanne.

Junior frowned. "You have to think outside the box, Suzanne. We're competing in a global marketplace now. The sky's the limit."

"Bah!" said Toni. "More like pie in the sky."

Junior waved a hand at them in dismissal. "Ah, you gals don't know a good thing when you see it. This here invention could make me a million bucks!"

"Good," said Toni. "You make your million and I'll take half of it in the divorce settlement."

Junior shook his head slowly. "Ain't gonna be no divorce."

"And why is that?" said Suzanne.

Junior focused a mournful gaze on Toni. "'Cause we're still in love, right, baby? There's a reason I spray-painted your name on that overpass."

Toni made a fist and said, "Junior!" in a threatening tone. But Junior just smiled and spun on his heels.

"Are you okay?" Suzanne asked. Toni was still scowling, but wiping at her eyes, too.

"Got something stuck in my eye," she murmured.

"And in your heart, too, I think."

"I don't know about that," said Toni. "All I know is Junior's got these crazy dreams and schemes that never work out."

"Amen to that," Petra called loudly from the kitchen. "If you ask me, I think your boy is a couple sandwiches short of a picnic lunch."

WHILE Suzanne and Toni quickly assembled chicken salad sandwiches for afternoon tea, Petra dashed outside with a bag of trash. When she returned she was rubbing her arms and briskly hugging herself. "Temperature's dropping and my lumbago tells me we're in for a whopper of a storm!"

"You don't have lumbago," said Suzanne.

"No," said Petra. "But I've got an itchy toe."

"And it's itching for a storm?" said Suzanne.

"Something's rumbling toward us," agreed Toni. "Has been for days."

"I just hope it's not a tornado," worried Petra. "There've been a couple of touchdowns in Missouri and Kansas."

"Uh-oh," said Toni. "Maybe we'll get a tornado and the Cackleberry Club will be swept off its foundation just like Dorothy's house in *The Wizard of Oz*."

"And we'll land in a magical new place?" said Suzanne.

"That'd be okay with me," said Toni. "Just as long as there's not a wicked witch in the picture. I couldn't deal with a stupid witch."

"Especially one who wears green pancake makeup," said Petra. "Ugh." She glanced at Suzanne. "You still going to Lester Drummond's funeral today?"

Suzanne nodded. "I thought I would."

"Well, it's a perfect day for a funeral," said Petra. "Rainy, dark, and gloomy."

"Who has a funeral at two in the afternoon?" said Toni.

"Aren't they usually bright and early in the morning—before anyone's had a chance to wake up and smell the coffee?"

Suzanne shrugged. "I guess Lester Drummond is still doing things his way—even from the other side."

ARRIVING at Hope Church, feeling a little out of breath, Suzanne paused in the vestibule to collect herself. And was immediately greeted by a pair of sober-looking ushers decked out in formal black suits with white carnations in their lapels.

"Good afternoon, ma'am," one of them said with great gravitas. "I'm afraid the service is already under way."

"Oh!" Suzanne cried. Had she gotten the time wrong? Or was she running late? "I'm sorry," she said. "I thought the service started at two P.M."

"Mrs. Drummond requested that it begin earlier," said one of the ushers, the older of the two men. "On account of the fact she isn't feeling well. So it all started about five minutes ago. She's up front now, with the, um—"

"Casket," put in the other usher.

How extremely odd, Suzanne thought to herself. *I've never heard of such a thing.*

As she made her way inside, she heard the quiet murmur of prayers being recited at the front of the church. There was Reverend Strait, of course, standing over the gunmetal gray casket draped with a white cloth. To either side were standing sprays of white flowers—lilies, roses, and carnations.

A small group of mourners occupied the front five rows.

But what really caught Suzanne's eye, as she took a seat discreetly near the back of the church, was the woman who sat front and center in a black dress and veil. Shoulders hunched and one hand clutching a hankie, her back appeared to be heaving as she crumpled over in grief.

Deanna Drummond?

Had to be. Yes, Suzanne was positive it was her, looking like a carbon copy of Carmen Copeland even from the back.

And sitting right next to Deanna, their shoulders practically touching, was a bulky man in a dark suit. Even from where she sat, Suzanne could see the man holding Deanna's arm, almost supporting the grieving woman's full weight as they sat there together.

Suzanne craned her neck to get a better view but couldn't make out the man's identity. Then he turned for an instant and she caught his profile.

Boots Wagner. Oh!

It made sense, of course, that Lester Drummond's former bodybuilding pal would be at the funeral. After all, the two men must have spent a lot of time together over the years, working out and pumping iron.

But didn't Carla Reiker say that Boots had been unhappy with Drummond's antics at the gym? Yes, I think she said that. I'm pretty sure she did.

So why was Wagner being so solicitous to Deanna Drummond? Was he just a nice guy helping a grieving woman get through a soul-crushingly difficult day?

Suzanne's mind flashed back to the mess of papers they'd seen spread out in Drummond's house last night. Had Deanna enlisted Wagner to help her sort through the detritus of documents?

Or was something more sinister going on? Could they be in collusion? Were the two of them responsible for Lester Drummond's death? Suzanne let this thought ramble through her head as she glanced about the church.

A few rows ahead of her, Deputy Driscoll sat watching the mourners with keen law enforcement eyes. Did he suspect something was brewing between Deanna and Wagner? Maybe.

Suzanne found herself fidgety and unfocused through the rest of the funeral. And didn't really get her head back into the game until a mournful tune thundered from the organ and the casket was wheeled briskly down the center aisle. Then she peered at the string of mourners who followed behind it, everyone dressed in somber black and white. Though, in her mind, nothing was really in black and white at all.

SUZANNE was scurrying for her car when Allan Sharp suddenly lunged out of nowhere.

"Suzanne, a word please!" Sharp barked.

Suzanne stopped in her tracks. Had Sharp been at the funeral? She didn't remember seeing him, but he must have been. He was dressed in a black sharkskin suit.

She turned reluctantly to face him. "What?"

Sharp glowered at her. "I understand you've been asking questions about me."

"Who told you that?" Suzanne said, working hard to keep her voice even.

"None of your beeswax," Sharp responded aggressively. "I just want to know why you've been poking your nose where it doesn't belong."

"I have no idea what you're referring to."

"I think you do," countered Sharp.

"Look," said Suzanne, "I'm just concerned about what's going on in our town. The murder, the investigation . . ."

"We're all concerned," said Sharp. "Especially since your little friend Missy skipped town."

"I really don't know anything about that," said Suzanne. She cringed inwardly at the direction this conversation was going.

"Oh yeah? My guess is she's in hiding for a reason."

Suzanne tried to stare him down, but Sharp just gave a nasty smile and continued.

"The reason being," said Sharp, "is because she's guilty as sin!"

SLIPPING in behind the wheel, Suzanne pulled away from the church, wishing she'd never stopped to talk to Allan Sharp.

What a miserable jerk. Heaping blame on Missy like that. On the other hand, he might have been trying to lay a smoke screen, trying to deflect blame from himself since there's a chance he might be involved in Drummond's murder!

Clutching the wheel, her knuckles almost white, Suzanne made the impromptu decision to stop and check on Doogie.

I've got to know how that big lug is doing, she told herself as she drove the few short blocks to the hospital. But when she tiptoed into Doogie's room, she saw that he was sleeping fitfully. He was lying on his back, snoring loudly. A blanket was pulled up to his chin, revealing his slack face, and his tousle of gray hair had turned into a veritable bird's nest.

Suzanne turned and found a nurse coming down the hallway.

"Are you one of Doogie's nurses?" she asked.

"I am," said the woman. She was fifty-something with a lined but caring face. As she stared at Suzanne, her professional courtesy suddenly morphed into curiosity. "Are you Suzanne, by any chance?"

"Yes?"

The nurse nodded toward Doogie's room. "He's been asking about you." Then she shook her head and said, "No, that's not quite right. It's more like he's been calling out for you."

"Really?" said Suzanne. "So he was awake earlier?"

"He was maybe a little more cognizant a couple of hours ago. But he's pretty much been in and out of consciousness all day."

Suzanne tiptoed back into Doogie's room. She sat down quietly near his bed, watching him intently as he slept. He was still snoring, sawing wood like crazy. He almost surely didn't know she was there. And yet . . . she felt a connection to him.

What would Doogie do? she wondered. *What would he do next?*

Suzanne's thoughts roamed to the murder of Lester Drummond, to Missy and where she might be hiding. Where indeed would she hide, in this small town where everybody seemed to know everybody else's business?

Slowly an idea began to form in her brain.

SHE drove as fast as she dared back to the Cackleberry Club. By now it was late afternoon and their customers had long since departed. Petra was in the Knitting Nest teaching a couple of women how to combine a knit stitch and a purl stitch into a ribbing stitch, while Toni swept up in the café. She was dancing with her broom, twisting and turning and belting out the lyrics to Taylor Swift's "We Are Never Ever Getting Back Together."

Suzanne walked into the café and called out Toni's name.

Startled, Toni said, "Oh, hey!" Then stopped abruptly, looking a little sheepish at being caught mid-shimmy.

Suzanne didn't beat around the bush. "Are you up for an adventure?"

"Sure!" said Toni. And then, more cautiously, "What kind of adventure?"

"An exploratory adventure. Call it a short road trip."

"Suzanne, what've you got up your sleeve?"

In a low whisper, Suzanne said, "I think I know where Missy is!"

CHAPTER 23

"IT's sweet of you to drive," said Suzanne. She wasn't thrilled about riding in the Frankencar again, but Toni had volunteered to drive and it only seemed polite to accept.

"Sorry I don't have a CD player," said Toni, as they jounced around a corner. "But Junior hot-wired in an old cassette player. It works pretty good."

"Yes, it does." *As long as you don't mind listening to old cassette tapes of John Denver, the Carpenters, and Sly and the Family Stone*, thought Suzanne.

"So where are we headed?" asked Toni, as she wheeled her way through downtown Kindred, kicking the stuffing out of the speed limit. "You're being awfully mysterious about this little trip."

"We're headed for Jessup," said Suzanne. "So take County Road 5 out of town." Jessup was some twelve miles away.

"What's over there?" asked Toni, grinding gears as she gunned her engine.

"That's what we're going to find out."

"Hah! I bet you think Missy is holed up at the Motel 6 or something! Or maybe the Bide-a-way Inn, which I hear is kind of a hot-sheet joint."

"No," said Suzanne, allowing herself a smile. "But I have another idea."

Toni popped in an old Madonna cassette and they hummed and sang their way through the countryside and into the next town. Just a couple of Material Girls.

"Now what?" asked Toni. She eased back judiciously on her speed as they hit the Jessup city limits.

"We're looking for Grand Avenue," said Suzanne.

"Hmm," said Toni. "Seems to me that's the fancy part of town. Pray tell who lives . . ." She stopped abruptly. "Oh man, I get it! You think Missy's hiding out at Carmen's place, don't you?"

"Hey," said Suzanne, "you're the one who's always hot to creepy crawl old houses."

"You're darn tootin'," said Toni, grinning now.

They drove past a gray stone Gothic church, down a curving drive with spiffy-looking Cape Cod homes, and then up a hill where a few larger homes were comfortably situated. This was obviously the nicer, upscale part of town with wide, landscaped boulevards and old-fashioned wrought-iron streetlamps.

"Nice," said Toni. "Fancy."

Suzanne peered out the rain-streaked car windows, gazing at large homes and streetlamps that glowed like a string of rosary beads. She'd been to Carmen's home once before. Now if she could just remember which one it was . . .

They cruised past a large Tudor-style home, then a red stone manse covered with ivy. Suddenly, Suzanne blinked with recognition and cried out, "That's the one! Pull over!"

Toni cranked her steering wheel hard and bumped to a stop. "You mean the spooky-looking one with the tower room and widow's walk on top?" She looked a little askance as she gazed through her windshield.

Suzanne nodded. "That's the one. That's Carmen's place."

Toni narrowed her eyes. "What would you call that type of architecture? Mausoleum style?"

"Victorian," Suzanne said, practically laughing out loud. Toni really cracked her up sometimes.

"That place looks like it would be more conducive to a mystery writer than a romance writer."

"Maybe so, but this is what Carmen calls home." Suzanne stared at the large turreted house that was shrouded in darkness. Not a shred of light shone through the heavy draperies. Not even a yard light burned. Had she made a mistake? Had she misjudged her own hunch?

As if reading her mind, Toni said, "You really think Missy's in there? That Carmen is hiding her? Protecting her?"

"Carmen would never do such a charitable thing," said Suzanne. "Especially after firing her. But I happen to know that Carmen left for New York yesterday. So that would mean her house is empty."

"And maybe Missy had access to a spare key?" said Toni.

"That'd be my guess."

"Then we'd better go take a look."

They jumped out of the car and tiptoed carefully up the front walk to the house.

"Wow," whispered Toni, as they stood before Carmen's massive front door. "Why do I feel like one of the peons come to storm the castle?"

"Because we are," said Suzanne. She grabbed the bronze ram's head door knocker and slammed it hard against a brass plate. A deep boom seemed to echo from within. They stood there waiting, but no curtains parted, no sound of scuttling footsteps answered them. Suzanne banged the knocker again. Still no answer.

"Now what?" asked Toni.

"Maybe we should skulk around back and try your little trick," said Suzanne.

Toni's face lit up. "Now you're talking."

A brick walk led them around the side of the house, past overgrown gardens and a wrought-iron gazebo.

"This place would be gorgeous if it was, you know, fixed up a little," said Toni. "The gardens are a disaster."

"I guess flora and fauna aren't Carmen's forte."

"Or maybe her gardener quit," said Toni. She snorted. "Or was fired."

"C'mon," Suzanne whispered. "Let's try the back door."

They rapped on the glass and jiggled the brass doorknob, but to no avail.

"Rats," said Toni.

"We have to get a look inside," said Suzanne. "This is a huge place. Missy could be hiding in any little nook or cranny."

"The tough thing is, the windows are way up over our heads. We're gonna need something to stand on."

"What about that gazebo back there?" said Suzanne. "I think I might have seen a bench inside."

"Let's do it."

They ran back to the gazebo, hoisted up a wooden bench, and muscled it around to the back of the house.

"Here," said Toni, dropping her end. "Let's wedge it under this window."

They pushed the bench against the foundation and clambered on top of it.

"See anything?" said Toni. They both had their noses pressed against a window that was slightly rounded.

"Maybe a faint glimmer of light," said Suzanne.

"Could be a security light. Or a night-light."

"Maybe," said Suzanne.

"Wait a minute—I think I see a shadow moving!" said Toni. "Unless Carmen's got a cat or something."

"More likely an 'or something,'" said Suzanne.

Toni rapped her knuckles hard against the window. "Missy, it's us! Let us in!"

Suzanne gave a little tap for good measure and said, "It's Suzanne and Toni. Open up if you're in there." They waited for a good forty seconds, then banged on the window a little harder.

"We know you're there, Missy," said Toni. "So you may as well let us in."

They hesitated, peering into the darkened interior. Waiting, hoping. For all they knew their hunch could be totally wrong. But Suzanne didn't think so.

Finally, a light flashed on.

"That's it!" exclaimed Toni. "She's here!"

They dashed around to the back door and waited. Finally, after what seemed like an eternity, the door swung open a crack and a sliver of Missy's face appeared. "How'd you find me?" she said in a whisper.

"Open the door," said Suzanne. "We're not here to turn you in or anything. We just want to help."

Missy opened the door, but didn't look happy. She was definitely nervous and on edge. "How'd you find me?" she asked again.

"We took a wild guess," said Toni.

"Carmen blabbed to me that she was going to New York," Suzanne explained. "So I just put one and one together."

"Oh dear," said Missy. She closed the door and the three of them stood in a back hallway that had a black-and-white tiled floor and a brass coatrack. "If you can do that, so can Sheriff Doogie."

Toni glanced sharply at Suzanne, her penciled brows forming twin arcs of surprise. "She doesn't know."

"Know what?" said Missy. She frowned at them and shook her head. "What's going on?"

"Doogie was hit by a car last night," said Toni. "He's in the hospital."

Missy clasped a hand to her mouth. "No!"

"You don't know anything about that, do you?" Suzanne asked her.

"No, of course not!" Missy cried. "I wouldn't. I would never . . ." She pushed a hank of blond hair off her face. "You have to believe me!"

Suzanne decided that Missy's look of shocked surprise was genuine. This was obviously the first she'd heard about Sheriff Doogie. Of course, that still didn't explain why she was at Carmen's house.

"What are you doing here?" Toni blurted out.

"Oh." Missy waved a hand as though Toni's question was a particularly abstract thought. "It all just got to be too much. So I thought I'd hide out over here. But now it looks as if I didn't think it through all that carefully."

"Well," said Suzanne, "you really *do* need to think it through. Because Deputy Driscoll has the whole department out looking for you."

"That's right," said Toni. "So you better start figuring out the tough stuff. Like what are you going to do now?"

"You're not going to turn me in, are you?" Panic filled Missy's face.

"No," said Suzanne. "But I think this calls for some kind of plan."

"Maybe you'd better come in," Missy said slowly. She turned and headed down a wide, central hallway. "It seems we do have a lot to talk about."

They followed Missy down the hallway, past a living room that boasted damask sofas, an elegant gaming table that might have been Chippendale, and a spectacular white marble fireplace.

"This is like something out of *Lifestyles of the Rich and Crazy*," said Toni.

Missy led them into a smaller room, a parlor that had been converted into a cozy writing studio.

"So this is where Carmen writes her bodice busters," said Toni, looking around.

"Her office is actually an interior room," said Missy. "So I figured it was the safest place to hide."

"It's lovely," said Suzanne. There was another smaller fireplace with an ornate, carved mantel, a tall mahogany secretary stuffed with books, three tufted leather chairs, and an enormous desk that held two Mac computers, a color printer, and a scanner. The wood-paneled walls were hung with dozens of original oil paintings.

They sat down and pulled their chairs together to form a circle.

"Now what?" said Missy.

Suzanne looked at her. "Are you asking for my advice? Because if I give it, I sincerely hope you'll have the good sense to follow it."

Missy blinked. "Yes," she said. "I really do need help."

"Then you should probably get in touch with Deputy Driscoll first thing tomorrow," said Suzanne.

"That's not going to happen," Missy told her.

"Honey, it's the smart thing to do," said Suzanne.

Missy folded her arms across her chest and shook her head.

Toni glanced at Suzanne. "Plan B?"

"What's plan B?" said Missy.

"We don't actually have one," said Suzanne.

"But my gut tells me we better come up with one," said Toni.

They all sat in silence for a few moments until Suzanne said, "What's really at the crux of all this is, who killed Lester Drummond?"

"It wasn't me," said Missy bluntly.

"We know that," said Suzanne. "But the question still remains."

"We've got to figure out some answers," said Toni. "With Doogie laid up in the hospital, it's up to us now."

"Oh, I wouldn't say that," said Suzanne.

"Ho!" snorted Toni. "Do you really think Deputy Dawg— I mean Driscoll—is any kind of crack investigator?"

"Probably not," Suzanne allowed. "But that's only because he's young and inexperienced."

"But we're not," said Toni. "We're older and have some miles on us. So like I said, it's up to us." She rubbed her hands together. "Who's blipped on our radar?"

"For the murder?" said Suzanne. "You know I'm still suspicious of Allan Sharp. Especially since he was being sued by Lester Drummond."

"And there's Deanna Drummond," put in Toni. "The nutcase ex-wife who's lusting after an inheritance."

"And we did get accosted by Karl Studer," said Suzanne.

"Studer's son was incarcerated in prison when Drummond served as warden," Toni said as an aside to Missy.

"There really *are* a lot of suspects," said Missy. She sounded worried but hopeful.

"And there could be more," said Suzanne. "Trouble is, we don't know who exactly was under investigation. Doogie played his cards pretty close to the vest."

"Agreed," said Toni. "It could be some ordinary guy who's been rubbing shoulders with all of us."

"What do you mean?" said Missy.

"Like . . . any old goofball," replied Toni. She glanced at Suzanne. "Right? Could be somebody we see practically every day at the Cackleberry Club."

Suzanne gave a polite nod, but she was deep in thought, thinking about the various possibilities, turning the suspects over and over in her mind. Still, no hard evidence had piled up against any one of them. Just idle speculation that could slip off as easy as Teflon. She lifted her eyes and focused on one of the paintings on the wall. It was a combination of illustration, graphics, and wild paint strokes. She recalled how Carmen had bragged to her about collecting outsider art. Art that was naïve, self-taught, and eccentric—completely outside the mainstream.

Her eyes traveled to another canvas where a bizarre, cartoonish red dog clutched a blue building between its jagged teeth. She glanced at the crudely lettered signature in the lower right corner.

"Gantz," Suzanne said suddenly. She studied the signature again and murmured, "Jake Gantz."

"What about him?" said Toni.

Suzanne's mind was starting to hum. "What if he's the wild card in all of this?"

"What do you mean?" asked Toni.

"Gantz was incarcerated at the Jasper Creek Prison," said Suzanne. "Under Lester Drummond's watch."

"He was?" said Toni.

"Dale Huffington mentioned it to me," said Suzanne. "I kind of pooh-poohed the notion of Gantz being involved in this thing. But Doogie did seem interested in him . . ."

"Holy garbanzo beans!" said Toni. "You think Gantz could be the killer?"

Missy's eyes went round. "Could he be?"

Suzanne didn't much like the idea that was formulating in her head. Still, it was irritating her like a grain of sand inside an oyster. So it was a notion she had to pursue. "Jake's kind of a loner," she said in a halting voice. "He's a guy who pretty much lives off the grid. And he's ex-military."

"When you put it that way," said Toni, "Jake *does* sound like a viable suspect. He's in and out of all sorts of places and nobody pays much attention to him."

"That's true," said Missy. "He just sort of drifts around town looking down-and-out."

"But that doesn't make him a killer," said Suzanne, backpedaling a little.

"But what if it's all an act?" said Toni. "What if he's one of those guys who's seething with inner rage?"

"Suzanne!" said Missy. "You have to look into this!"

Suzanne shook her head. "I really can't do that."

"Why not?" said Missy.

"For one thing," said Suzanne, "I'm not a trained investigator."

"You're the next best thing," said Toni. "Heck, you've gotten this far. You've gotten further than anyone else in law enforcement!"

"You could at least *talk* to Gantz," urged Missy.

"Talk to him about what?" said Suzanne. "I can't just approach Gantz with the notion that he's a murder suspect. That might totally scare him away!"

"Maybe you could just talk to him about Lester Drummond and try to draw him out," said Missy. "See what his reaction is. Could you do that? Please?"

Toni was nodding in agreement. "We've come this far, right?"

"Maybe," said Suzanne. "Honestly, though, I don't even know where the man lives."

"But look," said Missy, pointing at the walls. "Carmen purchased several of Gantz's paintings, so she must have his address. She's a stickler for keeping records."

Toni and Missy pawed through Carmen's file drawers then, looking for anything that might help. Finally, in a file labeled "Art," they found a scrawled receipt.

"Is this Gantz's address?" Toni wondered as she smoothed a piece of crumpled paper. "It's hard to tell—his handwriting's so spindly and awful."

"Does this address say sixty-nine fourteen?" asked Missy.

"I think that's a seven," said Toni, scratching her head. "It's sixty-*seven* fourteen Sinkhole Road. But it's really rural. I don't have a clue where this might be."

But Suzanne recognized the address. "Toni, do you

remember that weird cult, the Neukommen Following, that used to live out on Sinkhole Road? I think this might be the same address."

"That cult moved away," said Toni. "Over a year ago."

"I realize that," said Suzanne. "But maybe Jake Gantz is the new tenant."

THEY bid their good-byes to Missy—when they would see her again, they didn't know. But they had to move on. Were motivated, in fact, to check out Jake Gantz's whereabouts.

So Suzanne and Toni drove back to the center of town, then followed a rambling blacktop road that eventually branched off to Sinkhole Road.

"I think we're in Deer County now," said Toni, struggling to get her bearings. "Be nice if we had GPS."

Suzanne popped open the glove box.

"Oh no," said Toni. "No GPS in there."

"Better than GPS," said Suzanne, unfurling a piece of paper. "A map."

"Ah," said Toni. "Reliable, old low-tech."

Sinkhole Road was lonely, dark, and dreary. Not many houses were out this way where the bluffs piled up, one on top of the other, sliced through by dark, fast-rushing streams. In the lowlands, thick stands of tamarack and scrawny pines indicated it wasn't exactly good farm country, either.

"Any minute now," said Suzanne. "Any minute." One eye was trained on the road, the other on her map. "The turn-off's here somewhere."

"But where?" wondered Toni. She'd been driving for a good twenty-five minutes and was starting to regret their slightly impetuous detour.

"There!" cried Suzanne.

Toni cranked her steering wheel hard and slewed into the turn, bumping onto a narrow rutted road they'd both almost missed.

"This is awfully remote," said Toni as they humped along a dirt road while wet tree branches slapped the sides of her car. Her car labored and groaned as the road twisted up through a fern-lined gully and then leveled out for a hundred yards or so on top of a woodsy hill. Another half mile of bad road through dark groves of burr oak and red maples brought them to their final destination.

"This is it?" said Toni, sounding disappointed as the car crept across a mixture of gravel and sticky mud. There were four dilapidated clapboard houses, a small building atop a far ridge, and an old-fashioned barn, the wood weathered and gone to silver.

"The road ends here," said Suzanne. "So, yes, this is it."

Toni rolled to a stop. "Nice little compound they got here. Rustic and outdoorsy, but without that slick Ralph Lauren feel."

"Funny," said Suzanne, as she gazed at the broken-down buildings. A light burned in the first house, all the other buildings were dark.

"Now what?" asked Toni. "Do we just knock on the door and say, 'Hi, how are you?'"

"I guess," said Suzanne. She pushed the passenger door open and stepped out. "Are you coming?" Toni's car was idling so roughly it was hard to hear her own words.

"Maybe I better wait in the car," said Toni. When Suzanne gave her a quizzical look, she added, "Keep it running in case we have to make a quick getaway."

"Yeah . . . right," said Suzanne. She stepped gingerly around a couple of mud puddles as she walked up to the door of the shanty. She drew a deep breath and knocked. Her nerves felt jumpy and frayed and she wasn't sure what to say or what to expect.

Suzanne waited in the dark for a few minutes, then knocked again. Nobody home? Or did they just not feel like coming to the door? On the other hand, how could anyone ignore the throaty rumble of Toni's car?

Eventually, the door creaked open and there stood Jake Gantz. He was barefoot, dressed in camo pants and a flimsy waffle weave T-shirt. He gazed at her, blinked rapidly, and said, "Uh . . . Suzanne?" He didn't just sound surprised—he sounded shocked.

"I was just, um, in the area," Suzanne began. She knew she was fumbling her words, sounding a little strange herself. "And I thought I'd stop by and have a quick chat. Maybe ask you . . ."

Gantz pushed open a battered screen door and peered into the darkness. He saw the idling car and inclined his head toward it. "Who's that?" he asked. "Who's out there?"

Suzanne turned and saw that she could just make out Toni's outline. "Oh, that's Toni," she told him. "You remember her. From the Cackleberry Club?"

"Toni," said Gantz, as if he were testing out the word. "Yeah . . . okay." He raised a tentative hand in greeting.

Sitting behind the wheel of her car, Toni looked startled by his greeting. She raised a hand just as her car began to roll forward.

"What's she . . . ?" began Gantz.

And suddenly, before Suzanne knew what was happening, Toni's car let loose a shuddering buck that seemed to rattle every nut and bolt that held the old buggy together. Then the engine revved loudly, a glut of blue exhaust spewed from the tailpipe, and the car backfired, producing an ear-splitting retort that echoed off the nearby trees and sounded like a rifle shot.

Gantz, a look of abject horror on his face, suddenly flung himself face forward into the mud. "Hold your fire!" he cried, his voice rising in a terrified, pathetic scream. "For gosh sakes, hold your fire!"

Shocked beyond belief, all Suzanne could do was gaze at Gantz as he lay cowering on the ground, his hands covering his head. And her single thought was, *Oh dear Lord, the poor man.*

CHAPTER 24

A hard rain drummed on the roof as Suzanne, Toni, and Petra bustled about the kitchen of the Cackleberry Club. It didn't matter how nasty it was outside, though, because inside, Canadian bacon sizzled, banana bread released its sweet aroma as it baked, and sliced avocados and a bowl full of eggs sat at the ready for Petra's Wednesday morning cheddar and avocado omelets.

This was the only sense of normalcy, however. Because Suzanne and Toni hadn't wasted a second in cluing Petra in on Missy's whereabouts last night. Then, of course, the story progressed to their woeful tale about dropping in on Jake Gantz. And how the poor man had reacted so badly to the noise from Toni's car.

"It was just a lousy backfire," Toni told Petra. "Happens all the time. Junior says it's 'cause of a crappy fuel pump."

"But Jake, that poor soul," said Petra, fretting. "For him to be so terrified of a noise that he immediately hit the dirt and covered his head! He must have really believed there was rifle fire coming at him."

"It kind of did sound like a rifle shot," Toni admitted.

"I'm not a doctor or a therapist," said Petra, looking a little mournful, "but I'd say that Gantz is probably suffering from post-traumatic stress. Like so many of our poor returning veterans."

"And I'm no Sherlock Holmes," said Toni, glancing at Suzanne, "but I'm guessing that Gantz is probably not a viable suspect anymore. A person who's that afraid of a little noise . . ." She shrugged as she continued to apply a set of silver Lee press-on nails.

"That's pretty much my feeling, too," said Suzanne. "Jake Gantz isn't a killer. He's just too timid and wounded . . ."

"Well, we didn't *really* shoot him!" broke in Toni. "It just *sounded* that way."

"I meant psychologically wounded," said Suzanne.

"I think you're right," said Petra. "There's no way Gantz could have ever gone up against a tough, intimidating guy like Lester Drummond."

"Then who did?" said Toni. When nobody ventured an answer she said, "Looks like we're back to square one."

"More like square one and a half," said Suzanne. "Now we also have the Missy situation to contend with."

"You're not going to turn her in, are you?" said Petra.

"I'm hoping she'll turn herself in," said Suzanne.

Toni shook her head. "I wouldn't bet on that."

"Then she'll be a fugitive," said Suzanne. "And we'll all be complicit."

"But some fugitives are completely innocent," said Toni. "Look at poor Richard Kimble."

"That was a movie," said Petra. "This is real life."

"A real-life mess," said Suzanne. She thought of Doogie still lying in the hospital and made a mental note to call and check on him.

Petra glanced through the pass-through at their handful of customers. A dozen or so souls had braved the rain so they could enjoy a home-cooked breakfast at the Cackleberry Club. "Toni, maybe you better go out and start taking orders."

"Consider it done," said Toni, as she gingerly reached for her order pad.

"And don't stab anyone with those fake talons!" said Petra.

"Please," said Toni as she hustled through the swinging door.

Petra cocked an eye at Suzanne. "Okay, what are *you* doing to do? About Missy, I mean."

"I'm still trying to figure something out," said Suzanne. "Maybe some sort of compromise." She lifted a hand, then let it drop to her side. "I'll noodle a few ideas around."

"While you're noodling," said Petra, "could you please pull that pan of blueberry muffins from the oven? I'm pretty sure they're done by now."

Suzanne slid her hand into a puffy oven mitt, opened the oven door, and grabbed the muffins. "Perfect," she said, as she placed the pan on the countertop. The muffins were golden and steamy and fabulous looking.

"Don't just eyeball them," said Petra, as she cracked eggs into a bowl. "Be sure to test them." Petra was a stickler for testing her baked goods for doneness.

So Suzanne grabbed a toothpick and poked the center muffin.

"Did it come out clean?" asked Petra.

"Clean as a whistle," said Suzanne, as a gust of wind suddenly whooshed against the building, rattling the windows on the kitchen's back wall.

"Good," said Petra. She reached up and turned on her radio. "This weather is driving me bonkers. It feels like something nasty is about to break loose. Like the ions in the atmosphere have all gone stir-crazy."

But Suzanne was still contemplating her next move with Missy. Should she call Deputy Driscoll? Let him in on the little secret that she'd located Missy? But if she did spill the beans, what exactly would the ramifications be? Would Driscoll want to speed over to Jessup, all crazy-ass lights and sirens, to slap a pair of handcuffs on Missy and drag her to jail?

Maybe I could reason with Driscoll. Make him understand that Missy is really innocent. And make it clear that law enforcement should be looking at the likes of Karl Studer or Allan Sharp or Deanna Drummond—or maybe even Boots Wagner?

Should she try that? Was her argument convincing enough?

Deep in her heart, Suzanne knew this was all just wishful thinking. No, the best thing, the smartest thing to do, was wait until Doogie had recovered and was well enough to rejoin the investigation. Then she could sit down with him and precisely lay out the situation. If she did that, Doogie would be able to figure out the next move.

"We're getting slammed!" Toni yelped as she hustled back into the kitchen.

Petra snatched the breakfast orders from Toni's hand and shot Suzanne a worried look. "Suzanne?"

"I'm on it," said Suzanne. She grabbed her long black apron, draped it around her neck, and was through the swinging door with one quick lunge.

The café was suddenly so busy that Suzanne had her work cut out for her. She seated two tables of slightly soggy newcomers, took several orders, explained the difference between Eggs Balderdash and Eggs in Purgatory to a traveling salesman, then slid behind the counter and hastily brewed another pot of Sumatran coffee. Strong and hearty, it was a good, fortifying blend for a stormy day like today.

Toni joined her at the counter, grabbing a pitcher of orange juice and filling two glasses. "Weren't you taking this afternoon off?" she asked. "Wasn't this the day you and Sam were supposed to go trout fishing?"

"I'm afraid we're going to have to change our plans," said Suzanne, wiping her hands on her apron. "You get this much wind and rain and all sort of little bugs and seeds get washed into the streams. When that happens, the trout are kind of overwhelmed by an easy food source."

"So your hooks or flies or whatever are totally unappealing to the little fishies, huh?" said Toni.

"That's about the size of it."

"Too bad."

"Guys," said Petra, leaning through the pass-through. "The storm is starting to intensify. WLGN has reports of a tornado being spotted some six miles southwest of here. Over near St. Helena."

"Oh man," said Toni. "That's right by Cappy's General Store."

"Has there been an actual touchdown?" asked Suzanne.

"Not yet," said Petra. She wrapped her knuckles against the counter. "Knock on wood."

Suzanne and Toni glanced out the front window of the Cackleberry Club. The sky was an angry swirl of low-hanging blue-black clouds.

"This does look bad," said Suzanne. Nearby poplars and small maples were being thrashed like crazy by the wind, practically being stripped of their leaves. She wondered if they should move customers away from the windows, just to be on the safe side.

"Aw, we'll be okay," said Toni, sensing Suzanne's unease. "Maybe we'll just have to request that our customers drink out of the southwest side of their coffee mugs." Still, her eyes flicked nervously as she said it.

"I'm going to turn the radio on out here, too," said Suzanne. She hopped up onto a straight-backed chair and spun the dial on their old Emerson radio. It was tucked up in the rafters on a shelf filled with colorful ceramic chickens. As a burst of static filled the air, several customers immediately quieted down, the better to hear the weather report.

Still, Suzanne and Toni moved about the café, gamely taking orders, joking with customers, keeping tabs on the storm outside.

Suzanne had just delivered a cheese omelet when her eye went to one of the craft items hanging on the wall. It was lovely paper collage depicting a food-laden farm table. The hand-painted calligraphy on it spelled out "Come and get it." Something about the calligraphy resonated with Suzanne, and she narrowed her eyes, studying it. *It's interesting*, she thought, *that in that particular style of printing, a C looks more like a G.* She blinked and straightened up. *Now why on earth is that suddenly pinging in my brain?*

Then it dawned on her the note in the cemetery! The note that had been left on the grave where Drummond had died. *Whoever signed that note signed it with the initial G. But what if it had really been a C? If so, who could C be?*

Before her brain could dredge up any sort of answer, there was an unearthly roar overhead, as if a hundred jumbo jets were about to crash-dive into the Cackleberry Club!

Suzanne glanced around, wild-eyed, and saw that everyone in the café had stopped eating and was casting fearful glances about, too. Then, before anyone could move a muscle, the entire building began to tremble. Water glasses rattled and crashed over on tables, ceramic chickens shuddered and shook on their narrow shelves. The atmosphere suddenly felt hollow and weird, but pulsing with dangerously charged electrical energy!

As every light in the place winked off, screams and cries erupted from the customers. But before Suzanne could move a single step, there was a tremendous, ear-splitting crash, as if a giant sledgehammer had been dropped on their roof.

And then a high-pitched rasping sounded—and one of the front windows completely shattered!

Tiny shards of glass burst in upon them with gale force, followed by a tremendous *whoosh* of damp, cold air and a swirl of rain, leaves, and debris.

There were sharp cries and moans from the customers, followed by Petra's cry of "Heaven help us!" from the kitchen.

In the darkness, panic seemed to reign for a few moments, until Suzanne grabbed a book of matches, lit a candle, and held her little torch aloft.

"Anybody hurt?" she called out, as Petra came flying out of the kitchen.

"What the Sam Hill . . . ?" began Petra. Then she saw the window, completely open to the elements now, and skidded to a halt. "Oh no!" she cried.

Everyone started babbling at once. "The window . . . the lights . . . the glass!" they all exclaimed. Customers got up from their chairs, looking scared and shaky and disoriented.

Luckily, Toni had the presence of mind to dig out a dozen little tea light candles. She quickly distributed them to all the tables, helping restore a semblance of calm.

But there were a few injuries. Dan Beckman, one of their regulars, had a nasty gash across his forehead.

"Petra!" Suzanne called. "Grab your first aid kit!"

"I've got it!" Petra called as she rushed to Beckman's side. She bent down and carefully inspected his head wound.

"That yellow plaster hen just came hurtling down at me," said Beckman. He was bleeding and shaken but trying to feign a casual calm. "Like some kind of kamikaze dive-bomber!"

"I'm so sorry," Petra cooed, pulling out strips of gauze and antiseptic.

"But I'm . . . I think I'm okay," said Beckman.

"Good thing you've got a hard noggin," said Petra, trying to make a joke even as her voice shook. "That chickie didn't really mean to hurt you."

Suzanne stood in the middle of the café and surveyed the chaos. "Are there any other medical problems?" she asked in what she hoped was a loud, clear voice.

Turns out there were.

"Sonja's got some glass stuck in her head!" called Toni. Sonja Winter, a retired librarian, was clasping a bunched-up napkin to the back of her head.

Suzanne hurried over, glass crunching underfoot, to inspect Sonja's injured head. "Toni, grab a bigger candle," she directed. "Petra, bring that first aid kit over here."

They all crowded around Sonja, as Suzanne ever so gently parted the woman's cap of gray curls.

"Doggone," said Suzanne, "there *are* a couple of glass shards."

"It's not too bad, is it?" asked Sonja, glancing hopefully at Suzanne.

"I don't think so," said Suzanne. "But they need to come out."

Petra took a closer look. "I can't do this," she said. "We need a medical professional."

"You're right," said Suzanne. "A nurse or doctor will have to pluck out those shards with forceps. Make sure none of the glass breaks off."

"I could use my manicure tweezers," offered Toni.

Suzanne held up a hand. "No, we really do need someone with medical training."

"Better call the clinic," said Petra. "Hopefully the roads are passable and we can drive Sonja and Dan over there. And whoever else needs patching up."

Suzanne tried the wall phone and found it was dead. "Lines must be down," she muttered. She grabbed her cell phone instead and quickly punched in the number for the Westvale Medical Clinic. She knew Sam would be there with his calm voice and rock-solid reassurance.

Esther, the office manager, answered in a shaky voice. "Westvale Medical Clinic."

"Esther," said Suzanne, "this is Suzanne over at the Cackleberry Club. We've got a couple of medical emergencies. One of our windows blew in and we've got people with cuts and embedded glass."

"We've got trees down all over the place, too," replied Esther. She sounded scared and a little frazzled.

"Is your power still on?" Suzanne asked.

"No," said Esther. "But our backup generator clicked on a few minutes ago, so we're good for a while."

"Is Sam there?" Suzanne asked. "Can he come over here or can we . . . ?"

"Dr. Hazelet's not here," Esther interrupted. "You just missed him. He took off something like three minutes ago."

"Where'd he go?" asked Suzanne. This was not what she wanted to hear.

"We received an emergency call from a very panic-stricken woman," said Esther. "Apparently there's been a three-car smashup out on County Road 28, right near that old church. Five people injured, some of them little kids. Anyway, you know Sam. When he heard there were kids, he grabbed his bag and took off like a jackrabbit."

"They called the clinic directly? Not 911 to get an ambulance?"

"Couldn't get through I guess," said Esther. "Some cell phones aren't working and the lines are down all over town. I suppose even at the Law Enforcement Center. Poor Molly must be going crazy!"

"But some of the nurses are still there? Still at the clinic?"

"Sure are," said Esther. "So if you can get your injured folks over here we're open for business. I bet there'll be a lot more injuries coming in, too."

"We'll be there," said Suzanne. She hung up abruptly and turned to face a dozen inquiring faces. "Anybody who's cut or injured, we're going to drive you to the clinic," she announced.

"Uh . . . I don't think so," said Toni. She grabbed a

wildly flapping curtain and pulled it aside as she peered out the broken window. "There are trees down all over the place. On top of cars, even blocking our driveway."

A few of the customers crowded around the window with Toni. It was, indeed, complete chaos outside. As if an enormous game of pick-up sticks had been played out in their parking lot.

"Probably straight line winds," said Petra, surveying the damage. "Looks pretty bad."

"And the wind's still whipping like crazy, blowing debris all over the place!" exclaimed Toni.

"What if there's another tornado?" someone cried out.

"My car's parked in back," said Suzanne, trying to remain calm. "We can get out that way."

"Go check," urged Petra.

But when Suzanne hurried through the kitchen and looked out the back door, her heart sank. A huge tree branch had been sheared off from the giant oak that stood in the backyard. While it hadn't damaged Suzanne's car, it was definitely blocking the driveway.

"Wow," said Toni, who'd followed her in. "I guess we're stuck here for a while."

Suzanne and Toni went back into the café to break the bad news.

"Looks like we're stuck here for a little while longer," Suzanne told everyone. "Until we can move some of these downed trees."

"I'm gonna try to call Junior at the garage," said Toni. "See if he can get some guys over here with chainsaws and pickup trucks."

"Good thinking," said Petra. She smiled at Sonja, who now had a red bandana tied around her head. "How are you doing, hon?"

"Hanging in there," said Sonja.

But Suzanne was pacing back and forth, still fretting. The storm and injuries had set her on edge . . . as well as Sam just taking off like that.

Petra pulled her aside. "What's wrong, sweetie?"

Suzanne chewed her bottom lip. "Just . . . I don't know. Call it a low-level vibe. A worry vibe."

"About . . . ?"

"Sam," said Suzanne, finally vocalizing her nervousness. "I'm worried about Sam."

"You shouldn't be," said Petra soothingly. "Didn't you say he was out tending to the injured?" She glanced about and let loose a sigh. "Lord knows, we sure could use him here."

Toni saw Suzanne's consternation, too. "Did you try his cell phone?"

"No, I didn't."

"Give him a buzz," she urged. "If you can get through to him, maybe it'll set your mind at ease."

Suzanne grabbed one of the tea lights and walked into the Book Nook. She pulled her phone from her hip pocket and hit Sam's number. No answer. She waited a minute and tried again. Still no answer. Suzanne stood there, staring dejectedly at her phone. When she heard soft footsteps behind her, she whirled around.

It was Toni. "Did you get hold of him?"

Suzanne shook her head. "No, but I guess I really didn't expect to. Esther said a lot of phones were out all over town. Even some cell phones. It was a miracle I got through to her."

"You think the phones are out at the Law Enforcement Center?" asked Toni.

"Sure," said Suzanne. "I suppose so." She stood there for a moment, considering this. Then she quickly dialed Doogie's direct line.

A man's voice answered immediately. "Law Enforcement Center."

"You've got phone service," said Suzanne, surprised.

"For now anyway," said the man.

"What about at the 911 call center?" she asked. "Is it working? Are people getting through?"

"They are as far as I know."

"Okay, thank you," said Suzanne.

They walked back into the café.

"Did you get hold of Sam?" asked Petra.

Suzanne shook her head.

"Where'd you say that accident was?" said Toni.

"Um . . . County Road 28," said Suzanne. "Near that old church."

"Huh," said Toni. "As the crow flies, that's like ten minutes from here." She gave Suzanne a reassuring smile, but it faded as soon as she saw the look of consternation on her friend's face. "Hey, you're looking a little jittery. You didn't get conked on the head, did you?"

Suzanne wasn't injured, but her mind was suddenly spinning out a strange scenario, a dark and evil scenario. First Lester Drummond had been put out of commission. Then Sheriff Doogie was laid low. And now . . . Sam had been called out? Boom, boom, boom. One, two, three? It couldn't be, could it?

Grabbing Toni by both shoulders, Suzanne said, "You stay here, try to get Junior working on those chainsaws, and keep everybody calm."

Toni's eyes went wide. "What are you talking about? Suzanne, hang on a minute! Are you *going* somewhere?"

"I'm going out," said Suzanne. With every passing second her nerves were strumming wildly and she was filled with an ice-cold fear.

"Outside?" Toni stammered.

"Out to check on Sam," said Suzanne.

Toni's face went completely blank. "Check on Sam?" she

choked out. "With our cars out of commission, how are you gonna do that?"

Suzanne was already halfway out the door as she hollered back, "How else? Pony express!"

CHAPTER 25

As Suzanne scrambled down the back steps, the wind caught her broadside and practically spun her around. Rain slashed painfully at her face and she was instantly drenched from head to toe. Still, Suzanne tore through the driving rain, skittering across the hardpan backyard that had suddenly become a sea of turgid mud. She ducked into the back strip of woods on her property, ignoring the branches that tore at her clothes, and ran out into a field of planted corn.

Clouds roiled overhead, lightning crackled, and thunder played a set of dark and ominous timpani drums.

Am I going to be struck by lightning? Suzanne wondered. *Am I going to keel over from all this stress?*

Still she pushed on. Running, sometimes stumbling, through the field, heading for the barn where Mocha and Grommet were stabled. Though the going was terrible and clods of mud kept building up on the soles of her shoes, Suzanne fought to remain close to the hard-packed line of earth that, in drier weather, served as a sort of road for farm vehicles.

Her breathing grew more and more labored as she ran. But she was definitely making forward progress and drawing ever closer to the farm, ignoring, as best she could, the sharp stitch of pain in her side. Because this was certainly no gentle jog around the park with an aging dog—this was a full-out race through a dangerous storm!

Finally, with a harsh gasp, Suzanne threw herself up against the rough wood of the barn and quickly muscled open the barn door. Ducking inside the shelter suddenly came as a huge relief! No more wind whipping her hair, no driving rain to make her eyes blink and her nose run.

Suzanne took a couple of minutes to dry off, then located an old riding helmet from a cubby on the back wall. She plopped the helmet on her head, grabbed her tack, and had Mocha saddled and ready to go in about two minutes flat. All the while, she talked calmly to Mocha. "It's okay, boy. We're going for a ride. I know we can do this, you and me!"

Giving a final tug on the cinch, Suzanne jumped on Mocha's back and rode him out of the barn, his hoofbeats ringing sharply against the cement. She took a deep breath, ducked her head through the doorway, and was, once again, back outside—heading into the teeth of the storm!

Mocha shook his great head in protest, spooked by the wind and rain, but Suzanne dug her heels into his flanks and they were suddenly off.

Suzanne knew it was maybe a fifteen-minute cross-country ride from the farm to the old church that served as a sort of landmark. That was where Sam was supposed to be, tending to the injured. So that was where she was headed. And, hopefully, when she arrived, she'd find that everything—especially Sam—was just fine.

Mocha was a big, powerful quarter horse. Which made for an easy gallop across a newly seeded field of soybeans.

Suzanne could feel his powerful haunches bunching beneath her, driving hard, kicking up clods of earth. Within minutes they reached the edge of the nearby woods.

This is the best way to go, she told herself. Cut through the woods, come out by that old church, and follow along the highway.

She spurred Mocha forward and headed into the woods. And found some blessed relief from the storm. The denseness of trees slowed the wind's terrible onslaught, while the canopy of leaves afforded her a little extra shelter from the rain. But the woods were tough going, too. There were fallen trees to negotiate, rocks to angle around, and stands of buckthorn that scratched and tore at their legs. Mocha kept pushing ahead, reading her familiar signals, carefully sidestepping obstacles.

Ten minutes into the woods, Suzanne worried that she might be turned around. The scenery all looked the same. Trees, thick underbrush, hills, and occasional ravines.

Where am I? Where's the old church? That would mark my way, wouldn't it? Only if I could find it!

Suzanne and Mocha splashed across a shallow, rock-strewn creek, kicking up mud and debris.

This way? I hope it's this way.

They plunged farther into the woods, passing through groves of sumac, the tiny red berries just beginning to form among the thick green leaves.

But where is that deserted church?

Branches whipsawed back and forth, beating at them ferociously. The wind had picked up again. In fact, it felt as if another tornado might be barreling down upon them!

Loosening the reins a little, Suzanne allowed Mocha to pick his way, slowly now, down a narrow twisted and turning path.

Maybe this is a bad idea, Suzanne thought to herself. *Maybe I should just turn around and forget . . .*

A dark, stone pillar, half obliterated by trees, loomed directly ahead of her.

What?

She gave Mocha a little kick and he instantly picked up the pace. As they drew closer, Suzanne saw that it was a stone statue. A statue of a man gazing up toward the heavens, both arms upraised.

Oh my—and there are more statues, too. I think I know what this is.

Though they were battered and broken, Suzanne understood that she'd stumbled upon an abandoned section of the church's stations of the cross. So the old church had to be close by!

They made their way slowly now, and Suzanne saw rounded stone tablets peeking out of the tops of bushes.

Gravestones.

Which meant the old church was *very* close by.

Soon, wet, soggy ground yielded to harder earth and Suzanne urged Mocha into a slow canter. Then, in no time at all, they flashed past the old stone church, half tumbled down, its broken roof open to the punishing elements. And a few moments later, they popped out of the woods and onto a narrow road!

Reining Mocha in, taking care not to let him stumble and lose his footing on the rain-slicked blacktop, Suzanne glanced left, then right, through the driving rain.

And saw—nothing. No accident, no Sam.

But Esther said it was *near* the old church, she told herself. Not *at* it. So she had a decision to make. Turn left or turn right.

Suzanne thought for a minute. Left would take her back toward town, but right . . .

She reined right, jabbed Mocha with her heels, and sent him cantering along the side of the road. The wind was at her back now, so the cold wasn't quite as piercing. And maybe, if she called out, Sam might be able to hear her?

"Sam!" Suzanne called as she cantered along. "Where are you, Sam?"

With the wind still howling, she worried that she wouldn't be heard. Still, it didn't hurt to try.

I don't care how crazed I sound, she told herself. *I just want to find him!*

She called out a few more times as the road curved this way and that. Still she saw . . . nothing.

Pulling back on the reins, Suzanne brought Mocha to a dead halt. And wondered again if she was being silly. Rushing out here in the middle of the storm because she'd had a crazy, weird hunch that something might be wrong?

I should go back, she told herself. *Before my horse slips and we both break our fool necks out here.*

As she dipped her head, trying to decide what to do, she suddenly spotted a hint of blue up ahead through the thrashing trees!

That has to be Sam's BMW!

Feeling relieved and a little embarrassed now that she knew Sam was perfectly safe, she walked her horse toward the car.

As she drew closer, she saw that Sam's BMW had been driven clean off the road. And directly behind it sat a red car. Strangely enough, both cars appeared to be empty and there wasn't a person in sight!

Cautiously, Suzanne approached the two cars.

So where was the accident? she wondered. *What was going on? Had an ambulance already arrived to haul away the injured?*

That's probably the exact scenario, she decided. And here she was, trying to charge in like the cavalry, when there was nothing left to do.

Okay, she'd simply circle the cars, make sure everything

was cool, and then cut and run. Try to forget this ever happened. That she'd overreacted like some kind of paranoid cuckoo bird.

That was the precise moment lightning crackled overhead, and a photo-strobe flash illuminated a pair of legs sprawled on the pavement ahead.

What?

As well as someone leaning over them.

Suzanne's heart suddenly lurched into the back of her throat.

Who's hurt? Sam? What happened?

Then the proverbial lightbulb winked on in Suzanne's head and she could think of only one terrible answer!

Tasered? Please don't tell me Sam's been Tasered!

That single word burst inside her brain like a thousand fragmented pieces.

She drew closer, hoping she was wrong, daring herself to look as she trotted past the red car.

And there, just up ahead, kneeling above Sam, holding a plastic bag over his face, was the slim form of Carla Reiker!

Suzanne didn't stop to scream. She didn't try to put two and two together because there simply wasn't time. Instead, she dug her heels into Mocha's flanks and sent her big horse into a wild, full-force gallop. Grasping the saddle with her right hand, she slapped the reins against his neck to drive him even harder. And like a medieval knight in a joust to the death, Suzanne charged directly at Carla Reiker.

Reiker didn't see her coming until the very last second. Maybe she caught a quick flash of Suzanne on her galloping horse, or maybe she felt the thunder of Mocha's hooves on the pavement. In any case, Reiker sprang to her feet like a scalded cat, her mouth grimacing in surprise.

Mocha's broad shoulder sideswiped Reiker hard as he galloped past, spinning her around and knocking her flat to the ground. Reiker was momentarily stunned, but not three seconds later, she clambered to her feet. She stared in shocked bewilderment, caught in the act. And, when recognition finally dawned, when she saw it was Suzanne who sat astride the horse, she screamed out, "Yoooouuuu!"

Suzanne reined Mocha into a tight circle and charged again. But Reiker was smart, wily, and highly trained in combat. This time, as Suzanne skimmed past, Reiker managed to lean over and deliver a hard karate chop to Suzanne's upper thigh.

The blow was dead-on and landed so hard Suzanne gasped in pain. Could she do this? she wondered. Could she fight against Reiker and win? No, she *had* to do this. Trying wasn't an option. Facing off against this woman and winning was what she had to do! After all, Sam was lying out cold on the pavement, helpless, with a plastic bag stretched across half his face!

Once again, Suzanne spun Mocha around, ready to drive hard at Reiker. But this time Reiker was more than ready for her. She stood in the rain, her feet spread wide apart, and with a look of triumph on her angry, determined face, held up her hand and brandished her Taser! There was a hum and a nasty crackle as she turned it on.

Suzanne's brain was in a whirl. *She's going to use the Taser on Sam again? Or on me? Or on Mocha?*

Feeling frantic now, Suzanne wondered just how many volts Mocha could absorb? How many volts could *she* absorb? And did she really have the guts to find out?

But Suzanne was determined to make a stand. There was no turning back now—the duel was on and there would only be one winner!

She guided Mocha down the narrow berm of the road, past Sam's car, and around Reiker's car. This was going to be it. She would regroup, make an all-out charge against Reiker, and take this crazy woman down once and for all!

Suzanne hunched forward like a jockey, knotting herself

into what she hoped was a smaller target. Then she urged Mocha into a fast trot, ready to kick him into a full gallop.

And just as she flashed past Sam's car, she saw his fishing rod, sticking partially out his back window. Quick as a snapping turtle, Suzanne reached out and grabbed the fly rod.

Out of the corner of his eye, Mocha saw Suzanne grab the whiplike rod and nervously crab-stepped hard to the left. But Suzanne was an experienced rider and quickly brought him back under control. "Easy, easy," she told the big horse, trying to settle him down as she spun the rod around and got a firm grasp on its cork handle. She hunched forward in her saddle again, gritting her teeth, unaware she was making a hum like an angry hornet. She gave one mighty "Hyah!" and sent her horse flying.

Using the fishing rod as a whip, she descended upon Carla Reiker like the Four Horsemen of the Apocalypse!

The first stinging blow opened a jagged cut on Reiker's cheek and drove her backward a good five feet. Stumbling, roaring in pain, the Taser suddenly flew from Reiker's hand. It hit the blacktop, cracked open, and rolled harmlessly away.

Eyes filled with rage, Reiker touched a hand to her face to check the trickle of warm blood. Jerking her hand away, she gazed at the bloody smear and let out a bellow like a stuck pig.

Not wanting to ease up on her attack, Suzanne spun Mocha around and slashed at Reiker again. This time she opened a huge gash directly over Reiker's left eye.

"Take that!" Suzanne cried as rivulets of blood coursed down Reiker's face.

Screaming bloody murder, wiping frantically at her face, Reiker backpedaled like crazy. In doing so, she stumbled on the broken Taser, tripped, and began to topple over backward. Her arms whipped out to her sides making futile gestures while her feet paddled in the air. But nothing would save her. She was out of tricks! Reiker hit the pavement hard, her head striking it first and bouncing like a ripe cantaloupe. A low moan escaped Reiker's lips and her hands curled into fists. Then, amazingly, thankfully, the maniac lay perfectly still!

Leaping from her horse, Suzanne flung herself down on the wet pavement. In one smooth and forceful motion she ripped the hunk of plastic off Sam's face and threw it aside.

He was white as a sheet and barely breathing. Suzanne didn't know if he'd been Tasered repeatedly or suffocated to the point of unconsciousness! But she knew she had to do something!

"Breathe!" she screamed. "Take a breath, baby!" And then, because she knew his life was totally in her hands, that no medevac helicopter was going to drop from the sky and assist her, she cupped her fists together, raised them up high, and brought them down hard against Sam's chest.

"Live!" she yelled out. "You've got to live!"

CHAPTER 26

HER hands pressed together, Suzanne began chest compressions as she knelt on the cold, unforgiving ground. She punched the center of Sam's chest with fast, forceful moves, alternating each hit by leaning forward and giving him mouth-to-mouth resuscitation.

He's not getting enough air, Suzanne thought wildly. He needs more air to bring him around!

Suzanne continued to labor over Sam, alternating compressions with breathing, for what felt like hours, though it was probably only a minute or two. And just as Sam let out a sharp gasp, she heard the sound of a vehicle pulling up behind her, of someone stopping.

Now what? More trouble?

She managed a quick glance and saw an old pickup truck. And was truly stunned when she saw Jake Gantz's face bobbing toward her through a sheet of rain.

"Jake!" she cried out.

Jake shuffled closer. His mouth hung open and surprise

lit his face. "Is that the doc?" he asked, looking down at Sam. "Is he hurt bad?" His eyes shifted to Carla Reiker, who was still out cold on the pavement. "Is she hurt, too?"

"I'm trying to . . ." Suzanne had run out of words because she'd practically run out of breath.

"I . . . I'll get a blanket!" said Jake, as Suzanne kept working.

Her shoulders were burning, her breath was coming in short, stuttering gasps, but she wasn't about to stop. But she was still scared to death. Oh yes, she was scared as she mumbled a hasty prayer. And though she wasn't able to recall her exact words later on, she knew they were something to the effect of, *Please help me, dear Lord. You're all I've got right now!*

Suddenly, just as Suzanne was starting to despair, just as she was about to let fear overwhelm her, Sam's eyes fluttered and he let loose a low groan. Then his lips parted and he sucked in an enormous glut of air.

"That's it!" Suzanne whispered excitedly. "Breathe! Just breathe!"

Sam's chest lifted as he gulped more air and his eyes fluttered again. And then, seconds later, when he appeared to be breathing just fine on his own, he opened his eyes fully and stared directly up at Suzanne.

"I'm here, Sam. I'm here for you," she said.

He continued to look at her, to practically drink in her every feature.

"Do you know where you are?" Suzanne asked as she peered at him anxiously. *Please answer me. Please don't have brain damage or something awful like that.*

Sam slowly raised his right hand, crooked his head, and gave her a questioning look. Then he touched his fingers to his forehead, almost as if he had to confirm that he was still very much alive.

"Do you know where you are?" Suzanne asked him again.

"I think so," Sam rasped, finally answering her question.

"Do you remember what happened?"

Sam licked his lips. "Crazy lady tried to suffocate me." His voice was hoarse and papery, but a little stronger now.

He'd come back to her. Yes, he had!

"That's exactly right," said Suzanne. Relief flooded her voice and she allowed herself a small smile. Her hands were patting his chest now, making little involuntary circular motions as hot, salty tears coursed down her cheeks. "But she won't ever touch you again!"

And then, out of the blue, a lopsided grin suddenly spilled across Sam's face. And he croaked out, "Suzanne. Sweetheart. What took you so long?"

WITH Sam sitting cross-legged on the pavement, breathing much better now as he slowly regained his bearings, Suzanne turned her attention to Carla Reiker.

"Did she hurt the doc?" asked Gantz. He was eyeing Reiker's still form, stretched out where she'd fallen.

Suzanne nodded. "She sure tried to."

"You want me to tie her up?" asked Gantz. "I've got some rope in my car."

"We better check her pockets first," said Suzanne. "Make sure she doesn't have any sort of weapon."

"You do that," said Gantz. He backed away from Reiker as if she were a poisonous snake.

"Be careful," Sam croaked out, as he pulled the blanket tighter around his shoulders.

Suzanne knelt down beside Reiker and stuck her hands in the woman's jacket pocket. She probed around gently, looking for a knife or a gun. When her fingers hit something cold and hard, she frowned.

"What?" called Sam. "Did you find something?"

"I don't know," said Suzanne. She wrapped her fingers

around an object that felt more like a large tube of lipstick and pulled it out. Only it wasn't a lipstick at all. It was a vial of clear liquid.

"What's that?" said Gantz. He took a tentative step closer.

Suzanne turned the vial over and stared at a small white label. "It says Dianabol." She glanced over at Sam and said, "Does Dianabol mean anything to you?"

"It's a synthetic steroid," said Sam slowly. "A performance-enhancing drug. Wrestlers use it. So do weight lifters."

Suzanne's brain pinged and her eyes locked onto his. "Drummond!" she cried out, recalling his bulging physique, thinking back to her conversation with Boots Wagner about performance-enhancing drugs. "Reiker must have been Drummond's drug dealer!"

"Drugs?" said Gantz. He sounded frightened.

"That's why Reiker killed him," said Suzanne. The pieces and parts of the puzzle were suddenly dropping rapidly into place for her. "Reiker was always right there at the Hard Body Gym, so she must have been his drug connection. But something happened between the two of them. They had a serious falling out."

"So she killed him," Sam said slowly.

"Like she almost killed you," said Suzanne. "And Sheriff Doogie."

Sam looked confused. "I can understand why she went after Doogie, but why me?"

"Because Reiker thought you were handling the autopsy," Suzanne said abruptly. "She figured you were in charge of the whole thing. She was afraid the drugs would show up in the final toxicology report and the whole thing would lead back to her and the Hard Body Gym."

"You think?" said Sam. He was having trouble buying into her scenario.

"Wait a minute," said Suzanne. With Gantz following her, she walked back to Reiker's car and looked inside. On the backseat was a small black nylon gym bag. Inside were two small boxes of vials. All with the label "Schedule 3—Rx only."

"Wow," said Gantz, giving Suzanne an admiring gaze. "You're some smart lady."

JAKE Gantz turned out to be a real prince of a guy. He not only grabbed a rope from his car and tied up Carla Reiker, but he wrapped his blanket around Sam and helped him limp over to the passenger side of his car.

Suzanne, meanwhile, pulled out her cell phone and called the Law Enforcement Center. Then she had a very terse conversation with Deputy Driscoll.

When Suzanne was finished, she walked back to where Jake was standing. He was half guarding Reiker, who seemed to be slowly regaining consciousness, and keeping a watchful eye on a still-dazed Sam.

"I just talked to Driscoll at the Law Enforcement Center," said Suzanne. "Told him all about Carla Reiker and the drugs." She nodded at Sam. "And about how she tried to kill you, too."

"And what was Driscoll's reaction?" asked Sam. "Now that you've solved the case right out from under him?"

"Actually, I think he was a little relieved," said Suzanne.

"He should be," said Sam. His good humor seemed to be back in full force.

"He also asked if one of us could stay here with Reiker," said Suzanne. "Until he can get out here and pick her up."

"I'll stay," volunteered Jake. "You take the doc to the hospital and get him checked out."

Suzanne made a small gesture at Mocha, who had wandered over and poked his nose halfway into the car where Sam was sitting. "My horse. He's . . ."

"Don't worry about him, ma'am," said Jake. "I'll take care of him, too. There's a barn over yonder that belongs to a farmer named Drucker. I've done odd jobs for him in the past and I'm sure he won't mind sheltering your horse for a day or two."

"You're sure?" said Suzanne.

"You just take care of the doc," said Jake, nodding his head. "He still looks a little unsteady, like he might need some medical attention." He reached out and tugged gently at one of Mocha's reins. "We'll be okay, won't we, boy? We'll wait here for Deputy Driscoll, then get you settled in a nice, dry stall."

As if in response, Mocha let loose a loud snort.

"I can't thank you enough," Suzanne told Jake, as she climbed into the driver's seat of Sam's car. She was trying to remain brave but felt emotionally wrought, nearly on the verge of collapse.

"That's okay," said Jake. "Just trying to be helpful."

Sam shifted around in his seat until he was practically facing Suzanne. Then he reached out and clasped her hand. "Are you okay?"

Suzanne blew out a breath and nodded. "I think so. As long as you're back with us."

"I'm good," said Sam. "I am now, anyway."

"That Jake," continued Suzanne. She watched as he jiggled Mocha's reins and gave him a pat. "What a lifesaver he turned out to be."

Sam gripped her hand tighter. "I think you have that mixed up, my dear. It seems to me *you're* the one who did the lifesaving."

CHAPTER 27

IF everyone hadn't been so dinged up, it could have been old home week back at the hospital. As it was, Sam was checked out in the ER, given a quick EKG and a few toots of oxygen, and pronounced good as new by a third-year resident.

Then Sheriff Doogie, who'd heard about Suzanne's daring rescue via the hospital grapevine, was wheeled down to join them. He'd made excellent strides in the last twelve hours, regaining his color as well as his feistiness.

"Reiker was the one who waylaid *me*!" proclaimed Doogie. "Here I thought she had car trouble—and it turned out she wanted to clobber me with a tire iron! Tried to run me over, too, I guess."

Suzanne gazed at Doogie. "So you knew it was Reiker who assaulted you?"

"Oh yeah," said Doogie nodding. "I knew it. Trouble was, my poor muddled brain couldn't get the words out to tell anyone. I tried to tell Driscoll . . . and then when you came to see me yesterday morning, I tried to tell you . . ."

"You did try!" exclaimed Suzanne. "You mumbled something about drugs. Only I thought you were referring to the drugs the doctors had given you."

"Naw," said Doogie. "Once Reiker attacked me I had this weird . . . whadyacallit? . . . flash of insight that she might have been involved with Drummond that way. Just because he'd gotten so big and burly lately. Trouble was, I couldn't spit out any words."

"The whole thing's just crazy," said Suzanne, shaking her head. "And I can't wait to call Missy and tell her she's off the hook!"

"Yes, she is," agreed Doogie.

Suzanne was ready to go home, but Sam was busy recounting his rescue to a few more members of the ER staff, embroidering his tale here and there, tossing in a few extra smatters of excitement. Suzanne wasn't sure whether to bask in his praise or be profoundly embarrassed.

Fortunately, Doogie interrupted.

"Excuse me," he said, puffing out his chest and addressing Suzanne directly. "But weren't you warned to stay clear of this matter? To not step on law enforcement's toes?" His words sounded harsh but his delivery was rendered with a merry twinkle in his eye.

"I don't remember anything about toes," said Suzanne, trying to keep a straight face. "My recollection was you asked me to step in and handle things."

Doogie shook his head and let out a relieved wheeze. "Carla Reiker dealing drugs. Holy baloney. Who would have pegged her for a drug dealer? Or a killer?"

"None of us did," said Suzanne. "Until I went looking for Sam, that is, and found her trying to kill him, too!"

"She came charging in on a white horse," whooped Sam.

"You should have seen her! Like something out of *Indiana Jones*!"

"Really," said Suzanne. "Mocha is a distinct chestnut color."

BUT the surprises didn't end there. Because ten minutes later—after Doogie threatened to do a wheelie in his wheelchair and was finally taken back upstairs by one of the nurses—the rest of the gang showed up!

"Oh my gosh!" Suzanne exclaimed as Toni and Petra piled into the exam room to embrace her and cluck over Sam. "How on earth did you . . . ?"

"Jake brought us," said Petra.

"That's right," Toni piped up. "Jake stopped by the Cackleberry Club and filled us in but good." She shook an index finger at Suzanne. "It seems you've been a busy girl!" Then she turned toward Sam. "And you, you've got to be a lot more careful when you make house calls!"

Sam grinned. "If you say so."

"But what did you do about all the injured people at the Cackleberry Club?" asked Suzanne. "Dan and Sonja and whoever else?"

"Oh, we brought them with us," said Petra. "They're down the hall in the ER right now. Getting patched up."

"What about all the trees that were blocking the driveway?" said Suzanne.

"Junior came through with his chainsaw gang," said Toni proudly. "His guys are over there right now, working on the downed trees. But first he cleared a kind of pathway, so the customers could get out."

Suzanne was stunned. "So they're all . . ."

"Gone home," said Petra. "They just sort of carpooled their way home."

"So," said Toni, shuffling closer to Suzanne and Sam, "Carla Reiker was seriously dealing drugs, huh?"

"Not recreational drugs," said Sam. "Performance-enhancing drugs. Sad to say, there's a big market for that kind of thing."

"You mean like steroids?" said Toni.

"Afraid so," said Sam. "They're wildly popular."

"Wow," said Petra. "Who would have thought?"

But Toni didn't want to let it go. "So you guys think Reiker was dealing drugs to Drummond and that things went bad between them?"

"It certainly looks that way," said Suzanne.

"It *was* that way," said a voice suddenly from the doorway.

They all turned to see Jake Gantz standing there.

"Jake!" said Suzanne.

"When Deputy Driscoll showed up to haul that lady away," said Gantz, "he popped the lid on her trunk and discovered all kinds of vials in there. Some of it was like that stuff you found in her pocket, but there were other things, too. Maybe . . . Oxantho-something?"

"Oxandrolone?" said Sam.

"Yeah," said Jake.

Sam let loose a low whistle. "There you go."

"What I still don't get," said Toni, "is why Reiker went after Sam?"

"Because Reiker thought Sam was in charge of Drummond's autopsy," Suzanne explained. "I suppose she just got nervous. She figured Sam was eventually going to find drugs on board. Drugs that were used to increase muscle mass and performance. And that it would all lead back to her."

"Jeez, Suzanne," said Toni. "If you'd have kept on investigating, you might have been next on her hit list!"

"There's a happy thought," said Petra.

"Toni always looks for the silver lining," joked Sam.

"I'm just glad it all ended well," said Petra. She turned and beamed happily at Jake. "And you! From now on you're cordially invited to dine at the Cackleberry Club for free. And to order whatever your little heart desires!"

Jake looked stunned. "Me? What'd I do?"

Suzanne reached out and grabbed his hand. "You turned out to be a true friend."

"That's for sure," declared Petra. "And in the recipe of life, friends are the most important ingredient!"

But Jake just ducked his head. "Looked to me like that horse of yours was the real saving grace."

"Mocha was absolutely . . . terrific," said Suzanne, fighting back tears.

"I'm going to paint a fine portrait of him," said Jake. "To enter in the Hearts and . . ."

"Sold!" said Sam.

He squeezed Suzanne's hand. "And I'm giving it to you."

"Thank you," said Suzanne, with love in her eyes. And then, whispering so no one else could hear her, said, "I love you, Sam."

"I love you, too," he whispered back. "I love you, too."

Recipes from the
Cackleberry Club

White Bean Breakfast Hash

4 slices bacon
¼ cup chopped onions
½ red bell pepper, chopped
1 tbsp. butter
1 can cannellini beans (15 oz.), drained and rinsed
2 eggs
Salt and pepper to taste

Cook bacon in frying pan until crisp, then remove. Add onion, red pepper, and butter to pan and sizzle for 5 minutes. Add beans to mixture and stir. Crumble bacon into bean mixture and stir. Push bean mixture to side of pan. Drop in eggs and fry. Scoop bean mixture onto 2 breakfast plates and top each with a fried egg. Makes 2 servings.

Chocolate Chip Quinoa Breakfast Cookies

4 large ripe bananas
1 tsp. vanilla extract
2 tbsp. almond butter
½ cup coconut sugar
1 cup cooked quinoa
1 cup uncooked quinoa flakes (or oatmeal flakes)
1 cup unsweetened, shredded coconut
Pinch sea salt
½ cup chocolate chips

Preheat oven to 375 degrees. In a large mixing bowl, mash bananas with a fork and add vanilla, almond butter, and coconut sugar. Add quinoa, oatmeal, coconut, and pinch of salt. Mix until well combined. Stir in chocolate chips. Line baking sheet with parchment paper and drop batter onto baking sheet. Bake for 25 to 30 minutes.

Stuffed Green Pepper Soup

1 lb. ground beef
1 envelope dry onion soup mix
1 can diced tomatoes (14.5 oz.)
1 can tomato sauce (15 oz.)
2 large green peppers, chopped
1 beef bouillon cube
⅛ cup brown sugar, packed
1 cup cooked white rice
mozzarella cheese

In a large pot, brown ground beef thoroughly. Stir in soup mix and heat. Add all remaining ingredients, except rice, and bring to a boil. Reduce heat and simmer for about 35 minutes or until peppers are soft. Add rice and heat for another 5 minutes. Spoon into bowls and sprinkle with mozzarella cheese. Makes 4 servings.

Chicken Meatloaf (Chicken Chickenloaf?)

2 lb. ground chicken
1 cup soft bread crumbs
½ cup onion, finely chopped
2 eggs
1 cup tomato sauce
Salt and pepper to taste
¼ cup melted butter for basting

Preheat oven to 350 degrees. In large bowl, mix together chicken, bread crumbs, and onion. In small bowl, beat eggs. Add tomato sauce to eggs and mix. Pour egg mixture into ground chicken mixture, add salt and pepper, and mix well. Pat chicken mixture into 9" × 5" loaf pan and bake for approximately 1 hour, basting occasionally with melted butter. Remove loaf from oven and pour off liquid. Let loaf rest for a few minutes, then turn out onto a serving platter.

Suzanne's Breakfast BLT

Toast a slice of French baguette. Stack with slice of bacon, lettuce, and tomato. Spread on a little bit of spicy mayo. Add a fried egg and serve open-faced!

Bacon Cornbread

1 cup flour, sifted
1 cup cornmeal, yellow or white
3½ tsp. baking powder
1 tsp. salt
3 tbsp. sugar
1 egg
1 cup milk
¼ cup butter
½ cup crisp bacon, chopped

Preheat oven to 425 degrees. In large bowl combine flour, cornmeal, baking powder, salt, and sugar. In separate bowl combine egg, milk, butter, and bacon. Pour egg/bacon mixture into flour mixture and mix just enough to moisten dry ingredients. Pour into greased 8" × 8" × 2" pan and bake for 35 to 40 minutes.

Crazy Quilt Bread

1½ cups sugar
1 egg
1¼ cups milk
3 cups packaged biscuit mix
½ cup candied fruit (mixed)
1 cup walnuts, chopped

Preheat oven to 350 degrees. Mix sugar, egg, milk, and biscuit mix together by hand. Add in the candied fruit and chopped walnuts. Pour batter into a well-greased 9" × 5" loaf pan. Bake for 45 minutes or until a toothpick comes out clean. Cool before slicing. Spread with regular butter or honey butter and enjoy.

Petra's Cranberry Muffins

1¾ cups all-purpose flour
⅓ cup sugar
½ tsp. salt
2 tsp. baking powder
2 eggs
¾ cup milk
¼ cup melted butter
1 cup dried cranberries, chopped
1 tsp. grated orange rind

Preheat oven to 400 degrees. Sift together flour, sugar, salt, and baking powder in large bowl. In a separate bowl, mix together eggs, milk, and melted butter. Make a center well in the dry ingredients and pour in the wet ingredients. Mix until moistened. Fold in cranberries and grated orange rind. Spoon batter into greased muffin tin and bake for 20 to 25 minutes.

Petra's Goat Cheese and Pimento Tea Sandwiches

10 oz. goat cheese, softened
¼ cup heavy cream
¼ cup pimentos, drained and chopped
1 tsp. Tabasco sauce
Salt and pepper to taste
8 slices of bread

Using a spoon, mash goat cheese, then blend with cream, pimento, Tabasco sauce, and salt and pepper. Spread cheese mixture on your favorite white or wheat bread and cut into tea sandwiches. Makes 16 tea sandwiches. (Note: If you're unsure about goat cheese, you can use cream cheese or any other soft white cheese.)

Easy Cream Scones

2 cups all-purpose flour
1 tbsp. baking powder
4 tbsp. sugar
½ tsp. salt
⅓ cup butter, chilled and chopped into bits
1 cup heavy cream

Heat oven to 425 degrees. In a large bowl, mix together flour, baking powder, sugar, and salt. Cut butter into mixture until mixture is coarse and crumbly. Stir in heavy cream until dough begins to form—this should take about 45 seconds. Place dough on floured work surface and knead for 10 seconds until it forms a ball. Flatten dough gently and cut into 8 wedges. Placed wedges on ungreased baking sheet and bake on center rack for 12 to 15 minutes. (Note: You could also add ½ cup of dried cranberries, ½ cup of raisins, or ½ cup of chopped currants if you like.)

Petra's No-Bake Peanut Butter Fudge

2 cups sugar
½ cup milk
¾ cup peanut butter

1 tsp. vanilla
½ cup chocolate chips

Place sugar and milk in pan and bring to a boil. Boil for about 2½ minutes. Remove from heat and add peanut butter, vanilla, and chocolate chips. Stir until well mixed. Pour into greased pan. Cool and eat!

Toni's Pineapple Dump Cake

1 box angel food cake mix (16 oz.)
1 can pineapple chunks (20 oz.), not drained
Whipped topping

Heat oven to 350 degrees. Dump cake mix and pineapple chunks into an ungreased 9" × 12" baking pan. Stir together until well mixed. Bake for 25 minutes. Cool in pan. Scoop out and serve with a dollop of whipped topping. Easy!

Beer-Battered Chicken

1¾ cups all purpose flour, sifted
1½ tsp. salt
½ tsp. pepper
12 oz. beer
Vegetable oil
1 chicken, cut in pieces

Combine flour, salt, and pepper in bowl. Beat in beer using a wire whisk, then let stand for 30 minutes. Add about 1 inch of oil to frying pan and heat to 375 degrees (medium-high heat). Dip each piece of chicken in beer batter and place in hot oil. Fry chicken, turning only once, for about 30 minutes or until done. (Note: Chicken can also be fried for less time—10 minutes—to create a crust, then baked in oven at 350 degrees for 30 minutes.)

Resources

BOOKS AND MAGAZINES

The Good Egg—Author Marie Simmons offers two hundred fresh approaches to preparing eggs—everything from breakfast to dessert.

The Fresh Egg Cookbook—Jennifer Trainer Thompson explores recipes for using eggs sourced from farmers' markets, local farms, and your own backyard.

Home-Made Vintage—Christina Strutt provides a guide to giving your home a vintage air and a country cottage appeal.

Modern Country—Nancy Ingram and Jenifer Jordan show how to add a clean, modernist edge to classic country decor.

Country Living—Magazine devoted to home and decorating, food and entertaining, antiques and collectibles. (countryliving.com)

Country Sampler—Magazine with country decorating and lifestyle articles. (countrysampler.com)

Living the Country Life—Homes, gardening, and the country life. (livingthecountrylife.com)

Mary Janes Farm—Charming magazine about crafts, decor, and organic living. (maryjanesfarm.org)

WEBSITES AND INTERESTING BLOGS

Cottagehomedecorating.com—How to turn secondhand and rescued furniture and objects into charming, comfortable cottage style.

Mypetchicken.com—The how-to's of raising chickens in your own backyard.

Joyofbaking.com/eggs.html—All about cooking and baking with eggs.

Incredibleegg.org—American Egg Board's site with egg facts, fun, and lots of recipes.

Fresh-eggs-daily.com—Blog about eggs, chickens, and tasty recipes.

Bedandbreakfast.com—Your getaway guide to more than 11,000 country inns and bed-and-breakfasts.

Cookingwithideas.typepad.com—Recipes and book reviews for the bibliochef.

Jennybakes.com—Fabulous recipes from a real make-it-from-scratch baker.

Baking.about.com—Carroll Pellegrinelli writes a terrific baking blog complete with recipes and photo instructions.

Garden-of-books.com—Terrific book reviews by an entertainment journalist.

Lattesandlife.com—Witty musings on life.

Turn the page for a preview of
Laura Childs's next Tea Shop Mystery . . .

Steeped in Evil

Coming March 2014 in hardcover
from Berkley Prime Crime!

THEODOSIA Browning didn't consider herself a wine connoisseur, since tea was really her forte. Fragrant Darjeelings, malty Assams, and her current favorite, a house-blended orchid plum tea that tickled her fancy as well as her taste buds.

On the other hand, how often did a girl get invited to a fancy wine tasting party at the very upscale Knighthall Winery?

Rarely. In fact, tonight was a first for Theodosia. And her invitation to this lushly groomed vineyard, located a leisurely drive from Charleston, South Carolina, came at the behest of Drayton Conneley, her right-hand man and tea expert at the Indigo Tea Shop. Luckily for Theodosia, Drayton happened to be a dear friend of Jordan Knight, Knighthall Winery's slightly flamboyant proprietor.

"You see?" said Drayton, grabbing her elbow and steering her toward an enormous trestle table set under a spreading live oak. He was sixty-something and still debonair with a prominent nose and thatch of gray hair. "Jordan managed to produce four completely different varieties of wine." Wine bottles beckoned like shiny beacons and attentive waiters were more than willing to fill glasses. "Amazing, wouldn't you say?"

"Amazing," Theodosia echoed. She didn't know if five varieties was a feat worth celebrating, but Drayton certainly seemed impressed. And the grounds of the winery did look absolutely magical this September evening, all lit up and sparkling like a scene from some elegant Austrian fairy tale. Plantation oaks and pecan trees were iced in silvery lights, candles floated in a free-form pool, a string quartet played lively music, and a handsome magician in white tie and tails amused guests with fluttering, disappearing pigeons and sly card tricks.

Drayton handed Theodosia a crystal flute filled with white wine. "This is Knighthall's White Shadow," he told her. "Although I'd call it more of a Reisling."

Theodosia took a small sip and found the wine to be utterly delicious. Crisp and aromatic, with hints of apples and citrus. Not unlike a fine oolong tea. "It's spectacular," she replied.

"I told you," said Drayton. "Lots of folks thought it would be next to impossible to grow grapes out here on Wadmalow Island, but Jordan's definitely proved them wrong."

If tea plants could grow here and flourish, Theodosia thought to herself, why not grape vines? Although perhaps a sandier soil was needed? Wasn't a sandier, rockier soil supposed to prove the true mettle of the grape?

They stepped away from the tasting table and looked around, enjoying the warmth and excitement of the evening and the rather excellent people-watching.

"I'd say the crème de la crème of Charleston is here in full force tonight," said Theodosia. Tanned and toned women in chiffon dresses drifted by, wafting perfumed scents that hinted at lilies and lilac. Men in seersucker suits also wandered the elegant grounds, sipping wine as well as an occasional tumbler of bourbon. Of course, Charleston folk being the congenial sort, everyone seemed quite preoccupied with the exchange of air kisses and pleasantries, pretending not to notice if they themselves were being noticed.

"The beautiful people," Drayton mused. "Dressed to the nines just in case a society photographer should happen along." Of course, he was also dazzling in a blue and white seersucker suit—a sartorial Southern statement that was punctuated by his trademark red bow tie.

Theodosia would have denied it, of course, practically laughed in your face, but she was also one of the beautiful people. With an abundance of auburn hair that might have inspired a painter like Raphael, creamy English skin, and sparkling blue eyes, she looked like she might have slipped in from another, earlier, century. She was bold yet tactful, filled with dreams and yet practical. Her only flaws were that she tended to wear her heart on her sleeve and often rushed in where proverbial angels feared to tread.

"Jordan!" Drayton called out, as Jordan Knight, the owner of Knighthall Winery, came up to greet them. "Congratulations on such a fine turnout." He turned to include Theodosia. "And this is Theodosia Browning, I don't believe you two have met."

"Thanks for coming," said Knight, as he shook hands with each of them. He was mid-forties, with a shock of salt and pepper hair, watery blue eyes, and a slightly pink complexion. He'd removed his jacket, loosened his tie, and his manner seemed to veer between nervous and ebullient.

"I'm pretty sure I just convinced the owner of the Lady Goodwood Inn to carry my wine," Knight chortled. In his other, more practical life, he was the CEO of Whizzen Software. Knighthall Winery was his most recently established passion.

"Well done," said Drayton, clapping his friend on the back.

"Your winery appears to be thriving," Theodosia told Knight. Being a business owner herself, she knew how difficult it was for a company to succeed, let alone flourish in today's tough business climate. And the deck was stacked against upstarts even more.

"We're starting to gain some traction," Knight responded. "We have distribution to thirty liquor stores in something like five states. And my son is in the process of helping to negotiate a potentially large deal with a Japanese distributor, as well." Knight gazed about distractedly. "You've met my son, Drew, haven't you?"

Drayton nodded yes. Theodosia shook her head no.

"I'd love to say hello to him," said Drayton. "Is he here tonight?"

"Drew's around here somewhere," said Knight as he cast a quick glance at the large crowd and shrugged. "He's no doubt managing all the behind-the-scenes activity." Now he glanced nervously at his watch.

"Relax," Drayton told him. "This is your big night. Enjoy it!"

Knight grimaced. "I'm a little antsy about my presentation."

"What is that?" Theodosia inquired politely.

"In about five minutes," said Knight, "we're going to do a special barrel tasting of our new Cabernet reserve." He flashed a perfunctory smile. "We're calling it Knight Music."

"Catchy," said Theodosia.

"We're pinning all our hopes on this one," said Knight. "Going for broke."

"I'm guessing that several of Charleston's food and wine critics are in attendance tonight?" said Drayton.

Knight nodded. "We invited anybody and everybody who can give us a mention, article, or shout-out. After five years of moving heaven and earth to produce four varieties of Muscadine grapes, it's all come down to this one make or break moment."

"Good luck to you then," said Theodosia, as Knight hurried away.

Theodosia and Drayton edged their way slowly through the crowd, in the direction Jordan had gone. A makeshift stage had been set up just outside a large, hip-roofed barn and two workers were rolling out an enormous oak barrel. Two Japanese men, both wearing white suits and standing ramrod-stiff, stood nearby, watching intently.

Theodosia gave Drayton a nudge. "Those must be the Japanese distributors your friend Jordan mentioned."

Drayton nodded. "I read a recent article in the *Financial Times* about how the Japanese are suddenly head-over-heels crazy for wine. Particularly the pricier ones."

"*Sake* being so last year," said Theodosia.

"Everything is cyclical," said Drayton, trying to sound practical.

"Except for tea," said Theodosia. "Tea just seems to keep gaining in popularity."

"And aren't we glad for that," said Drayton.

"Excuse me . . . Theodosia?" said a voice at their elbow.

Theodosia turned with a smile and her eyes met those of a good-looking man with piercing green eyes and a mop of curly blond hair. Kind of surfer dude meets buttoned-down lawyer. He was smiling back at her, and with a kind of instinctive knowledge, she realized that she knew him. The man's name was Andrew something. Andrew . . .

"Andrew Turner," said the man, filling in the blank for her, bobbing his head. "We met at my gallery a couple of weeks ago."

"That's right," said Theodosia. "Max brought me to one of your openings—you were featuring all sorts of dynamic, contemporary oil paintings as I recall."

"Where you undoubtedly feasted on cheap white wine and stuffed cherry tomatoes," said Turner. "The hopeful gallery owner's stock in trade."

"I don't recall the wine," said Theodosia, "but I do remember a wonderful painting that you had on display. All reds and purples and golds. Subtle but also very visceral. The artist was . . . James somebody?"

"Richard James," said Turner. "You have a very keen eye. And as luck would have it, that particular piece is still for sale if you're interested."

"Let me think about it," said Theodosia. She hastily introduced Turner to Drayton, then they all paused as a passing waiter stopped with his tray of hors d'oeuvres to offer them mini crab cakes and shrimp wrapped in bacon.

"Why don't you drop by again during the Paint and Palette Art Crawl," Turner suggested. "You know it kicks off this Wednesday."

Theodosia was about to answer, when Drayton quickly shushed them. Jordan Knight was standing on the stage next to an enormous weathered oak barrel. And it looked as if he was about to begin his speech.

The crowd hushed en masse and pressed forward to hear his presentation.

"Thank you all for coming," said Knight. "This is such a proud moment for me." He clasped a hand to his chest in a heartfelt gesture of appreciation. "We've labored long and hard to cultivate grapes here in South Carolina."

There was a smatter of applause.

"And our newest vintage, Knight Music, which you are all about to taste, would never have been possible without the hard work of my manager, Tom Grady, and our many dedicated workers." Jordan extended a hand toward a lovely red-haired woman who stood off to the side. "And, of course, I must thank my wonderful family. My wife, the lovely Pandora Knight, and my son, Drew Knight." He smiled as his eyes searched the crowd for Drew. When he didn't find him, he said, "Though my son seems to be missing in action at the moment."

There was more laughter and guffaws from the crowd.

As Jordan continued his speech, two workers began to tap the large barrel of wine. They fumbled around on the top, trying to get a spigot going, but it didn't seem to be working.

"Of course," said Jordan, playing to the crowd now, "our winery is not without problems—as you can plainly see."

One of the workers tilted the large barrel up onto one edge. The other worker, looking frustrated and brandishing a crowbar, suddenly popped off the round, wooden top. The heavy lid went airborne, spinning in the air like an errant Frisbee, and then hit the stage with a loud bang. At that very same moment, the entire barrel seemed to teeter dangerously.

"Whoa!" Jordan shouted. "Careful there! We're going to sample that fine wine!"

But the giant barrel, unbalanced and heavy with wine, was more than the workers could handle. They fought valiantly to right it, but were beginning to lose their grip!

Slowly, the barrel tipped sideways and viscous red liquid began to spill out, sloshing across the stage and spattering the crowd. There were sharp cries of dismay from the guests as everyone tried to jump out of the way!

Jordan Knight scrambled for the barrel in a last ditch effort to avert total disaster. He leaned down and tried to muscle his shoulder beneath the huge barrel. Unfortunately, the laws of physics had been set into motion and he was clearly too late. The barrel continued to tip, rolling over in slow motion like a sinking ocean liner making a final, dying gasp.

The barrel landed on its side with a deafening crash and torrents of red wine gushed out like rivers of blood!

Now horrified gasps rose up from the crowd as Jordan Knight seemed to stagger drunkenly. He crumpled to his knees, landing hard, and his entire face seemed to collapse. Then an agonized shriek rose up from his lips, blotting out the music and even the gasps from the crowd.

Curiosity bubbling within her, Theodosia pushed her way through the crowd to see what on earth was going on.

And was completely shocked to see the body of a dead man lying on the stage!

He was curled up, nose to knees, like a pickled fish. His head was tilted forward, his arms clutched close across his chest. The man's skin, what Theodosia could see of it, was practically purple from being submerged inside the barrel of red wine.

Who? and *What?* were the first thoughts that formed like cartoon bubbles deep in Theodosia's brain. And then her eyes flicked over to Jordan Knight, who was kneeling in the spill of wine, his pants legs completely soaked with purple as tears streamed down his face and his arms flailed madly about his head.

From the look of utter devastation on Jordan Knight's face, Theodosia was pretty sure he'd found his missing son.

Watch for the next Cackleberry Club Mystery

Scorched Eggs

A flash fire becomes a deadly inferno and a dear friend is killed. But when firemen sift through ashes and charred ruins, it appears the fire was deliberately set. Did the perpetrator have murder on his mind? Was it a crazed firebug or a bizarre cover-up? Or something else entirely? With Sheriff Doogie still on the mend, it falls to Suzanne and her Cackleberry Club cohorts to solve this crime!

And watch for Laura Childs's next
Scrapbooking Mystery, too

Gossamer Ghost

There's nothing spookier than Halloween in New Orleans. But with a killer wreaking havoc in the French Quarter, does scrapbook maven Carmela have a ghost of a chance of catching him?

Find out more about Laura Childs and her
Tea Shop Mysteries, Scrapbooking Mysteries,
and Cackleberry Club Mysteries at laurachilds.com
and become a Friend on Facebook.